Gabriel Lock:
BOUND BY FATE

By: D. & H. Cancio

 @d.h.cancio

 thegabriellockseries  @TheGabrielLock

g D. & H. Cancio

© 2025 David N. Cancio and Humberto Cancio, Jr.

All rights reserved.

ISBN: 978-1-962825-75-7

This book is a work of fiction and non-fictional events based on expression. Some of the names, characters, places and incidents are products of the writer's imagination or have been used fictitiously. Any resemblance to persons, living or dead, actual events, locale or organisations is entirely coincidental.

All rights are reserved. No part of this book may be used or reproduced in any form by any electronic, mechanical, or any other device now known or invented hereafter without the permission of the author, except in the case of brief quotations embodied in critical articles and reviews. These forms include, but are not limited to xerography, photocopying, scanning, recording, distributing via internet means, information storage and retrieval systems. Because of the dynamic nature of the internet, any web address or links contained in this book may have changed since publication and may no longer be valid.

The Gabriel Lock Series:

1. Bound by Law – September 2024
2. Bound by Fate – November 2025
3. Bound by Will – April 2027

Upcoming…

4. Bound by _____
5. Bound by _____
6. Bound by _____
7. Bound by _____

A novel inspired by
true events.

Any similarity to any specific person, occurrence or event is purely
coincidental.

Dear Reader,

At the beginning of our book, you find two statements that at first glance seem contradictory. These are: (1) A novel inspired by true events and (2) any similarity to a specific person, occurrence, or event is purely coincidental. It is important that I explain why they are not inconsistent.

All lawyers must adhere to specific ethical obligations, particularly regarding client confidentiality. These rules govern the disclosure of any information about a client, including their identity, personal details, and certain communications between attorney and client. Due to these requirements, there are many matters I cannot share—even with David, my son and co-author.

I became a lawyer in 1978. As you can imagine, in a career that spans 6 decades, I have had many clients and cases. In law, like in everything, situations and conflicts tend to repeat themselves over time, and while each one has its own particularities, the longer you participate in legal cases, the more you can pick out the patterns and the tendencies. Once you recognize the connections, plausible contradictions, unlikely concurrences, and you exclude the oddities of each case, you recognize the workings of the cases themselves. You take those mechanisms, mix them in the brain, add imaginary characters, combine modified particularities from other cases, and you have a unique storyline.

Still, this does not make the narrative an accurate depiction of reality. The essence that must always remain in every one of our novels is our description of the true feelings and reactions of the individuals involved in similar situations. David and I believe that this is the indispensable element in maintaining the core of the drama that inspired our fictional tale. All the rest is probable, credible, and trustworthy storytelling based on involvement, knowledge, and experience.

Are Thomas and Gabriel David and me? No, definitely not, though each of us has traits in common with both. I can honestly say that the only real character in any of the books in the series is 1980's Miami. I hope you enjoy our story.

Humberto Cancio, Jr. Esq.

Miami, 10th of October 2025

Bound by Fate

A Novel

D. & H. Cancio

Chapter 1: The Confession

Miami, Florida: October 1966

Thomas genuflected as he entered the church. Taking a knee, he raised his eyes to the crucifix hanging behind the altar and bowed his head with respect. He heard traces of whispers as some knelt on the cushioned hassocks with their fingers laced while others preferred the comfort of the rock beneath them and knew that some prayed while others sat in adoration. Thomas stood and lingered in the center aisle, searching for the line for the confession booth; he had never been to this church before. Finding it, he turned to his left and strode toward the side of the church. The candles gave a dim glow behind their red cases, and the smell of incense filled his nose as he walked through the mist of smoke.

He reached the confessional and sat. As he waited, his mind wandered and he tried to control it, but the thoughts wreaked havoc all the same. The door clicked, and he focused on it. A man, dressed in black Roman robes and with grayed hair smiled at him.

"Have you come for confession, my son?" he asked with a soothing voice.

Thomas eased and took a deep breath.

"Yes, father, I have."

The priest's smile broadened.

"Please, just through that door," said the priest, pointing to the door that lay on the other side, "When you're ready. No rush as you can see." Thomas Lock looked around him, through his spectacles, he saw no one in line or even near the confessional and he didn't know what to think. "People believe that they've been especially good today, but come tomorrow, I'll have a line out the door. So, don't feel ashamed. We've all been where you are."

Thomas nodded and rose from the pew. Making the sign of the cross, he entered the box and knelt on the cushion. The smell of incense faded as he shifted on the kneeler and waited for the priest to speak. A moment passed before the confessional screen opened.

"Help me father for I have sinned," said Thomas looking up at the screen.

"Thank you for coming. It is not an easy thing to admit fault. I am Father Bianchi, and I will hear your confession today."

"Thank you, Father."

"How long has it been since your last confession?"

"One month, Father."

"What do you confess?"

Thomas looked up at the screen and then back down to his hands. He recounted his sins of the last month, of showing anger toward his son in frustration, of not praying more often, for missing mass for two Sundays in a row, and for other venial things.

"Are those all of your sins?"

"Yes, Father, at least since my last confession."

"Please recite your Act of Contrition."

Thomas closed his eyes and recited his act of contrition, apologizing for offending God with his actions and affirmed his resolution to sin no more.

"As your penance, you will speak with your son and ask his forgiveness for your frustration if you haven't already, you will then think of three people who need closeness to Christ, and you will recite one decade of the rosary for each of them. Do you accept this penance?"

"I do, Father," answered Thomas.

"Then you are forgiven in the name of the Father, the Son, and the Holy Spirit. With your prayer of thanksgiving, you are free to go."

"Father, before I go, may I ask for some advice?"

"Of course, my son."

"Years ago, my wife and I almost became the adoptive parents of a little girl, Enara. She was the daughter of friends of ours. We had her in our home for a month when the adoption agency had approved us. I even have a photograph of her playing with my son, Gabriel in the back yard."

"Go on," said the old priest.

"At the end of the month, we received word that her uncle had been found, and he wanted to care for her, so we had to give her up. It nearly broke our hearts, but we accepted it and gave her back. I guess I'm here because I feel guilty over it all. I have faith, but from time to time, I doubt that giving her up was the best thing. My wife and I promised her parents that we would take care of her if anything happened to them and I struggle with knowing if we could have done more."

Father Bianchi leaned back in his seat, removing the silhouette of his head from the screen. He thought for a moment before replying.

"I understand how you would feel that way and I cannot tell you if she has a better life or a worse one, but that is our perspective as humans. What we know is that her uncle accepted the blessing of raising this child and we must have faith in our Lord that what happened was best for everyone."

Thomas nodded and accepted the old priest's words.

"If you still doubt, then I invite you to pray and ask Mother Mary to intercede on the child's behalf. It never hurts to pray for one another."

Thomas thanked Father Bianchi and rose to exit.

"Wait, where are you going?" asked Father Bianchi.

Thomas, surprised, answered.

"I thought that you were finished."

"I am," retorted Father Bianchi, "but you're not, you still need to recite your Thanksgiving prayer."

Embarrassment flushed Thomas' cheeks red. He knelt back down and completed his Thanksgiving prayer before Father Bianchi dismissed him, and he left the confessional. As he left the little church, he retrieved the rosary he carried in his pocket and began his penance. When he finished the decades, he thought about the Blessed Mother, asking her for her intercession on Enara's behalf and for the strength to handle the guilt he carried.

Chapter 2: The Client

Miami, Florida: Early January 1982

Gabriel leaned back in his chair, staring at the Christmas card Rosa and Joaquín had sent him weeks before. He smiled as he read the words and remembered the new joy in their lives. The events of the past year played in his mind like motion pictures. He and Rodrigo had made the difference for Joaquín. His mind skimmed quickly through the cases and clients from his first year: Valerie, Rozália, Franco, and the other clients he had represented. He leaned forward, and, allowing the smile to fade, he placed the card in the envelope and returned the gift to its resting place in his top drawer.

The mountain of case files to his left invaded his periphery as he sat straight in his chair, and he let out a small sigh. *It never ends*, he thought to himself. Glancing at his watch, he grabbed the Wallace case file from the stack. Opening the file, he rested it on the desktop and took a pencil from its place and began examining the contents. *Jacob will be here in a little over an hour*, he thought as reviewed the next page.

He spent the next half hour delving into the file, breaking from it only when hearing a knock on the door.

"Come in, Susana," he said recognizing the familiar knock.

"Jacob Wallace will be here in…" began Susana, poking her head through the door.

"Half an hour," finished Gabriel, smiling back at her as she turned her head toward him.

"Yes," she affirmed. "Did you complete the billing that I requested for December?"

"All of it."

"Good. How's the workload for this week?"

"Well, considering that it's the Monday after New Year's, I'd say that it's a mountain's worth," he joked, gesturing at the stack of casefiles still piled on his desk.

Susana giggled and then asked if Gabriel wanted Cuban coffee to start the day.

"Is my father going to have some?" he asked. Seeing her nod in agreement, he accepted her offer and watched as she exited, and closed the door.

Jacob arrived a few minutes before the hour, and Gabriel heard the familiar tone speaking with Susana from the waiting room. He closed the file and removed the stack from his desk, placing it on the floor next to his chair before Jacob entered. When the knock came, Gabriel opened the door, allowing Jacob through and extended his hand to shake his. Jacob's short blonde hair shone beneath the light which illuminated his grey eyes, and made his smile seem warm.

"Good to see you, Jacob," greeted Gabriel, "please sit."

Jacob thanked him and took a seat at one of the chairs. "Thank you for meeting with me, Gabriel. I am ready to put this thing behind me and next week can't come soon enough."

"You've suffered enough, Jacob, these are the last steps."

"It's hard. I never wanted it to be this way, but I can't keep giving Belinda chances and when I found out that she had moved on, I knew that there would be no way back."

Gabriel nodded his head and opened the file. "Let's step into the conference room so you can review the agreement, "he said, making his way to the door. Jacob followed.

"I've reviewed your file and the notes leading up to this moment and want to tell you that the agreement that your wife's lawyer sent over looks to be in order. Please review it and let me know if anything is missing. Also, if anything new has come up since we last spoke, then please say so now," he said, signaling to the first chair on the right side of the conference room table, handing Jacob the agreement in a manila file.

"Nothing is new with me, Gabriel, but let me make sure that this is in order," he replied, taking the agreement and reviewing it.

Gabriel returned to his office and sat for a few moments, processing the remaining items of his to-do list in his mind while Jacob read. As he checked off the cases, billing, and motions, Jacob shifted, and Gabriel came back to the present. He stood and returned to the conference room.

"Everything seems to be in order, Gabriel. After I sign this, what is left to do?"

"It's an uncontested divorce, since you have divided the assets you have, and you have agreed to give her $10,000,00 to get back on her feet. All that you have to do is answer the seven questions that we reviewed previously in front of the judge. The entire process should be over quickly. It's a simple divorce, honestly." Gabriel picked up the phone from the receiver and called Susana, instructing her to enter his office. He turned and grabbed a pen from his desk drawer and handed it to Jacob, who took it, and signed his name. Gabriel signed the line next to his as a witness and right on cue Susana entered the room, grabbed the pen Gabriel held out to her, and glancing at Jacob's signature, signed as the other witness. She then scooped up the document and left the room.

"What do we do now?"

"Nothing for now, at the hearing we will present this to the court, enter it into evidence and the judge should admit it without problem."

"Okay," said Jacob smiling, "with me at the wedding and at the divorce. After all that's happened, it was about time."

"Well, you didn't have children, and you never really got to integrate your lives together because of all the problems."

"It took a long time for me to begin to move past my marriage, but I'm finally ready to start another life."

"And now you'll have the chance to. Forgive me for not asking earlier, but would you like some coffee?"

"Would love some, thank you. Should we walk down to the corner store or is Susana making it?"

Gabriel checked his watch, "Susana should have finished it by now. Hold on." Gabriel rose from his chair and walked over to the door. Poking his head through, he called out to Susana, and she turned to him, holding one hand on the mouthpiece of the telephone. "Susana, is the coffee ready?" he asked in Spanish.

Susana responded, "Yes, it is, sorry. Your grandmother is on the line and wants to know if you are still meeting her for lunch at 1:00pm. Can you make it?"

"Sure" and nodded.

"Yes, he'll meet you there," she said speaking Spanish into the receiver. When she hung up the phone, she turned back to Gabriel and told him that she would bring the two coffees. Gabriel acknowledged, explained the situation to Jacob who joked back.

"When you've lived in this town long enough, you pick up a thing or two about Spanish. My mother-in-law never spoke English. No problem, Susana," he said in heavily accented Spanish.

Susana laughed and Jacob gave her a thumbs up. Gabriel returned to his desk, and they continued to speak.

"How's the new position?"

"Not bad," answered Jacob, "construction is picking up in the town so moving up to assistant project manager is great and I've enjoyed the company since I've been here. They also allowed me to handle the issues with Belinda and understood a lot of what I was going through. Unfortunately, the owner experienced the same thing with his son, so he had a lot of grace in dealing with me."

"Is his son okay now?"

"Yeah, he is, but it took a while for him to overcome it."

Gabriel paused and neither man said a word. Before the silence became awkward, Gabriel opened his mouth to speak, but the door opened and Susana entered, carrying two Cuban coffees. The Espresso cups were intricate porcelain of white and blue that sat on small saucers with small silver spoons next to them. A napkin lay beneath each of the cups and the quality overall impressed and surprised Jacob.

"Sorry ma'am," he said, taking his cup from Susana's welcoming hand, "in construction, everything's Styrofoam or plastic."

"We do a lot of that here also, but every once in a while, we celebrate," joked Gabriel, taking his cup from Susana and raising it. The two men sat back in their chairs and sipped. Gabriel glanced at his watch and still had some time before he had to call his next client, which was luckily on the way to lunch. "What are you going to do when the divorce is finalized?" he asked, after taking a sip.

Jacob lowered the cup to the saucer on the desk. "I think that I'll take a vacation and head up to Tennessee or North Carolina and spend some time in the mountains. I'm originally from Northern Alabama but came down here with a friend and never left. Belinda did that to me. I had never met a woman like her before."

"I've never been to any of those states before."

"You should take a trip up there, Gabriel. The Appalachians are a sight to be seen. The Blue Ridge is God's country for sure. Maybe you need a vacation."

Gabriel chuckled as he took another sip from the cup, feeling the sweetness grow as he neared the bottom where the sugar caramelized, "Lawyers don't get days off unless their wives force them, and seeing as I don't have a wife or girlfriend right now, I'm not sure that I will."

Jacob laughed a dry laugh, "Amazing the power they have over us."

"Amazing indeed," agreed Gabriel.

Jacob departed a few minutes afterward and Gabriel found himself staring at his watch listening to the second hand as it ticked its way across the numerals. When he found the time, he picked up the phone and called Franco Mirabal, his client and new boxing instructor.

"Wild man!" shouted Franco from across the line.

Gabriel laughed and took a second to confirm that the deal with Santiago had gone well.

"So, when did they move in?" asked Gabriel. He took notes on his legal pad as Franco explained the move and the adjustment to the first level only, but Gabriel surmised that it was positive, and Franco explained that some of the higher-level executives of Santiago's different enterprises appreciated the quality of the Mirabal furniture and had even granted Franco contracts to design rooms in their homes. "So, it sounds like it's gone very well." Franco continued for a few moments longer before Gabriel glanced at his watch again and realized that he had to leave for lunch soon. "Franco, before I go, I can't make it to the gym tonight, but I can go Thursday. Does that work for you?"

Franco agreed and Gabriel jotted it down on his pad.

"Thursday at 6:00pm, I'll see you then."

Gabriel hung up the phone, turned in his seat, and grabbed his sports coat from his chair. *The rest of the day is pretty clear, so I can enjoy lunch with Abuela*, he thought as he exited the office and then the building. Climbing into the Regal, he turned the key, checked his mirrors, and left the parking lot, strolling onto Coral Way and off to lunch, eager to see his grandmother.

Chapter 3: The Lunch

Miami, Florida: Early January

Gabriel arrived at Abuela's with time to spare. As he climbed the stairs of the building, he heard the familiar toddlers playing in the breezeways and heard the clangs of serving spoons beating pots and pans on stovetops and smelled the aromas of beans, meats, plantains, and yucca. Before reaching Abuela's door, he heard the anchors from Univisión, Telemundo, and Radio Mambí discussing matters of state and economy. Reagan was now a full year into his presidency, and the tax cuts had only dented the stagflation. *Prices are still up, but at least people have more money in their pockets,* mused Gabriel as he left the news behind and tapped on Abuela's door.

He heard her from the other side and entered, greeting her as the smells of his summers in Asturias welcomed him. "Pulpo?" he asked. Abuela turned to him and nodded. Her light grey hair still had some black wisps but now bore more white than black and even more gray. He looked around the apartment, still decorated with a Christmas tree and even some stockings on the bookshelf, but otherwise it was the same. He strolled over to his grandmother, and they exchanged customary kisses on each cheek.

"I'm going to be a few more minutes, so take a seat. I'll call you when I'm ready to serve," she said, ushering him back to the sitting room. Gabriel preferred to stand and drew closer to the bookshelf, examining the novels that occupied each level. He glanced over the familiar names of Machado, Quevedo, Cervantes, Bécquer, and Teresa de Ávila, among others. *Few novelties*, he joked with himself as he realized that much of what sat in his own personal library mirrored what Abuela and Abuelo had collected over the years. At the end of the shelf sat his grandfather's favorite, Calderon de la Barca and he recited to himself:

¿Qué es la vida? Un frenesí.
¿Qué es la vida? Una ilusión,
una sombra, una ficción,
y el mayor bien es pequeño:
que toda la vida es sueño,
y los sueños, sueños son.

He raised his eyes to the top shelf where a duplicate of the photo he now had in his office stood. There stared his grandfather's face, eyes beaming at the camera as they had years before. The stocky man of pale skin and sharp eyes sporting his linen shirt, woolen pants, and ascot cap with an arm resting firmly on Gabriel's shoulder. He smiled before shifting to another photo of himself as a child, laughing with his eyes closed as Abuelo held him to his cheek. *The only child of his only child*, thought Gabriel, realizing that he was all that his grandparents had. He gazed at the family photos for a little longer when Abuela called him to the table. He heard her say a few things in Spanish before walking over to the set table with the plates of food in her hands. Laying down the octopus, shrimp, and other tapas, Abuela smiled and returned to the kitchen, retrieving two glasses and a small pitcher of water. She eyed him, commanding him to sit first, but knew that she would lose. He pulled her chair out and she complied before he took his own.

"Whenever you look at the books on my shelf, I hear you recite those lines, even when you say them to yourself like now. I read them in your body. Your grandfather was the same way," she said, chuckling as she accepted his manner.

"As is my mother."

"Yes, you all live those lines," she said with a slight smile. "You are so much like both your parents, but this romantic streak comes from your mother. May I?" she asked, extending a hand toward him.

He took his plate from the table and handed it to her. She served him the assortment of food, taking small portions of each for him.

"And the salad that I forgot is on the counter. Where is my mind, Gabriel?"

"Hopefully here for a little longer," joked Gabriel, "even if it's not as sharp as it used to be."

Abuela rose and walked back to the kitchen, grabbing two small bowls of salad. She handed Gabriel his and then placed hers on the table, served herself the other food she had prepared. She sat and Gabriel followed suit.

"You or me?" she asked.

"I'll say it this time," he said, taking the hand she offered to him. "Bless us, O Lord, and these Thy gifts, which we are about to receive from Thy bounty through Christ our Lord. Amen."

"Beautiful," remarked Abuela in her thanks. "So, how is work?"

"Not much has changed since we last spoke, Abuela. Busy after the new year, but otherwise, I don't have any exciting cases."

"How is Joaquín?" she inquired before taking a shrimp to her mouth.

"Good. Really good. Walter called me earlier this week to tell me that Joaquín was a great find and that he really appreciated him as the new manager."

"I prayed for them a lot."

"I know, Abuela, as did I." He pierced one of the pieces of octopus with his fork, drawing it to his mouth and eating as the familiar taste soothed him. He chewed for a few moments and Abuela watched him, hanging on his critique. "Yes, it's very good; it's always good," he spoke, answering her silent question.

She brushed a wisp of hair from her face with her fingers, tucking it behind her ear. "Not as good as home," she stated.

"Don't be so hard on yourself," dismissed Gabriel, "anything you make is delicious."

"Octopus in Asturias is better than in Miami," she declared in gruff tone.

"Anything you say."

"Exactly! You learned well."

Gabriel raised an eyebrow as he tilted his head slightly downward, giving her a playful gaze.

"What?!" she joked.

He held his gaze, and the staring contest began. Seconds later, Abuela surrendered.

"So, when are you getting married?" she inquired flatly.

"I don't know, ask God."

"I do, often, but he's not really answering me."

"Maybe he's telling you to be patient," counseled Gabriel, taking a forkful of salad.

"I'll have to light more candles for you at mass," she said, shaking her head. "Do you carry the rosary that I gave you?"

"Yes, in its case, and I carry it in my pocket at all times. And I have one in my car, hanging from the rear -view mirror on the windshield."

"And the holy water?"

"In the glove compartment of my car, like I always have, but none of those things will get me married you know."

"Oh…Well maybe you need to speak with Father Lázaro."

Gabriel laughed aloud.

"It's really serious, you know!"

"It is, Abuela, I know that it is, but my focus is on my work. When the right one comes along, you'll be the first to know."

"At this rate, I'll be dead," said Abuela, rolling her eyes.

"Of course you will be," retorted Gabriel. "Come on, let's talk about something other than my love life, please. I don't want to be the cause of any more of your grief."

"Okay," agreed Abuela, ending the conversation.

They sat in silence for a few minutes, eating their lunch and savoring the cooking. When they had finished, Abuela took the plates and carried them back to the kitchen, scraping the remaining food and sauce into the garbage can before running water over the silverware and plates in the sink.

"Are you still working out with Franco?" asked Abuela, returning to the table.

"I see him Thursday."

"Not tonight?"

"No, I've got to stay late at the office to finish some work."

"Would you like me to pack you some dinner?"

"It's fine, I've got leftovers at home."

"You'll have more," offered Abuela.

Gabriel politely declined, "I can't. If I take your leftovers, then I won't eat mine, and I don't want the food to spoil."

"Your loss."

"I know," said admitted Gabriel. He allowed a sly smile to escape him and Abuela bade him to loosen up.

"I'll light a candle for you at mass tomorrow morning, maybe two."

"Make it three for good measure."

"For good measure! –Now go or you'll be late."

Gabriel checked his watch and knew that he was pushing it. He turned to head out the door and as he opened, he heard Abuela one last time.

"It's been long enough; you need to let it go."

Gabriel did not turn back to her. He paused, held the door for a moment, and answered.

"Some things don't fade with time, Abuela; they fade with answers."

"They fade when you face them. Don't forget that."

"I won't. I promise." Gabriel closed the door behind him, and, making his way to the Regal, departed back to the office, processing Abuela's words and the choice he had to make.

Chapter 4: The Long Timers

Miami, Florida: January 1982

The week leading up to Thursday dragged on. Work pushed his plans further than he had hoped, but everything that everyone pushed off to the new year needed the speed of the old one and so the comfort of hard worked late nights only came when his head hit the pillow. As he exited his car, he watched the sun appear from behind the clouds, and, remembering that Susana wouldn't be in until after 10:00am because of a medical appointment, decided to make his way down to Versailles for breakfast.

Gabriel expected less people on a Thursday morning, but it didn't bother him. Finding a seat in front of a mirror, he took a moment to examine the menu and his mood. He debated between a few options when a familiar voice sounded from behind him.

"Good morning, *Doctor*," said the voice in Spanish.

Gabriel looked up to see Santiago's dark eyes and tanned face with his rough, hairy hand extended toward him.

"Good morning," responded Gabriel, rising from his chair and offering his own hand to shake.

"May I?"

"Please," said Gabriel, gesturing toward the empty chair across from him. Santiago sat and within a few minutes, the waiter greeted them, took their orders, and brought them coffee, orange juice, and water. Gabriel took a sip of his water as Santiago cracked the knuckles on his hands. His rings shifted slightly as he bent his fingers into crooked positions and Gabriel noticed a fresh scar across his left hand.

"What happened to you?" he asked, using his chain to point at Santiago's hand.

"Nothing major, just the usual work," he joked, massaging his left hand with his right.

"Building something else now?"

"Always."

"Even in your sixties, you don't stop," said Gabriel, reaching for his coffee cup.

"The moment a man believes he's old, his days are numbered, believe me. The trick to life isn't to die old, it's to die young, just late."

"Ah, young at heart," surmised Gabriel, taking another sip of his coffee.

"A young heart equals a young mind, and a young mind equals more time."

"I'll keep that in *mind*, Santiago. Thank you."

Santiago chuckled at the change of tone.

"Your father has a young man's spirit, but then again, he's about ten years younger than I am."

"He'll be fifty-two soon, in March."

"And in September, I'll be another year later," joked Santiago.

Both men laughed and a few moments later, the waiter brought them their breakfast, somehow managing several plates on his arms, but not one fell to the floor or clattered into another.

They ate while sharing stories, with Santiago speaking at length about how he rebuilt his life in exile.

"So much of what I have now is because of three things, Gabriel," he said, raising his thumb, index, and middle fingers from his palm. "First, my faith. My life could have gone so many different ways, but God smiled on me and answered my prayers. Second, my wife and kids. They are the joy that pushed me to work as hard as I have. And third is your father. Without his legal advice and the cases he's won for me, only a part of what I have would be mine."

Gabriel sat back in his chair, absorbing Santiago's words, and the gravity of their meaning.

"I never really understood just how much his counsel affected your business."

"The three people critical to your success in business are your banker, your accountant, and your lawyer. You should always have those three people, and you should see them once a month and at least once per quarter. I think that I speak with your father once a week if not every other week and when things get crazy. it's even more."

Gabriel nodded, reflecting on his clients from the past year. None of them had contacted him other than Walter but his needs were more frequent than the other clients. There was a lot of contact during the cases, but once the cases had finished, so did the calls.

Santiago grabbed his fork and began to dig into his breakfast and Gabriel followed suit. They ate and Santiago began telling Gabriel stories his father had never shared. Most of the anecdotes were about problems or comical situations that life gave on occasion, but a few were stories about his father's personality. "Your father," said Santiago, "one time was with me at a gas station that we started building before the permits were finalized. He kept telling me that I needed to cease and desist, but I didn't listen. He then went inside to grab water, and at that moment an inspector from the county walked up and stood next to me as I was replacing the storage tanks for the gasoline."

"What happened?"

"Well, he asked me who I was and when I told him that I was the owner, he said he was the inspector." The corners of Santiago's mouth curled into a bashful smile. "Needless to say, he asked for permits."

"And you didn't have them, did you?"

"They were in processing."

"What was the inspector's reaction?" asked Gabriel, taking a sip of water from his glass.

"Luckily much better than your father's."

"How did you manage that?"

"I showed him the tickets that I bought to Mexico and told him that I was going to be leaving for a month for my daughter's wedding and my second honeymoon and told him that my general manager had just retired, so he understood that it wasn't a usual thing."

"So, what did he do?"

"Luckily, the Dolphins game that he was going to was about to start, so he cut me a break and let me off with a warning, but it should have been much more."

"And my dad's reaction?"

"Nearly killed me and nearly had a heart attack."

Gabriel held his laughter, remembering that they were in public.

Santiago chuckled for a few moments longer and then continued, "I've put your father through a lot with my businesses. Poor man. His heart is bigger than you know, Gabriel. Much bigger."

Gabriel's expression thanked Santiago for the kind words.

"You'll have the kind of relationship with your clients, your more loyal ones at least, that your father does with his. I'm sure of it. Your stories with your long timers will be just as good if not better.

"He's told me the same things," answered Gabriel.

"I'm sure he has," said Santiago, wiping his mouth with his napkin, "but know that he doesn't say it because you're his son. He says it because he believes it."

Gabriel nodded.

Within half an hour they had finished, and Santiago paid the bill with Gabriel promising to pay the next time. As he made his way from the table to the Regal, he felt a sense of keen pride over his father's reputation. Santiago was one of the most successful businessmen in all of Miami. Of all the lawyers and firms in the city, he chose the little office on Coral Way, the one that now bears Gabriel's name.

When Gabriel arrived, it was only half past eight, and, remembering his list of things to do, he figured that he would greet his father and then get down to work. When he called out to him, he only heard silence in return. Walking over to his father's door, Gabriel knocked gently, waited, and, after not hearing anything, opened the door. *Strange*, he thought.

He checked the desk, searching for a clue as to where his father had gone or as to what might have delayed him, but found nothing. Realizing that Thomas must have had an appointment that he had not recalled, he walked back to his office, and, while rounding the corner of his desk, saw the note written on his legal pad.

Left to see Raúl Morales. Will be back this afternoon.

Raúl was a name he had known but hadn't heard in years. *What could Raúl want that would make Dad drive to see him?* He entertained the possibilities and questions that flowed through his mind and after a while dismissed them. *Speculation is pointless. I'll have the facts this afternoon*, he thought as he sat down at his desk and began to work.

Susana arrived shortly before 10:00am, greeting Gabriel and asking where Thomas was.

"Dad will be back this afternoon. He went to see Raúl Morales," said Gabriel as Susana pushed the ajar door to his office until it lay fully open.

"He drove to Naples?" she asked, not hiding her surprise.

"Possibly, but I doubt it. Two of Raúl's kids still live here in Miami, so he's probably meeting him somewhere around close by."

"I forgot that he still had family here. He moved so long ago it seems." She took a seat at her desk and placed her purse on the far side of her desk.

"One of his daughters and one of his son's. The other two live in Naples."

"Where do you think that they are meeting?"

Gabriel thought about his answer, calculating where Thomas would agree to meet. Knowing the early hour, there were only a few places that they could meet on this side of town.

"Best guess, they are meeting at one of the daycare centers. I do not think that they are having breakfast. If it's important, they might grab lunch, but I would not count on it." He lowered his eyes back to his files while Susana nodded and agreed.

"Do you have much on the docket for today?" she asked.

Gabriel, not raising his eyes from the file, spoke.

"Yesterday I knocked out most of what I had today, so the later part of the afternoon is open. I might just leave early so that I can train a little longer at Franco's."

"How is that going?"

"Well. Really well. I have gotten stronger and have toned up a bit more despite gaining a few pounds."

"That's muscle mass, not fat."

"Sure, but I prefer to remain lean. Do you know how much it costs to buy new suits?" he joked.

"You can afford it," she teased.

"I can, but it doesn't mean that I'd like to, and it seems like Miami's only getting more expensive."

"It is. Every day," she affirmed.

As she finished speaking, she turned back to her desk and Gabriel resumed his examinations, hoping to finish them before his lunch hour.

Thomas returned just as Gabriel opened his last file, hearing his father's voice greeting Susana before stopping in front of Gabriel's office door. He raised his eyes to his father's and Thomas gestured with his head and arm, signaling that he should follow him. Gabriel held up two fingers and Thomas understood, giving his son the time he needed to complete his work.

Thomas sat behind his desk, ruminating and pondering the cycle of events Raúl had described to him. A knock came at the door, and the noise interrupted his train of thought. "Come in," he said, shifting his gaze to the door.

"I imagine that you want to talk about Raúl Morales files?" asked Gabriel as he entered.

"Yes, please. Take a seat."

Gabriel sat in one of the chairs in front of Thomas's desk. Thomas glanced down at the small stack of files to his right.

"Raúl Morales called the office a while ago and seemed very worried about a new matter. We agreed today that we are all going to meet this coming week but just know that the events are fairly serious. I would like you to investigate these files before then," he said, placing his hand over the stack.

"Which day are we meeting?" asked Gabriel.

"Either Wednesday or Thursday, he has to check with his kids to see who can come."

"So, it is fairly serious then?"

"Yes."

"Care to shed some light on the gravity of the problem?"

"Not yet. I would like you to become familiar with the businesses, how they developed and their legal problems in the past. You don't have to do a full dive but enough to get a sense of their business and most of all, the work done for them in the past."

"And you think that not telling me about the issue will make it easier for me to read all of this?"

"I want you to be focused on the paperwork. Irregularities, patterns, etc. I want you to focus on everything instead of searching for something related to the issue at hand because if you search for it, you may miss something else."

"I understand," affirmed Gabriel.

"Do you have the time to start this now?"

"I do. I don't have to leave for Franco's until 5:00."

"What are you working on at the moment?"

"Just finished signing some motions and letter Susana prepared for me; I just have my regular pile of files but nothing pressing."

"Then work on these until you leave for Franco's,

and when you see him, give him my best and tell him to also give my best to Alfonso."

"Will do."

Thomas turned to the stack of files and lifted them toward Gabriel.

Gabriel nodded and stood, grasping at the stack of files and trying to collect them all in his hands. Once he had secured them in his arms, he moved toward the door.

"Wait, I almost forgot. Here, take this." Thomas called out as he handed Gabriel another litigation file. "This was the first and biggest case I handled for them."

"Right. I'll get on this."

Gabriel returned to his office, closed the door behind him, and dug into the files. It was unusual for this father to throw things on him like this. Thomas had not detailed what he was supposed to look for but knew that he trusted him to find the anomaly. Putting down the first file he grabbed the thick folder labeled *Trial*, but before he could open the expandable, there was a knock on his door.

"Come in."

Susana emerged from the doorway and Gabriel peered up at her.

"You have a couple in the waiting room wanting to see you: a Mr. and Mrs. Adegboye." She announced.

Gabriel lowered the file onto the desktop.

"Mr. and Mrs. Adegboye you said?"

Susana nodded.

"Please tell them I'll be right with them. I'll fetch them when I've put these up," he said, pointing to the stack beside him."

"Should I set up the information for a new file?"

"No, not yet. These folks were the victim's family in the last case I handled at the State Attorney's office."

Susana followed his train of thought.

"You got it."

"Susana, better yet please set them up in the conference room and prepare coffee for them."

Susana nodded and closed the door.

Gabriel leaned back in his chair, caught between the emotions of the Adegboyes coming to his office and the mystery of the Morales files. More than a year had passed since he last saw them. *What could they possibly want with me?* he thought to himself. As he rested his head on the top of the chair, the memories of Leonard's harsh words came to him, flooding his mind and filling him with remorse. The corners of his eyes started twitching as he recalled the moments in the Gerstein building and the brief conversation with Donovan, the meeting with his old boss, Drakos, and the sorrow of a plea instead of justice.

He let out a long breath, wiped small beads of sweat from his brows, and calmed himself. *Come on, nothing you haven't handled before*, he thought.

A few minutes later Gabriel walked into the conference room. Leonard and Sharice were sitting on the far side of the table and rose as soon as they saw him. Leonard extended his hand toward Gabriel. "So good to see you, Counselor."

Gabriel smiled a little, attempting to conceal his surprise, took his hand, and said, "Good to see both of you again."

Sharice walked around her husband and hugged him.

Gabriel could not conceal his astonishment any longer as intrigue and bewilderment betrayed his impassive intent.

"I don't blame you for your surprise in seeing us, Gabriel," stated Leonard, pulling out his chair and taking a seat.

Sharice and Gabriel followed suit.

"The last time that we saw you, I was angry, too angry to see the reason why you had left us last December."

Sharice placed her hand on Leonard's, signaling she wanted to speak. Leonard nodded and Sharice adjusted her glasses before allowing her sweet voice to fill the room.

"It was hard for us. We had worked with you for so long that nothing made sense. How could the lawyer who fought so hard for our family just leave the case to another lawyer? I knew there was a reason why you would not give us answers and seemed so detached last December. Nothing made any sense, and then Mr. Donovan came in and told us that he would be taking the case and within fifteen minutes had told us that we had to accept the plea deal that we refused to take."

Gabriel listened to every word but held his silence. Sharice smiled, understanding his limitations, and continued.

"Anyway, we have friend from church that has a friend that works at your old office and through her we found out that you left that job on the same day you spoke with us. She said that you were the talk of the office, an incredibly good prosecutor with a very good future and no one expected you to leave. She said that everyone was so surprised."

"We know that you can't really say anything, and that you probably signed something when you left," began Leonard.

"But we know that you only resigned because you refused to force us into taking the plea," finished Sharice.

Gabriel kept silent for another moment, grateful for their words, but forced not to address it. He finished calculating his words and spoke.

"Thank you, but you know, it wasn't really the place I was looking for." answered Gabriel.

"No, you were looking for a place with your name on the door not once, but twice." interjected Lenoard with a grin. They all laughed. "I owe you an apology for the way I treated you."

"You do not owe me a thing, Mr. Adegboye. The truth is that I am very happy here and working with you made me realize that this was more important than I thought. Had it not been for your case, I would not have learned what I needed to earn a place here."

The three of them exhaled as Gabriel unloaded the truth.

"We understand that, very much so," admitted Sharice.

"And we've thought about it and your honesty a lot since then," continued Leonard.

"Thank you, Mr. Adegboye. So, what brings you by?"

"You mean besides the apology?" said Leonard.

Gabriel did not know exactly how to react.

"My dad passed."

"I am so sorry to hear that."

Leonard rose from his chair and began to pace around the table, clearing his throat to speak.

"Thanks, but you know he lived a full life. In the end he forgave the man that wounded him, and he asked me to thank you for everything you did. On his last night, he kissed his grandchildren goodbye and slipped away during the early morning, almost at dawn." Leonard wiped his eyes. "He was content to be on his way to be with my mom. My father was a good man. He taught me to work hard and to do the right thing. I will be forever thankful for those lessons, and I work hard to do the same for my children." There was silence for a few seconds as all three reflected on their memories of him. "We are here for his estate, and we hope that you do that type of work."

Gabriel paused for a moment, holding it long enough for Sharice and Leonard to hang on to his words.

"Unfortunately, I don't do estates; they say that it's for older lawyers, So…"

Sharice and Leonards' eyes widened toward him.

"My father does our estate work, instead," joked Gabriel.

Sharice sighed in relief and Leonard laughed, his booming voice echoing in the room.

"You almost had me there," he admitted.

"Oh, I had you, but you can hold on to your pride."

Leonard waved him off and Sharice looked at him from her chair.

"I want to meet the man who raised you," exclaimed Sharice, "Can we meet him?"

"He might be tied up, but he is here. I'll ask Susana to see if he can spare a minute."

Gabriel walked to the door, opened it, and called for Susana to check his father's availability. She complied and he saw her rise from her desk.

"Before we go any further, I assume that you have the death certificate, correct?"

"We ordered them through the funeral home. They said we would need eight to ten certified copies. We ordered ten. What else?"

"Collect all the ownership documents for everything he owned, deeds for houses and land, titles for cars, boats, and anything else of that nature. You want to get his last two tax returns, any bank account statement you can find within the last year, check books, savings booklets, safety deposit box paperwork and keys, retirement plans, investments in bonds, stocks, and all other bank related paperwork. The most important thing is to get information on any and every bank or investment brokerage where he may have had an investment," he said as Sharice was opening her bag for a paper and pen. "We have a list."

Turning to the door of the conference room he poked his head out and requested the list from Susana as she returned from notifying Thomas about the Adegboyes. He faced the Adegboyes and spoke, "Susana will give you a comprehensive list of items before you leave for you to start working on."

Sharice and Leonard nodded and leaned back in their chairs, waiting for Thomas.

He entered a moment later, sporting his famous suspenders and thick spectacles.

"So, these are the famous Adegboyes?" asked Thomas extending a hand to Leonard and receiving a hug from Sharice. "I've heard so much about you."

"Hopefully only good things!" hoped Sharice.

"Only the best, Gabriel told me that you were his favorites when he was at the State Attorney's office."

"Favorites?" pressed Sharice.

"I'd swear it in a court of law," joked Thomas.

The four of them sat for a little while, talking about the estate, Gabriel's childhood, Thomas' practice, and the other things that curiosity and comfort bring. Gabriel leaned back as they spoke, absorbing the moment and enjoying the peace it brought to him. The weight of that day at the Gerstein building lifted with their forgiveness and his in return. As they finished, his father left to collect the papers from Susana and Sharice followed him, leaving Leonard and Gabriel by themselves.

"I see where you got your values from," said Leonard.

"Yeah, he's quite the lawyer and a better Dad."

"I believe you, Gabriel. Thank you for accepting our apology and for allowing us to work with you."

"There was nothing to forgive, Mr. Adegboye. It was a tough situation that neither of us wanted."

"You're right, but still, it takes a great man to forgive."

"As it does to ask for forgiveness."

They smiled at one another, and Gabriel outstretched his hand.

"Thank you for giving me your time today," said Leonard.

"It was our pleasure, but seriously, you don't need to thank me, Leonard."

"We owe you our thanks." Gabriel nodded and escorted Leonard back to the main area where Susana, Thomas, and Sharice chatted, list in her hand.

"Ready, Lenny?"

"Ready, Love."

The Adegboyes departed while Gabriel, Susana, and Thomas watched them. They heard the chatter as the clients made their way down the hallway and into the parking lot. Gabriel turned to his father who congratulated him.

"They're good people, Son."

"I know, Dad. I just didn't expect to see them again, especially after all this time."

Thomas smiled and stared at his son, the cerulean eyes magnified by the spectacles, "I get the feeling that they'll be with you for a long time, Son. Just you wait and see."

Chapter 5: The Gym

Miami, Florida: January 1982

Gabriel arrived at Franco's early and began stretching as soon as he entered. Rigo had greeted him as he was cleaning some of the punching bags with a rag, offering no more than a wave as the sound of Rock music blared through the speakers and echoed off the walls. Off to the side a few young guns pounded each other in training while their girlfriends talked and showed off their nails and hair.

Crossing to the locker room, Gabriel did not see Franco anywhere and figured that he hadn't arrived yet. *Great,* he thought, *so I've got some time to myself first.* He entered the room and opened his usual locker, using the key from his chain to remove the lock. Stashing his briefcase and suit, he changed into his T-shirt and boxing shorts, removing his cross and a pen he had forgotten in his pocket. He glanced over at the mirror in front of the sink and saw the definition in his frame that had improved over the last few months. He worked out with Franco three days per week and, despite Franco pressing him for more, three was all that he could manage.

Turning on the faucet, he washed his hands and face before staring into the mirror for a few moments, grateful for what he saw in the reflection. He looked less stressed, and he noticed it in the lines that had lessened on his face. *This is the least stressed that you have been in a long time*, he thought.

He dried his face with one of the clean towels on the table of the locker room and then chalked his hands. He walked back into the gym, gloves and wraps in his hands and laid them down next to the ring. Rigo met him as he made his way to the first station and picked up a jump rope. Rigo held up five fingers to Gabriel while pointing to the digital clock that hung above. *Five minutes*, thought Gabriel. Rigo glanced down at his watch and then lowered a finger as each second passed until he closed his fist and Gabriel began. Sweat slithered down his face, wrists, and hands as the rope rhythmically beat the base of the mats on the floor. He jumped for a minute, then alternated from leg to leg for another minute longer, then switched it up, crossing his arms every fourth jump.

"Now you're just showing off, Wild Man!" yelled a familiar voice over the booming rock music.

Gabriel raised his eyes to see Franco waving at him from the second-floor overlook. He smiled back at him and pressed on.

"Rigo, warm him up, good. I need him to spar with one of guys in twenty minutes," said Franco in Spanish.

"With Adalto?" questioned Rigo, continuing the Spanish.

"Yeah!"

"Okay."

"Who is Adalto?" asked Gabriel also in Spanish.

"One of the fighters here, he's a newer kid. He's aggressive but controlled. Very mature for nineteen."

"Good to know."

"Don't worry, he's about three weight classes beneath you and is respectful."

"Does Franco train anyone who's not respectful?"

"Not really, but there is one kid who's pretty arrogant."

"Who's that?"

"Savio. He only trains in the morning, but he trains for two hours five days a week and competes on the weekend. He's working his way through amateur level until he finds enough sponsors to take him pro."

"Is he close?"

"Yeah, both to sponsors and to becoming pro."

"Will he stay if he goes pro?"

"No, he'll go, but Franco doesn't need the money, and he'd probably want less of a headache."

"Is he that bad?"

"All of our fighters are controlled except him. He's the only one that has ever lost control."

"What did he do?"

"He was sparring with a fellow fighter and didn't stop hitting him. Franco had to rush in and throw Savio off him. Nearly banned him and there was so much blood."

"Did the other guy leave the gym?"

"Yes, and Savio was suspended for three months."

"And he chose to stay?"

"He didn't have a choice. when the other gyms found out, no one would take him, regardless of his talent."

Gabriel nodded and jumped rope until the five minutes ended.

Then Rigo ran him through the rest of the warmup, from step ladders to shadow boxing; they did it all.

A few minutes later, Franco returned with Adalto, and strapped Gabriel with a body pad and headgear. Franco collected his hair and repositioned the hair tie, moving the knot higher up on the back of his head, and spoke.

"Adalto, Gabriel, this is sparing to prepare Adalto for his fight next week. Adalto is nineteen, Gabriel is twenty-nine. Adalto is a Bantamweight while Gabriel is a Light Heavyweight. For today, we'll do six rounds. Three minutes as usual. Adalto, because of the difference in class, don't hold back on the body shots, but pull back the face. Gabriel, Adalto needs the training, give him hell.”

“Isn’t weight class too much?”

Franco looked at Gabriel and rebutted his argument.

“Have you been training as a professional fighter?”

“No.”

“Then do as I say.”

Franco looked back to Adalto.

“Why do I have to watch his face?” questioned Adalto.

“Because his is better looking than yours!” answered Rigo from the back.

They laughed.

“Because Gabriel needs his face in court.”

“Okay,” answered Adalto.

The fighters nodded and entered the ring. Once ready, Franco stood between them, they touched gloves and began to spar. Between Adalto’s speed and his endurance, Gabriel fought on the defensive, giving one jab to every three of Adalto’s and rarely landing a cross. Sweat soaked Gabriel as he watched Adalto circling around him almost dancing, his movement smooth and water-like yet brazen at the same time.

By the time the rounds ended, Adalto stepped out while Gabriel collapsed on the mat. Sweat and exhaustion poured out of him while his arms throbbed. His body felt sore from his ribs to his wrists and though Adalto spared his face, he punished his body, even with the padding. Rigo and Franco checked on him as he lay spreadeagle in defeat. Franco climbed into the ring and sat on the mat next to him.

“Are you dead?” joked Franco.

Gabriel tried to raise his arm to him but could barely lift it.

"The Wild man ain't wild no more," affirmed Franco, laughing. "Let me help you with those."

Franco removed Gabriel's gloves from his hands and helped him to a knee. He led him and leaned him against the post at one of the corners of the ring. Handing him a bottle of water with a straw, Gabriel drank for a moment, savoring every drop as his breath pained his ribs.

"I should have made it three rounds instead of six," cursed Franco, lamenting his decision and taking the bottle back from the seated Gabriel.

"I've taken worse licks in the courtroom," admitted Gabriel, coughing. "And given much worse in return. This is my penance for the beatings I've given, I'm sure of it."

"You think?" Franco's brow rose as the shock set in.

"Yeah, you walk into the courtroom like you slip into the ring, ready to fight. In the ring you fight with your body, in court you fight with your mind. You must convince the jury that you are telling them the truth, and, by implication, the other side is not. The evidence and testimony are colored by the impression you transmit in your questions, words, gestures and even objections and expressions. If the jury feels that you are the truthful person in that room, you win the case. But, if, at any moment, someone asks a witness an innocuous question at the wrong time, or you take just a little too long in reacting to a slightly incoherent answer, your bubble of truth bursts and you are lost."

"But you have no way of knowing that, right?"

"No lawyer does, but it doesn't make it any better when you're down looking up."

Gabriel tried to raise himself from the mat and pain shot from his ribs all the way down to his legs. He knew that it was only a matter of time until his sciatica flared and knew that he had to stretch. Franco helped him up and supported him as he leaned forward, stretching the compressed muscles and doing all that he could to release the tension.

"How bad is it?"

"Not as bad as I thought," confessed Gabriel, reaching down to his toes and holding the position until his face turned red from the rushing blood. "It's gotten much better since I started training with you. The attacks come less often, and when they do they go away quicker."

"Good to know. You've also put on some muscle since you started coming here more regularly. That's what you need to help your core hold you up. You've still got a long way to go, but not bad."

"I'm not trying to go pro, Franco, but I'm glad that I've got some more muscle."

"I know that. I meant that you've toned up but still have some more work to do."

"As long as my practice lets me, I'll be here," said Gabriel, spreading his legs shoulder-length and twisting back and forth in dynamic stretch.

"So, what's been new with you?"

"Just work, really. Dad's got me working on files for some new clients, my responsibilities have increased, and the cases have become more complex, but they're good. Some of my old clients from the State Attorney's office came in today after not seeing them for a year."

"That's nice, to say hi?"

"That and to give us some work."

"Not bad, Wild Man, not bad. What happened to that girl that you helped last year? –The one that was not really your client."

"The one in the wheelchair?"

"That one!" shouted Franco.

"She's fine," said Gabriel, grabbing a small towel from his bag and wiping the sweat from his face. "My client keeps up with her more than I do, but I ran into her lawyer last week on the way to file some papers at the clerk's office and he told me that the renovations to her home have gone well and that she started dating the general contractor who did the work."

"Really?"

"Yeah, apparently he was smitten by her and didn't care about her condition."

"A shot at a new life there."

"He works in mysterious ways."

"He does, like providing you with penance through the fists of a 19-year-old."

"Yeah, what a mystery that is."

"At least he didn't call you old man."

"Nope, he just made me feel like one."

They both laughed. Franco held the rope up and Gabriel exited the ring, doing the same for his friend before they walked over to Rigo who swept the floor next to the locker room.

"Next week, Champ?" asked Rigo as Gabriel approached.

Gabriel nodded.

"Wild Man, thank you for this favor. Want to see Adalto's fight?"

"When is it?"

"Next Friday."

"Time?"

"He's a Bantamweight, so it's early."

"Time?"

"Six O'clock."

"I've got plans, but I will see what I can do. I will call you if I can make it, but otherwise, count me out."

"Alright, I guess friends are like leftovers. Some you want as soon as you see them and others you skip out on."

"Wise ass."

"Especially with you. Now get dressed and get out of here; you've had enough for today."

Gabriel made his way to the locker room and in a few minutes had changed into the sweatpants and sweatshirts he brought to spare his suit and tie. Removing the formal wear from the locker, he made his way back to the parking lot, climbed into the Regal, and turned the key. The engine sputtered a few times and Gabriel cursed the motor. Franco, with a garbage bag in his hand, moved toward him.

"Want me to throw the car out along with this bag?" he joked.

"It's been giving me trouble for a few weeks now. Ever since Christmas. I've taken it to the mechanic twice, but they can't seem to figure out the problem."

"I've got a guy who specializes in these."

"Buicks?"

"American cars, but yes, Buicks."

"Where's he located?"

"I'll take you next week if you can spare the time. Think it will last that long?"

"It should hold for one more week at least."

"Okay, pick me up next Friday in the morning and I'll take you to him. You can do Friday morning, right?"

"Yeah, the morning's free, and if not, I'll move around whatever I need to move around, because I need to fix the car."

"Done deal."

"See you next week."

"If I don't hear from you sooner," stated Franco.

Gabriel smiled, turned the key one more time and the motor roared.

"Wild Man, let it ride!"

Gabriel shrugged him off, turned the wheel, and headed home, ribs sore, but grateful for all that had happened that day.

Chapter 6: The Complaints

Miami, Florida: January 1982

The weekend and the early part of the week came and went, and Gabriel's ribs delayed as long to heal. He had met with his father on Tuesday morning, debriefed him on the Morales files, and, to both of their satisfactions, had found no anomalies in the history of their businesses. Now he sat in his office just after lunch and waited for Thomas to return so that they could prepare for the Morales meeting.

Thomas entered his office at half past the hour, and Gabriel raised his head to find his father sitting in one of the chairs opposite his desk.

"Unusual seeing you in one of those."

"I can imagine so."

"They'll be here soon?"

"Yes, in the next half-hour or so."

"The hearing went well?"

"Deposition."

"That's right, the hearing's tomorrow."

"9:00am sharp."

"Want me there?"

"No, I've got this one. Should be routine," finished Thomas, removing his glasses and wiping the lenses clean with the spare cloth from his pocket. He massaged his eyes and then the bridge of his nose where his glasses rested, doing his best to remove the indentations that spectacles often left behind.

"Care to review the Morales files one last time?"

"Review?"

"Discuss," corrected Gabriel, focusing on his father's divided attention.

"Yes, let's."

Gabriel flipped his notepad to the sections he had prepared and began reading through the highlights. Thomas asked a few questions every so often, but nothing more than clarification.

"In everything that Raúl's done in building the family business, not a single piece has fallen out of line. No anomalies, violations, fines, or anything out of the ordinary. Of all the lawsuits that you handled for him; the wins were fair and the settlements clean. Everything that I read through was by the book and all loose ends tied."

"And the numbers?"

"From what I could tell, perfect."

"Good," affirmed Thomas, "I had thought as much."

"What's so important that you couldn't tell me about anything about the case?"

Thomas smiled and peered at his son. He reached over to Gabriel's notepad and took it, reading the notes slowly from beginning to end, and speaking when he finished.

"Raúl is going to fully retire and transfer the ownership to all four of his children. Each one will now own a different childcare center. Under his leadership, they have won award after award for years, reaching the highest levels of recognition and certifications, fulfilling all government contracts, and far surpassing expectations. Competition is fierce. Until this point, all the locations had his name, so competitors did not dare, but as you know, any succession of an empire has enemies, and our job is to make sure that this transition goes as smoothly as possible. That is why I had you go through all the files and figures without an explanation. I'm sorry for the suspense and secrecy, but I needed this to be airtight."

Gabriel leaned back in his chair, ran his hand through his hair, and massaged his face for a moment.

"I've seen you this intense only a handful of times and normally those times are with Santiago, McCrocadoo, or with last minute favor cases."

"Generally, yes."

"I know that Raúl's been your client for a long time, but what don't I know?"

Thomas took a hand to his chin and massaged it for a moment. Relaxing a bit, he stared at the files, formulated his thoughts, and confessed.

"Before Santiago's business started booming and before the Buendía's came to me, your mother and I lived very humbly. You were just born, and we didn't have a lot of money. One day a large client of mine called me and told me that he and his family decided to use a much bigger firm and that the work I would do for them would end at the end of the month. At the time, it was eight days away. Where was I going to make up for twenty-five percent of our income in eight days?"

Gabriel remained very still, listening to his father's every word, processing the story that he had never known.

"It was then that Raúl came to me. He had told me that he no longer trusted his previous lawyer and wanted to know if he could trust me. When I told him that he would have to take a leap of faith, he believed me, and we have worked together ever since."

"Was it that bad?"

"Not that month, but when twenty-five cents out of every dollar is suddenly gone, all of a sudden you're having to choose which bill you want to be late on, and that's not a good place to be in."

Gabriel nodded, unsure of what to say.

"Not that I have to tell you, but not a word of this to your mother."

"She doesn't know?"

"How could she? I lost the client on a Wednesday but gained Raúl on that Thursday. There was no reason to tell her, but it does not mean that I wasn't scared."

Voices echoed from the secretarial area and the waiting room. Thomas rose from his chair and moved towards the door of the office. When he reached the doorframe, he saw Susana leading a tall, lanky man with white hair, into the big conference room, followed by a much younger brunette. At that moment, Thomas signaled for Gabriel to come out of the office and signaled for him to go first. Gabriel nodded his head and moved forward toward the conference room Leading his father.

Morales was crouching to sit down but had not reached the seat of his chair when he saw them coming through the door, stood upright, and began rounding the table. Gabriel stepped to the side and Thomas shook Raúl's hand first.

"Good to see you, Thomas. It has been a while."

"That it has," agreed Thomas.

"This is Mirella, my youngest," said Raúl, turning to the brunette that accompanied him. "She runs one of my centers now."

Both Thomas and Gabriel shook her hand as Raúl moved to the side.

"And this young man is?"

"Raúl, this is my son, Gabriel. I think that the last time that you saw him, he was seventeen," said Thomas, turning and moving so that Gabriel could shake Raúl's hand, "Gabriel is now my partner."

"Yes, I gathered that from the addition of the second Lock on the door. I am sure you couldn't get it up there quickly enough. As for you, son," he began, shifting his eyes to Gabriel, "You were very young when I last saw you and no longer a boy. Thomas…" Raúl kept his eyes on Gabriel while addressing Thomas.

"Yes, Raúl?"

"How long have you had that sign?" he asked. Thomas chuckled.

"His mother claims I bought the sign when he was three."

"Did you?"

"When he got into law school at Florida."

Raúl turned and gave Thomas an amused look. Thomas opened his palms and shrugged.

"Okay, I've had it since he graduated high school."

"You know, Dad," spoke Gabriel, raising an eyebrow toward his father, "that really does explain a lot."

Raúl cut him off.

"Nothing wrong with that. Most of my kids kept the businesses, so there you are."

"Yes. Please, take a seat," said Thomas, gesturing at the chairs around the table.

As everyone sat, Susana came in with a colada and a set of thumb-size plastic cups.

"Cafecito anyone?" she asked as she began to serve. "I just brought it from the corner café, so it's still hot."

"I'd like some," answered Raúl, "And Mirella as well, please."

Thomas and Gabriel both nodded and, a few moments later, Susana departed, leaving them to sip their Cuban coffee in private.

"So, how is the rest of your family?" asked Thomas, looking at Raúl as he placed his coffee down.

"Everyone is great, thank you for asking. Martica added two more children since we last visited, so now I have seven grandchildren," he said with a broad smile. "More than a basketball team and two away from a baseball team and the range is twelve years from oldest to youngest."

"Not a bad spread," joked Thomas. "How old is the oldest?"

"Seventeen in two weeks' time. They grow up fast."

"Yes, they do." Thomas smiled at Gabriel as he replied to Raúl. "Are you still puttering around in the garden?"

"I sold the house here in Miami, and bought an apartment near Martica, and Juan, my eldest, which I use whenever I'm in town to be near the kids."

"Where are you most of the time?"

"In Naples. I bought a much smaller house there. Prices are very reasonable, and I was able to buy it outright without financing. So, Martica and I come in during most weeks, and different groups of kids and grandkids come and visit me on weekends."

"Well, you know, when people retire, they only worry about getting sun and seeing the grandkids."

"Ideally, yes."

Thomas saw that Gabriel had pulled out a yellow pad and a pen and was ready to take notes.

"So Raúl, I imagine that you'd like to discuss the transfer of ownership?" Thomas scanned Raúl's thin face. He had changed over the years. His face had become thin, and more wrinkled while his eyes had sunken in and had not aged well. He resembled little of the man Thomas fought for years ago.

"That was the plan for today, but I'm afraid that we have had a visit from the Department of Health and Rehabilitative Services regarding a series of letters they have received concerning our treatment of the children."

"Why didn't you mention this last week?" inquired Thomas.

"Because we were only made aware of them yesterday. According to the inspectors, the letters say that we have been careless in letting them wander around the school. One of the accusations points to a swing that is just outside our fence and claims that we let the children play on the swing without supervision. The inspector knows that is not true because we have that swing scheduled to be removed and have even paid a substantial deposit to the company that is going to remove it. It is old and was left outside the fence when we remodeled the outside playground on purpose because it is unsafe." He stood up and began pacing back and forth. "The inspector that I've known the longest also feels that it is a planned attack against our company because there were four letters sent to his office, one for each center, with different names but you can tell they were typed by the same machine."

"Do you have copies of the letters?" asked Gabriel.

"The inspector could not go that far," said Mirella, interjecting, "all the material is supposed to be confidential. He knows we do an exceptionally good job for those children in a place where few daycares establish themselves because of the low socio-economic status of the area. We depend on government subsidies. If someday they are stopped, the number of children will be reduced by fifty percent. Most owners do not want to take that risk, but we designed our business plans, and our leases permit us to reduce our costs if the subsidies stop, in order to continue the service."

"How can we help?" asked Thomas.

"I want you to please send a letter to the Florida Department of Children and Families saying that we want to find out who is trying to ruin our reputation," replied Raúl.

"I could do that, but what would be the effect?"

"An acknowledgement that we're rectifying the situation."

"True, but they know that since they know you and have known you for a long time, but I'm afraid that a written letter from our office would only have the opposite effect."

"How so?"

"They may think that since you involved your attorney, you might have something more that you are hiding. If it is an easy solution and you have had their trust for a while, why would you need me?"

Raúl rose and began to pace around the conference room, pondering about the details of his conversation with his contact.

"I know you're under a lot of pressure old friend, but at least you know that the accusations were not taken seriously now."

"But they may in the future and especially the near future," interjected Raúl. "This goes beyond a simple transfer of ownership. My business is in line for an award as the outstanding daycare of Florida. It is something really special. It even appeared in the papers and got a big write up and we are all counting on those awards to help the transition from my wife and I to the kids as the new owners." Raúl held his hands with his palms up. "I thought that an accusation like this could ruin all that, but I guess you're right."

"We just need a plan. Give us some time and we will handle this." said Thomas.

"I trust you. I just do not understand why someone would want to do this."

"Neither do we, but we can't do anything to change what they do, only how we respond, so give Gabriel and me some time to work on this and come up with a solution."

Raúl nodded his agreement and looked over at Mirella.

"Stepping away from this is hard enough, I don't want it to be even harder for my children to take over."

"We'll do everything we can," reassured Gabriel, rising to shake Raúl's hand. Raúl took it before meeting Thomas's outstretched hand.

"We know." Raúl turned back to Mirella. "Come on, let's leave them to their work."

"Thank you both," she said, joining her father as they exited the office. Thomas followed them out as Gabriel leaned against a chair, contemplating the reasoning behind the attack. *This is personal, but from who?* he thought.

"Gabriel when you started at the State Attorney's office did you take a turn at juvenile court?"

"Yes, I did and yes I can talk to some people over at Children and Family, but it won't be today, I have to head downtown for a hearing."

"That's fine. Get started when you can. In the meantime, I'm going to see if I can find any leads from a few contacts that I know. I want to know if their property is being targeted by a company looking to lower the value for a cheaper buy. I will have to check with county zoning."

"I hadn't thought about that," admitted Gabriel.

"Wait until you start getting some of the cases that I've been dealing with."

"You know Dad, we could start now."

"You may be my partner, but you are still the junior partner. You need some more experience first. Regardless, let me know what you find tomorrow morning."

"Will do," answered Gabriel. He left the conference room, grabbed his belongings from his office, turned on his heel, and left for downtown.

Chapter 7: The Simple Divorce

Miami, Florida: January 1982

Gabriel walked with his briefcase in his right hand as he sauntered up the steps to the courthouse. The meeting with Raúl and Mirella was still present on his mind as was the visit to Children and Family. No leads had come from it, but he had put the idea into their minds, and it would be on the radar. Checking his watch, he stopped and waited for Jacob to arrive. Last Monday felt longer than a year ago as he thought about everything that had transpired since then. *And tomorrow I will meet Franco about the Regal. The weekend cannot come soon enough*, he thought.

Knowing that he was a few minutes early, he observed the people that made their way to and from the entrance. A few paces beside him, two men in sports coats drew in smoke from their cigarettes. Two ladies sized him up as they walked past him, playing with their hair, and fixing their gazes on his cerulean eyes. Small smiles followed and, for a moment, he debated chatting them up. During his self-argument, a tall broad, blonde, and young man approached him.

"Gabriel?" asked the man.

Turning his attention from the women, Gabriel realized that it was his client, Jacob Wallace.

"Jacob, sorry. I did not realize that you were already here. I figured that you would be coming from the other direction."

Jacob brushed it off, waving his hand in front of his face while looking slightly off to the side.

"It's no problem, Gabriel. We are both a little early. I was anticipating heavy traffic. Are you ready to get in there?"

"Of course, Jacob."

"Belinda and I have been separated for a year, we've agreed on the division of assets, how much simpler could this be?"

"Honestly, the fact that we are here is more of a formality. Usually, in cases like this neither the client nor I come. You both made this quite easy on me and I'm sure the opposing side would agree. Are you ready to go inside?"

Jacob paused for a moment as he inhaled deeply and removed a lighter from the breast pocket of his jacket.

"Let me smoke a quick one before we go in."

Gabriel and Jacob entered the courthouse just after Jacob exhaled the final bit of cigarette smoke from his lungs. Popping a Tic Tac into his mouth, Jacob offered one to Gabriel who declined. Rounding the corner on their way to the courtroom, Gabriel spat out his gum in a nearby trashcan. When they arrived, they saw the opposing counsel, which Gabriel did not recognize. She stepped forward and stuck out her hand. He shook her hand. Her grip was firm but gentle. Gabriel looked up to meet her caramel-colored eyes. A hair-tie pulled her hair into a ponytail, except for her bangs which hung down to just above her eyebrows and curled to the sides. "My name is Sarah Jensen.

"Good to meet you Sarah, my name is Gabriel Lock." said Gabriel, outstretching his hand. "This is my client, Jacob Wallace."

"Sarah, where is Mrs. Wallace?"

"She's just powdering her nose. I am sure that she'll be back in a moment. We are a little early."

Gabriel, Jacob, and Sarah broke into small talk about the Dolphin's chances of winning another Superbowl. As they debated and reminisced about the perfect season, a young woman with dark brown hair and freckles walked up to them.

"Hello, Belinda," said Jacob, greeting her.

"Hey Jake, how are you?"

"Fine, thank you. And you?"

"Good, doing just fine. Are we ready to get started?"

"Sure thing, let me just let the bailiff know," said Sarah, walking down the hall toward Judge Samuel Siegal's chambers. Belinda went to retrieve her purse from the chair at the end of the waiting room.

As she departed, Gabriel turned to Jacob and ran through the questions that he would have to answer to finalize the divorce. Jacob answered them easily and when Sarah returned, the four of them entered the courtroom.

As they found their places, the bailiff announced the entrance of the Honorable Judge Siegal, who found his place and began proceedings.

"Ahem," he began, clearing his throat, "To my knowledge, this is an uncontested divorce between two amicable parties. Am I correct in this assertion?"

"Yes, Your Honor," answered Gabriel and Sarah in unison.

"Good, then we may begin the questioning and resolve this quickly."

"Mr. Wallace, since you are the petitioner, I will begin with you. Counsel," said Judge Siegal, turning his attention to Gabriel. Do you object to me speaking to your client directly?"

"No, Your Honor, I do not." Judge Siegal took a moment and brushed part of his gray hair to the side as he leaned forward in his seat. Judge Jay and Jacob ran through the questions in no more than a few minutes' time.

"Thank you for your answers and brevity, Mr. Wallace. Mrs. Wallace, I will now move on to you if Ms. Jensen has no objections to this proceeding?"

"None, Your Honor."

"Good! Now, Mrs. Wallace, what is your name and address?"

"Belinda Wallace, 2510 Blue Heron Dr."

"For how long you have continually resided in the State of Florida?"

"All of my life, Your Honor."

"Are you married to your spouse, Mr. Wallace?"

"Yes, Your Honor."

"Are there any children born of this marriage?"

Before Belinda could speak, Sarah interrupted.

"Well, Your Honor, not exactly born of this marriage, but Mrs. Wallace did give birth to a baby boy during this marriage."

Judge Siegal's eyes widened, and his eyes drifted slowly to Jacob, whose face bore a shocked expression. Gabriel shook his head for a moment, trying to recall Octavio's words.

"Uh, Your Honor?"

"Yes, Mr. Lock?"

"Permission to speak directly to opposing counsel?"

"Granted."

"Ms. Jensen, I am sorry. Did you say that there was a child born during this marriage?"

"Yes, Counsel. The child is not of this marriage. We are not claiming your client is the father and my client is not looking for any child support or to impose any obligation on his with reference to this child."

"Your Honor," said Gabriel, turning his attention from Sarah back toward Judge Siegal. He could sense disbelief emanating from Jacob, whose face had changed from shock to incredulity. "The fact is that the parties have been separated for a year and a half as is stated in my petition and have not had any contact. We had no knowledge as to the existence of the child."

"Well, given Mr. Wallace's expression, I would say that that's pretty clear, Counsel." Sarah spoke, adding onto the judge's assertion.

"Your Honor, my client knows for a fact that the petitioner, Mr. Wallace, is not the father of this child."

"Understood, Counsel," said Judge Siegal, focused on Sarah. "Mr. Wallace," he said, returning to Jacob's face, "Are you prepared to raise and support this child despite your petition to divorce your wife, Mrs. Wallace?"

Taken aback, Jacob fumbled around his thoughts as he processed Judge Siegal's question. After a moment he responded.

"But, Your Honor, the child is not mine. She admits it," he said, rising from his chair and pointing across the aisle toward Belinda, "we have not seen each other in a year and did not have relations for at least two months before that.

"I'm sure that all of what you have stated are facts, but under Florida law, if a child is born during a marriage, he is the child of the husband and wife unless the biological parent steps forward, swears the child is theirs and agrees to become responsible for the child under oath. If not, the husband is responsible for a child that is not his biologically. So, I am going to ask you once again, are you sure that the child is not yours?"

"I'm sure that the child is not mine, but, Your Honor, please, this cannot be the law!" petitioned Jacob, looking from Judge Siegal to Gabriel and back.

"Counsel, please explain to your client that he is responsible. So, I am adjourning this petition for divorce until the parties have cleaned up this mess." Raising his head and moving his eyes from party to party, Judge Siegal surveyed them. "Am I clear?"

"Yes, Your Honor," stated Gabriel and Sarah again in unison. Judge Siegal slammed the gavel and left the courtroom to head back to his chambers. Jacob slumped his chair, disbelief and defeat left him disillusioned as he gazed into space, his mind taking in the gravity of the judge's words and Belinda's actions. Sarah leaned over her chair toward Gabriel.

"Gabriel, let me get Belinda out of here for a few minutes. Can we meet somewhere and sort this out?"

"Let's meet in an hour at your office. Do you have a conference room?"

"I do, and it's free all day."

"Good, then let me try and cool things down with Jacob before we head over there."

Gabriel glanced over to Belinda, who also slumped in her chair. He could see the tears sliding down her cheeks from her puffy eyes.

"One hour," he said to Sarah, "we need to settle this mess."

Sarah shook her head and, taking Belinda gently by the arm and ushering her out of her chair, left.

Jacob held his head in his hands and stared at the desktop. Gabriel took a hand and placed it gently on his shoulder.

"Are you okay?"

"How can anyone be okay when you find out that your wife gave birth to another man's child and the judge forces you to take care of him?"

"I don't know the answer to that, but what I do know is that we are going to get some answers and if you can brave it, we'll have them in an hour."

Jacob nodded but stared at the desktop.

"Come on, let's go for a quick walk, get some fresh air, and then head over to Sarah's office in Coral Gables."

They rose from behind the desk, exited the courtroom, and left the courthouse to get some air and some answers.

Gabriel made his way across the street to the small Cuban cafe behind the Courthouse with Jacob. Both sat across from each other at the two-person table at the very back of the restaurant.

"Where do we go from here Gabriel?"

"Like I said before, we will know more when we meet in an hour."

"Can I really be held responsible for that child as if I were his father."

"Yes, because since the birth occurred during the marriage, then legally you are his father unless the biological father steps forward, volunteers to become the legal father and takes full responsibility for maintaining the child."

"So, what you are telling me is that, by staying married to her so she could be covered by my insurance and giving her a place to go home to if things really went south for her, I am repaid for that with being morally, financially and other wise responsible for a child that is not mine."

"Yes. The road to…" Jacob rose from the table in one swift move.

"Gabriel I am not hungry, and I will not be attending that meeting," he said cutting Gabriel off. "Feel free to attend or not attend. At this point, I don't care."

Before Gabriel could say anything, Jacob walked out of the restaurant.

Chapter 8: The King of '66

Miami, Florida: January 1982

Franco stood outside of the office of his family's furniture store. It felt unusual seeing him there instead of at the gym. He stopped the Regal long enough for Franco to get in and within seconds of being in his car he had already touched the stereo and changed the station.

"Just like in high school," laughed Gabriel, reaching for the dial and lowering the blaring music.

"What? Live a little, Counselor."

"Franco, it's early in the morning."

"It's Miami, bro. Nobody sleeps here anymore, especially on a Friday?" he asked, rhetorically.

Gabriel did his best not to laugh and validate Franco's claim, failing terribly in the process.

"So where is this place?" asked Gabriel, not taking his eyes off the road.

Franco had pushed the seat as far back as it could go, almost lying down.

"My buddy and his dad own it; it's on the corner of Coral Way and 78th street."

"The gas station?"

"Yeah, they've got a garage on the back side with a lot too."

"I never noticed it."

"Because you're too focused on point A to notice the rest of the alphabet," said Franco, chiding him.

"Any chance you want to sit up like a decent person?"

"Zero. Wake me when we get there," said Franco, turning to his side and using his hair to shield his eyes.

The traffic held them up longer than they expected but still arrived before the hour. Gabriel parked in front of the gas station and followed Franco as they made their way to the mechanic's shop. As they passed through the door, they found a kid, no older than fifteen, wearing a Dolphins cap backwards, chewing on a Big League bubble gum, and wearing a gray work shirt with his sleeves cut, standing behind the counter.

"Pauly!" yelled Franco sticking his hand in the air for a high five.

"Hey Uncle Frankie," said the young man as he met Franco's hand in the air.

The clap of the high five echoed off the walls and Franco smiled.

"This is my friend Gabriel," said Franco, introducing Gabriel.

"Nice to meet you, Pauly."

"It's Paul, only Uncle Frankie calls me Pauly, but it's nice to meet you too."

"Yeah, what's this about Frankie?"

"Pauly, Frankie, they rhyme, ya know?"

"Sure thing," affirmed Gabriel.

"Your dad back there?" asked Franco, taking the attention off the nicknames and back to the matter at hand.

"Yeah, he's probably under a chevy right now," said Paul. "Let me get him for you."

Paul walked through the door behind him and into the garage. Gabriel saw him pass the other mechanics and cars before he got to the back wall where only the orange and teal of the Dolphins hat showed fully. He could not see Paul's mouth move, but he could tell that his father was under some vehicle giving instructions back as Paul's head nodded every few seconds. Gabriel turned his attention back to Franco who stood behind him, facing the back wall and staring at old black and white photos of cars the shop had maintained over the years.

"Some crazy ones, here, no?" asked Franco, gesturing Gabriel to take a gander.

Gabriel approached the photographs. He saw a 57 Ford Thunderbird, a 50 Jaguar XK120, a 59 Aston Martin DB4 GT Zagato, and a 55 Chevy Bel Air among others that were parked in front of the garage. In one of the other's, he saw the three Ford GT40s of Le Mans 66.

"I mean, I get why he has the gas station, but this is what he really lives for," said Franco, appreciating the business.

"Those are some pretty nice ones for sure," stated Gabriel, not recognizing the majority of the cars in the frames.

"The lesser-known ones are my favorites," said a voice from behind them. Gabriel turned to see a burly man with black hair and tanned skin with smudges of oil on his face. He offered a hand to Gabriel who shook it.

"Pablo's my name, and you are?" said the man in heavily accented English.

"Gabriel, we can speak in Spanish if you prefer," replied Gabriel.

The answer caught Pablo off guard.

"He looks gringo, doesn't he?" shot Franco, cackling.

Gabriel smacked Franco who laughed it off.

"As you prefer," continued Gabriel in Spanish and Pablo nodded.

"I'm sorry, the pale skin and blue eyes are not typical of Franco's company," admitted Pablo, switching to Spanish.

"No problem; I understand. So, Franco tells me that you are the guy to see about car trouble?"

"I am, what's wrong with the car?"

"Whatever costs the most!" yelled Franco, cackling again.

Gabriel resisted the temptation to smack him again.

"Pablo, it's outside if you would like to see it. I think that it's the starter and hopefully that's it."

"Take me to it."

The three of them walked outside and to the car. Gabriel popped the hood, and Pablo lifted it to see the engine below. He looked at it for a moment, eyeing each part and searching for anything obvious.

"What's wrong with it?"

"The Starter gives me trouble. It sputters instead of roars." muttered Gabriel, "I can't tell if there's anything else."

"Starter isn't too bad if that's all it is, but I'll have to really look at it."

"How long do you need it?"

"A half hour if you're in a rush, an hour if you can spare the time."

Gabriel glanced at his watch.

"An hour's fine."

"There's a good restaurant around the corner if you'd like to grab breakfast."

"Perfect, I haven't eaten anything," said Franco, "which way, Pablo?"

"Down Coral Way," explained Pablo, pointing west, "under the expressway and you'll find in the next building over a little restaurant called Galicia."

"That sounds great said Franco with the natural enthusiasm of a hungry man."

Gabriel rolled his eyes as Pablo laughed, and Franco led the way. They strolled over to the small restaurant, laughing and reminiscing about old high school memories. As they entered, a young woman greeted them, and blushing as she saw Gabriel, grabbed two menus, and led them to a booth. They sat and she placed the menus on the table, lingering on Gabriel's eyes, before walking away to bring them water.

"Still got it," declared Gabriel, snickering.

"Only because she saw my ring. Otherwise, you will always be Sancho Panza."

Laughter roared through the little café and as they laughed, men and women at the counter stared at them, grateful for the scene. Gabriel's ribs ached and he saw Franco wipe his watery eyes, allowing the amusement to get the better of him.

"I needed that, I truly did."

"Anything, Wild Man."

The friends enjoyed breakfast over the next forty-five minutes, leaving a few minutes before quarter till. As they left the restaurant, the young woman from earlier waved goodbye to Gabriel and wished him a good day.

"Sancho, let's get going," chided Franco as Gabriel waved, bidding farewell.

"She was cute, you know."

"Of course she was, but what more are you going to do?"

Gabriel kept silent, knowing what Franco implied.

"She still there?" asked Franco.

"Always."

"You have got to let her go. Either work it out or let it go."

"I've let it go."

"No, you haven't, that's why she's still there, and until you do, you'll never move forward."

As they approached the garage, Gabriel saw the Regal parked in the front.

"Chat about this later?"

"Anytime you wish," said Franco.

Pablo emerged from the front door, holding a can of Coca-Cola in his hand.

"How was breakfast?"

"Filling," answered Franco, "how's the car?"

"Well, not great. The starter needs replacing, the transmission is failing too, and the air conditioning might need replacement in another four to five hundred miles. You really beat up this car."

Gabriel smacked his forehead with his palm.

"That's the truth, I drove it back and forth to Gainesville while I was at the University of Florida and then I gave it a lot of wear while at the Prosecutor's office, driving to crime scenes, to see witnesses, and victims, and though now I do a lot less driving, I think it's telling me that it's time for a change."

"Luckily you came now and not after everything broke down."

"How much are we looking to replace it?"

"A lot," answered Pablo.

"How much is a lot?"

"Cheaper parts and labor with a discount for being Franco's friend, $750. Good parts and labor with a discount, just under $1,200."

Gabriel grimaced.

"I just got comfortable with not having a car payment. Do I have to do the AC too?"

"If I do it now with the other two, it'll be cheaper as you'll save on labor."

"Great," added Gabriel flatly."Should I try and trade it in?"

"If you're open to it, I've got something in mind."

"What are you thinking?"

"I got a trade in last month after a good client of mine had to buy a bigger car because he's got another child now and couldn't keep the fun car anymore."

"What did he trade in?"

"The King of '66. Come, follow me."

The three of them walked to the backside of the station to find a few cars parked in the back with covers on them. Pablo ducked his head underneath a few covers until he found the right one.

"I wouldn't blame you for changing the paint on it, but this baby will be a classic someday."

Pablo removed the cover to reveal a 1966 Ford Mustang.

"Woah," said Franco before whistling at it.

Speech eluded Gabriel. He stepped toward the Mustang, placing his hand on the top of the car and appreciating the legacy in front of him. "I had thought of buying a new car but had never would have considered this car for an everyday car."

"She may not be the GT40 of Le Mans, but everybody knows that the Ford Motor Company was the king of '66."

Gabriel stared at the interior, taking it all in from the white seats to the radio, the steering wheel, and everything else. Seconds went by in silence as all three of them examined the car.

"How much do you want for it?"

"Give me your Regal, plus what I put into it and some legal advice about what I want to do with this building, and I'll call it even."

"What are you going to do with the Regal?"

"Sell it. A Regal will flip easy, but this car is one that the average person with a family either can't buy or won't, but you are no average man from what Franco tells me."

"Just hardworking," corrected Gabriel. "I've only got one major concern."

"Name it."

"Maintenance. She's a beauty, but she is sixteen years old, and while the mileage is fine, how do I know that she won't have a problem?"

"That's a good question and a fair one, but she won't give you any problems, and if you promise to keep me in mind with any of your lawyer friends who want to buy other cars like this, I'll take care of any of your car's problems for one whole year."

Gabriel raised his eyebrow at the words.

"A whole year?"

"I'm that confident. I have worked on this car for the last two months."

Gabriel looked over at Franco who gave him his approval.

"You'll give me that for a promise?"

"And a Regal, $900, and legal advice. Besides, what lawyer doesn't keep his word?"

Franco hooted and Gabriel nodded.

"You've got a deal. When can I pick it up?"

"Leave me the Regal and take it today. Bring it back next week. I have a document in the office showing this as one of my loaners while your car is here. I take cash or check."

"I can agree to that," affirmed Gabriel, stretching his hand to Pablo who took it.

The two men shook hands and Franco clapped.

"Alllllrrrriiiiigggghhhhttt!" yelled Franco. "The Wild man is back!"

"You know you are bad for my reputation as a serious man," cracked Gabriel with a wide smile.

"Give me a moment to grab the documents and the keys," said Pablo as he walked over to the garage and disappeared behind the door.

Gabriel looked at Franco who looked back at him.

"Damn, Counselor. After this, you are taking me to lunch and dinner for the whole week."

"Yeah well, you did good."

Gabriel turned back to the Mustang and smiled. He never thought that he would drive something as special as this.

"Wait until my dad sees this."

"Wait until Santiago sees this when you drop me off at the office."

"That's right, he'll be there."

"Yes, he will."

"How's it going with him?"

"Best partner we've ever had."

"That good?"

"Oh yeah, we are turning a profit and a lot of his executives, and their relatives have come looking for entire homes of furniture. We have made a lot of money just from them, let alone the clients that we have been able to bring in. Besides, do you know what it is to have his company name on the top floor and ours below? –That alone has brought business."

A moment later, Pablo returned, holding a papered clipboard, a pen, and a set of keys. Gabriel removed his car keys from his keychain and placed the new Ford's on it instead. He signed the paperwork on the clipboard and promised Pablo that he would tell his friends about the collection he had here. In a few minutes, they bid farewell with Gabriel and Franco now seated and ready to go.

Gabriel turned the key, and the motor roared to life. Franco looked more excited than he did, but he didn't care. He pressed the gas, and the motor thundered.

"Ready to hit the road?" asked Franco.

Gabriel smiled, and floored it, taking off on Coral Way with the King of '66.

Chapter 9: The Complication

Miami, Florida: January 1982

A week came and went with Gabriel signing over the Regal and receiving the Mustang in return. He had taken his parents and even Abuela for a ride, but not before his mother and grandmother blessed it with holy water. Now he pulled up to the office enjoying his morning commute much more than he had before. Sitting in his office and examining his files, he heard a knock at the door and looked up.

"Yes," he said, bidding entry.

Susana opened the door.

"Jacob is here."

"I will come out and get him. Is the conference room available?"

Susana nodded, backing away from the doorway and returned to her desk. Gabriel grabbed a yellow pad and a pen and rose from his chair. He walked through the doorway of his office to the waiting room. He saw Jacob rising from the sofa and extending his hand.

"Come on in," said Gabriel as he turned and pointed toward the conference room. They entered and Gabriel, taking the chair at the end of the table, signaled for Jacob to sit next to him.

"When you came to me, it was just a simple divorce. No property in common, no debts in common, and a short-term marriage with no children. I did not really have to ask many questions past the where, when, and how, but now things have gotten a little more complicated."

"I understand, and again I want to apologize for my behavior after the hearing."

"Nothing to apologize about."

"Have you heard from her attorney?"

"As you know we did not meet that day because Sarah said it was no use. She did not have a chance to speak with Belinda because she left too quickly with eyes full of tears. There was no new knowledge to gain from that meeting and the reason I asked you to come here is because I am expecting a call from Sarah in twenty minutes to discuss where we are going from here." Gabriel looked at his watch. "But I need some more information with this new development."

"What do you want to know?"

"When was the last time you saw Belinda before the hearing last week?"

"About fifteen months ago. I got home from a meeting," he said, shifting uncomfortably in his chair, "and found her high as a kite. The new TV I had bought for the room was missing and she was asking me for more money. I think she had a strong reaction to her new medication, but I had never seen her like that. I did not get angry, but I was disappointed. She saw the disappointment through the haze, so she ran out of the apartment and headed for the stairs."

"Go on."

"I thought I would be able to beat her to the lobby if I took the elevator, but I missed her and that was the last time I saw her until the hearing. I would do anything for her, and I could not believe she was running away."

"How did you get in touch for the divorce?"

"I got a call from her four months ago at the apartment," he said, defeat crippling his voice. "She said very simply, I am not coming back, so file for divorce. I will call you in three weeks to give you the attorney's address and phone number. I contacted you, and we filed. So, tell me, Gabriel, what are the chances I will be responsible for that child?" he asked, placing his hands flat on the table.

"Depends on who the father is, his condition, and his relationship to her. Most of all, it depends on if he wants to be responsible." said Gabriel, setting his elbows on the table and interlocking his fingers in the air before him.

"So, a man I do not know and who does not know me holds my future in his hands?"

"Yes."

There was a knock on the door.

"Ms. Jensen is on the line for you, Gabriel," said Susana from the door.

"I will take it in my office. Jacob do not go anywhere," he said, rising from the chair and quickly crossing through the door and disappearing into his office.

He sat in the farthest chair in front of his desk and picked up the receiver of his phone.

"Sarah, how are you?" He said then listened for the response. "Glad to hear. I have my client in my office, and he is obviously anxious to know what is going on." Once again, he listened intently. "Still? Well, I understand that if he is out of town on a business trip, it is difficult for her to speak about this with him. When will he be back?" Again, he pressed his ear to the phone. "Alright, please let me know once you have something." There was a response, and Gabriel nodded his head in agreement, "Take care."

He made his way back to the conference room and as soon as he walked in, Jacob leaned forward in his chair.

"Well?" he said before Gabriel had a chance to sit down.

"The biological father is on a business trip out of town and will not be back until sometime next week. She will talk to him then."

"I guess that if he is a businessman, he will probably take responsibility, and it will not be up to me."

"Unfortunately, all kinds of seemingly respectable guys walk away from children without looking back every day. So, while this is a favorable thing, it does not really determine what he will do."

"So basically, nothing gained today? There is no certainty one way or the other?"

"No closer to knowing your fate, no." said Gabriel opening his palms wide, "But at least there's no bad news."

Jacob rose.

"You know if I at least had the man's decision in my hands I might be able to start accepting whatever my fate may be. Of everything that is going on the hardest part is the uncertainty."

"It always is," said Gabriel, rising also.

"Thank you, Gabriel," said Jacob, turning and striding out of the conference room.

By the time Gabriel got up and followed, he could hear Jacob closing the outer door of the office. He walked back to his office, closed the door, and, sitting in his chair, thought to himself, *How quickly life changes. One moment Jacob was trying to help the woman he loved and the next, he could be raising someone else's child.*

Chapter 10: The Old Colleague

Miami, Florida: February 1982

The brisk air of the passing cold front hit Gabriel as he took the short walk from the parking area to the Juvenile courthouse and offices of the Department of Children and Family Services. It was late morning but refreshing as the crisp air brought a small change to the usual heat. As he entered the building, he saw lawyers milling around waiting to be called in what was a very informal system. Questions about the complaints rattled his mind as he and his father had no idea as to why anyone would have malice against Raúl and his family. *Hopefully, Pearl will be able to give me a hand with this*, he thought to himself as he passed by the windows of the assistants calling up the waiting lawyers. *Great, she's not here.*

He strode through the outside trailers until he found the office he sought.

"Pearl how are you?" he asked as he entered through the door.

"Well, if it isn't the sweetest blue eyes in town. Did I just win the lottery, and you are running to represent me? There is no other reason that a high-flying lawyer like you would be here with me."

Before replying he looked at the warm face that always greeted him happily. Her black hair fell to her jaw in a bob that rounded her thin face and brought out the best of her elegant features. Her long, purple-colored fingernails, contrasted with her yellow blouse.

"How can you say that, Pearl? Didn't we both promise that if we reached thirty-two and neither of us were married that we would have a child together."

"You promised me that when I came back from my honeymoon."

"But I still meant every word."

"Yeah, all the ones you said and the ones you didn't say right?"

"You know me too well,"

"So, what's going on? What brings you back here? —I thought that you were long-gone from this place."

"You know the Morales family? They run three or four daycares down near homestead."

"I do. Fine people. They run those things right for all the kids. Most of the kids wouldn't have a place to go if it weren't for that family. The parents have nothing but good things to say about them. They are up for an award, aren't they?"

"My father has represented them for many years at the firm, and he asked me to look into these complaints that came in."

"I know those well."

"You do?"

"Yes, I reviewed those when the second one came through. I figured that one was a fluke, but a second one? And then a third? Those were very strange. Supposedly they were individual and separate accusations originating from different centers. The accusations, however, were repetitive or parallel. All of them were, in essence, a child getting away from the personnel at the center. When we spoke to the parents, they had no information that any incident had occurred with their child. Lastly, we found that the address on the envelope did not match the address of the parents, or the child attended a center different from the one that was accused of the violation. Anyone with a little experience could see right away that the allegations were made up. The pattern of complaints did not fit with the way complaints occur normally. Complaints about four different places, from four different people all at the same time were hard enough to believe, but once we looked at the details, we knew they were not real. Still, we investigated by the book and all our suspicions proven to be true. Somebody is trying to hurt them, but they won't find a sympathetic ear here. Like I said, these are good people."

"Any idea as to who might have done this?

"Not really. And it was not worth the time and effort to find out."

"Do you have the results of the investigation," asked Gabriel, leaning closer to her.

She looked at him, looked down at her desk, and then back.

"I know the department sent letters to the centers saying that the investigation was closed," he said defensively, "and that officially it found no basis in fact for the complaints, but do you think I could have copies of the notes on the investigation and the interviews?"

The muscles in her face tightened and her eyebrows rose as she processed his words.

"You know that I can't do that, Gabriel."

"I know that normally these things are confidential, but I have a bad feeling about this. I think it's more than just an attack from a competitor or a disgruntled individual. I think doing these people profound harm is something dear to this person's heart."

"You think this person could harm the kids?" asked Pearl.

"I don't think so, but who knows what they are capable of."

"Don't worry so much, Counselor, things like this always blow away as soon as they arrive."

"So do hurricanes and yet it sometimes takes years to repair the damage."

"You feel that this is that serious? I can always make a request to see if they will let you review the file, and we can make an exception. Do you have any evidence that might bolster the request?"

"Not really. It just makes no sense. Each daycare is under a different corporate name, and they are run by different people, no common staff, or paperwork. Raúl has only been to one of them in the last four or five years and is retired living on the west coast near Naples. How does the accuser know they are related? Someone has been digging into them way beyond what is normal in these cases."

"Good points. I'll get right on it. Call me in a few days."

"I will," he said turning toward the door.

"See you soon."

They smiled as they bid farewell and Gabriel left the trailer, hoping that he would have something in a few days' time for her. None of it made any sense to him. The files had yielded no anomalies to neither him nor his father, yet these complaints had every bit of malice in them.

Let's hope that Dad found something, he thought to himself.

Chapter 11: The New Shareholders

Miami, Florida: February 1982

Three days had passed since his visit to Pearl and Gabriel sat working through files and thinking about the clients that he had to deal with. Depositions, hearings, and disputes filled his schedule over the next week and somewhere in the madness he had to make time for billing or Susana would have his head. A knock came at the door, forcing Gabriel to raise his eyes from the dossier occupying his attention.

"Yes?" he called out.

Susana opened the door and closed it behind her. Gabriel widened his eyes and raised his eyebrows. "Yes?" he asked again.

"Jacob Wallace called a few minutes ago to let you know that he's prepared and ready for the hearing next week."

"He didn't wish to speak?"

"He said he was in a rush and asked if you would call him after 4:00 this afternoon."

Gabriel glanced down at the calendar beneath his pen. He scanned the date, finding nothing for the late afternoon.

"I'll call him then. Did he say anything else?"

"No, but I thought that I should let you know that your father will be in a little later, he's tied up with Mr. McCrocadoo until after lunch."

"That man always needs something."

"I'm pretty sure he pays the light bill for the year," she joked. A sly grin formed from the corners of her mouth as Gabriel tried to remain professional.

"That's okay, Buendía pays for the building."

"And probably my salary," she added.

"Something like that."

"How's he doing, by the way?"

"Buendía?"

"Yes."

"He's good," said Gabriel, rising from his chair. He stepped around the desk and leaned on its side. "He is still a little shaken up from everything that happened last year, but he is doing well. He and the family flew to Argentina for the holidays, and he told me that we would meet again in the coming weeks to discuss the sale of his business, but he doesn't plan to leave for another two years at the earliest."

"Didn't he want to get out immediately?"

"At first, but he does not want to sell to anyone that's just going to buy his portfolio and fire all his employees. He is looking for the right buyer and that takes a while."

"Is he definitely going to sell?"

"He may not. He has thought a lot about this. His wife does not want him to sell, so that helps, but he just needs to put the trauma of two big accidents behind him and, as you can imagine, it's not an easy thing to do."

Susana nodded as she inhaled deeply. Silence filled the next few seconds before she spoke again.

"How's the girl?"

"Katerina?"

"Yeah."

"She is doing better. I spoke with Hamilton at the end of last week and he mentioned that the renovations were almost done and that she had improved tremendously with her physical therapy. She is doing better than the doctors expected and with her continued improvement, they believe that she may become strong enough to have kids."

Susana's brows rose.

"You're serious?"

"I assume Hamilton was. It is what he told me, and he sounded pretty resolute on the phone."

"With the devastating accident she had, it's nothing short of a miracle."

"I know," affirmed Gabriel, reaching for the cross that hung beneath his shirt.

"Poor thing needs some good news in her life."

"Well, she's got more than just that, Susana."

"What do you mean?"

"She's got a fella now."

"She what?" asked Susana, jaw dropping as far as it could go.

"Yeah, exactly that. The foreman who is doing the renovations asked her out and they have been going strong ever since. Got her father's blessing and everything."

"I am happy for her. God's looking out for her."

"For sure."

"Wasn't she engaged to a doctor before the accident?"

"Something like that. He gave up on her when things got tough, but God had other plans and she seems to like them," he said smiling.

"Sometimes it's the one that you least expect that turns your world from upside down to right-side up."

"Always," echoed Gabriel.

"She is going to invite you to the wedding you know. –And your favorite client, Walter, too."

"I doubt it, Susana," contested Gabriel, now sitting a bit straighter in his chair.

"Watch it happen. Good deeds stick with people." Susana leaned against the doorframe and squinted her eyes with intensity.

"Yes, Susana?"

"Did you call Franco back?"

"For?" toyed Gabriel.

"Your boxing match."

"I think that this is the first time that you've ever encouraged me to fight."

"First time that I encourage you to use your fists," she said, raising hers. They stared at each other for a few more moments before Gabriel surrendered.

"I'll call him after lunch if it makes you happy."

"It would be good for you to get back in the ring. You could use the workouts."

"I already took a beating from a kid; would you like me to have another?"

"No, just want to make sure that you are sharp. Your enemies go beyond the courtroom, you know."

"Who says I have enemies?"

"Doesn't every lawyer?"

He looked at her but changed the subject, "Any other messages for me?"

"No, but I believe that Mirella will be coming by this afternoon. Did you and your father figure out what you were going to do?"

"We have our plan, but Mirella called at the end of last week saying that she found something. Maybe it will be significant, but we'll see."

"These complaints are odd. I have a feeling this will take many twists and turns" said Susana, nodding. She pulled the door open a little wider but spoke before slipping through. "Call Franco, Gabriel. He has already called twice asking for you to spar with him."

"I'll call him, Susana. I promise."

"Good. I will send Mirella through when she arrives. In the meantime, please get started on your billing."

He smiled and nodded, and then she left, closing the door behind her and leaving him to work.

A few hours later, Susana heard Mirella's familiar voice exchange greetings with Susana. He hurried to finish his notes on the Wallace file for the court appearance next week, but the door cracked open before he could finish the last line.

"Mirella is here to see you," began Susana.

"Send her in, I was just finishing my notes for the Wallace case."

"Remember to call him in the next hour."

Gabriel stared at his watch; a quarter past three.

"I won't forget, Susana."

"Then I'll send her in."

Mirella entered and Gabriel rose from behind his desk to greet her, offering his usual handshake. They shook and he invited her to sit in one of the chairs in front of his desk.

"How are you, Mirella?"

"Since last week? –Better but still worried about the complaints. You?"

"Struggling to breathe," he admitted as he gestured to the larger pile of cases stacked neatly to his right.

"I don't envy you at all."

"I do not blame you. How is your father?"

"Good. Dad and Mom are getting ready to retire to a little place he has on Long Boat key."

"The good life."

"They have worked hard enough so now it is time for sand and sea. Dad is an avid fisherman and they both love it there."

"What brings you by?"

"Well, I know you haven't finished looking for the people responsible for all those complaints but your dad's preparing the paperwork for the transfer of shares of each of the daycares from the folks to each one of us. Your dad said he could keep everything in escrow until this complaint was cleared up. I came to pick up the paperwork so everybody can sign before they take off."

"Have you been in yet?"

"No."

"Come on let's get you into the conference room." Gabriel opened the door to the secretarial pool and walked through it stopping just after the door to the conference room. Signaling Mirella to go in and then moving inside himself, he pointed to the end chair at the near side of the table, and she sat down while he took the seat beside her.

"Now that we are here, did you have any further information about the complaints?" she asked.

"No, everything is quiet and nothing else has been filed against your dad or the daycares, but I think whoever it may be, might be taking their time planning their next attack."

"You really believe they are out to get us? Could it be a discontent parent?"

"Every business has unhappy clients, but the protests and retaliations don't normally take this form. Usually, they are directed at a person because of an incident that happened. In this case they directed fictional accusations at the institution. It does not fit the norm."

"Makes sense," she said, resting her weight on her left elbow. "I understand."

"Did you beat a rival for a contract or a location?"

"We have had the same locations for three years, and everyone that has the right credentials is in predetermined areas of the city to get the subsidies. So, we cannot figure out what is up."

"Do any of you have a personal problem with anyone that might want to get back at the family?" "Has anyone tried to buy you out?"

"No."

At that moment, Thomas came into the conference room carrying a series of manila folders in a brown expandable file.

"How are you, young lady. I am sorry I had you waiting but your dad called me just yesterday and I have been working hard to get this ready for you."

"Thank you so much. I kept reminding him, but he was convinced that he was going next weekend and not this weekend."

He placed the expandable file on the table and took one manila folder out.

"Since he can't come into the office, I drafted all the paperwork, made copies, and wrote out on the copies where the signatures have to go, and what has to be written into each line on the paperwork." He showed her the sample. "Is it clear?"

"Yes, very much so. But all that work."

"I was glad to do it."

"I better get going because I do not want to drive those last few miles in the dark. Those houses near the beach are not always lit up well."

They all stood up together, and Gabriel accompanied her to the door.

"Listen," he said, "I don't expect to come up with anything, but I will keep on digging."

"I know. Thank you very much, both of you," she said, nodding to Thomas who had appeared behind them. She exited through the main door and as Gabriel turned back toward his office, Gabriel heard Susan's voice say, "Jacob Wallace is on the line."

"I'll take it in a second. Do you have much left for the day?" He asked his father.

"Not terribly much, no. What about you?"

"I've got this call which will last just a few minutes," said Gabriel, checking his watch, "Do you and Mom have dinner plans?"

"Not that I can remember."

"Would you like to?"

"Are you buying?" asked Thomas with a smug smile.

Gabriel blanked, surprised by the question.

"Yes," he answered.

"Oh, good. Normally when you invite us out, I pay."

"Give me a raise and I'll pay more often."

"Do well on these cases and we will talk about it, but not now. Go take your phone call."

Gabriel grinned and returned to his office to call Jacob and discuss their new strategy.

Chapter 12: The Orphan

Miami, Florida: February 1982

A few days later, Gabriel sat behind his desk, examining the stacks of papers and files surrounding the yellow pad in front of him. Organizing the priorities in his mind, he sorted through the names and dates of his clients, planning the time that he would need to devote to each one and calculating the billing per hour. As he pondered, a small knock came from his closed door.

"Yes?" he asked. No response came. "Come in," he said a little louder.

"You're here early," said a female voice, opening the door.

Gabriel looked up to see his mother, Laura.

"Hello, Mom," he said in Spanish, rising from his chair to greet his mother. "What brings you to the office? And especially this early." Gabriel hunched over to hug his mother and as he embraced her, he kissed her on the cheek. "Did you get a day off from work?

She smiled and looked up at her son, choosing to respond in her accented English.

"I had to take Bertha in for a tune up, so I took the day and your dad, and I decided that he would drop me off here while he went to the zoning meeting with Mr. Reyes. That would give me the chance to see you and then after he finishes his meetings we will go out to dinner."

"That's nice. I wish that I could take the rest of the day off," he grinned.

"You do realize that tonight is Friday, right?"

Gabriel raised his eyebrows, not realizing that Friday had come so soon.

"I am glad you'll be here for a while. I have not seen you, for… wow the last time that I saw you was almost three weeks ago."

His mother sat in one of the client's chairs.

"You know, son of mine, you never forgot about your mother like this at the State Attorney's office."

Gabriel lowered his eyes and accepted the guilt.

"There's no excuse, Mom, and I am sorry for that. I've been a little swamped and really have not had time to do much except work."

"And play poker on Thursdays with the guys."

"I actually haven't played in the last two weeks, but aside from work, all I've done is exercise, sleep, and do billing."

Laura examined her son's face and tone, accepting the truth he gave her.

"Well, I have already heard it from your Abuela. She is not happy with you, and you know how she gets when you don't call her."

"I know, Mom. I owe it to Abuela to go and see her. I just must remember not to eat for two days."

They both laughed.

"It doesn't matter how old you are, Abuela is going to feed you like you're a little kid because in the end, that's what you'll always be to her."

"Right. I am a child to her until she tries setting me up with another date."

"She still does that?"

"Don't act like you don't know, Mom. Do you understand how many times I have had to run out from the office when I am working late because she set up a reservation for me at a restaurant?"

"She's only looking out for you."

Gabriel raised his eyebrows at his mother. There was much of his grandfather in her. Even if her black hair and dark eyes were his grandmother's, but her milky white skin, facial expressions, and her gestures, were all Abuelo's.

"You know, Mom, if by looking out for me, you mean adding a great grandchild to the family, then you are spot on." He leaned back in his chair and brought the fingertips of both hands together in front of him. "I promise you that I'll call her before the end of the day."

"Don't mention I told you because I'll hear it for that."

"I promise. As for not staying connected with you, I will do a better job of it but just know that last year was a serious adjustment for me. I went from just practicing law to having to worry about bringing clients through the door, convincing them to trust the intimate practice instead of the massive firm, and then persuading them to refer more clients to us. And that's the easy part. Managing my cases and time with the utmost efficiency, keeping track of my time to bill, sending out billing, collecting the billing, and in the midst of all of that, actually doing my work is what takes up the majority of my time. Dad depends on me, bringing in a certain amount of money to support myself and help him support the firm. Luckily, these last couple of months have been good, but I wonder from time to time if I have been more of a burden than a blessing."

"You are not a burden, and your father wouldn't have it any other way. You don't think you are the only one that has continually dreamed of Lock and Lock, do you? I am surprised that your father didn't order the Lock and Lock sign when you were three." Laura shuffled in her seat and leaned forward, fixing the folds in her dress as she spoke.

"I know that it was always his dream for me to practice with him, but I thought that he wanted that after I told him that I wanted to go to law school." Gabriel leaned back in his seat and waited for Laura's reply.

"He never pushed you and I give him a lot of credit for that; it would have been unfair for him to push you as your father, but he always dreamed about it."

"Now, after almost a year, how do you like this practice instead of criminal law?"

"Well Door Law is very different animal."

"What's Door Law?"

"Taking anything that comes through the door."

Laughter erupted from within Laura and Gabriel loosened up a bit.

"Well, your father doesn't practice that anymore. Believe me, when he started, I would go to the tiny office in Little Havana, and he had to take everything that came in the door just to pay the rent. I would finish teaching my kids and then I would run out of my classroom, hop in my car, and hightail it to the office until nine or ten. He could not afford a secretary when he first started, and we were just two kids when we got married so it's not like we had a lot saved. After helping your father, we would go home, go to sleep, and then we'd do it all over again."

"I did not realize that. I didn't know that money was that tight."

"How were you going to know? You could not even walk then, and it wasn't until you started speaking that our finances got better. Abuela and Abuelo helped us a lot by taking care of you. Abuela loved holding you and caring for you. Do you remember how sick you used to get as a child?"

Gabriel nodded, recalling how he would spend large swaths of his childhood in his parents' bed and eating soup.

"Your father worked so hard to make ends meet for us. If you think that you are working hard now, you should have seen your father. There is nothing that he wouldn't have done for us."

Gabriel nodded and closed his eyes for a moment, remembering his mother and father by his side when he was in the hospital with pneumonia when he was seven.

Silence filled the room for a few moments before Gabriel changed the subject. Rising from his chair, he opened one of the files on his desk. "So, what do you plan to do this morning?"

"I was going to invite you to go have breakfast, but I guess that you already ate."

"I've been trying to eat healthier and save a little cash, but I'd love to go and grab a cup of coffee with my mom."

Laura's eyes became full as she smiled, revealing some of her teeth.

"I am sorry that we haven't done this more often, Mom. I do want to tell you that I have a client coming in a little later, so we will need to be back by 10:00 a.m."

"No problem, son."

The journey to the nearby coffee shop on Coral Way lasted no more than a few minutes. Finding the café nearly empty, the waitress escorted them to their table and took their coffee orders quickly. Laura shuffled in her seat, finding the most comfortable position while Gabriel leaned back against his chair and the wall as he sat in an open pose, diagonal to his mother.

"So, who is this client that you have to see next?"

"A brand-new father by the looks of it."

"Well, that's definitely exciting, congratulations to him, but since when do you need a lawyer to have a child, I used a doctor."

Gabriel half-snickered as he looked at his mother from the corners of his eyes. The waitress returned to them carrying their coffee mugs on a tray hoisted at eye level and evading the maze of tables and patrons that paid her wages.

"One latté and one black coffee," Laura said to the waitress, placing the mugs down and moving the small container of sugar from a nearby empty table to theirs. "Anything else that I can get you both?"

"Just a small glass of OJ for me, thanks," said Gabriel, trying to remain professional. The waitress grinned back at him.

"I would like your breakfast sandwich on a croissant please," said Laura.

"I'll be back with the OJ in just a moment and a little longer on the sandwich "My name is Melisa, and I'll be taking care of both of you," she said smiling and tucking the tray underneath an arm and walking back toward the kitchen.

Half an hour later, Gabriel and Laura returned to the office. As they entered, they found Susana warming up a pot of coffee and trying hard not to yawn.

"Good morning."

"Good morning, Susana," they both replied in unison. As Gabriel and Laura passed her toward his office, Susana called out to them.

"Gabriel, Jacob called you to confirm his appointment."

"Thanks."

Turning off the coffee machine, she tiptoed over to her desk and pulled a small piece of paper handing it to him. "He didn't say anything else but said to call him back when you had a moment."

"I've got some time before my next appointment. Let me finish with my mother and I'll call him back and confirm personally. Any other messages, Susana?"

"None. I'll be sure to let you know if any calls come in while you and your mother are finishing up."

"Thanks." Gabriel returned his attention to his mother.

"So, what is this appointment that you have at ten?"

"Just a client that I need to finish some things up with."

"Come on, Gabriel. I have been your mother for almost thirty years; you can't fool me. What is really going on that's bothering you?"

"I guess that I've got a good poker face for everyone but you, huh?"

"No one reads a poker face like a mom, I'm sorry to say."

Gabriel looked down at the yellow pad on his desk and contemplated the information in his mind, deciding on which information he would be allowed and want to disclose. He chose another approach.

"Mom, how do you feel about shared responsibility?"

"Concerning what?"

"Raising a child?"

"Like shared parenting?"

"Something like that."

Laura took her hand and placed it on her chest.

"Your father and I have managed to be good parents to you, but just because we are your parents does not mean that we are the only ones that raised you. We had a lot of help from Abuela and Abuelo, your teachers, our neighbors, friends, and the church. Yes, the church helped us a lot with you."

"How do you mean?"

"Think about how hard it is to be a person in society. Between competition and other people telling you who to be without knowing who you are it is tough on a person. I look at what girls must deal with these days, how things are changing, and it makes me feel odd because somethings are easier, but others are much, much harder."

"A client of mine found out on Monday that he's going to have to raise a child."

"Well, that's wonderful news. Is he excited?"

Gabriel recalled Jacob's facial expressions from Monday.

"It's just a little different because the child is not his."

"Oh," she said, pausing. Collecting herself, she reverted to her previous tone, "The lord works in mysterious ways, Gabriel. Think about that child. Is the child's father in the picture?"

"Doesn't look like it."

"Then maybe it was a blessing from God that now, your client gets to be a father to a child that would be otherwise fatherless."

"You know, I hadn't really thought about it that way."

"It's hard to when you're supposed to be on your client's side and his side only."

"Mom, if someone that you cared about asked you to raise their child, would you?"

"Yes, and your father and I almost did."

Gabriel sat up in his chair, surprised by what Laura had just said.

"What do you mean almost?"

"When you were a little more than four, there was a couple that your father and I were friends within church. The Zubizarreta family from Spain. They had moved from San Sebastián a few years after you were born, and your father and I got to know them well at church. They had a little boy of five and a little girl of two when they got into a car accident on the road to Key West and died. Only the little girl, Enara, survived." Laura exhaled, pushing through the recollection of memories. "It was horrible, Gabriel. Enara was in the hospital for a month and in that time, the diocese did everything that they could to contact their family in Spain. For weeks, the church tried everything but couldn't find any family in San Sebastián or the surrounding areas, so there came a point where the archbishop, Joseph Patrick Hurley of Saint Augustine, met with us and other families to see if we would want to adopt Enara and raise her as our own."

"Wouldn't that go to an adoption agency in Miami?"

"Of course, it did, but a catholic adoption agency was going to help process the adoption and make sure that child was going to be looked after and raised Catholic like her parents. I remember him speaking with your father and me, asking us questions about you, our family, if we would be good Catholics, everything you could think of. Before your father and I could finish the final step to adopt, the church was able to find her father's cousin, Eneko Zubizarreta. He had moved to Rome a few years earlier, which is why they had such a hard time finding him, but in the end, he came to claim her. For a moment, your father and I were relishing having another child."

"Because of what you went through when I was born."

"Yes, I always wanted three kids, but fortunately, one was enough."

Gabriel leaned forward in his chair staring intently at his mother.

"If Eneko hadn't come to claim Enara, would you and Dad have been chosen over the other families?"

"Actually, we had already been chosen when we learned of the cousin. Every child deserves the best life they can have, and every child deserves love, regardless of who the parents may be. In your case, your client may be the one selected by God to give that child that love.

"Did she stay at the house?"

Yes." We took care of her for a month. She was with the church for the first two, at St. Aloysius and later St. Philomena, but we had her for the last month when we were chosen as the new parents until the church found her uncle, Eneko, who wanted her."

Laura finished speaking and Gabriel kept quiet for a moment, knowing the agony hidden behind his mother's pleasant smile.

"I don't remember her though," said Gabriel forcing a puzzled look.

"Remember the first year you went to Asturias?"

"I was five, so my memory is not very clear, but I do remember I went with Abuelo and Abuela and stayed for a long time."

"You didn't come home sooner because we did not want you to come home until the adoption was decided one way or the other. What would have happened if you had met each other, bonded and then she had to go? Both of you would have suffered and she was very fragile after losing her parents and her brother. You got to know her for the last two weeks of her stay with us." Gabriel heard fierce protection in his mother's voice for him and for her and thought, *Mom wanted Enara, but she really wanted to protect me.*

Laura and Gabriel paused for a moment. They had spoken for about twenty minutes, and Gabriel, sensing that they had been at it for a while, looked down at his watch.

"Mom, I've got a little less than twenty minutes to prepare for my client and make that phone call, but I appreciate everything that you just told me. I may use it to comfort him if he is still not over the news. Do you mind either going to Dad's office or the conference room until I finish with him?"

Laura looked behind her, then at the door leading to the mini conference room.

"I'll just wait in your father's office. Not a problem."

Laura got up and left Gabriel's office, closing the door on her way out. Gabriel retrieved the slip of paper that Susana gave him and thought about Enara, wondering how different his life would have been. Drifting off into what could have been, he recollected himself and dialed the number on the slip. The dial rang for a few moments before a woman's voice came through the other line.

"Hello, Molina, and Schwartzmann's office. This is Renae speaking; how may I help you?"

"Hello Renae, this is Gabriel Lock from Lock and Lock. My secretary, Susana, told me that someone from your office had called. Was it Ms. Jensen?"

"Yes, it was. I can transfer you to her extension. Wait one moment, please."

Gabriel waited a few moments until there was a voice on the other line that he recognized as Sarah's.

"I'm good, Sarah. Yourself?" Sounds came from the receiver as Gabriel nodded periodically. As Sarah finished on the other side, Gabriel nodded his head one last time. "Thank you for letting me know, Sarah. I will be sure to tell him." Gabriel returned the phone to its cradle and stood up from his chair. He took a moment, walked across the room, and thought about opening the door. Turning back to his desk, he checked his watch and realized that Jacob was probably already on his way. Gabriel returned to his desk, sat down, and looked through the file one more time as he waited for Jacob to arrive. *I could have had a sister,* he thought. *I found out that I could have had a sister after all this time.*

Chapter 13: The News

Miami, Florida: February 1982

Gabriel sat in his office on Monday morning, still recovering from the shock of his mother's confession and processing the phone call he had just had with Sarah. Imagining how his life could have been compared to what it was perplexed him, and the stress of the unknown caused his sciatica to flare and his lower back to throb. Leaning forward in his chair, Gabriel hoped to stretch the nerves and muscles as he pushed his chair back and brought his upper body as parallel to the floor as it would go. Dinner with his parents and the weekend seemed to have dissipated as quickly as the ticks on his watch in the hour. A few minutes after two, Susana notified him that Jacob Wallace had arrived and was early for his appointment.

Jacob Wallace entered Gabriel's office teeming with excitement and before Gabriel could say anything, Jacob broke into his monologue.

"Gabriel, I wanted to tell you something that I didn't tell you when we were in court. Something important."

"What is it?"

"Look, I've been thinking a lot about this. Maybe this is what I needed. At the courthouse, I didn't know what to think. I was angry, uncertain, and, for a moment, I almost felt betrayed." Jacob began pacing from side to side. "I thought that Belinda and I would have children together or adopt. She was the love of my life, but that didn't mean that I was hers. She and I argued for the year leading up to our split, but I knew that we weren't drifting apart like she had said. I knew that it was something else and now I know that it was that she wanted her own child. She didn't cheat on me while we were still together and I know I was a bit difficult at the courthouse during my last visit, but I've been thinking about this a lot. What if this was God's chance to give Belinda what she needed and what I always wanted?"

Gabriel did his best to follow.

"Jacob, something doesn't fit. Why would you say that Belinda wanted her own child, wouldn't she have her own with you?"

Jacob swallowed hard, allowing the lump in his throat to leave him and clear the air.

"I'm sterile, Gabriel. I knew that if I ever had a child, he would not be of my blood but could still be mine. I would raise him, teach him how to play sports, go fishing, and everything else that fathers do with their sons. In the end it wouldn't matter that he wasn't mine, but could carry on the family name, and it's a good name."

Gabriel waited for a moment, allowing Jacob to settle his emotions.

"Jacob, I think that's great, that you have this compassion, and I think that you would make a great father. You are already a good man, but I just got off the phone with Sarah, Belinda's attorney just before you entered. She informed me that the father wants to be in the boy's life. He's apparently signed the documents, and they are being faxed to me as we speak. If that is the case, the child will no longer be your responsibility."

"Is she sure?"

"The man apparently signed the documents in Sarah's office."

Tears formed in Jacob's eyes as Gabriel finished, and he bowed his head for a second. He raised his head and swallowed hard, peering out of the window.

"I can't say I'm not disappointed," he said as he looked for a seat but found none.

"Life is like that," continued Gabriel. "It throws the unexpected at us and just when we get used to the idea, it changes it up on us all over again."

Jacob finally fixed his gaze at his lawyer and there was a soft knock on the office door. "Come in," said Gabriel.

Susana opened the door and without looking at Jacob she quietly crossed the carpet to Gabriel's desk and handed him some documents. She turned around and left quickly while he looked over the affidavit for admission of paternity.

"It's all here. Jacob. Would you like to review them?"

"No need, Gabriel. Thank you for letting me know. Send me the billing for your work and let me know when we return to court to settle this divorce."

Gabriel nodded and did not say a word.

"Have a nice weekend," he said, turning away and heading out the door.

"You know the right woman will come along and then you can adopt as many children as you would want." Gabriel said after him,

Jacob turned and smiled weakly.

"Yes, there will be plenty of time for that. Thank you for reminding me my friend." Jacob made his way to the door. Gabriel saw Susana escorting him to the door and shut it behind him. *I can't believe all that has happened today and it's not even 11:00 o'clock.* He thought for a moment and then he picked up the phone and, looking at the information at the bottom of the pleading, called Sarah.

"Hey Gabriel, calling back so soon?"

"Yes, to tell you that Jacob just left my office but told me that he will sign the documents to close the case."

"I bet he was so relieved."

"Actually, he wasn't."

"What do you mean?"

"It turns out that he never thought he would have a child and after he got over the initial shock, he really liked the idea. Then, when he found out that was not going to happen well..."

She was quiet for the moment.

"Would you like to go for a drink with me sometime?"

Momentarily he was caught off guard.

"Ah yes, I would."

"Teaming with enthusiasm, Counselor?"

"Sorry, it's been an eventful day."

"Well, I am swamped this week but next week, you can tell me about it over a mojito."

"How did you know Mojito's are my favorite?

"You see, we already have two things in common."

"What's the other one?

"We are both willing to wait a week for a good thing."

Gabriel laughed. Sarah had a silent smile on the other side of the line.

Chapter 14: The Owners

Miami, Florida: October 1978

Dwight sat across from Steve on the other side of the desk in the upstairs office. The mahogany paneling contrasted with the cream-colored linoleum floors giving the office a warm feeling. Steve sat in his leather desk chair and Dwight sat in one of the well-cushioned armchairs facing Steve.

"Got all your notes, Dwight?" asked Steve, putting a hand through his greying hair.

"I am ready. You?" replied Dwight in their shared southern drawl.

"Ronald should be here in the next ten to fifteen minutes."

"Feels weird being here on a Saturday," added Dwight, inhaling deeply.

"I'm sure that talking to your brother about his role in the company is a weirder feeling."

"Probably the hardest thing that I will ever have to do."

Dwight and Steve spent the next few minutes going through the pictures and paperwork, the summaries, and the invoices, taking notes on their papers and reviewing the list of subjects. Preparing themselves for the confrontation with Ronald.

A knock came from the door.

"Come in," said Steve, rising from his chair. Ronald entered the room.

"Close the door behind you, Ron, please."

Ronald turned back and placed a hand on the flat of the door, pushing it gently.

"Hey Ron, how are you?" asked Dwight, embracing his brother as he neared the empty chair.

"I'm good, thanks. How are you, Steve?" he asked his cousin after hugging Dwight and turning to his cousin.

"Good. Thanks, Ron."

"So, what's going' on? It's unusual to have a meeting on a Saturday."

"Well, it is important, Ron. We wanted to talk to you about something that came to our attention and think that we need you to be aware of."

"Go ahead, shoot."

Ronald glanced at Dwight, searching for a hint of an explanation, but Dwight stared only at Steve, who opened one of the drawers on his desk and retrieved a manilla file.

"Ron, the other day, we received a call from one of our clients saying that they didn't receive one of their shipments."

"Which one?"

"Mr. Miller called, from USA TV & Company in Daytona, remember him?"

"Sounds familiar. I normally deal with Arty, though."

"Arty?"

"Arthur Feuer, the store supervisor."

"Understood. Anyway, Mr. Miller called and told me that he did not receive his shipment of TVs."

"That does not make sense. All the TVs were packed in the truck that took off on Tuesday."

"Not all of them, Ron," began Dwight, meeting his brother's eyes.

"Mr. Frank Miller," continued Steve, taking a hand and stroking his chin, "explained to us that he was missing a few TVs. We asked him how many, and he said that we were five short. I thought, 'well, that's strange. Ron always takes extra care with the Miller order. In fact, Ron takes extra care with all the orders.' So, I started digging. I looked at the security footage from the loading dock, and I noticed something a little different one night."

Ron kept silent.

"I found' footage of you carrying' TVs over to the truck and noticed that you took one back. When I first saw it, I thought that maybe one had gotten damaged, no big deal, but as I kept watching the tape, I saw you carry another one back. Same model. Same box. I thought, well if one is broken, I can deal with it. Two, well that is some rotten luck, but when I saw you carrying number three and number four back, I just said to myself, 'Now what in the blazes is Ronald, my cousin, doing with all those TVs?! –They can't ALL be broken, can they?'"

Steve finished and rose from behind the desk to make his way over to the small television set behind him. He bent over to press the button on the VCR. The television set flashed for a moment as he turned it on.

"Hold on, let me fast forward a bit." "Here it is!" announced Steve.

They all stared at the screen, watching Ronald moving the television sets from the truck on the loading dock back to a small room in the warehouse.

"Now look here, Ron. If you wanted a few TVs for yourself, all you had to do was just ask. I mean, come on, Ron. We're all family here. We all want to make some money, but doggone it, Ron. Why didn't you say something?" Ronald kept silent, not uttering so much as a sound. Steve stared at him straight in the eyes. "Dwight, you want to say something. You've been at this much longer than I have."

"Look, Ron. We aren't going to come down that hard on you, but I just want to know why ya did it?"

"It was just a couple of TVs. I didn't put them on the truck because I wanted to put them in my house. Lori and I have been changing the TVs in the house, and these were nice TVs. We had overstocked the truck anyway, and when I counted them up, I figured that I could just pay the company back in the following week. I didn't mean anything by it. I figured a couple-hundred would fix it all square."

"That's it, Ron? That's all it was, just a couple hundred?" asked Dwight, raising his brow at his brother.

"That's it, Dwight. I swear."

"You swear?"

"Hell, I swear on my wife."

"You don't like your wife, Ron."

"Okay, I swear on Grand pappy's grave."

"Ronald Altheus Pilkington, you just lied to your cousin, you lied to me, and you just swore that you didn't steal from the family company."

"I didn't lie to you!"

"Then why do we have tapes and tapes upon tapes of you stealing from the company, hmm?

"Are you calling' me a liar?" barked Ronald, clenching his teeth and fists. Veins surged in his temples, and blood turned his face red.

"You're a damn liar!" yelled Steve, staring his cousin down.

"Enough!" screamed Dwight. Ron and Steve found their chairs again. "Enough with the hollering and yelling. Ron, we have evidence of you stealing from the company repeatedly. We don't just have the tapes, but we have the receipts for transactions and all of the records on you. Read 'em and weep, Ron."

Dwight dropped a file with all the evidence onto Ronald's lap. He opened it and began scanning all of them. The sworn testimonies of Arty, Garland, and all the other members of the clients that he had bribed and split profits with.

"Mr. Miller fired Arthur as soon as we got the statement. Most of the other accomplices were fired as well, Ron. We added all the figures up, and we estimate that you stole a little under eight hundred thousand dollars' worth of goods in the last six years. It's over, Ron. We've got everything."

Silence emanated through the room. Steve took a drink of his water, and Ron fumed in his chair.

"Were you havin' money problems, Ron?" asked Dwight in a low voice.

"No, I wasn't havin' no problems with money, but we," he said, pointing at them both before returning his fingers to himself and making a triangle. "We was havin' money problems."

"What do you mean by that, Ron?" Ron reached for a pen from Steve's desk and took it in his hand. Removing a piece of paper from the file that Dwight plopped on his lap, he leaned onto the desk and began to write.

D 25%   S 50%   R 25%

"See these numbers, right here?" he asked, pointing at them with his index finger.

"What about them?" asked Steve.

"This is our split. When our dads started this company, they took fifty percent each and worked this way, both until they both retired. We kept the same percentages. You took fifty percent as the only child," said Ron, pointing at Steve, "but we took twenty-five percent each. Now, I don't hate that we kept the percentages the same, but I do indeed mind that I was working' my tail off to put food on my table, and you walked out on us, Dwight, eight years ago when you decided that you'd go do something else and not help us out over here. Instead of sticking with the family business, you just walked out and kept your money. Meanwhile, Steve and I were over here working and working and working away. Then, out of nowhere, Steve," continued Ron, pointing back to Steve, "You decide to solidify this when we had the company retreat four years ago that Dwight was fine to do what he was doing. So, all of this happened, and I'm over here, working like a dog, wondering if I'm ever going to get out o' this here mess. So, one day, I figured that I'd take the property that was excess and get my side business going. I was going to approach you to buy you out, my dearest brother, and then Steve and I would be fifty-fifty. That would give me enough of a reason to stick it out instead of watching you do your life's joy and still making out like a bandit." "But you stole from the company, Ron. Steve and I did the calculations, and we've concluded that you stole nearly eight hundred thousand dollars. As there's no insurance coverage to recover what you stole, you are going to surrender your twenty-five percent to us, and you will be removed from the company."

Ron's eyes broadened, processing the words that Dwight spoke. He choked on his words as he tried to utter them, doubling back in his chair, shifting, and twisting in disbelief.

"You going to take this away from me? You are serious, aren't you?

"We're serious, Ron," confirmed Steve, his dark eyes projecting his disgust. "All of this could have been avoided if you'd just called us an' told us how ya felt. We could have worked something out, Ron, but now we are here, and you gone."

"What if I pay it back?"

"You are going to, but we can't take you back, Ron. Can't trust ya wortha shit anymore."

Ronald bowed his head and nodded.

"No changing it is there?"

"Ya had five whole fuckin' years, Ron. Ya didn't change it then an' ya sure as hell won't now."

Ronald leaned back and made a gesture of resignation. He knew that he had lost.

"Listen, I'll walk away from this, but I want one thing promised to me. My shares in the company are greater than what I stole. I want a document statin' that I will be paid out for the remainder of my shares."

"It's already been drafted. Ya just need to sign on the dotted line," urged Steve, passing Ronald the documents, "I even highlighted them all for you just to make a little bit easier. Dwight, anything you want to say?"

Dwight raised his head and looked at his brother square in the eyes.

"You Are My Brother. Always will ya be my brother, but I don' want to see you ever again 'round here. Ya hear me?"

"Loud and clear, Dwight."

Ronald took all the documents and signed them all, one by one, initiating where he had to and signing where he didn't want to. After a few moments, he surrendered the pen and the papers to his kin and, without saying a word, walked out on his family.

Dwight and Steve sat in silence for a moment. A tear left Dwight's eyes, and Steve put a hand on his cousin's shoulder.

"There was nothing we could have done, Dwight. He's a thief. Had a damn good reason, better than most, but in the end, he's a thief. He done us wrong and soiled our family name. He even swore on Grand pappy's grave and didn't think twice about it."

"I know," choked Dwight, wiping his eyes with his sleeve, "I just figured he would have chosen different. Hell, done something other than steal from his family."

"Me too, Dwight. Me too. Either way, your fixing' to have thirty-seven and a half percent of the company, I figure that we should move to make it a fifty-fifty split. Thoughts?"

"I'd like that, but I can't move from the Miami PD just yet. I'm close to a promotion, and I can't buy you out for the twelve and a half percent. I don't have the cash just yet."

"How long do you think it will take you?"

"At least two years, maybe three."

"Well then, get to saving, partner." Steve rose from behind his desk and outstretched his hand toward his cousin. Dwight looked down at Steve's hand, and, taking it in his, thanked him, before they left the office.

Chapter 15: The Ring
Miami, Florida: March 1982

Gabriel paced around his office, holding a contract in his hands and a pen behind his ear as he patrolled in front of his desk. Muttering to himself, he placed the document on the desktop and underlined a phrase. He tugged his sleeves back up his arms and resumed his analysis. A knock came at the door, and Susana's familiar voice mentioned Rodrigo Vivar being at the office.

"Sure, let him in, Susana. Thank you."

A moment later, Rodrigo walked in.

"Rolled sleeves, unbuttoned collar, and a pen sitting on your ear? –You're getting sloppy."

"Tell me about it," admitted Gabriel, not bothering to look up at Rodrigo's smug face. "Want to sit down? I am almost finished with my thoughts on this contract."

"I've got something fairly big for you, so I can wait a few minutes."

Rodrigo waited for Gabriel to finish the contract, and Gabriel, preferring not to force his best friend to wait, fired through the pages, summarizing and jotting down facts before scribbling his conjectures.

"Alright, Rod. I'm all ears," said Gabriel, laying the contract on his desk and leaning against it, folding his arms across his chest.

"Thank you for your undivided attention. Anyway, do you remember that client that I talked to you about the other day at Cacique's?"

"Jog my memory a bit."

"The one about the theft from the electronics store. The owners are all middle-aged men with southern drawls. Come on, you remember Old Miami, right?"

"The guy ended up being part of a stealing ring with the employees that he oversaw, right? You just went to court with this, didn't you?"

"My client flipped, got immunity, recorded the others, and he will be testifying against them when their criminal cases come up, but now the owners are coming after them in civil court, including my client."

Gabriel inhaled and processed the facts.

"You've come here because you want my help?"

"Either you or your dad."

Gabriel nodded and tilted his body on the desk, twisting to find his planner. He shuffled through the pages for the next couple of months, looking at his different court dates and appointments.

"How intense are you expecting this to be?"

"It's going to take a fair amount of work."

"Do you think that the evidence is in his favor?"

"There's something off about this case. It doesn't make sense to me that they wouldn't only go after them in criminal court but then in civil. Not that it doesn't happen, but these guys are all blue-collar workers; they don't have that kind of money."

"Is something else at play?"

"Could be, but I can't find the angle nor invent one."

"Can you get me the details of what you have so far?"

"When do you want to meet the client?" asked Rodrigo, taking a step back and sitting in the chair.

Gabriel glanced at his watch and recalled that his afternoon was clear.

"Can he be here in a few hours?"

"He lives in Hialeah." Gabriel nodded.

"What's his number?" asked Gabriel, moving behind his desk and taking the phone from its cradle. Rodrigo fed Gabriel the number who called the client and handed the phone to Rod.

"Mr. Melendi? Hi, this is Mr. Vivar, your criminal attorney. I am speaking with Gabriel Lock from Lock and Lock on Coral Way about your civil case. He has time to meet you at…"

Gabriel held up three fingers.

"Three o'clock this afternoon. Are you available? Okay. I'll need you here at three. Your case is going to be a tough one and we need to get a jump start on this."

The muffled words from the other side of the line got louder and Gabriel knew that Melendi protested against the drive.

"Yes, I know that you live in Hialeah and that traffic is really rough."

Melendi said a few more words, and Rod continued.

"Good lawyers are really hard to find, Mr. Melendi…"

The protest ended and the line held silent for a few seconds. Rodrigo's face changed and Gabriel could tell that the client had surrendered.

"Thank you, Mr. Melendi," Finished Rodrigo, handing the phone back to Gabriel, who placed it in its cradle and returned his gaze to his waiting friend.

"Do you really think that he'll be here in at three?" Gabriel looked down at his watch again.

"He'll be here at quarter to three; I'm sure of it."

"I'll ask Susana to order some lunch for us from the corner place just down the street, and we'll get to work."

"You buying?"

"Think I can win this thing?"

"No."

"Then sure, I'll buy, but if I win, you buy the tickets for both of us at our next playoff game, deal?"

"That's a lot."

"I thought that you said that I couldn't win?"

"You can't."

"Then why gripe about sure money?"

Rodrigo measured his response for a moment, calculating Gabriel's chances. He nodded and Gabriel sauntered from his desk over to his door and asked Susana to place an order for two from the restaurant down the street.

An hour and a half later, Gabriel and Rod were preparing for Melendi's arrival. As they straightened out their files and notes, Gabriel's phone rang. He picked up and found Susana on the other line telling him that Melendi had arrived. Gabriel instructed her to send him in, and within a few moments, a stocky, black-haired man in his thirties advanced toward him while carrying a parcel. He stuck out his free hand to shake Rodrigo's and Gabriel's hands. Gabriel noted the man's movements and intensity as he opened his mouth to speak.

"Antonio Melendi, but my frens call me Tony. Rodrigo told me about ju, and I hope you trus' me a little and, ju know, help me out. Ju understan' me?"

Gabriel hesitated for a moment. He understood the speech well because he spoke Spanish, but the accent was the strongest he had ever heard. *Lord help us if we get Judge*

Smith or Judge Lebowitz; they won't understand a word, he thought.

"Yes, I understand you, but would you prefer Spanish, Mr. Melendi?" asked Gabriel.

"No, Mr. Lock, *Englitch* is fine. I practice, an' I talk in court. All de days I speak Englitch with my frens at work, and wit' family at home. I must practice. Ju know?

"I know, Mr. Melendi, would you mind taking a seat?" asked Gabriel lowering his arm to point at the desk. Melendi sat down and Gabriel began his questioning.

"Rodrigo performed a bit of a miracle with your case. You were the head of the ring that stole more than a quarter of a million dollars from your employer, and you walked away without doing a day in jail."

"Jes, a big, bery big, miracle. I tink, I gonna be…how you say…behin' bars."

"In jail," added Rodrigo, sarcasm writhing through his voice, knowing Gabriel had understood it.

"Jes, for a long time, and now not'ing; no bars. Amazing. We stole a quarter of a million and me, not one day. *Un* fenómeno dis guy," he said, putting his hand on Rodrigo's shoulder. "My boys go crazy for playing ball. We play every day. I tink no more baseball with my kids, den noting happens, so I play wit' dem every day. So, I cannot pay enough to dis man for dat, ju know?" nodding his head towards Rodrigo. "Fantastic, no? Because prison cost me my life. If one of dose big guys," he said, putting his hand above his head to signify height, "come to me and wants something with me, I give my life before I nobody's wife, ju know? My boss, Mr. Steve, send dese papers wit' a police officer." Tony opened a brown envelope and took out a set of documents. "Wit' what Mr. Rodrigo say to me. dey are lying," he glanced at Rodrigo.

"The lawsuit is a lie." he interjected.

"Jes, suing me for *juan* million dollar..' I answer all deir questions, Mr. Lock. We finish in court. I no understand dis!"

Melendi retrieved the lawsuit from the parcel and placed it in front of Gabriel, who began reviewing the documents.

"Mr. Melendi," began Gabriel.

"Tony, my name is eh, Tony. Please, Mr. Lock, call me Tony."

"Okay, Tony. They needed you to cooperate to catch everyone involved. Without the evidence you gathered with the wire you wore; they could not have convicted everyone. Most of the things captured on film and caught by the accountant could have been mistakes unless they analyzed them as parts of a pattern. Only you knew everyone involved and how it functioned. You got lucky they needed you specifically to make sure that all the people were caught, including your fence and outside people. That's why you didn't do a day in jail."

"I know my case don't look so good, ju know? But I believe in him," he said, pointing to Rodrigo. "He told me dat you are the flame, and dat is good enough for me."

Gabriel, momentarily lost in Cuban slang, glanced at Rodrigo, who mouthed *the best*.

"And I ask me 'where I going to take a million dollar' to pay? I don't have dem buried in the ground. *De* most important thing is that we don't steal a million in merchandise. *dey're* playing a game *dere* wid us. Dere a cat locked up dere."

"Jailed cat?" asked Gabriel, looking at Rod. "All the time I've spent in Spain at my family's place, I've never heard that."

"Something fishy. Very Cuban."

"Got it."

Melendi continued.

"Imagine. I tink dis was close. Everyt'ing Okay, finish. Den, yesterday a policeman come to my house, and give me dese papers and I see dat dey wanna million dollars. Dis is ridiculous. When tink dese people dat we steal a million in TVs, espeakers, an' radios? Ju steal dat, ju empty the warehouse."

"Tony let's get back to earth," said Gabriel, reeling Melendi in, "You and your buddies stole around two hundred and fifty thousand dollars. That's a lot of money. I would be pissed too if I were them. You were the ringleader that got away with no jail time, remember? "

"Okay, I was de leader. But why are all of us in the suit? Why say we stole one million dollars? *Das* no true!

"If they prove the loss, they can make an insurance claim against their carrier. It's called a Fidelity bond; a type of insurance that covers a company against theft by employees. Whatever the insurance doesn't cover, the company takes that loss as a deduction from their taxes. I think what they are trying to do is to obtain a judgement against the employees, and then, once they have a final judgement, they will make the claim either against the insurance, or the IRS, or both. While they're at it, they can make you an economic prisoner by pursuing you with the judgement or letting the insurance company do so. They may feel, for some reason, that a claim against the insurance company won't be enough. They may not be expecting much of a payoff, and so they must be getting the judgement for the IRS also."

"Bankruptcy for me?" asked Melendi, trying to find a solution.

"Bankruptcy can't get rid of judgements that have to do with fraud or theft. The law won't permit it."

"Are ju kidding me?!" bellowed Melendi, rising from his chair and raising his hands to his black hair.

"I'm afraid not, Tony. They are suing you and all your cohorts and claiming that you had a conspiracy to steal from the company. They want to get a judgement against each one of you."

"How long do dat last?"

"Twenty years."

"Dey can spend twenty years harassing me to collect?"

"Yes."

"Dat's not right, Mr. Lock!"

"Better than becoming someone's wife in jail," answered Gabriel.

"I nobody's wife, Mr. Lock, NOBODY'S!"

Melendi removed his hand from his head and took a deep breath in. He pondered everything, analyzing what Gabriel had just told him, and recalled everything that they stole. Taking one more deep breath, he sat back in his chair and calmed himself.

"Okay. I no wanna be nobody wife in prison, so what can we do?"

Gabriel rose from his chair and began to pace around the room. He rifled through the papers that Melendi had given him and began doing arithmetic in his mind. As he paced and calculated, he measured the timeline of what Melendi had told him.

"How much did you say you guys stole?

"Two hundred and fifty t'ousand dollars, Mr. Lock."

"They are claiming a little over a million."

"No, das not true!"

"How long did you say you worked at this place?"

"Two years."

"They are claiming the stealing went on for five years."

"No way José! I was not there five years."

"Actually, what they are saying is that the stealing started with your co-conspirators before you got there, and you just formed a part of it and slowly became the head guy."

"But dats not what happen. No *señor*, I was not dere for the estealing; liars!"

"Well, if it is a conspiracy, you are responsible for everything that everyone does in that conspiracy, even if you weren't there at the time of part of the crimes."

"Dat can't be!"

"That's the law."

"Can you do something, like we did with de jail?"

"I might be able to do something."

"I would appreciate dat very much."

"You can count on it, Tony. That's my job. Now let's begin with the facts. Tell me every detail."

Chapter 16: The Refuge

Miami, Florida: March 1982

Tony stood in his driveway several hours later admiring his house he thanked God for his blessings in it. Twin palm trees swayed with the wind, and for a moment, he felt hope. As he walked toward the front door, he paused and took a deep breath. Opening the door, he heard music playing in the kitchen and called out for his wife.

"I'm here," he shouted, as he walked through the doorway.

Putting down the things he had brought from his car; he walked toward the kitchen but found no one. Raising his head and letting out a deep sigh, he gazed out the window and saw his boys playing catch in the backyard. Listening to the radio, he could make out the lyrics to *Keep on Loving You* by Speedwagon. He began to groove to the music when he heard the sound of heels clicking on the floor tiles.

"Hi Love," he said in Spanish, opening his arms to greet his wife, Amalia.

"Hello Babe," she answered, embracing her husband and kissing him, "How was the meeting with the new lawyer?"

Tony met her questioning eyes.

"Good, he will do good." he explained. He looked up and saw his two sons playing catch in the backyard. "How did they behave?"

Amalia snickered.

Tony exhaled through his nose and cracked a smile at her answer. It was never a question that their boys would behave just like him. He returned his focus to Amalia, kissed her again, and released her to walk over to the backyard.

His kids, Anabel and Álvaro, drew their eyes from their basketball hoop to look at their father. Tony peered at them with his dark eyes, reached for the ball with one hand, and undid his tie with the other. Rolling up his sleeves and balancing the ball on his left hand, he stepped on the cement and looked at his younger child. The small boy lingered for a moment before pulling his thick, curly, black hair to the side and grabbed the ball from his hand.

"¿Me la vas a pasar?" asked Tony, waiting for his son to invite him to play. Álvaro looked down at the ball in his hand, then to his brother.

"Yes, Papá."

Shooting it with his all his strength, the ball hit the backboard with a loud thud, and the three of them began to play until the sun gave way to the moon, and the stars and Amalia called them in for supper. When they finished their game, Tony collected the ball and placed it in the bin along with all their other toys, next to the door. Anabel opened the door and bolted through it to wash her hands while Álvaro never left Tony's side.

"Let's go Alvarito, your hands."

Alvaro nodded and trundled off to join his brother and clean up for dinner. Tony sat at the kitchen table, placing the napkins down next to the placemats and already set plates.

"You haven't played with them in a while, Tony."

"I haven't had the mind to in a long time, baby," he admitted, massaging the palm of his hand and working out the sore muscles. Remembering all the places that he applied to with no luck, he stared down at his folded arms on the kitchen table.

"This will also pass like everything else. You made a big mistake in robbing the store, but I know you will not be doing it anymore and I *know* you learned your lesson. We're going to turn the tables. Don't give up."

Tony raised his eyes from his arms and hope spread through his face. Acknowledging the wisdom in his wife's words, he knew that he had to turn the tide, that Gabriel and Rod had brought hope, and that they, as a family, would overcome his surrender to temptation. He would, once again, feel comfortable in his own skin.

"I love you," he told his wife.

"I know," she answered. Anabel and Álvaro burst back into the kitchen.

"Look Mamá, we washed our hands," they said, running to their mother to demonstrate their half-washed hands, soap dripping onto the floor tiles with each step. Anabel giggled and Amalia grabbed a hand towel from one of the cabinet drawers. She dried her children's hands after running them under the kitchen sink to properly wash them.

"Who wants food?"

"I do, Mamá," yelled the kids, excitement gushed through their faces as they sat in their seats and adjusted their superhero cups. Amalia gathered the platters and plates of chicken and rice, sweet plantains, and yucca. Tony sat back in his chair lost in the fragrances of home as he watched his family excited for dinner. Gazing at his real wealth, small tears formed in his eyes as he looked at the world, he almost lost.

"Alvarito, wait for papa to pray," instructed Amalia.

Alvaro took the fork from his mouth and placed it next to the plate.

"Sorry, Mamá."

Amalia, Anabel, and Álvaro waited on Tony. Tony extended his hands to his family, and they all bowed their heads in prayer. As he thanked God for all that they had and for the food.

Anabel interrupted.

"And that Papa finds a job…"

Tony looked up at his daughter.

"Quickly!" Jr. added,

They all laughed. Tony looked up at the crucifix hanging above the pantry door and bowed his head again.

"And God, may we always follow in the path of good, Amen."

As he finished the prayer, he asked that God's light would lead him through the darkness that lay ahead.

Chapter 17: The Two Sisters

Miami, Florida: March 1982

Gabriel and Jacob exited the courthouse in unison, stepping to the side as they walked past the entrance to speak while Belinda and Sarah walked past them toward the street. Everything had been settled, Jacob was no longer responsible for the child, and it was all over. Jacob leaned against the stone wall and looked down at the floor, taking a moment to himself while Gabriel watched Belinda peering up and down the street as Sarah tried to speak with her. Down the road, a grey pickup truck approached the curb, stopped, picked her up, and drove her out of Jacob's life. Gabriel recognized the father of her child from a picture of his driver's license in Sarah's file.

"I guess that's it," said Jacob, loosening the knot in his tie and unbuttoning the top button.

Gabriel turned to him, offering his client as much comfort as he could, but to no avail.

"I want to thank you, Gabriel, for handling all of this. I don't know how clean this was compared to your other clients, but I appreciate the effort and professionalism."

"There's nothing to thank me for, Jacob. I'm sorry that all of this unfolded in the way that it did."

"So am I." Jacob exhaled all the air out of his lungs and then inhaled fully as if drawing in a fresh existence. "And with that, I start my new life."

"Best of luck, Jacob."

"Thanks."

A swarm of people exited the courthouse, and Jacob took that as his opportunity to slip into the crowd, fading among the arguing faces. The judge's signature on the final judgment had torn the last ties between Jacob and Belinda and from now on they were only memories of each other's past lives. Gabriel knew that this was the best thing that could happen since she had already started a new life, and now, he could have one too.

As he watched the crowd move down the steps and onto the sidewalk, he felt a hand touch his shoulder. He turned and saw Sarah with a slight smile.

"You always take your client's problems this hard?" she asked.

"I do, if I'm not careful, but this one got to me. He was really in love with her, and everything he used to know is now lost to him. How can I not feel for him?" said Gabriel, turning to face her.

"I can understand that, but he was ready for this, wasn't he?"

"It's not really something you are ready for when you're the one still in love, but he was ready enough, I suppose. Yet, when the child came into play, it shattered him. He ended up with a child he didn't expect and once he began to like the idea of having a kid, fate tore it away from him. Still, once the pain is gone, I think he will learn that there is a possibility of fatherhood for him with the right woman and he will really want that."

Sarah nodded, taking a moment to process what Gabriel said.

"Belinda's reaction was so relieved that I didn't have to work with her emotions through this. It was straightforward."

"She was the one that was loved. Always the easier of the two."

She looked at him quizzically. "So, where are you parked, mister Lock?"

"My car is parked down the street. Yourself?"

"I'm down the street at well?"

"Under the overpass?" he asked.

"Not quite, but close." A hint of playfulness echoed in her voice and Gabriel cracked a sly grin.

"You're not really parked down there, are you?"

"No, counselor, I'm not."

"Your car's far away?"

"Something like that."

"Would you like me to drive you to it?" inquired Gabriel, pausing to turn his attention from the street to her.

She met his eyes and squinted hers, examining his facial reactions.

"Why don't we grab some dinner at Joe's Fish House by the river, and I'll tell you where it is?"

An amused look rippled across Gabriel's otherwise stoic face. He looked down at his watch.

"It's a little early for dinner."

"But not happy hour," she fired back.

The amusement turned into laughter and Gabriel agreed.

They made their way to the Mustang where Gabriel opened the door for her, pulling the seat back to make it more comfortable."

"Your mamma taught you manners," joked Sarah.

"Those I learned from my dad."

"Mamma's proud right?"

"Every day. So, you're okay with Joe's Fish House?"

"Never been, so it's an adventure."

"Excellent." Gabriel turned the key, and the motor roared. Sarah reached for the radio and raised the volume as In the Air Tonight, played.

She began singing along and Gabriel laughed to himself as he maneuvered the car into position and they left the lot, heading to Joe's Fish House and blasting the radio all the way down the street.

The trip lasted five minutes, they drove into the restaurant's little parking lot where the valet quickly walked over and handed Gabriel a ticket for later. He and Sarah walked past the lobsters in their tank and the hostess asked them, "Would you prefer to sit in the dining room or on the terrace?

He looked at Sarah and without a word he knew her preference.

"Outside please."

The young lady smiled and guessing they did not want to be disturbed, led them to the last table next to the veranda with a wonderful view of the river and the buildings on either side. She led them to some shortened picnic tables on the far side and then she was gone, having taken their drink orders and leaving the menus for them to read and discover the specials that had been caught that morning.

Sarah glanced down at the menu before bringing her eyes back to Gabriel.

"Before, when we were talking about Jacob, you lingered on his child and how it was unexpected to him. Why was that?" asked Sarah..

Gabriel measured his response first and then spoke.

"A funny thing happened to me during this case. I found out that Jacob almost had an unexpected child, and I found out that I almost had an unexpected sister."

"Really?" Sarah's eyes enlarged as she saw the shock of the coincidence set in. "What happened?"

"My parents almost adopted a girl, whose parents died in an accident of some kind. They were in the final steps of adoption when the Church found an uncle or some type of blood relative and they asked my parents to withdraw their request so the child could be raised by her own family. My parents, believing it was the right thing to do, withdrew their petition and so I almost had a sister."

"And you never found this out?"

"No, my parents didn't think it was right to tell me. I remember having met her one time at mass with my family as a little boy, but I never saw her again beyond the one time that she came to our house."

"I'm surprised that they didn't tell you."

"I think it was because it coincided with a 3-month period I spent in Spain, as a little kid, with my grandparents and my mother's family. I was five or six at the time, so it wasn't difficult to get time off from school. I was attending Saints Peter and Paul Catholic School, and I got an excused absence if I passed a test when I came back which I did apparently. I only missed the first two weeks of school but still had to pass the test."

"And you just found this out?"

"Yeah," said Gabriel, leaning back and taking it in. It appears that since it didn't go through, my parents thought there was no point in telling me."

"Your parents didn't try for more kids?"

"No; after me, my mother couldn't have another one. My birth was tough on her and the doctors told her that another might kill both her and the new baby. The news broke their hearts clean in two, so when the adoption did not go through, it gutted them. Their convictions and faith got them through, but it wasn't easy. I now know that it was even harder than I thought."

"Oh, I'm sorry, I got carried away with the questions."

"No harm done. I always wanted a sibling, but I guess it was not to be. What about you? Siblings or only child?"

"I was lucky. I have a sister who gave me a nephew and a niece," she said wistfully. "She and I are very close."

"Can't say I don't envy you. Life crafts paths for you to choose from, and well, my parents chose the one they thought was the right one for that child," he said quietly.

"I get it," she said, proceeding to change the subject. "So, did you always want to be a lawyer like your dad?"

Gabriel opened up and she had guessed right. He began to get caught up in her work stories and by the time the drinks arrived he was laughing and being the Gabriel that she hoped he would be like. They spoke for the next hour and when it came time for dinner, they decided to stay, ordering the specials for the day and delving into each other's lives and dreams until Gabriel looked up and saw their waiter discreetly standing near the next table. Looking around they finally noticed that everyone else was gone.

"Do you close during the day?"

"Yes, about forty minutes ago," said the waiter with a grin as both of them laughed. He smiled and continued, "We close between lunch and dinner, but you were so into each other that I didn't have the heart to interrupt, so I helped the day crew pick up. They have to prepare for dinner, and we have to clean this area."

"No problem, we're leaving now."

They got up quickly, and as they made their way to the door, Gabriel handed the waiter a twenty-dollar bill, a subtle thanks for not interrupting them. Sarah and Gabriel exited the restaurant and made their way down the sidewalk back to their cars.

Chapter 18: The Video Tape

Miami, Florida: April 1982

Gabriel sat behind his desk, doing everything that he could to focus on his work and not think about Sarah, but was failing beyond measure. The night at Joe's Fish House kept him lightheaded and smiling, *If you act like this at poker night, the guys are going to eat you alive*, he thought to himself as he brushed off the infatuation. *There's nothing worse than a fool in love, and right now, you're acting like a fool.*

The intercom sounded with Susana's voice, "Raúl and Mirella Morales are here."

Gabriel snapped out of it.

Thank God, he thought to himself. *I need something else to focus on*, "Please move them into the Conference room and advise my father," he said back into the intercom.

"Already have on both counts."

Gabriel came out of his office with a pad and pen in hand and met his father before entering the conference room.

"Is something going on, Son?" asked Thomas, pausing.

"Nothing at all," answered Gabriel, processing his cases in his mind for errors, "why do you ask?"

"Your step seems lighter."

Gabriel paused, torn between revealing Sarah to his father and lying. Before he could answer, Thomas cut him off.

"Actually, tell me afterward, Raúl and Mirella are waiting."

"Sure thing, Dad," answered Gabriel, smiling as he turned.

"So many years since we've seen each other and now this is three times in a few months." said Thomas with a smile, reaching for their hands and greeting them. Gabriel followed suit and they stood for a moment.

"Please, take your seats," offered Gabriel. They all sat in the chairs around the conference room table.

"Well, as you know when I retired, I gave each of the kids their own daycare. I don't get involved in business much but, I happen to be at Mirella's daycare when they had the problem, so I told her that we had to come straight here to see you. It may be connected to those letters sent to the Children and Family Services."

Thomas knew that more lay behind Raúl's words than what he spoke but opted to let it slide. Gabriel turned to Mirella.

"Can you tell me what happened?"

She faced him, straightened her glasses, and began to speak.

"About three weeks ago I hired a temporary replacement for one of my teachers that had to go on maternity leave. According to the paperwork and documents she gave me; her name was Graciela Argüello. Supposedly, she was 27 years old, born in León, Nicaragua, and was fully qualified. The first couple of days she had what I would call light duty, filling in lunch times, breaks, and assisting in different classes. On Monday morning, Reina, one of my other teachers, had a fender bender coming to work and could not come in, and that's when I began having my doubts."

"Why is that?" inquired Thomas.

"Because for the first time I was able to observe her directly and I realized Graciela was not as experienced as she should have been according to her documentation. The next day Reina was still feeling the effects of the accident and did not come in. Again, I saw hesitation in Graciela's actions and reactions when she was alone with a child. One of the kids caught his finger in a toy and there was trepidation in her movements and fear in her eyes as she handled the situation, not so much at the incident, which was nothing but at the child's crying. These are the normal reactions of someone just starting to handle children, not of an experienced childcare worker.

"So, the paperwork did not match the employee you were observing?"

"Not at all."

"Did her apparent inexperience create a situation?"

"No, but her false papers did."

"What do you mean?"

"I became suspicious and so I requested an expedited search with the Department of Health and Rehabilitative Services to send me her documents from their file. Before the papers arrived, we had an incident."

"What happened?"

"We thought that one of the smaller children, Héctor, a four-year-old, made it out of the front door without anyone seeing him. It did not make sense at the time because the handle of the door, as well as the lock, are beyond his reach and the door has a buzzer when the door is not in contact with the frame for more than thirty seconds. Luckily, we have surveillance cameras and when we looked at the tape, we saw what really happened," she finished speaking and then reached into her large purse and handed Gabriel a video tape.

"You have a record of the incident?"

"We do. This is everything."

Gabriel walked over to a covered part of the side piece and moved the door to one side, revealing a TV and cassette player. He took the VCR tape and placed it in the player. The screen showed a wide-angle picture of the front of the location. Within a few seconds a blonde mestizo woman in her early twenties appeared on screen. Her clothes and makeup made her look older but her looks betrayed her age.

"That appearance made sense since she had to be old enough to match the experience detailed in her documents," remarked Mirella, verbalizing everyone's thoughts.

They watched as they saw the young woman hold the door and was immediately followed by a little boy in blue jeans and an orange shirt. He held her hand and they walked to the swings on the front side of the building. She helped him sit on the bucket seat swing, fastened him in, and then began to swing him. They watched as she pushed the swing back and forth, checking her watch from time to time. Suddenly, she looked up to something beyond the screen, and left the boy swinging on his own, jogging away. Seconds ticked by as the child swung on his own until it lost momentum before coming to a stop. The child began to look around, realizing that no one was there. In the silent video, the boy reached for the bar that secured him, and began to fidget, struggling to remove the restraint. He continued, shifting his body and using his arms to push himself free to no avail. In the mute video, he flailed, desperately trying to free himself. He raised his little hands to his crying eyes, opened his mouth, and in their minds they could hear him scream. No one said a word as the disturbing images continued. Thomas shifted uneasily in his seat as Gabriel's stomach jerked. What seemed like a minute later, a couple came into view. Hearing the crying they glanced over to the swing set. When they saw the child and realized he was by himself, the woman ran toward him, and the man ran toward the building. The tape turned into a mixture of black and white dots before going dark.

"That was yesterday morning at 11:30, just before lunch and nap time. The woman that picked up the boy is one of the moms. It was her daughter's birthday, and she was there with her husband to pick their daughter up early. Had they not been there to get Dora, who knows how long

Héctor would have been alone outside?" pressed Mirella, anger filling her voice.

"I can't believe that anyone would harm a child," whispered Raúl, sorrow tinging his tone.

"Where is the woman with the questionable paperwork?" inquired Thomas, raising his eyebrows and widening his eyes.

Mirella paused and formulated her words with caution.

"I do not know, but what this clip does not show is me instructing her to take Héctor to the general room and put him down to sleep. I had to return some phone calls from the office, and I guess that the moment I went into the office to make my calls, she did this," explained Mirella, pointing to the dark TV screen.

"She knew she was being filmed?"

"I have signs all over the school. I have had the cameras ever since I had an incident between two divorcing parents that had a mix-up in their scheduling and almost went at it in the pickup line. So now, I announce the surveillance and people behave very politely."

Gabriel chuckled at her answer.

"Well, the good news is that the child is all right. Still more puzzling is why this young girl got fake papers to work for you."

"The question is why go through all that trouble to commit a felony, while being filmed. The chances that she will eventually get caught are high even though she was able to walk away. Even if she would not have done this, there is no longevity in that job because, as you said, you had already caught on that her experience did not match her resume. Clearly the job was not her motive so was she there just to create this problem. That was her motive." said Thomas.

"So, that's what she was doing there?"

Gabriel spoke up for the first time since they had watched the video, "Can we see the tape again?" No one objected so he walked to the machine and hit rewind. When the tape stopped, he hit play and moved to one side but remained within an arm's length from the machine. The tape rolled but just before the mystery woman disappeared, Gabriel stopped the tape. "Please look at her face just before she runs off. She seems to be looking for something or someone in the distance." Gabriel rewound the tape to just before her disappearance and hit play again. "Observe her eyes and the tilt of her head. See how she is looking into the distance? Then she looks at the child as though she was checking that he is okay and then she runs off." Mirella, did she know these people were coming early to pick up their daughter?"

"Yes, she must have."

"What if she was waiting for that moment to disappear and leave the child by himself?" continued Gabriel.

"What does that mean?" asked Raúl.

"Well, it was either about the child or about your business," continued Thomas, "and she had the chance to take Héctor, or hurt him, and she really didn't do either. Gabriel's observation points to her not wanting to injure the child, just you. So, it's about your business and nothing else. That means that there is a good chance she may be, either the person who sent the letters, or she is tied somehow to that person."

"She knew that Dora was being picked up at that time, so by placing Héctor out there when she did, she knew Dora's parents would see a little boy alone and unattended," said Mirella, "So, why would she want to hurt my business?"

"It must be personal?" said Raúl.

"Well, I had never seen that woman in my life, prior to ten days ago. So, it can't be personal on that level."

"I think that she knew that you were on to her, and she had to go before she was caught by the authorities," added Thomas.

"I concur," remarked Gabriel, "but that does not explain the splashy exit."

"You're right because something like this makes me more likely to pursue her!" Anger bellowed through her voice.

"Still, she could have been sent by a competitor to create a problem that would be fatal to you, like a misplaced child."

"Then why leave him out there at a time when she knew other parents were coming?"

"That's true," responded Gabriel, nodding his head. "Although she did not want to hurt the child, just you, so her actions were perfect for that."

"You know, she seems familiar somehow. I get the feeling that I have seen her before," murmured Thomas.

"From where?" asked Raúl, perking up from his chair.

"I'm not sure, but I feel like she is familiar in some way. She is obviously not a client of mine or Gabriel's and she's too young to have been an old client of mine, but I'll think about it. There has got to be something somewhere."

"What are we going to do? Should we close the school?" asked Raúl.

"No, Raúl, there's no need. She won't be back."

"How do you know that?"

"She knows that she would get caught, and to me, the quick retreat indicates she has no intention of getting caught. Gabriel and I will investigate this situation and see what we can find."

"Some quick questions and homework," said Gabriel, pen in hand and legal pad ready. "Do you have any competitors in the area?"

"This is the daycare that is farthest away from the others and there is no room in that market for two daycares there since the government reduced their subsidies. Maybe, two years ago when the subsidies were widespread, but not anymore. If we weren't already established there, we would be thinking about closing. This daycare is in a low-income area and daycare is too costly for most of these people without assistance from the government."

"Okay so has your landlord spoken to you about needing the space for any reason?"

"As a matter of fact, the owner has a space that is even bigger than ours that has been vacant for close to a year. He has reduced the asking price on the rent several times."

"Then it's personal. So, have you kicked out any children within the last three years or had a problem or situation with any parent?"

Mirella was shaking her head at Gabriel with every question.

"Have you fired any teacher within that same time period?"

She continued shaking her head.

"Have you had any argument with any neighbor there?"

"No, Gabriel, we have not had any problems other than making ends meet during the winter months, when the attendance from our afternoon programs goes down due to Christmas vacation. We haven't had any issues or problems with anyone recently."

Thomas smiled to himself and lingered on her last word. He sighed and rose from his seat.

"We can begin to look other places to see if we can produce a real name. Maybe she has a record. Raúl, why don't you look through all your papers to make sure it's not about you. Also look through your records and make a list of all those people who have worked for you throughout the years. In the meantime, we will investigate the individual she was impersonating to see if we can get anywhere with that. We can also look at the applications for licenses to see if she may have filed for one at some point."

Raúl and Mirella nodded before rising from their own seats to shake Thomas and Gabriel's hands before departing. Gabriel escorted Raúl and Mirella out of the conference room and out of the building. Thomas's thoughts returned to the face of the woman from the video tape. He persisted for a moment, staring at her face. and thinking about every client he ever had, every adversary he ever faced in court, and nothing came to his mind. The face stayed with him as he wondered, *Who are you and what do you want with the Morales family?*

Chapter 19: The Lists

Miami, Florida: April 1982

Thomas sat behind his desk, ruminating, and pondering the cycle of events from seeing Raúl again to the contents of the video. The possibilities wracked his mind, not giving him a moment to focus on anything else. The young woman's face engraved itself in his memory and became the subject of all present attention. He broke and called Susana on the intercom.

"I'm going to step out of the office for a while. I feel like I could use some fresh air. If Gabriel asks for me, tell him that I will be back in an hour or so." He got up, grabbed his suit jacket from the hook behind the door, and walked out, waving to Susana as he left the office.

Thomas drove up Coral Way until he saw *Sergio's* restaurant on his left. He spied on the empty outside seat and decided on it over any other place around. Finding a parking spot, he strode up to an open table and made his presence known. When the young server came out to his table, he placed his order and turned his attention to the traffic and the scenery.

The videotape played in Thomas's mind as he waited for his food. When the server returned to check on him, he asked for a café con leche and a glass of water. The blonde woman etched herself into his thoughts. He knew her. He had seen her before but could not recall where.

"Who are you?" he asked himself aloud, posing the question as much to her as to his subconscious to uncover her identity. "Why do this now, and what is your motive? What are you trying to prove?"

This was someone who was affected in some manner by Raúl, one of his kids, or one of his deals. But why she looks so familiar is the piece that does not fit. Raúl and his daughter did not seem to recognize her so why would he. Could someone that has beef with him be taking it out on his clients? That would be endless after nearly twenty-five years of clients. But I have seen that face before. It was younger, but how much younger?

He raised his left arm, and the server came quickly to his table.

"May I have the check, please?" he asked in Spanish.

"But your food isn't here yet," she countered, surprised by his request.

"I know, but I'm in a bit of a hurry; I've got to make it back to the office and I like to be quick."

The server smiled, sensing his apprehension. She reached into the side pocket of her apron and, taking out her book, added the figures, writing the total with a flourish. She placed the check before him and with a smile he took out a twenty and told her to keep the change.

Questions and thoughts rushed through his mind as he waited for his food. His eyes dried from the intensity of his thoughts as he forgot to blink, causing them to burn faintly. He removed his spectacles and massaged his eyes and nose, still thinking about the face.

His food arrived a few moments later and he did his best to savor the flavors and the effort of the meal as he shook off his thoughts and prayed before eating. In his prayer, he asked for the Lord's blessing over the food, but also to allow him to be present at every moment and not so dismayed with the past. When he finished his prayer, he genuflected, and for a moment, felt peace. The aroma of the meal humbled him, and he began to eat.

Walking to his car his mind kept exploring thoughts and possibilities. He parked without caring where the white line was and walked toward the office. He swung the door open and, walking into his office, decided to start at the beginning.

"Susana, could you get Raúl on the phone, I need to speak with him."

Without a word she lifted the phone and dialed. As he walked into his office, he heard the intercom and lifting the handset, he hit the switch on the base and asked, "Do you have a minute?"

Noise came from the other side.

"I have been reviewing what I saw in the videotape all afternoon in my mind, and I wanted to speak to you again because even though you said in our meeting that you did not connect this young lady to anyone, I can tell you with all certainty thar I have seen her before, but I cannot pinpoint where or when."

Confusion and inquiry came from Raúl's voice.

"Yeah, I am sure that I have seen her before."

More noise echoed from the receiver.

"I'm sure I have made a lot of enemies in my years of practice but if they are after me, why attack you? Right now, I'm not handling any case or dispute for you. Therefore, the attack is against you directly I think or at least you are the key to solving the identity of the attacker."

Silence followed his statement and Thomas held firm as he waited for Raúl to respond. When he did, Thomas listened carefully and considered what Raúl had pointed out. Thomas considered his options and then spoke.

"I have not heard from anyone else, but I will ask Susana to make discrete inquiries after we hang up. Still, it could be from a negotiation, a contract dispute, a business deal gone bad, a problem with the parent of a child, or even a teacher you fired and had consequences such as a disputed unemployment claim. Maybe I wrote the letters having to do with the dispute and somehow saw this young woman at a hearing or negotiation without realizing who she was."

Raúl began to say something, but noise sounded in the background.

"Raúl, hold on, I'm going to put you on speaker phone, I'm having a hard time hearing you."

Raúl paused a moment and then spoke, his voice echoing through the speaker like a megaphone.

"That's possible, I opened my first daycare twenty years ago."

"Do you think this is just against your daughter? If it were someone, she was familiar with then your daughter would have recognized her, but she didn't."

"I agree, she would have. She's making her list to make sure it was not her, but she received her master's degree in March and has only been overseeing her daycare for six months. This is the last one I worked full-time, before I moved to Naples, and why I am so involved. When she took over is when I stopped coming, but I was part-time until then.

"Would you make a list of all the people who fit the categories we talked about or any other situation that might have drawn me in and we can go over that? I know I asked you to look at these same things in our meeting but please redouble your efforts because if she was willing to endanger a child who knows what else she may be ready to do."

"I thought Gabriel was going to investigate."

"He is, but if more than one client engages in this revenge, it will be that much harder to track down, so I think it's best if we work it from all angles."

"I will get the kids to make their own lists, and I'll have my wife help me. She has an amazing memory."

As soon as he placed the handset in the cradle he walked toward Susana's desk.

"Susana, please call my most regular clients and discretely inquire if anyone has had a problem at his or her business that is out of the ordinary?"

"Any particular order?"

"Oldest clients first; especially clients that I've had more than ten years and have businesses open to the public."

"Sure thing, I'll get right on it."

Thomas went back to his desk. and picked up a pen and a yellow pad and began to write. The list of people involved in Raúl's cases was small and he was done in a few minutes. He picked another client and started a list for them. He knew it was probably a waste of time, but he had to do something on his end. Images of emotional clients and vehement adversaries flashed through his mind. He wrote them down, analyzed wins and losses, and because this could be apparent friend or undeclared foe, he left nothing to chance. Two hours later, he looked up and thought, *The past never does leave you. When you least expected it comes back and invades your thoughts, determines your actions, and sometimes, even defines your life.*

Chapter 20: The Division of Corporations

Miami, Florida: April 1982

Gabriel and Rodrigo sat across from each other at a table in Cacique's restaurant. Playing with the salt and pepper shakers, Rodrigo fidgeted in his seat as his stomach lurched.

"You alright there, man?" asked Gabriel, raising his eyebrows at his best friend.

"I am starving. I haven't eaten since last night."

"That's kind of what happens between dinner and breakfast the next day."

Rodrigo shot him an impolite look and Gabriel chuckled.

"Give it a minute, Rod. I am sure it'll only be a few minutes; Esmerelda is usually quick with our food."

"Have you given Tony's case much thought?"

Gabriel straightened up in his chair and took a sip of his coffee before formulating his thoughts.

"The claim is obviously too high which means that there is going to be a creative solution to this thing. I think that I may have figured it out."

"What makes you so sure?" asked Rodrigo, "It's a lot of money that they're suing for if you're wrong."

Gabriel took the pepper shaker from the table and caught Rodrigo off guard.

"Just a hunch: but there is no defense to the stealing that went on so, we need to move in one of two directions: the first is to try to reduce the amount they are claiming our client and his cohorts stole by going through the company paperwork, The second is to be able to present to the court evidence that the company was inflating the claim to defraud the insurance company and my hunch is that this is what those greedy guys did" he said, smirking.

"Great, so the entirety of our Tony's defense is based on your hunch. Brilliant."

As the words came out, he saw Esmerelda making her way toward them with plates in her hands.

"Here you go boys," she said to them both., "I've got the eggs benedict with extra onions and cilantro."

"That's for onion breath here," joked Rodrigo, gesturing at Gabriel.

Esmerelda snickered and handed the plate to Gabriel.

"And the big steak omelet is for you then." Esmerelda placed the plate in front of Rodrigo and peeked at their coffee cups. "Aside from some more coffee, can I get you anything else?"

"Ketchup if you can spare it."

"Sure thing, my little love." Esmerelda set off and Rodrigo shot Gabriel another look.

"Lock, ketchup with an eggs benedict?"

"For the home fries, Rod. Who eats potatoes without ketchup?"

"Civilized people, Lock, that's who."

"I'm not civilized; I'm refined."

They laughed until Rodrigo's stomach lurched again.

"Look, one of the accusers is a cop. He likes what he does because, if not, having fifty percent of a business like this, why would he be out on the street risking his life every day? Secondly, being a cop, if they go down, his cousin may avoid major problems, but he won't."

"That is true. but their records are probably so messed up and confusing that we will not be able to find clear proof." said Rodrigo, now paying very close attention to what Gabriel was saying.

"So, we may not find enough proof to put them in jail for fraud, but if we have enough to make Mr. Police Officer think that the trail will reveal something improper on their part and he will have a problem with internal affairs, that should bring us a settlement. This will only happen if I am right about their intent to defraud. We may not find any evidence. In that case, we won't accuse anyone of anything. However, if I am right, then we just have to have enough inconsistencies for them to cave."

Half an hour later, Rodrigo and Gabriel crossed the street and opened the door to the offices of the Secretary of State Division of Corporations, Miami Office. They stepped down the hallway toward the elevator of the north tower. They entered and Gabriel pressed for the third floor and when the doors opened, they greeted the person at the desk and parted down the short hallway to the stacks of files they needed to see.

"Feels a bit strange being back in here," chimed Rod.

"How so?" asked Gabriel, stopping at a filing cabinet marked with the correct year and alphabet. Opening it, he fingered through the files as Rod spoke.

"I normally just ask the assistants to pull this kind of information for me."

"How often does that happen?"

"Seldomly," answered Rod, shifting his weight from both legs to one and leaning against the wall. "So, what are we looking for?"

"The filings for Sunshine Electronics and its ownership."

"Why is that relevant?"

Gabriel withdrew a file from the cabinet and opened it on a nearby table. Rod left his post on the wall to examine the findings and peered over Gabriel's shoulder.

"Because," began Gabriel, turning his chin slightly and shifting his eyes to the peering Rod, "the math in the claim does not make sense. Tony stole for a year, if you tripled that from the sales in the previous year, it would still be short of one million.

Rod, immediately catching on, finished the thought, "but the owners would have caught on sooner and then the two-hundred and fifty thousand wouldn't have happened. Something doesn't add up."

As Gabriel scanned the documents in the file, he came across the original filing by Jeremiah and Hiram Pilkington.

"See Rod, this is what I was looking for," he said as he read the names aloud. Taking the next page, he found the listings for Steven, Thomas, and Ronald Pilkington before finding a second one in 1979 for Steven and Thomas Pilkington. Gabriel snickered.

"What are you so happy about?"

"I think that we need to pay a visit to our new friend, Mr. Ronald Pilkington."

"Got an idea on where to find him?"

"No, not yet.

"I've got a guy who might," said Rod with a smirk.

"Why doesn't that surprise me?"

Walking over to the copy machine, Gabriel copied the relevant pages from the file. He returned the documents to their folder and closed the cabinet. Sealing it behind him and grabbing his bag, He said goodbye to the clerk behind the desk as he and Rodrigo departed down the hallway back to the elevator. Now they had a lead to follow and maybe a way to win this thing.

Chapter 21: The Exile

Circa Stamford, Florida: April 1982

A few days had passed since Gabriel and Rodrigo discovered the files at the Division of Corporations, spoke to Tony, and got Ronald Pilkington's address. It was now Friday, and they found themselves driving on the highway in the Mustang. As Don't Stop Till You Get Enough played on the radio, they chatted back and forth about different cases and Rodrigo's troubles with Arlene as the car thundered down the road.

"I don't think that I'll ever understand women," admitted Rodrigo, shaking his head and accepting his lost position.

"You forgot about your anniversary, ordered flowers at the last minute, they arrived a day later, and Arlene got mad. This is a completely normal reaction for a woman to have."

"But I ordered them for our anniversary."

"Yes," said Gabriel, drawing out the word, "but…you made a classic rookie mistake in that you didn't make up for it by getting her a backup gift."

"Because they were supposed to get there on time."

"Dude, I'm not the one mad at you, I'm just telling you that it's easy to understand why she'd be a little ticked off."

"Yeah, well what do you know? You have been single for so long that you do not have any skin in the game," said Rodrigo, brushing Gabriel off.

Gabriel grinned and laughed keeping his mouth shut and offering no reply.

Rodrigo, bewildered by Gabriel's lack of response, shifted his weight against the passenger door and gave him a quizzical look.

"Wait a second, why are you smiling like that?"

"No reason at all other than laughing at you."

"No, there's a reason. I've known you long enough to know that you haven't mentioned Her while talking about girlfriends and love interests plus you didn't say anything about the solemnity of single life, so…" Rodrigo began adding everything in his head, "You're dating a client?"

Gabriel nearly pulled the car off the road in shock. Rodrigo held onto the dashboard and the handle above the door, until Gabriel corrected the car.

"No, not a client. Your reaction was too strong but it's someone you like but feel funny about dating. Well maybe I'm wrong."

Gabriel fumed and gave him a look, that clearly said, *don't go there*. Rodrigo saw him furrowing his brows from the intensity of his stare.

"But you are dating someone?" he repeated with a triumphant look.

Gabriel allowed the anger to vent like steam before answering.

"I've gone on a few dates, yes."

"With whom?"

"A lawyer I met in passing."

"I'm not going to lie, I'm both surprised that you'd date another lawyer, and completely understand it at the same time."

"Why is that?"

"Because another lawyer means that all that you'll talk about is work, but on the flip side, since all you do is work, who else would you meet besides a secretary or office aid?"

Gabriel chuckled but knew that Rodrigo was right. He did not get out much and his workaholism had been a problem ever since She left.

"Either way," continued Rodrigo, "I'm glad to hear that you're dating someone and I'm sure that she's terrific if you're actually consistent about it."

"She is."

"Great! –The question now is: will you give her a real chance, or will She get in the way again?"

"Honestly," said Gabriel, turning his eyes to him for just a moment, "Sarah deserves the best."

"So, her name is Sarah?"

"Yes, it is."

"Does this Sarah have a last name?"

"It's classified."

"Oh, one of those need-to-know, right?"

"Something like that."

"Okay, Gabriel. Whatever you need, pal."

"We'll talk about it on the way back. The house is just ahead."

"Deal," said Rodrigo, reaching for his briefcase in the back of the Mustang.

Gabriel and Rodrigo pulled up to the house in front of the lake and confirmed that the number on the mailbox was the one they were looking for. They stepped out onto the asphalt of the long terracotta-colored driveway. Beside them, facing a lake, stood the massive ranch-style residence of Ronald Pilkington.

"So, this is how the other half lives," said Rodrigo, turning his head from side to side, taking in his surroundings.

"Yeah, this is how the other half lives, and if I'm right, this could have been more."

"Bigger than this?

"Oh yeah and in a way, we are here to find out why it's not."

Gabriel and Rodrigo gathered their briefcases from the back of the car, straightened out the wrinkles in their suit jackets, and walked toward the front door. Scrub jays and warblers chirped in the distance and Gabriel peeked over at the water from behind his aviators, seeing ripples from the fish as they surfaced for food. Taking a step up from the pathway onto the front steps, the lawyers rose onto the front stoop and rang the doorbell.

A few moments passed before they rang again. Rodrigo shuffled his stance as they heard a voice from behind the door.

"Gimme a minute, boys. I had to bleed the lizard!"

"Well, we found Ronald. No doubt about that," joked Rodrigo. Gabriel chuckled silently to himself. A moment later, the door opened and before them stood a beer-bellied hillbilly wearing American Flag swim shorts and a tank top that said Back-to-Back World War Champs.

"Good afternoon, fellas. Come on in," said Ronald, opening the door and letting them enter. Rodrigo entered first followed by Gabriel and then Ronald as he closed the door behind them. The interior was starkly different from that which Ronald's character suggested. From wooden floors to crown moldings and crystal chandeliers, lavish decorations led the eyes to the flow of the house from one ornate room to the other.

"I was just outside and fixing to set up some poles, slug a few beers, and get my Friday on if y'all want to join me on the back deck. I've got some PBRs back there."

"No thanks, Ronald," began Gabriel, changing the subject, "unfortunately, we have to drive back and can't risk anything."

"I understand, gentlemen. Don't you worry. I understand completely. Now, firs' thing's firs'…do not call me Ronald. Ron's the name. Ronald was my father's –his middle name anyway. Lord knows he hated Hiram an' holy shit on a shish kabob, it is that an ugly name."

Gabriel and Rodrigo did their best to conceal their laughter. From their conversation several weeks prior, Gabriel recalled the drawl and eccentric personality but didn't expect to find himself face-to-face with a man sporting a tank top that said *Back-to-Back World War Champs* for a business meeting.

"Listen fellas, I know that my attire is a little loud, so to speak, but looky here, it is, but my family is out of town, and I celebrate the freedom of the stars with a couple stripes," he said, holding up the PBR can and pointing at the red and blue.

"All of your family?" inquired Rodrigo.

"My wife is at the salon with her friends retouching her nails while my kids are still in school. They get out around three and they will probably be here a little closer to three thirty by the time Ms. Wilma drops them off. Did you mean something by it?"

"Just asking out of curiosity."

"Ye mean because of my brother, Dwight, and my cousin, Steve?"

"Yes," answered Gabriel, "we'd rather not run into them here while we're questioning you."

"Ah, you ain't got nothing to worry about. Haven't shot the shit with them fuckers in a few years. Nearly lost it all when I left the family business."

"You left or were you left out?" pressed Gabriel, meeting Ronald square in the eyes. Ronald stared back without so much as a blink.

"You know, I like you a lot, you son of a bitch. You're sharp. I can just tell it in your eyes. Come outside and find a seat. I'll fix you both some water." Ronald pointed at the glass door that led to the back deck.

Gabriel and Rodrigo nodded and headed for the back deck. They found their seats next to the fishing poles and sat with their backs straight up instead of against the chairs. Gabriel raised his briefcase to the small nearby table and withdrew the copies that he needed. Glancing down at his watch, he heard the calls of the warblers as they flew by.

"This is a nice place," said Rodrigo, reaching for his own briefcase to gather his own materials.

"By the way, I'm getting you a shirt just like his for the next 4th of July."

"Sure thing. I'll be sure to grow my mustache and mullet too. It will fit well when I visit my mother in Hialeah in the morning before coming to yours."

"I'm sure that Arlene will love it too."

"Nothing turns her on like business in the front and party in the back." Ronald emerged from the house with a tray of glasses. He lowered it and offered refreshments to them.

"I was fixing to bring you some H 2 O but said Fuck it, these boys will like some southern sweet tea better. Lemons for your squeezing boys, drink up."

"Thank you, Ron," they said in unison before squeezing their lemons and taking sips of their sweet teas.

"So, y'all want to talk to me about' my family business, don't you?" "Not a problem. What do you want to know?" Ronald sat down next to them in one of the chairs.

"Why did you leave the company in 1979?" queried Gabriel.

"Was forced out. Got caught stealing from the company and they forced me out."

"Just like that?" asked Rodrigo.

"They had me on tape. Nothing I could do to get out of it."

"How did you resolve it?"

"They bought me out using my share in the company against the merchandise that was stolen."

"How much?"

"Eight hundred thousand dollars."

"Your shares were worth that?"

"No sir-ree, I had twenty-five percent. My shares were worth a little over a million dollars. They absorbed my shares and then wrote me a check for five thousand dollars per month."

"Are they still paying?"

"No, they did for a little while but stopped paying after month number six."

"They just stopped?" asked Gabriel. Ronald nodded. "So, if you owned twenty-five percent and then had to cash it out, what did they split the money as, fifty-fifty?"

"Hell no! Steve is an ambitious son of a bitch, and he would never, ever let my brother get fifty-fifty. No, they probably split my share down the middle and took twelve and a half percent each."

"What does Dwight do for a living?"

"He's a detective in the police department."

"Does he work at the store?"

"He would need special permission from above to do both. So, he didn't bother. He left ten years ago and never looked back. He got to do what he wanted to do and collected his twenty-five percent. See, we didn't collect salaries, we just took home our shares." Ronald rose from his chair and walked over to the edge of the deck and leaned against the wooden railing. "I haven't talked to Steve since. I honestly couldn't give three flying shits on shingles for that deplorable man, but I've got to be honest with you. Not talking to Dwight breaks my fucking heart every time I think about it. Whatever it was in fuckin' tarnation that convinced me to steal from the company is beyond me. I jus' got tired of the same old shit – working my hiney off like my life an' the company's depended on it only to see Steve and Dwight walking' out with so much of the profit. Dwight should have reduced his part when 'e became a detective. He didn't at the beginning' cause he wasn't making' shit on the street wearing' the blue so we let him keep the twenty-five to pay his bills an' make sure that Shannon didn't walk out on him, but then he should have reduced his share."

"So, if they're paying you, do you think that they'd move to fifty-fifty?"

"Sure, now that I'm gone an' Steve's living really well, it wouldn't surprise me if he'd be willing to split the company fifty-fifty."

"How do you know that Steve is living really well?" asked Rodrigo, bewildered. "I thought you said that you don't talk to him."

"Just because I don't talk to him don't mean I ain't seen him. Shit, if 'e was an inch taller, he'd be round." Ruckus emanated from the burly man as he cackled at his own joke. Gabriel kept his laughter to himself but knew that Rodrigo hadn't gotten the punchline.

"Did you not get the joke, Rod?" Rodrigo shook his head and gave Ronald a blank stare. "Rod, work with me here. Think hard. Do you see it now?" Rodrigo again gave a blank stare. "Dammit, Rod, 'e's living so well, they could roll him down a hill."

"Ah," said Rod, now understanding the explanation.

"You know that your old company is trying to claim that my client stole your stuff too."

"Yeah, Steve would do something like that."

"That means he would get paid two times over, one from the insurance and one from you when he deducted it from your purchase price."

"When I left, he said I had to pay because the insurance won't cover a thieving owner. He wants to make an extra eight hundred grand. Get his cost and his profit."

"The math makes sense, Ron. I've got it now. Do you have copies of the insurance policies from the time that you were there?"

"Yes, I do."

"Great, I need copies of all those papers. Did anyone help you steal anything? Did any of the employees do anything?"

"No, sir. I acted alone for fear of suspicion."

"I have some options that I can follow. I can make you come to a deposition and have you testify on the record but then it would be public, or you can come by the office and sign a sworn affidavit that I can use if any negotiation comes up."

"If you take my deposition and it becomes public, that puts my brother in danger that he could be implicated in Steve's fraud. I don't want to do that, even if he participated with Steve, he is my brother."

"Okay, then I need you to meet me at my office. Can you meet me next week?"

"What's in it for me?"

"Oh, I don't know, Ron, your brother and cousin accused my client of stealing one million dollars from their company. Now they want to blame him for what you did. You don't strike me as a man who would let someone else carry his wrongs.

"Did he steal from them?"

"Yes, he did, but not a million dollars' worth."

"I like him. He is a good man?"

"Pretty honest for a crook. He's got a good wife and two ball playing kids that deserve a dad at home."

Ronald thought to himself for a moment and exhaled deeply.

"Alrighty then, Mr. Lock. I'll meet you at your office next week on Wednesday afternoon at 1:00 an' I'll bring you those copies. I hate Steve an' I know that if he's putting this on your guy, something ain't right. That being said, anything else you boys want to talk about?"

"Not that I can think of it, why don't you let me take the policies so I can make copies, study them, and have them for you when you come by."

"Fair enough. Let me get them."

He came back a few minutes later and both Gabriel and Rodrigo were standing looking out from the back porch.

"Well, you boys are welcome to stay for supper. Wife's fixin' something that smells like possum that we shot in the backyard yesterday if you'd like some," he said with a grin.

"Hmm, possum. Sounds lovely," said Rodrigo grinning right back.

"I wish that we could, Ron, but we've got to make it back to Miami. It's going to be a long haul back but thank you for meeting with us and thank you for the hospitality. We'll see you next week."

"Sure thing. Y'all drive safely now," said Ron, waiting to escort them out.

Five minutes later, both men were on the road and looking for a gas station.

"Do you think that he's going to change things in our favor?"

"He's the key to helping Tony, assuming that he has the copies that I'm looking for."

"What's your strategy?"

"I'll explain after we review those papers, and I make sure that what we need is in them."

"How do you know that they still carry the same insurance?"

"If they didn't, they probably wouldn't be able to join the claims and that would defeat the purpose of this lawsuit."

"Alrighty then," joked Rodrigo, making his best Ron impression.

"We'll see what happens next week."

Chapter 22: The New Possibility

Miami, Florida: April 1982

Gabriel glanced at his pants and brushed some stray pieces of lint from himself, taking a moment to fix the wrinkles. Choosing not to delay any longer, he unbuckled his seatbelt, opened the door, and made his way across the still traffic toward the café across the street where they had agreed to meet.

The bell above the door rang as he entered and the cashier alongside another blonde behind the counter giggled before Sarah turned her head and eyed him. Her lips parted, allowing her teeth to show as her cheeks grew full and rosy. Gabriel smiled back and gestured at an empty table. Sarah winked and nodded at the one before the counter instead. He acknowledged and moved toward the table, waiting for her. She continued her conversation with the cashier.

Gabriel ordered a cortadito and people watched for a few minutes, hearing the usual topics of family, sports, and gossip from the patrons. Two men played chess in the corner and from his seat, could tell that one could have the other in three moves. He stared, shifting in his chair to get a better view, and watching to see if white would take the knight that baited the trap. The knight fell and Gabriel snickered to himself as the man playing black moved a bishop onto the right square. White moved again, black countered, and eyes grew wide. The victor folded his arms and the trapped examined the board calculating where it had gone wrong.

"Enjoying the game?" asked Sarah as she sat across from him at the small table.

"Very much."

"Do you play often?"

"I used to. My father and I played often and, before he died, I played with my grandfather."

"I'm sorry to hear about him."

Gabriel met her eyes, shrugging off the loss. The light from above reflected off her hair and bits of red brightened among the strands of brown.

"The cashier your client?"

"Yes, in fact. I have been helping her in claiming her little boy and girl from Honduras. "They have been on the waiting list, but it seemed to her that they have been passed over several times. I am looking into it. Shall we go?"

Sarah rose from the chair and Gabriel watched her. She paused, turning her gaze from the register to the corner and back to Gabriel.

"Winston and Carlos are their names. They come every other day or so and love challengers." A smile broke across Gabriel's face to match the one she gave him. Sarah returned to the counter as Gabriel rose from his chair and strode to the gentlemen at the counter, introduced himself, and took Carlos' chair as Winston waited on his move.

"Boy you must really come here often."

"I eat from here practically every day that I am in the office. Many times I'll come and have a morning or afternoon coffee. That is when I see them. They have become a fixture of the restaurant and an attraction that patrons sit and watch."

"Are you ready to go?"

"Let's."

Half an hour later, Gabriel parked on Miracle Mile and turned off the engine. Sarah unbuckled her seatbelt as Gabriel exited the Mustang and strolled over to the passenger side to let Sarah out. She took his hand as she stepped out onto the asphalt of the parking space, turning to peruse and enjoy the merchandise and clothed mannequins behind the thick panes of glass in the boutique shops along the road.

They walked down the sidewalk hoping to enjoy El Tablao before the dinner crowd rushed in. They entered the dimly lit restaurant through a heavy set of wooden doors with brass designs. Small figurines of Don Quixote, Sancho Panza, El Cid, and others occupied the shelves and nooks scattered around the restaurant. Ceramic tables lined the interior while the flames of an open hearth rose and fell in the corner. Burnt gold walls with cherry wood booths and paneling emboldened the aim of an aged Spanish tavern. Sarah's focus engaged every spot in the room.

"Have you never been here before?" asked Gabriel.

"No," answered Sarah, fixating on the details of El Tablao's interior. moments later, a young brunette crossed the floor from the bar and greeted them.

"Sorry for the delay, we're just getting set up for dinner." Sarah and Gabriel nodded and watched as she reached under the stand. "Just the two of you?" They nodded their answer. "Booth or high-top?"

"Indoors, please," answered Sarah. The blonde guided them to a single table in the far corner of the room. Gabriel knew that it would be another half hour before more patrons would arrive and he preferred the emptiness to a large crowd of people.

"Fermín will be with you in a moment," announced the hostess, placing the menus on the table.

"Thank you," they said in unison.

She gave a big smile, bowing her head an inch or so, before departing back to the stand at the entrance.

"So why bring me here on a Tuesday for lunch and not a Saturday for dinner?"

"Because you appreciate art and design and it's easier to see when the place isn't full." Sarah lit up and Gabriel gave a sly smile. "I try to pay attention to the things you say."

"Who's my favorite painter?"

Gabriel gave a blank expression and Sarah giggled.

"Rembrandt," he answered, and Sarah smiled.

"Favorite Painting?" she tested.

"The Storm on the Sea of Galilee."

"Why?"

"The shadows."

"What else do I like?"

"In paintings?" he joked.

"Yes, just in art."

"Magical realism and Caribbean, especially Haitian."

"Well done, Counselor."

Gabriel nodded his head, and his eyebrows rose as he began to smile.

"And your favorite painting?" she asked.

"Abraham's Sacrifice," he uttered.

"The hands?"

"God's mercy."

Sarah's eyes sharpened and her head tilted.

"So profound and so dramatic, Counselor," she said.

Gabriel did his best to conceal his smile.

"Do you know what one of my favorite things about you is?"

"What's that?" she asked, tilting her head to the side and blinking her eyes like a cartoon character as she inquired.

"How playful you are."

"Me, playful? Gasp!"

"You don't like deep topics, do you?"

Sarah raised her eyebrows for a moment. A man with gray hair strode up to them before she could answer.

"Good afternoon, I am Fermín, and I will be attending you this evening," said the waiter in a thick Spanish accent.

"Good afternoon, Fermín," they both replied.

"I will begin by bringing you some bread and water." Fermín left to fetch bread and water while Sarah eyed Gabriel.

"I love deep topics, Gabriel. I love talking about things that people will appreciate, but sometimes it is overwhelming so I can only share it with some people and only some of the time. Besides, life isn't supposed to be so serious."

Gabriel crooked his head and did not know what to answer. Sarah continued.

"Do you know why people distance themselves from deep friends?"

"Because they can't handle it?" answered Gabriel.

"No, because they're afraid they won't be seen as the same or accepted for who they are."

"Is that why you keep it light?" prodded Gabriel, hoping Sarah would open up. She smiled and took his hand in hers.

"Will you marry me, Gabriel?"

The wrinkles around Gabriel's eyes tightened and he coughed for a moment.

"I…"

"Of course not, you just met me, but if you met some girl that you really cared about and dated her for over a year and then you asked her to marry you, do you think that she'd have the same reaction that you did?"

"Probably not."

"It's the same in all relationships. You must open up in the right amount of time. Too much depth and you drown people."

"Do you think that I can't swim?"

"If you go to the beach for day, do you swim the whole time?"

"Not when there are sharks."

"The boy can be trained!"

"That's a plus, isn't it?"

"Definitely not a minus."

"Some water and bread for you," said Fermín, placing two glasses filled with water and ice on the table. Removing a basket from his forearm, Fermín placed the bread in between them and withdrew a small notepad from his pocket and a pen from behind his ear. "Ready to order?"

"Can you give us a few minutes?" requested Sarah.

"Sure." Fermín returned his materials to their original places and set off back toward the bar area.

"Sorry about that. Have you had Spanish food before?"

"Just once. What do you recommend?"

"Jamón Serrano, Gambas al Ajillo, and Croquetas to start. Small plates are the best for Spanish, Portuguese, and Greek food."

"Sounds delicious."

"Sangria?"

"Dynamite."

Moments later, Fermín returned and took their orders. Gabriel surrendered the menus that they barely viewed and sipped his water.

"So," began Sarah, "aside from trying cases going to quaint restaurants, and playing cards with your friends, what else do you do for fun?"

"I like traveling, playing racquetball, soccer, running, going to the beach, working out, and occasionally playing chess, oh, and people watching just to name a few. What about you?"

"A lot of the same, but I would add fencing, dancing, equestrian riding, and reading."

"Is that all?"

"For now. Don't want to drown you."

"Unwrapping slowly, are we?"

"Something like that. You will learn in enough time. I promise."

"A woman of mystery."

"Well behaved women are rarely remembered."

"As are predictable men."

"You know what I love about you?"

"My cerulean eyes?"

"They're alright," joked Sarah. Gabriel eyes opened a bit, and the corners of his mouth rose. "Your manners."

"My manners?"

"You could speak to all of these people in Spanish, but you choose to speak to them in English when you're around me and that's because you care enough to make sure that I can understand."

"Just being polite."

"When most men don't think twice about it."

"So, you like empathy?"

"Empathy is sexy so, yes, I do."

"Know what else is sexy?" asked Gabriel. Sarah widened her eyes, and Gabriel leaned in. They brought their faces an inch apart. Breaking eye contact, Gabriel moved his head toward her ear and whispered. Sarah's widened eyes closed for a moment, as she lowered her head, turning it toward his slightly. Her body tightened and her lips parted as a surprised smile spread across her face. Satisfied, Gabriel finished and leaned back in his chair. Silence engulfed them for a moment and, upon seeing Fermín arriving with their food, Gabriel brought a finger vertically to his lips, signaling for Sarah to restrain herself. Fermín raised his eyebrows and gave a sly smile but said nothing as he placed the plates on the table.

"Please enjoy," he said, and walked away. Sarah waited until he was out of earshot.

"I didn't think a church boy would be so forward."

"There's nothing more determined than a church boy." finished Gabriel, winking.

Sarah grinned.

Chapter 23: The Victim

Miami, Florida: May 1982

May greeted Miami with the usual warmth it always had, yet Gabriel found himself free of sweat as he climbed up the familiar stairs at the criminal courthouse. He was going to meet Moses at the little restaurant downstairs and was running behind. He looked at his silver Bulova; it was a quarter past eight.

He walked into the downstairs lobby of the building and made his way around the offices in the center to the back where the restaurant was located. He walked through the double glass doors to search for his friend. He saw a deep brown hand go up, walked towards it, and slid into the chair across from Moses, taking a sip from the coffee that waited for him.

"Thanks for meeting me this morning, Mo. It means a lot."

"No problem, Lock, but I am in a bit of a hurry, so we do need to make this quick."

Gabriel nodded and placed his briefcase on the table. He retrieved the copy of the video that Mirella had made for him.

"This video contains a child endangerment crime," he said handing the video to Mo. "It was done on purpose though it has some mitigating factors. This was done by a temporary worker hired by my client to replace a regular teacher at her daycare whose out on maternity leave. It turns out that the papers she presented were falsified, using someone else's documentation. We believe she may have previously applied for the license and been rejected, or the license was not being processed quickly enough for her needs. Representing the daycare, I have been in touch with Children and Families, and I am on my way to find the woman whose paperwork was falsified."

Moses tapped the table with his fingers in sequence and processed the severity of the allegations.

"This is not light stuff, Lock. This isn't something easy to deal with and you may be interfering with a police investigation."

Gabriel met Moses' eyes square on, his cheek twitching as he readied himself.

"That's not possible, Mo."

"Why would you say that?" Moses furrowed his brows, his dark eyes squinted at Gabriel, piercing his argument.

"Because the police investigation hasn't started yet." Gabriel grinned slowly.

Moses fumed. "It's a thin line that you walk, Lock."

Gabriel wiped his face with one of the table napkins, removing the perspiration the morning had created. "Justice is always a thin line, Mo. That's why people hire lawyers."

Moses conceded and segued. "Do you have anything else for me?"

"Here are copies of some of the documents that the client gave me. They're the ones that the impersonator gave my client."

Moses examined the documents as Gabriel handed them to him, snatching a table napkin to clean the lenses of his red glasses.

"Cool specs, Mo," said Gabriel, pointing at the readers. "I didn't see red as your color, but they fit your look."

"You know that I fit my clothes to what specs I choose to wear. Anyway, I will watch the video and see what I can do. If I find her, I will let you know." Mo looked at his watch. "I've got to run, Gabriel. Court starts soon and I have got the trial ahead of me."

"Good luck, Mo."

"This guy is sick man. Hopefully, we'll put him away for a long time."

"I hope that you do."

"Let's hope that the jury feel the same way." Moses rose from the table, shook Gabriel's hand, and walked out.

Gabriel thought about leaving the table when the server reached him, chiding him for not having paid for the coffees. He laughed to himself, pulled a five-dollar bill from his wallet, and told her to keep the change, before walking out.

The walk to Children and Family Services lasted just a couple of minutes as once again, he found his way to her office through the trailers. He knocked on the door. "Come in." she looked at him in surprise. Twice in one month? – Oh, this is either awfully good or awfully bad. Come on in sugar."

Gabriel walked in the door with a Video tape in his hand.

"You still have that VCR here?"

"I do."

"I want to show you something."

"We'll have to go into the boss's office, but she won't mind."

Gabriel opened his briefcase and for a second time, he handed a government official a copy of the video tape. On this occasion he made no preamble and simply stood while Pearl watched.

"Oh my God, she left that child by himself and just took off. What is wrong with her?"

"My Father and I have been on the case since yesterday when the daycare owner came to see us." Gabriel summed up the past day's events before explaining the next course of action. "I personally delivered the tape to the State Attorney's office this morning."

"You gave it to Moses?"

"He'll take care of it."

"If you went to Moses already, why are you here?"

Gabriel reached for his briefcase again. From within, he retrieved a copy of the documents that Mirella had given him.

"Here are the papers she gave my client. She used someone else's papers to be able to take the position. Since it is a temporary job for less than a month, the standards are a little relaxed. Here's the point."

Pearl interrupted his explanation. "She had to have had access to the lady who really holds this license, and she must have known that there is a little leeway for temporary substitutions. So, it is a good guess that at some point she studied the requirements and that means she was going to take the exam and that means that we have a record of her application."

"That is what I'm thinking. It also means that you have the information on the real license holder, so, I figure that if you give me the address for the real holder, I can go and speak with her. That might lead us to the woman who is behind all this mess. If we are lucky, she will know who took her papers but if not, you may run across her name when you check applications."

"Now, you know I cannot give you any information for the licensee without permission from my superior.

"But you're not giving me information as to the licensee. She is not the one I am interested in. You are giving me a lead to find an impostor.

"That's true." Pearl returned to the main room toward her desk to go through some files under the impostor's fake name. When she found them, she revealed the address to Gabriel and wrote it on a slip of paper. "Now, leave before I have to explain why you shouldn't be here."

"Thank you, Pearl. You really should have waited for me."

"I'm sure that my husband would feel the same way. Now leave, but as always, it is nice to see you again, bright eyes."

Gabriel slid into his car and looked at the paper with the address 910 SW 19th Avenue, Unit 1. He turned the key and left. Arriving at the six-apartment, two floor building. He couldn't help but notice the 1950's design including the metal columns rising from the stucco half wall in the front of the structure, the open hallway between the units and the brick designs placed into the stucco finish on that half wall and the sides of the building. He stopped the car and ambled to the last apartment on the right. He knocked and heard a voice tell him to come in through the row of jalousie windows. He turned the handle of the door and stepped onto the terrazzo floor of the apartment. The air-conditioning unit was humming as it threw cool air into the pace. The slightly overweight woman sat on an aluminum rocking chair watching a TV that sat on a two-shelf bookcase right above a black VCR. She looked at him and asked in Spanish. "How many I help you?"

"My name is Gabriel Lock. I am an attorney. I am looking for Graciela Argüello," he said in English. She switched to English and Gabriel heard the familiar Cuban accent.

"Why are you looking for me?"

"Were you ever a childcare specialist in the state of Florida."

"Yes, for many years."

"I am Gabriel Lock an attorney from the Lock and Lock law firm. My firm represents the Dream Day Daycare."

"I'm not looking for a job. I am a little old for that, as you can see."

Gabriel smiled.

"The reason that I am here is that although you are retired your license has been at work for the last ten days."

No expression came from her face for a moment.

"What do you mean?" she asked in a low intrigued tone.

"Someone applied and worked at my client's daycare for the last ten days using your altered papers and license to be approved for a temporary position."

"I don't understand what you mean."

"May I open my briefcase and show you?"

"Of course."

Gabriel opened his briefcase for what felt for the hundredth time and displayed the documents for Graciela to see.

"These are the documents that were presented to my client as the basis for the young lady's application."

She looked through them vigorously, and when she reached the end, she looked at them again but this time very carefully and patiently.

"It seems that the only things Eleonor bothered to do was to change the picture and the date of birth, all the rest of the information is mine. I will say that she left the annex off which listed the rest of my jobs. Had she submitted those; she would have had to be at least in her forties."

Gabriel grinned.

"How did she get access to your papers?"

"Because her mother is my caregiver, and Eleonor has occasionally been here to see me when she has been in the proper frame of mind. That, I am sorry to say, is not often."

Gabriel took out a yellow pad and got ready to write.

"What is her complete name?"

"Eleonor Cuesta." the name jogged his memory.

"Do you happen to know her mother's and father's names?"

"I know their names; didn't you hear her mother is my caregiver? Her name is María Elena Cuesta, and her father was Luis Cuesta. Her father died in a terrible accident."

"Is there a way I can speak to María Elena?"

"She will not be in this week or the next because her mother is ill, so Elena is in Colombia visiting her. I will have a person from an agency here to help me with things."

"May I call you in order to return then?"

"Yes, write down my number. Call me at the beginning of September. She should be back by then."

"September?!" fired back Gabriel as he grabbed a pen to write down the number.

"Is there something wrong?" she asked.

"Yes, her daughter endangered the life of a child."

"Oh, my Lord. How could this be?"

Gabriel paused.

"Yes, and it is serious. I was hoping to speak with María Elena before I spoke with the authorities," he answered.

"María Elena's own mother is fighting for her life in Colombia, where she is now, so you won't be able to speak with her."

Gabriel nodded in comprehension.

"I'm sorry to hear that, I truly am."

"I've known María Elena's daughter for a long time. Consistency is not her strength, and I don't believe that your clients will have any more issues going forward. But I am sorry for what happened regardless of whether it was her."

"What makes you so sure that she won't do something again?"

"Anything more would put her own life in danger. This was bad, but the worst that she is capable of. She won't risk trouble with the law, but a scandal for a company is a different story."

"But endangering a child is more than a scandal," pressed Gabriel, giving her a stern look.

Graciela could not match his intensity and gazed at the floor. Gabriel saw the break in her guard and had to approach gently, appealing to her love of children.

"Graciela, you've cared for children all your life. I'm not trying to hurt María Elena or her family, but I do need to know if this young woman has done anything wrong before, anything like this?"

"No, she has never done anything like this. She's had personal problems, but she has never hurt anyone."

Gabriel felt relief, but didn't show it, maintaining his poise as he led her in his questioning.

She left the child unattended because she knew that other people were coming, so what Graciela's telling me fits. Maybe this was her first time, but why?

"Graciela, is she close to her grandmother?"

"Yes, very much so. She's been here several times, especially through the hard times," she said, beginning to stare off in the distance, lost in thought.

Gabriel noted this and decided not to press the issue further as it would be several months before María Elena returned.

"May I have your number, so we can keep in touch about this?"

Graciela gave him her number and Gabriel thanked her for it. As he turned to make his way to the door, he looked back at her, said goodbye, and walked out.

Graciela waited until she could no longer hear his footsteps and prayed to herself silently. When she finished, she thought about Eleonor and prayed aloud, "Oh my Lord, child. Where are you?"

Chapter 24: The Files

Miami, Florida: May 1982

Gabriel flipped on the switch, and the dark office became visible. The clock struck seven but did not make a sound as he walked toward the filing cabinets behind Susana's desk and began rummaging through the folders until he found all of them. He grabbed the stack and headed toward the conference room. He laid them across the table in chronological order. He noticed that the first pile was labeled Morales v Cuesta. He began looking through the first one labeled *Pleadings*, then he searched through the next one labeled *Discovery*, and again he could not find what he was looking for. He reached for a file named *Trial Prep* and examined it in vain. Gabriel heard Susana come into the office and seconds later, she walked to the door of the conference room, stuck her head in, and spoke, "Well good morning, you don't have anything in court today so what brings you in so early?"

"I've been reviewing the Morales' files looking for something that I thought I saw in there but so far I haven't found it."

Susana looked at the piles strewn across the big table.

"I'll make us some Cafecito."

"Could you please? That would be great."

As he began to look through the third file labeled trial, he found the name Elena Cuesta in his father's trial notes. Just then he heard Thomas' voice saying, "Hey can I have some of that?"

"Is everyone getting an early start today?" asked Susana to Thomas.

"What do you mean?" inquired Thomas, unsure of what she meant.

"This is for Gabriel, but I'll get you one right away."

"Gabriel is in already?"

"In the conference room."

"How long have you been here?" asked Thomas, walking into the conference room.

"Since a little before seven. I wanted to review the Morales' files one more time."

"Why?"

"How important was this Cuesta litigation?" pressed Gabriel, ignoring his father's question.

"Those were hard times and both companies were struggling. We had a mix of rampant inflation with a stagnant economy. Not a good mix."

"Do you have a minute?"

"I have all the time you want," he said sitting in the chair next to Gabriel. I have nothing scheduled."

Susana walked in with the Cafecito. Gabriel looked up as she placed it before Thomas.

"Have you had breakfast, Dad?"

"No."

"And you Susana?"

She shook her head.

"Susana, do you think you could order breakfast at the bistro for all of us?"

"Are you buying?" joked Thomas.

"Yes, I am," answered Gabriel, playful annoyance in his voice.

Susana giggled.

"Sure. We are not open yet, so I can pick it up if you want?"

"Thank you, Susana," answered Thomas.

Gabriel nodded and turning to his father he asked, "Tell me a little bit about Morales v Cuesta. How did it start?"

"Well, Morales needed a location for his new daycare. Parents from that area had mentioned that they had to drive too far to his first location. Another thing that led him to this was the waiting list at his first location. He knew this new one would go well, and he could extend his services to the area which would be looked upon favorably by Children's and Youth Services who controlled the permits at the time."

"Understood."

"Everything was going well until the landlord refused to make the repairs on the exterior of the building and so after an exchange of letters between his attorney and me, there was no choice but to file litigation. I must admit that I thought that it would settle as soon as I filed the complaint, but to my surprise, it didn't."

"And that's when it all started?"

"Yes."

"Can you tell me about the trial?"

"Sure."

Chapter 25: The Agreement

Miami, Florida: May 1982

Gabriel and Rodrigo sat across from each other in the conference room, waiting for Tony and Ronald to arrive. Thomas entered holding a stack of files in one hand and his sports coat in the other. Placing the files down on the table and hanging his coat on the back of a chair, Thomas loosened his tie and sat down.

"I need to get a pair of those," said Rodrigo, pointing to Thomas's royal blue suspenders. Thomas looked down and smiled. Taking his thumb and placing it behind his right suspender, he pushed forward on the suspender and held it out for a moment before removing his thumb and releasing it. A loud snap sounded as it slapped against his shirt.

"Love these things. I get new suspenders, ties, and bowties all the time from my friend Jeremy at his formal wear store. I'll take you and Gabriel after this."

"That sounds like a solid plan," responded Rodrigo.

Susana opened the door to the conference room.

"Mr. Melendi and Mr. Pilkington are here. Would you like me to send them in?"

Thomas turned back from her to Gabriel.

"Please, Susana, send them in," requested Gabriel.

Susana nodded and set off. A few moments later, Tony entered wearing black slacks and a white button-down shirt. Ronald followed closely behind him wearing an AC/DC T-shirt with ripped blue jeans.

"You know, Ron, I was really looking forward to seeing the Back-to-Back World War Champs shirt again," said Rodrigo, rising to shake Ron and Tony's hands.

"You know, Hot Rod, if you wanna get one, I can call my buddy Caleb and ask him to get you one."

"You'd do that for me?"

"Yes *siree*, I would. We can seal the deal and sock a fat one to my goat-fuckin' fat bastard of a cousin, Steve."

Thomas nearly choked on Ronald's words.

"Thank you so much for joining us, Ron. We appreciate it, sincerely." turning to Tony, Gabriel spoke. "Tony, how are you? Are you ready?"

"Yes, Mister Lock. I been practicing my English very much to make it very good, but I have a question, Mister Lock. I don't know how to say in English."

"Tell me in Spanish," said Gabriel.

Tony smiled.

"I don't understand him," said Tony in Spanish, using his eyes and eyebrows to signal towards Ronald. Tony whispered, "he has a very bad accent."

"Don't worry, if needed, I'll translate," answered Gabriel in Spanish.

Tony nodded and looked back at Ronald who smiled wide.

"¿Qué pasa, Mufasa? You don't understand me?"

"My English is bad, but I think yours is worse."

They all burst into laughter and after a while, Ronald looked over at Tony.

"I speak Español," said Ronald before switching fully to Spanish. "We can speak your lingo instead of mine!"

Ronald's accent in Spanish was the thickest southern drawl Gabriel had ever heard.

"No, English is better. I tink my English is *much* better dan your Spanish," pleaded Tony.

"No problemo, compadre," said Ronald, nodding in agreement.

"Great," said Gabriel shifting the subject, "I want to thank both of you for meeting with us today. The evidence that you provide is paramount for Mr. Melendi's defense." Gabriel said, turning to Ron, "and for us to make it air-tight, we need to make sure that we have all the dates and amounts fitting perfectly together. Did you bring the copies of the insurance policies?"

Ronald nodded.

"Great. Tony, did you bring me the itemized list of everything that you stole?"

Tony nodded also.

"Fantastic, please give me those documents," finished Gabriel.

Tony and Ron handed him the documents and Gabriel laid them out for everyone to see. As he read, he pulled the insurance policy closer to him and jotted down a couple of lines on the legal pad in front of him. Raising his eyes from the document, he peered over to Ronald, who had removed a can of dip from his pocket and had placed it on his gums.

"Ronald, I have reviewed the policy, and it says that it is from this period, so are you sure that this policy was in full force and effect during this whole period of time and that is hasn't been cancelled and then reinstated somehow?"

"Yessir! –That is the insurance policy from that time."

"And you, Tony, can you tell us everything again, from the beginning?"

"Yes, Mister Lock."

Tony told his story, and Ron smiled the whole time. As Tony finished, Susana reentered, having finished certifying Ron's affidavit.

"Good, thank you," said Gabriel accepting the pen from him. "Ron, one last thing. Would you want to be my rebuttal witness for Tony's case?"

"I cannot wait to see the look on Steve's fat face! Yes, sir! Count me in!"

"Thank you, Ron. With everything in place, we've got a solid plan."

"Great," said Thomas, "I think that it is about time for lunch, so I think that I'm going to walk down to the corner restaurant. Anyone interested in joining me?"

"Are you buyin,' Daddyo?" asked Ronald, beaming a smile at Thomas.

"I guess so," laughed Thomas. "What about you, Rod?"

Rodrigo looked down at his watch, "yeah, I'll join. I've got time."

Gabriel nodded and began to get up when Tony reached for him.

Everyone paused.

"We'll catch up, Dad. Give us a minute."

Thomas, Rodrigo, and Ronald all nodded, pushed in their chairs, and left through the conference room door.

Tony and Gabriel sat in silence for a moment as Gabriel waited for Tony to collect himself.

The thief exhaled and stared at the table, before speaking in Spanish. "Look, Mr. Lock, I have been thinking about this a lot since you took my case. I know that you are Rodrigo's friend and are doing this as a favor to him, but I am not a good man. I have made a lot of mistakes, selfish ones. I lied and stole for two years for nothing more than my pride. I know that I said that it was for my family, but it was much more than that after a little while. Your job is to defend people, but this is more than just defending me, this is more than I could have asked for, and more than anyone else would do for me. Why all of this for me?"

Gabriel closed his eyes for a moment, processing the depth of Tony's words and final question. He thought about all the answers he could give and, in the end, chose the only one that mattered. "Tony," he began in Spanish, "there is a lot behind why I serve you and my other clients to the best of my ability, why I lose sleep over their futures and the consequences of my decisions, whether it's strategy or execution. Either way, I lose sleep and bury myself into the files. I could tell you that it's because I am brilliant, but I'm not. The truth is that all of us are equal in the eyes of the law. In the bible, Leviticus 19:15 says 'You shall do no injustice in court. You shall not be partial to the poor or defer to the great, but in righteousness shall you judge your neighbor.' You are my neighbor, Tony. That is why I practice law, not to punish, but in defense of my clients, as my father before me."

Tony took a deep breath and tears formed in his eyes as he covered his mouth with his hand, trying to stop the emotions from escaping. After a moment, he collected himself and through watery eyes, spoke, "Thank you, Mr. Lock."

Gabriel nodded and stood, stretching out his hand.

Tony took it and they shook.

"So, are you hungry?"

Tony nodded.

Gabriel walked around the conference table and put his arm around Tony, giving him a slight hug, "Then let's get something to eat, I'm STARVING!"

Chapter 26: The Crooks

Miami, Florida: June 1982

Gabriel and Tony arrived early at the courthouse. Rodrigo was at a Motion to Suppress hearing in criminal court but would try to arrive before it started. As Gabriel and Tony made their way past security, Gabriel realized that the opposing counsel had not yet arrived. Taking Tony by the arm, he pulled him to the side.

"Tony, look. I know that I told you this before, but the proceeding is going to be heard in the judge's chambers, and there won't be a jury."

"Do you think there will be a trial?" asked Tony.

"Not if they have any sense."

Tony nodded and they both walked into the courtroom.

Brett Kannady, the opposing counsel, walked in, and the process server followed behind. He waited for Kannady to find his seat at the Plaintiff's table before giving the opposing counsel a document and then coming over to Gabriel and handing him a copy. On the top of the page was printed the word *Subpoena* in bold lettering. Typed below it was the name *Ronald Pilkington* and across the page in handwriting it said, *Served: June 10th*, yesterday's date, *7:32 p.m.* The processor's signature lay at the bottom. Gabriel looked over to see Kannady examining it before reaching over to his two clients, Dwight and Steve Pilkington. Steve remained still while Dwight's eye began to twitch. He turned and whispered quickly to Kannady, and he saw him shuffling in his seat and stood up.

Gabriel grabbed Tony's sleeve and pulled him toward the witness stand at the far end of the courtroom. Kannady followed them, and as planned, Gabriel raised his palm, indicating to Kannady that he was busy talking to his client. The attorney politely walked back a few steps. Gabriel turned and moved deeper into the courtroom with Tony, speaking with him in Spanish to give the allusion that it was relevant to the case. He placed himself on the other side of his client with his back to the witness stand so that Tony was between him and everyone else in the courtroom. From his position, he saw another slight man enter the courtroom and walk toward Steve. He knew that was the company accountant. Gabriel saw Dwight get up and approach Kannady. Dwight's eye still twitched, and his face turned red. He was talking low but gesticulated vigorously. His hands moved quicker than his lips. He looked up for a second, saw Gabriel staring at him, and stopped.

Taking Tony by the arm again, Gabriel angled him like a wall, shielding his facial expressions.

"Tony, we're going to leave the courtroom now. As we walk by, the opposing counsel is going to ask me to speak with him. I need you to go to the hall and wait for me there. Say nothing to no one. Understood?"

Tony nodded his head, and the pair set off for the courtroom. As they passed by, Kannady touched his arm.

"Counsel, may we have a moment in private?"

"Sure. One sec." Gabriel signaled for Tony to continue walking and when he saw him leave the courtroom, he turned.

"Listen, I can't believe you have just served a subpoena on a witness that we have no knowledge of as a potential witness in this case. Do you plan to put him on the stand?"

"I do."

"I will have to object."

"I am sure the judge will not see a problem with him testifying as he will be a rebuttal witness and I have listed rebuttal witnesses if needed on my pre-trail catalogue. I am going to tell the judge that, in question thirty-five of the interrogatories that I sent you, I asked your client if anyone else, other than the individuals identified in any other response, are aware of, or have any knowledge of, the theft of any of the merchandise claimed in your complaint. Your guy said no, and no one is going to believe that your guy just *forgot* this witness."

"Who is this witness?"

"He's your client's cousin and brother. That is, Steve's cousin and Dwight's brother."

"So what?"

"Well, I'm sure this isn't the first client who's lied to you, and it won't be the last. It happens to me a lot."

"What is it you think you know that I don't seem to know?" As Kannady pressed him, the bailiff opened the door of the courtroom and called out, "Pilkington Wholesalers vs Melendi, the judge is ready for you."

"Can you give us a minute please?" asked Gabriel to the bailiff.

The large man nodded.

"I can give you five minutes counsel, but not too long. Her Honor would like to get started."

"Thank you."

As the bailiff returned to the judge's chambers, Kannady stepped back and leaned against the wall.

"What is it that you know that I don't know?"

"I had a real nice talk with Ronald Pilkington, a week ago. Like I said, he's your client's first cousin and the other one's brother. It seems that he was a shareholder at Pilkington Wholesalers until two years ago. He left just before Tony started working there. He used to run the warehouse operations while Steve handled the office. Ronald was cast out because he was stealing from his partners. He only held twenty-five percent you see, because Ronald's brother, Dwight held the other twenty-five percent. But Dwight didn't work there. Steve, the owner that you've been dealing with owned fifty percent. Their fathers, from whom they inherited the company, didn't have salaries so they continued the tradition. Therefore, Ronald was working the same as Steve but getting only half of the money because Dwight and Steve decided that it was fair that no one got a salary. At first, Ronald started to steal to make things even, but he realized that unless he could buy his brother out of his share, his life wouldn't change. Not having the liquid assets, he continued to steal and by the end, his theft amounted to eight hundred thousand dollars.

"This guy admitted to you that he stole this stuff?"

"He didn't just admit it." Gabriel paused and opened his briefcase. Finding the right file, he removed a document and held it up for Kannady to see. "He swore it."

Kannady took the affidavit and examined it.

"They turned the theft into a business deal and agreed to buy Ronald out using the amount he stole as a down payment for his part. But it gets better. Besides the dates coinciding, your client has a Fidelity Bond for employee theft, but there is no coverage if the employee stealing is also an owner. Ronald assured me that none of the accused in this case ever helped him steal and he has no love for Cousin Steve."

"So, you think the numbers my client has come up with are all of it put together?"

"The summaries presented by your guy's accountants are all a lie and he is trying to pin Ronald's stealing on my client's group in order to collect the insurance and deduct anything they don't recover from the IRS."

"Why would he talk to you, Lock?"

"Because your guy agreed to a buy out, they signed papers and then they never paid him in full. They promised him copies of the agreement and never sent them. Instead, the papers disappeared, and they stopped paying him after three months. I think they figured that Ronald would never take them to court because of his stealing. Dwight and Steve split Ronald's shares fifty-fifty to make it basically a sixty-forty split for themselves. The total stock was worth about two million but because of the stealing they agreed to the price of a million, so they still owed him around two hundred thousand. They screwed him over, so he wants payback."

"You think I'm in the middle of a fraud?"

"If you push this, given the information that I've given you, you'll risk being a participant in attempted insurance fraud."

He just glared at Gabriel.

"I'm sorry man, I just don't believe you or this affidavit."

"Go confirm it with your client. Because, once you put your client, or his accountants, on the stand to testify to all the nonsense, you will become a participant."

"So, you are making sure that I am aware?"

"I am not assuming you knew before we got here today. Unfortunately for you, that is different from what everyone else is going to think, including the judge."

The scrutiny between the two men was hard. Finally, Kannady's stance broke.

"Give me a minute and let me talk to my guy."

The lawyer signaled to his clients and the accountant, then walked out of the courtroom into the hallway, opened the metal door leading to the stairwell and the four of them walked into the stairwell closing the door behind them.

Gabriel left the now empty courtroom and went to look for Tony in the hall. Just as he was reaching his client, the bailiff appeared from the judge's chambers.

"Counsel we're ready."

Gabriel strode toward the Bailiff and made a hand gesture signaling that they needed just a little more time.

"Mr. Lock, the judge needs to get started if you are going to get through the testimony today and she doesn't have another date until the summer. How much time do you need?"

"Ten minutes?" answered Gabriel.

"You've got five, Counselor."

From his new position in the hallway, Gabriel looked through the large, thick, rectangular window in the metal door that separated the hallway from the stairway. Dwight was at the rear of the group, but Steve was engaged in conversation with the accountant and Kannady. He saw Steve's face redden as he was talking to the attorney and the accountant. The accountant shook his head vigorously and looked at the cement floor of the stairwell for a second. When he looked up his face was as red as Steve's and Gabriel knew that the accountant had realized that he'd be implicated in the fraud if he testified.

The man shook his head again. Steve advanced toward the accountant and poked him with his index finger. The accountant slapped the finger away. Shaking his head and directing himself toward Steve, the accountant raised his fists as his face turned scarlet. Kannady stepped between them and spoke to press his point, but it was Dwight who stepped forward shaking his head. He seemed to be making it very clear to all that the case was stopping now. He turned towards his cousin and looked at him intently. Sensing the conversation's end, Gabriel turned and walked quickly toward Tony.

When the metal door opened, Gabriel and Tony sat in the hall chairs, purposely engaged in conversation. Kannady dismissed his clients and the accountant before standing a few feet from them.

"Gabriel, can we speak for a moment?"

"Sure thing." Gabriel rose and walked toward the side hall.

"What do you want out of this?"

"To go home."

"I can't do that."

"Fine, then I'll inform the Bailiff that we're ready to start."

"How about a judgement for ten thousand dollars?"

"Not a chance," said Gabriel, confident that the accountant was not willing to testify as to the amount stolen. "I don't care what you do with everyone else. You will get defaults against them in this case, but, in truth, their obligation of repayment will be adjudicated and decided by the criminal court. What your client testifies there is his problem. As part of their sentence each defendant will have to repay part of what was stolen as restitution. As far as my client goes, we are done here today. We both walk away."

"It's just not right."

"If your client wouldn't have gotten greedy and tried to commit insurance fraud, we wouldn't be having this conversation. He's the one that took a winning case and lost it. The question is, do you want to be complicit in their greed?"

Kannady was silent for a second. Losing wasn't a state that Kannady enjoyed being in.

"Let's tell the judge we're settled."

"Good, then we can all go home."

Kannady and Gabriel walked down to the judge's chambers to find the bailiff. Upon entering the antechamber, they turned to their right to find him seated in a chair behind his small desk.

"Marvin, we are settled. Would you inform the judge that we'll submit an order, please?" said Gabriel, waiting on the bailiff's agreement.

"Wait here, let me make sure that she agrees with that," he said, heading into the judge's office.

A few moments passed before he reemerged.

"Her honor has stated that you may submit your settlement and the order affirming it, but to have it here by Friday at noon."

"Thank you," both lawyers said.

Kannady and Gabriel departed the chambers into the hallway.

"I'll draw up a simple dismissal with prejudice as to your client and default judgements as to the others," Kannady said.

"Good. I appreciate your candor in cooperation."

"Don't get smug."

"I don't have to Kannady, I already won."

Gabriel left Kannady in the hallway and walked back to the courtroom. Not finding Tony there. Gabriel found Tony seated on a bench outside of the courtroom. As Kannady entered to find his clients, Tony moved to leave, but Gabriel placed a hand on his forearm and stopped him.

"Stay seated and let them leave first."

As Kannady, Steve, the accountant and Dwight left, they stared Tony and Gabriel down, disgust and anger rued Steve's face.

Gabriel waited until they left the courthouse before saying a word.

"So, Tony, how does it feel to know that you won one over *the man*?"

"Good, Mr. Lock. Very good."

"Ready to go home to your family?"

"Yes. Yes please."

"Then let's get out of here."

Chapter 27: The Melendi Notion

Miami, Florida: June 1982

A few days had passed since Gabriel and Tony settled out of court and everything swirled in Gabriel's head. He hadn't seen Sarah in over a week and hadn't even talked to her with how busy both of their schedules had kept them, and he had missed going to Franco's for over two weeks. He hadn't even taken the Mustang for a wash and detail or even a visit to the mechanic's and he felt as if he were behind on the rest of his cases. *I haven't even had lunch with Abuela in two weeks*, he thought to himself. Between juggling his cases, Sarah, his family, and his outside life, he didn't know how he managed it all. The AC blared in the background, and he realized that the sweat on his forehead came from more than just his cases, as he looked through the window in the office and could see the heat wafting off the tops of cars and jaywalkers on Coral Way. He checked his watch and realized that Tony would arrive shortly, and before he could even straighten up his desk, he heard the intercom sound.

"Mr. Melendi is here," Susana announced.

"Have him come in, please?" asked Gabriel. Through the door, he could hear her walk toward the waiting room, welcome Tony and Rodrigo, and let them both into Gabriel's office, closing the door once they entered.

Rodrigo waited for Tony to shake Gabriel's hand as he came around his desk to greet them.. Gabriel acknowledged Rodrigo and they shook before Gabriel returned to his seat.

"So good to see both of you." said Gabriel, gesturing toward the empty chairs. "How's the family? your wife, the kids?" asked Gabriel in Spanish.

"Everyone is great, thank God. Planning a weekend at Disney. We all need to get away and clear the mind." answered Tony, grateful for the question.

"I agree. How's the job search?"

"I'm prepared to start over, but I had been having trouble finding a job until two days ago when a friend of mine from middle school reached out to me. I met him at a restaurant, and I could not believe it; I had not spoken to him in years, and he reached out to offer me a job. I guess he heard that I needed help."

"Did he know about what happened?" asked Rodrigo.

"Not in complete detail, but I came clean and explained everything that happened. He asked me if I was planning to continue with my career as a thief or if I wanted a future that made sense?"

I told him I was through trying to take shortcuts and that all I wanted now was a steady straight way to make a living and support my family. He asked me, 'Are you going to steal from me?' I said, no." murmured Melendi, "and he offered me the job."

"You took the job?" asked Gabriel.

"He has a build materials company, and he needs an experienced person to handle the loading dock for him. Someone he can count on and who will have his back."

"Are you going to have his back?" asked Rodrigo quietly.

"I gave him my word." It is the only thing I have left to give so it must count. Everything I did led to nothing except grief for Amalia. I never wanted to see that look in my wife's eyes when I told her what was going on. She forgave me, and stood by me, but that was my one mistake, and I know there can be no more. I must be clean, for her, for the boys but mostly for me."

"Good then." added Gabriel with a smile. "So, you want Rod and I to be part of your crew at the loading dock?"

"Not exactly," grinned Melendi. "I don't think you could do a full day Gabriel."

"You'd be surprised," retorted the lawyer.

"When I went to confession this Saturday besides almost giving Father Antonio a heart attack from the surprise of actually seeing me at church, he and I had a long talk during confession about everything I did at the warehouse including wearing a wire and involving and then implicating everyone in my sin."

"Yeah, but everyone participated willingly," observed Rodrigo.

"I was the Pied Piper leading everyone into the water to drown. Anyway," he said looking at Rodrigo, "Father Antonio asked me if there was no way I could help them? I told him I did not think so, but when I got home, and spoke with my wife, she asked me if the information Gabriel used to settle my civil case would be useful to either get them out of their criminal trouble, or at least, reduce the gravity of their problems."

"It might," said Gabriel.

"They don't have to forgive me for leading them down the wrong path and then betraying them. I think that would be asking too much, but I can at least make up for it, you know, as much as I can, by giving them this information."

"You did not tell them what to do or say," commented Rodrigo.

"I taught them how to do it and then I wore a wire and got them to confess on the recording in exchange for walking away without consequences to me while they all go to jail. What a nice guy I was." finished Tony, looking down at his hands as his legs trembled.

"We understand the guilt," said Rodrigo.

"But we did sign a non-disclosure agreement together with the settlement and if we breach the non-disclosure, they could set aside the settlement," inserted Gabriel.

"There are no exceptions?"

"Well, if you get subpoenaed to testify, then you are obligated to tell the truth about everything you know."

"I have a feeling that all it would take would be a subpoena to take Tony's deposition." ruminated Rodrigo. "I'll talk to the defense attorneys. I've known a few public defenders since I worked with them at the PD's office. We can be discrete, and I can talk to them without being obvious and breaking the non-disclosure."

"Done," said Gabriel.

"Thanks guys. I can't believe everything you've done for me. And now this."

"You understand we are not doing this for you right? It's for your wife," answered Rodrigo.

"For whatever reason," chucked Tony.

"If this helps you find your way for you and your family, then it's worth it," answered Gabriel, settling the matter.

"Thank you," finished Tony, rising from his chair to shake their hands.

"Go home, Tony, and spend the rest of the day with your wife and kids. Don't do anything else except be grateful for them. Understood?"

"Yes, Mr. Lock, I promise."

"Good man. Rodrigo and I will take care of a few things here, but he'll call you when they're finished."

"Thank you, Mr. Lock and Mr. Vivar. Have a nice day."

With that, Tony turned and left through the office door, bidding Susana a good rest of her day and leaving the office.

"Do you think that he'll change?" asked Rodrigo.

"I do."

"Yeah, me too. I don't know what you said to him last week, but it meant something to him for sure."

"Nothing more than what he needed to hear."

"Got a lot to do this week?"

Gabriel snickered, thinking about everything he had to deal with, "Something like that. I've got a date this weekend with Sarah to see the Venetian Isles."

"That a boy! That will be a good time."

"I hope so. We haven't seen each other for a week."

"I'm sure that it will go well. Don't sweat it."

"I won't. I promise."

When Tony arrived home, he looked for the gloves, balls, and bats in the garage. He could not find them. He went into the back yard to see if they had left them there from the night before and the netting was gone. He went into the kitchen and found Amalia and the boys sitting around the table. Where is the netting? Where is the baseball equipment?"

"We got rid of it," said Pedrito, his oldest. "Gave it to the YMCA in east Hialeah. They needed it for the season."

"We also gave them the TV's and the VCR's." said Amalia.

"The Boom Box was the hardest to give away," added Miguelito, the youngest. "I love that deep base on the music."

"But we gave it all away, to show you that we don't need those things to be happy. We just need you. We never want to lose you."

Tony lowered himself slowly into the open chair and placed his head on his forearm. At that moment, he knew he had it all.

Chapter 28: The Venetian Isles

Miami, Florida: June 1982

Gabriel waited outside of Sarah's apartment building, watching a pair of students walk down the sidewalk. He knew that he was a little early. He opened his wallet and took out the picture and wondered if it was time to take it out of his wallet. He heard shoes tapping on concrete and turned to find the red in Sarah's brown hair glistening in the late morning sun. He placed the picture back in the billfold and looked up as she stopped a few steps in front of him and scanned his appearance, delaying when her eyes reached his ankles.

"You're one of those people?" she teased through the glint in her eyes.

"One of which people?" asked Gabriel. Sarah tilted her head and gestured her chin toward Gabriel's shoes. "What's wrong with my shoes? You don't like boat shoes?"

"The shoes are fine, but the socks are not."

Gabriel glanced down at the white crew socks that reached midway up his pale shins.

"If you ever burn the tops of your feet like I have, then you'll wear socks too."

"Ankle high ones?" she pushed.

Gabriel shook his head, gestured to the car, and walked over to the passenger side to open the door for her.

"What a gentleman," she teased.

"Just get in," said Gabriel, chuckling and closing her door. As he made his way to the other side, he stopped just before the trunk and rolled down his socks as far as they could go. When he started the car, Sarah shuffled and peered down at his legs.

"Much better."

"Yeah, yeah," said Gabriel, brushing her off. Sarah fastened her seatbelt, and the Mustang glided down the street heading toward the highway. They were delayed twenty minutes before reaching Biscayne Boulevard where they saw a few cruise liners docked at the port.

"Ever been on a cruise?" inquired Sarah, facing the ships.

"Once, with my parents and grandparents. I had to have been fifteen or so."

"Where did you go?"

"Puerto Rico and a few of the Virgin Islands, nothing too crazy. You?"

"Took one around the Mediterranean once, but it wasn't too special."

"Didn't like the stops?"

"They were fine, but nothing compared to the passenger ship I took with a few of my friends from Southampton to New York once. That is the best trip I have ever taken; at least on a boat."

"When did you do that?"

"In college when I did a semester at Oxford."

"Oxford?" Gabriel turned his eyes from the road to look at her before shifting back to the traffic. The Mustang moved into the right lane as they came to a stoplight.

"For one semester. I did it during my junior year at Yale."

"I'm impressed."

"Why?"

"Because they're great schools."

"Nothing else?" invited Sarah lightly while Gabriel shook his head. "Thank you."

"For what?"

"For seeing the person and not the gender."

"It's impressive for anyone."

Sarah's pupils dilated and Gabriel met her eyes for a moment, connecting with them.

When they arrived, they parked in one of the spaces beneath the palm trees just before a small dock where a group of people waited for the tour guides.

"This should be it," stated Gabriel, allowing Sarah to pass first. They joined the group and settled in at the back of the line. A large man with a larger stomach, a straw hat, and a tropical shirt walked from the dock, untied the rope in front of the line, and faced the crowd.

"Good morning, everyone," he began, wiping a bead of sweat from his forehead, "I am Jared Klute, and I will be guiding your tour this fine day." Some of the crowd nodded, greeted him with scattered words, while others waved. "Welcome and thank you for joining us today at Jared's Miami Cruises or JMC for short. Today we will be taking a cruise of some of Miami's most exclusive living locations, checking out some of the intercoastal islands where the other side lives." Some of the crowd cheered while Sarah giggled. "Lastly, if you all wouldn't mind showing your tickets to this fine young gentleman to my left," he pointed to a teenager who resembled him greatly, except for the missing stomach. "My nephew, Kean, will take them from you." A new line formed in front of Kean, and tickets flashed in people's hands, bidding entry.

"This looks like fun," chimed Sarah.

"I think that you'll enjoy it."

They migrated from the end of the line closer to Kean and a few moments later boarded the double-decker boat.

Twenty minutes passed before they cast off from the dock and headed toward the islands. Gabriel leaned against one of the poles on the back of the lower deck. Sarah leaned against the half wall, smiling, and brushing the loose strands of hair from her face as the salty wind whipped it back and forth.

A voice sounded from a set of loudspeakers instructing the passengers on where to look and what year the first island was built, but Gabriel couldn't hear properly over the sound of the intercoastal waves and the hum of the engines. Sarah tugged on his shirt and signaled him to follow her up the stairs to the upper deck. The breeze muffled the sound of the loudspeakers but neither one cared. Sarah took out a bottle of Coppertone and began spreading it on her arms and legs. "If I'm not careful, I'll burn." As she finished her arms and legs, she reached for her back with no success,

"May I?" asked Gabriel, holding out his hand.

Sarah looked at him, seeing his amused face.

"Sure, Counselor," she answered handing him the sunscreen.

"You don't get much sun in New York?" asked Gabriel, squeezing the sunscreen onto his open palm.

"It's just not as direct."

Gabriel took the sunscreen in his palm and spread it between both hands. He placed his hands gently on her skin as she held her hair up, massaging it onto her back and her shoulders. As he moved his fingers from her shoulders to her neck, he rubbed in the cream evenly.

"You give a good massage too, don't you?" asked Sarah as he finished.

"Something like that."

"Did you get it all? I don't want any red patches on skin. I burn easily."

"I didn't, but if you'd like, I can do it again," he answered as she turned to him, asking for the bottle.

"Slow down, Counselor."

They smiled at each other for a moment, and he handed her the bottle. Sarah placed some of the sunscreen on her fingertips and began spreading it on her cheeks and nose. Gabriel noticed that she covered her freckles. "Want some?" she said extending the small jar toward him.

"Sure thing," answered Gabriel, taking it. He began applying it on his arms and the back of his neck before moving down to his legs. The boat jumped a bit over a small wave, and they found themselves staring at the Venetian Causeway nearing Biscayne and San Marco Island.

"Over here is the Venetian Causeway, folks," said Klute over the loudspeaker. Built in 1925, the Venetian passes through the man-made islands, or Venetian Islands, of Belle Isle, Rivo Alto, Di Lido, San Marco, San Marino, and Biscayne Island. In front of us and to your left is Biscayne Island which is the first island coming from the Florida mainland." The boat drew closer to Biscayne Island and Sarah leaned forward to get a better view of the buildings. Passing beyond Biscayne Island, they approached San Marino Island. A large house with covered terraces overlooked the water as the sun reflected off the large floor to ceiling windows. Sarah's teeth showed and her dimples indented, hidden somewhere among her freckles and sunscreen.

"Enjoying yourself?" he said.

"Not really."

Gabriel felt his back tense. "I'm sorry to hear that." Sarah blushed.

"No reflection on you. I'm just worried that Jean Robert's death will also mean the end of the family dream and a return to Haiti, and I promised him that I would make sure that he and his family would be able to legally stay in the states. Now I am not so sure."

"Why would the status change?"

"Because the family's status was based on his. He is the one who won the lottery and the extension of that privilege to his family after his death is a judgement call, no matter what the law says." Not stopping to catch her breath, the rest came tumbling out. "So, now that he has passed there is a creeping doubt, especially if his involvement in the drug trade is confirmed. That is why..."

"I don't think he is involved but I have not removed all doubts. You know the workmen's compensation people are going to try hard to say he is because that gets them off the hook. The adjuster investigated that angle since she arrived on the scene the day of the shooting. I would not be surprised if that is their initial conclusion." Gabriel gazed at her and continued evenly. "You know you could let me go to their home and talk to the Widow and the kids. That would give me a better idea of who he was and what he was, or was not, doing." She focused on his eyes seemingly reading what lay behind them.

"And if you find he was involved?"

"I would not go out of my way to hurt the family, but I need to do what I have to."

She was silent and she turned her gaze from "Am I going to be present?"

"You know I won't be able to talk to them in their home by myself unless you let me. Still, I will get a more dependable reading of the family if you aren't, and I won't push for them unless I am convinced that he was not involved. Your choice."

"I must think about that. Nothing personal but, leaving you alone with my client is not easy."

"My client has ordered me to help his family in any way I can, if Jean Robert was not involved, but if he was, well...just the opposite. Understand? Your presence will distort the interactions between the family members and taint any conversation we have. I won't get a sense of their lifestyle or morality and that is really what I need. You have told me these are straight up people. Let me see that. If I do not find that, I cannot help you, but if I do then… I am bound to do everything I can."

Once again, she absorbed his face with her look. "Cheers, Gabriel." Sarah giggled and leaned against him, wrapping her arm around him.

Gabriel relaxed as the tension in his lower back eased.

"Thank you, Counselor. I know how hard opening up must be for you." Sarah gripped him a little tighter as the boat journeyed around the islands.

Chapter 29: The Stakes

Miami, Florida: June 1970

The smell of peppermint and cigarette smoke wafted from Luis Cuesta's azure suit jacket as he rubbed his temples with his fingers. His elbows supported his weight as he leaned on the desktop from his chair. Raymond Levine pressed a legal pad in one hand and a pen in the other, jotting notes.

"Did you read the transcripts that I gave you?" asked Raymond, looking up from his notes.

"Of course," replied Cuesta, "I read all three of them carefully. Especially, mine, and the general contractor's testimony."

Raymond leaned back in his chair, stroking the bristled ends of his mustache with his hand. He moved his fingers from the tip of his mustache and pushed the bridge of his wire glasses higher up, revealing wrinkled skin near the corners of his dark eyes. His ebony skin furrowed as he closed his viridian eyes for a moment.

"I can't believe he has to call the general contractor to testify," said Raymond, upon opening his eyes.

"The man's not well, Raymond," added Cuesta.

Raymond rose from his seat for a moment and walked over to the far wall, staring at the framed diplomas from Miami and Columbia. He turned back to Cuesta.

"When I took his deposition, I realized that he was no longer all there. None of his responses made any sense and he had a hard time recalling what had happened. When I followed up, the word on the street was that he had been institutionalized and was losing his mind."

"Does he have a case without the general contractor, Raymond? I can't afford to lose this lawsuit. I'm in more debt than I can handle, and my family can't afford a disaster. Tell me that, without the general contractor, he has nothing."

"Luis, when Lock placed him on your witness list for trial, that confirmed that he had no choice, and he was going to need the general contractor's testimony no matter what."

"Are you sure?" asked Cuesta, removing his elbows from the desktop, and rising from his seat. The freed temples revealed bulging veins. Raymond raised an open palm in front of himself, just to the side of his tie, using it to ease Luis's nervous mind.

"Listen, Luis, this is how I see it. The Plaintiff will put on their case first and so we will review your testimony the night before we are scheduled to begin. My strategy is to contradict the general contractor and discredit his mental state. That will put the other side in a bind because he's their main witness. He will be unable to prove the degree of damage and will not be able to prove anything in the realm of what they are demanding. My cross-examination of the general contractor will follow the questions I asked in my deposition. Their best attack is the general contractor and if I can discredit his mental state, then they have one to prove their case."

Luis exhaled and began walking around the office, contemplating his next reply.

"From what I read, if this is his star witness's deposition, you are going to destroy their case."

"I can still win even if he doesn't go on any tangents. If he does, it'll give the judge reason to doubt him. The way that I see it is that Lock can't win without his top witness and expert. By now, Lock knows this because no one can build this type of case without that level of expertise. At this rate, neither of us is going to win fully. The case won't be dismissed because they may prove that we are liable for delays and expenses, but they can't win the full amount either, because their witness won't be able to testify. What we can do is minimize the expenses and the best that they can do is to get a partial win. I don't see them getting a judgement higher than we have planned for. You'll eventually pay, but it'll be a fraction of what they're asking for."

"Understand, Raymond, that I need to win this case. If he obtains a judgement in trial for any larger amount, I will lose that shopping center, and the other two."

"I know that you are overextended. If we lose, you'd go into bankruptcy, but I can't see how Lock can get a full win without the general contractor. He's the only one that he can build a case around."

"I had the structural engineer come out on a Sunday to look at the building and estimate the cost of the repairs. They would have cost me $75,000 which I did not have."

"I am very aware of the importance of this trial, Luis. I know how desperate this is. We're going to win, and you don't need to worry."

"I can't help it, Raymond."

"I won't lose, Luis. I promise."

Chapter 30: The General Contractor

Miami, Florida: June 1970

Thomas stared at the transcript filled with his witnesses' responses, ranging from the general contractor to the smaller subcontractors and bit players. As he read through their testimonies, he immersed himself in the general contractor's statements. He found no solution in them. Six months of making this man the centerpiece of his case, bolstering his credibility, and building the testimony of everyone else around his story, had come to a vicious end a week ago.

He rose from his desk and paced from it to the wall lined with the antique astrological maps that Laura's family had given him as a gift. As he stared at the imports, appreciating the details of the handmade work, while he weighed the options. *A month ago, I had a witness who was going to topple every attack and rebuttal that the defense could throw at me. Now, I've got a man who has lost all touch with reality. If I put him on the stand, we'll lose this, and my client will go under. Unbelievable!*

Looking down at the floor, Thomas closed his eyes, taking his thumb and index finger, he massaged his eyelids. They burned as he maneuvered but the pressure in the bags under his eyes did not cease. *God, how am I going to get out of this one? I've lost my witness and my expert.* Thomas shuddered in quiet exasperation. Taking a moment, he picked up the phone and called his client. The phone rang for a few moments before a voice answered.

"Raúl, it's Thomas. How are you?" The voice replied audibly. "Were you able to confirm anything?"

"Yes, his wife confirmed that he started losing touch with reality about a month after you interviewed him. He was institutionalized shortly thereafter and only released three weeks ago." Thomas buried his head in his hand while holding the phone tightly to his ear.

"Now I understand his answers. How could I have missed this?" Thomas sighed before remaining silent.

"Thomas don't beat yourself up. His wife told me that he is okay most of the time but when he feels any type of pressure, his grasp of reality diminishes greatly. He was probably fine for the initial interview and got worse with time. You can't change that and there's no way that you could have anticipated it."

"He lost it during the deposition, so can you imagine what will happen in a courtroom setting? I can't use him."

"I don't want to put him through that, but I can't afford to lose this case. You know that all my money was put into this place and when that wasn't enough, I borrowed a lot from my family to help build this place out. I can't extend myself or my family anymore. This new daycare was supposed to be the gold mine. It's the only one around for miles, and there's no other building in which to open one. Now, if this goes south, I'm going to be ruined."

As Morales finished, Thomas measured the severity of his words. He couldn't afford to lose this case either. If they won, then more clients would go his way. If they lost, his future and the success that it promised would move farther away from his grasp.

"I understand, but in my mind, there is no purpose in submitting this man to the pressure since I doubt his testimony will help us."

"I know it won't. What can we do?"

"I'll think of something."

"What does that mean?"

"Raúl, you asked me to help you. You came to me with this problem and trusted me over other lawyers in Miami. I promised you that I would solve this for you and I will."

Feeling the confidence in Thomas's voice, Raúl relaxed, and Thomas sensed the tension of the situation fade.

"Thanks Thomas, I know that you will. Have a good evening."

"You too, Raúl."

Thomas twisted away from the phone and concentrated on the paneling on the wall. A moment passed and he sat in his chair, staring at the fat brown expandable folder on his desk.

Brushing off the useless deposition that lay next to it, he reached for the expandable, found a thin green file, and opened it. He examined the list of the things he would have to prove in trial to win the case. The general contractor was the keystone of the case, but with him gone, he had to figure out how he could win without him. He grabbed a second expandable containing all the documents that would be presented at trial, including contracts, notifications, correspondence, and notes between the parties. Grasping inside, he retrieved a yellow file labeled *Lease agreement*. From there, he broadened his search to find *remodeling documentation* and *notifications from the county*.

Thomas sat back and smiled. The general contractor had been such an entertaining and knowledgeable witness in the first interview that the documents seemed like mere verification of what the witness was saying, but the more he read and reread the pages before him, the more he realized that the documents told the story he needed all by themselves. They were not as colorful or as interesting as the general contractor had been in that first interview, but they certainly did the job, and the judge would realize it. There would be no jury that he would need to keep interested, just a judge that wanted to hear the facts as quickly as possible so he could finish and go on to the next case. Thomas rose from his chair, grabbed his coat from the hook behind the door, and turned off the lights in his office.

"Susana," began Thomas.

"Yes, Thomas?" answered Susana.

"Please call Mr. Morales and his son-in-law and ask them to be here tomorrow at 1:00pm to go over their testimony for trial. Then, please contact all the subcontractors that worked on the job and make appointments for them on Friday, we need to review everyone's testimony. Those that can't come on Friday, have them come on Saturday and if they resist, remind them that they have subpoenas for trial. Would you make sure that Mr. Morales plans to be here on Friday and Saturday all day, if necessary. As for his son-in-law, I don't need him on Friday."

"Okay. Lunch on both days?"

"Friday and Saturday? –Yes."

"Will do."

"I might need you this weekend to help me rearrange my trial notebook." Thomas noticed that her face went pale and then he remembered. "Lord, it's your engagement party this weekend, isn't it?"

She opened her mouth to speak but he continued.

"Never mind, I'll ask Laura to come in and that way we can spend time together even if I have to work."

"Thanks Thomas," said Susana, smiling.

He smiled back and walked out the door into reception. A few seconds later, he closed the building door, got into the front of his Cadillac, and drove off, heading home to his wife and son that were waiting for him.

Chapter 31: The Cuesta Trial

Miami, Florida: June 1970

The courtroom brimmed with light as the Miami sun beamed through the windows on the western wall. Thomas stood before his client, Raúl Morales, testifying on the stand, as Judge Mathis looked at them from the bench.

"Did there come a time when you advised Cuesta Properties LLC, the owner of the building, that some work was needed on the exterior of the building?"

"Yes," responded Morales, staring at Thomas intently.

"Was that work necessary in order to make the outbuilding, the one that you rented, suitable for a daycare?"

"Yes, the leak in the roof ran down the wall and created mold inside it, and that would endanger the kids and the staff."

Thomas walked around the podium, leaving his notes behind.

"Did the landlord do anything in response?" pressed Thomas.

"He sent an unlicensed handy man, to patch areas that clearly required more work than just a patch."

"Objection and move to strike the response," began Raymond, standing from behind his desk, "Your Honor, unless the witness is a qualified expert in roofing and construction, he is in no position to testify as to what was needed in terms of repairs."

"Mr. Lock?" inquired Judge Mathis, looking at Thomas and waiting for a rebuttal to Raymond's objection.

"Your Honor, it does not take an expert to understand subpar and unlicensed work won't solve a major leaking problem. The witness is answering from his own daily observations, but he is qualified to answer as to the suitability of this space to be used as a daycare given the leaks and the mold as he is licensed in several locations."

"I'll allow it but be careful not to stray from that and request an expert response. Your witness does not hold a license in construction or roofing, does he?"

"No, Your Honor, he is solely the owner of the daycare."

"Understood, but please keep in mind that Mr. Morales is only testifying in his capacity as a daycare owner and not a construction expert and your questioning, in this regard, must be to the suitability of the space as a daycare only."

"Yes, Your Honor," responded Thomas, and shifting back to Raúl, continued, "Raúl, did the Defendant send a licensed roofer to make the roof watertight?"

"No, he did not."

"Did you send any form of communication to the landlord, expressing the need for a licensed company to do this work?"

"I sent him several notes and one formal letter, which you drafted, that I signed," he replied, pointing to the desk to Thomas's side. Thomas turned from Raúl to the table he pointed at. He signaled his desire to retrieve documents from Henrietta Little, the court clerk, who nodded her approval. Thomas moved toward the table, grabbed the evidence, walked over to the defense table, and handed the documents to Morris, who glanced at them and, nodding his head, returned them to Thomas. Thomas approached the stand and handed the pages to Raúl.

"Raúl, I am showing you a series of documents marked Plaintiff's Exhibit 4, 5, and 6 for identification. Do you recognize these documents?" he asked, handing a set of documents to Morales.

"I do," nodded Morales.

"There seems to be a signature on the bottom of each. Do you recognize those signatures?"

"Yes, they are all my signatures."

"What are these documents?" queried Thomas, opening his palms towards the ceiling, demonstrating that he had nothing to hide.

"They are the notices I sent the landlord." Thomas advanced toward the Judge's raised desk.

"I'd like to move these into evidence, Your Honor."

Judge Mathis turned to Defendant's counsel.

"Any objection Mr. Levine?"

"No, Your Honor," answered Raymond.

"Madame Clerk, please mark them, for the record," ordered Judge Mathis. "What are they?"

"Plaintiff's Exhibits 4, 5, and 6, Your Honor," said Henrietta. Her dark hand choked the pen as she scribbled on each page. After writing the word *Exhibit* and the corresponding letter at the bottom of each page, she handed the papers back to Thomas while the judge made his own notes.

"Thank you, Ms. Little," said Thomas, turning his attention back to the witness. "Did you ever receive any response to these letters?"

"No." He placed the letters back on Henrietta's desk and walked toward the witness stand. "Did there ever come a time when the work on the premises stopped?"

"Yes, about fifteen days after the last notice was sent to the landlord."

"What happened, Raúl?"

"I was at our other daycare when I got a phone call from my son-in-law, Elías. He told me that there was an inspector from the county to check the beam that we had put in. Elías told me that the inspector had told all the workers that work had to stop immediately as he was going to write a stop order and that work would not be allowed to continue. Of course, when he said that, I started thinking that there would be no way for me to get the place ready by the fall. I told Elías to keep the inspector there, that I would be there ASAP." Raúl closed his eyes for a moment and coughed into his hand before composing himself again. "Luckily, the daycares are only about ten minutes apart from each other."

"Why so close?"

"Because it is an underserved area. The state told us that if we expanded there, we would have a lot of clientele. There were a lot more families that had applied for subsidies to pay for the daycare and the area had no schools to place the children in. That's when we decided to expand."

"So, this is a daycare that the area needed?"

"Yes."

"When you arrived was the inspector still there?"

"Yes, he was."

"Did you speak with him?"

"I did."

"What did he tell you?"

"Objection, Your Honor, hearsay," interrupted Raymond, rising again from behind his desk to object. Cuesta's blank face did not twitch or move as Thomas continued with his examination.

"I'll rephrase, said Thoams at once. Could you continue the work?"

"No."

"Did he give you documentation to that effect?" Thomas fixated on Raúl's answer and hoped that Judge Mathis and the rest of the court did as well.

"Yes," affirmed Raúl, nodding his head in agreement. Thomas walked to the clerk's desk.

"Could you please hand me Plaintiff's exhibit 8 for identification?"

"Of course, Mr. Lock." She reached over to the end of the desk and grabbed the document.

He turned from the table, made a gesture toward Raymond, who nodded, and then Thomas walked back to the witness stand, glanced at the page, and pointed his index finger at a section of the document.

"Raúl, would you please inspect this paper and tell me if you recognize it."

"Yes, it's the document that was given to me by the inspector who stopped at the daycare to inspect the job."

Thomas walked to the clerk's desk.

"And where have you kept this paper since that time?"

"In my records for this construction," responded Raúl.

"I'd like to move this document into evidence." Thomas turned around to see Raymond's face, waiting for his next move but he made no objection.

"Mr. Levine," interjected Judge Mathis, "while I appreciate the nod, the court reporter needs a verbal confirmation from you for the record."

"Without objection," said Raymond flatly.

Thomas gave the clerk the first document. Then he grabbed a second document which she had placed on the far corner of her table. He turned and walked to the Defendant's table where Raymond declined to object. He glanced at the judge, who nodded, and Henrietta took the document and wrote *Plaintiff's Exhibit 9*. Grabbing both pieces of evidence, Thomas strode towards Raúl and showed him the first document.

"Do you recognize this document?"

"That is the order to stop working."

"Raúl, would you read this paragraph?"

Raúl grabbed the document and began to read in a very slight Hispanic accent.

"Arrived at the permitted location to inspect a load bearing beam in the interior of the space under permit MDC 043529. Because it was raining, in the process of inspecting the beam, this inspector observed water penetrating the interior space both from the ceiling and the exterior wall on the north side of the building. Upon closer inspection, mold was plainly visible, and it became evident that haphazard and unsuccessful repairs had been attempted for the wall. Due to the presence of the mold, I am halting any interior work and mandating that the building be vacated until the exterior is repaired and the mold removed by a licensed specialist. A letter will be sent to both the owner and the occupant of the space. Eduardo Palacios, County Inspector." Raúl finished reading and looked up at Thomas. "That's all it says."

"Did you forward the inspector's order to the landlord?"

"Yes."

Thomas received the document from Raúl and handed him another.

"Do you recognize this document?"

"Yes."

"I delivered the original personally and kept two copies. I just spoke about the first copy, and this is the second."

"Why two copies, aren't they the same?"

"No."

"How's that?

"That is the copy of the stop work order signed by the landlord's receptionist, also kept in my records with the other one. The delivery was to their main office. I had the receptionist sign the copy and date it. Look right here," he said, pointing to the bottom left-hand corner of the first document."

Thomas took back the second document and ambled back to the clerk's desk thinking. He handed her the documents.

"So, one is the copy you gave the receptionist to sign and then you kept it."

"Yes."

"Did there come a time when you were ever able to complete the work needed to be done so that you could open the daycare in the space you had rented from the landlord?"

Raúl lowered his head and tilted his eyes toward the floor before speaking in a soft voice a little louder than a whisper. "No, the work was never done because the stoppage was never lifted due to the outside repairs never being finished."

"How long did you pay rent for that space?"

"Eleven months."

"Were you ever able to open the daycare?"

"No."

"Why?"

"Because the landlord never did the work, so the inspector never lifted his stop work order and we couldn't open."

"He did not perform the repairs?"

"Never, and I lost everything I invested in trying to fix up the place, not to mention what I paid in rent."

"Thank, you Raúl."

Two hours later, after all the evidence was in and the lawyers had finished their closing statements, the courtroom was perfectly quiet. The judge, after finishing a few notes, looked up from his yellow pad, and addressed the parties.

"I have reviewed the documents, including the lease, the material from the building department and the summaries of expenditures. I have listened to the testimony carefully as well as the closing arguments on both sides. Based on all the evidence before me, I find in favor of the Plaintiff in the sum of $220,000.00. Mr. Lock, please draft the final judgement for my review and signature. Send a copy to opposing counsel for his review. Mr. Levine, I will wait five days before reviewing and signing the judgment so if you have any objections, please let me know immediately, and submit them in writing to my office so I can consider your comments in preparing the judgment."

Cuesta lowered his head and tried to hide his reaction. His wife behind him stood up to address the court but he turned and shot her a look that caused her to stop and sit back down. The attorneys stood up and thanked the court. Cuesta and his wife made their way to the door before Raymond could pick up his papers and collect his files.

Chapter 32: The Restaurant Down the Street

San Sebastián, Spain: June 1972

Thomas and Laura passed the sign indicating San Sebastián and breathed a sigh of relief. The ride from Asturias had taken longer than expected and they felt a pang of guilt in leaving Gabriel behind, but he would be okay with his grandparents and cousins.

"I know it's hard leaving him behind, but we need some time to ourselves, and we shouldn't involve him in this. He's still too young."

Laura held back the guilt as much as she could.

"We don't know what's going to happen, but let's pray that it goes well."

"Look at the bright side, you always wanted to go to San Sebastián," said Thomas, trying his best to lighten the mood.

"Yes, I always wanted to come here, and we have your new clients to thank."

Thomas moved over to farthest lane, pressing the brake a bit to allow another to pass him, so that he could take the exit toward their hotel.

"We got lucky that they decided to meet here and not in Rome. I guess the Italian company wanted to get out of Italy," he said, chuckling,

Laura laughed at the thought and settled her nerves a bit.

"I just hope that Enara and her uncle are okay and doing well."

"Be positive. It was a miracle that she survived, that the church found him, and that we're even here, so we must trust that the miracle is still going. We come to Asturias every summer, but what were the chances that this meeting would even be here? –This is from above."

They arrived at the hotel as the moon shone above them and from the higher elevation, they could see the lights of the city below as well as the sea meeting the bay.

"The summer home of the kings," said Thomas, taking the bags from the trunk of the car and handing the key to the valet. The young man assisted them with the rest of their belongings before taking the car to the parking lot. As they checked in at the front desk, Thomas left a tip for the valet and asked the receptionist to call a cab for him and Laura as they would be heading into the city shortly.

A short while later they had continued in the cab into a poorer section of the city. The cabbie had been very talkative, explaining how the neighborhood was a working-class area that was not rich, but knew how to live life. The cab came to a stop in front of a six-story building that needed a considerable amount of paint. They paid and thanked the driver for his company and walked toward the double doors. They were locked and could only be opened by a key or a person inside letting them in. They looked for the buttons on the wall and to their surprise the buttons only went as high as the first floor. Laura opened her purse and rechecked the note from Father Pedro. The address was clear; Enara lived on the sixth floor. "Well dear, it looks like we'll have to wait," said Laura, looking up at the building.

They were delayed fifteen minutes in finding their way into the old building. As they climbed, they noticed that the inside of the structure matched the outside and although the marble stairs represented a luxurious past, the stone was chipped and dirty and harmonized with the abandoned look of the dilapidated structure. The elevator was out of order, but five flights of stairs had gotten their blood moving and hearts beating. All the floors had an apartment on each side of the stairs but upon reaching the last landing, they found one door on the right and an opening to the roof top on the left. The door was small and did not even have the decayed luxury of the others, just old, scratched wood.

Several knocks on the small door brought no response, so Laura walked across the hall and on to the rooftop terrace. Thomas followed, after one last glimpse of the small door, and found Laura close to a half wall looking out into the distance. As he came towards her, a breathtaking view began to appear below. He could see a good portion of the city and in the distance, he could see a small strip of glimmering dark bluish green that he imagined was the bay. She smiled and put her arm around his waist. "What an unbelievable place this is. Being surrounded by history and beauty is a great way to grow up."

"As long as she gets to see it and enjoy it," he said in a somber voice. He turned, walked back in. Laura followed and they knocked once more. In response he heard a far-off female voice. He knocked again and the female voice responded like a mismatched echo. Suddenly, Thomas realized it was coming from below. Laura went to the top of the stairs, looked down, and saw an older woman looking up at her and signaling her to come down. She began down the stairs and this time Thomas followed.

As soon as they hit the landing below, she began speaking in rapid Basque.

"Do you speak, Spanish," asked Thomas in Spanish, hoping that she would understand.

"Of course, I do!" she said nodding her head, with a joyful look, "What may I do to help?"

"We've come from America to meet Enara and her uncle, Eneko. Do you know if they still live here?" asked Laura.

The woman gave them an uneasy look. Thomas, sensing her distrust, reached into his coat pocket and pulled out an old worn picture of Enara and her family from before their passing.

"Her mother, Itziar, was my friend when they moved to Miami years ago," said Laura, pointing to the picture.

The woman nodded and understood.

"Itziar was a good woman. I was sad to hear that she had died."

"You knew her?" asked Laura.

"A little. She would go to mass at the same time as my family. I remember when Enara was baptized in the basilica, Saint Mary of the Chorus, on Easter Sunday when she was little."

"Do you know where she is?" asked Thomas, pressing the issue.

"She works at a restaurant down the street from the basilica called, The Cepa. It's across from the basilica. It should be easy for you to find if you look for the church. She should be there now and maybe Eneko too."

"Thank you," said Thomas, shaking her hand. Laura thanked her with a hug and the couple set off, down the stairs and on their way to the basilica. Laura and Thomas made their way north, passing streets with small restaurants and boutiques as their shoes clapped against the stone ground of the old Donostian streets. They looked from side to side, searching for the basilica and from there they hoped to find The Cepa. Passing Calle Enbeltran, they looked up to see the top of the basilica and so continued down Calle Mayor, taking a moment to enjoy the streetlamps that illuminated the thin balconies that lined the street. Some apartments had plants and others sported nothing more than the walnut shutters on either side, but the view was gorgeous, and Thomas was happy that this part of town, where Enara spent most of her time, was nice. They arrived at the basilica and paused for a moment, taking in the view of the baroque architecture and stunning sculptures, but knew that they couldn't delay.

"Santa María del Coro," said Laura aloud, genuflecting as she said the name.

"The Cepa has to be around here somewhere," added Thomas, unsure of which way to go. The street stopped in front of the basilica, and they could either go east or west, but couldn't see any signs of The Cepa and the woman from the building didn't tell them to go left or right. An elderly man walked in their direction, so Laura called out to him. He smiled and nodded as she asked him for directions. He turned around and pointed down the street, gesturing that it would be on the right side as they headed east. Laura thanked him and took off with Thomas following behind her.

They walked for five hundred feet before they came to an awning that bore the name *The Cepa*. Through the window they could see the square tables surrounded by dark wooden chairs on the opposite side of a long bar where the wine glasses and meats hung from the ceiling. Patrons sat eating, talking, drinking, and laughing all in this restaurant tucked into the street. As they looked through the windows, searching for Enara, a blond, green-eyed woman smiled at them and said, "please come in, we are still open."

"Thank you," said Thomas, after a moment.

"Table for two?" asked the lady.

"Yes please," responded Laura.

"I am Amaya the manager and, I have the perfect one for you and I will take care of you myself. What brings you to my humble restaurant?" she mused and led them to the table next to the large window. Thomas pulled Laura's chair out for her and then sat across from her. "Some wine?"

"Yes, that would be wonderful," said Laura.

"Enjoy!" replied Amaya with a smile as she sauntered away.

"Its's almost as if she knew we were coming." commented Laura.

"The old lady from the building probably phoned her to say she gave us directions, and we were coming."

"Thomas Lock, you are so bad. The mind of a Lawyer, always suspicious."

He chuckled and then Amaya was back.

She came walking back with a bottle of white wine and three goblets, "What would you like?" she asked in accented English, placing the bottle on the tabletop and serving all the glasses. She turned and pulled a chair toward her.

Laura glanced at Thomas, surprised by the action and the English.

"You must be wondering how I speak such good English. Well, my husband, may he rest in peace, was an American volunteer soldier who fought during the civil war. He came in one day and never left." She chuckled, "He taught me English, and I taught him how to cook. He became a great chef, loving food until the day he died."

"When did you lose him?" asked Thomas.

"Five years ago, last March. He was the love of my life, but life goes on and does not wait for us to recover. I have always taught Enara that."

"So, you know Enara then?"

"Could you imagine if I didn't as the manager here? It wouldn't be so good if she worked for me and I didn't know her," she said, laughing.

"Do you know her well?"

"Yes, I've known her for years; she is a gift from heaven."

"What do you mean?" asked Thomas.

"She walked into my life. How did my husband used to say? Liter…something."

"Literally?"

"Yes. My Husband used to say this all the time."

"What do you mean?" inquired Laura gently.

"One Saturday morning she came into the restaurant. I had seen her walking down the street with a gentleman that I learned later was her uncle, but I had never met her. Even though most people in the neighborhood know each other," she continued turning to Thomas. ""That Tuesday morning, she *arrived* at my restaurant, and said to me, 'I am hungry, I did not eat yesterday. I did not eat the night before that; I know it's early for scraps, but do you have any leftovers that I could please eat?' I looked into her eyes, and I did not see sadness, just determination. It was before opening, so I sat her at this table," she said point down in a circular motion, "and gave her leftovers from a party we had held the night before. I asked her, 'don't you live with your uncle?" Amaya looked at each of them. "She admitted that she did and immediately defended him saying he was a good man who had made a great sacrifice for her. So, I said, 'I do not understand, why can he not feed you?"

Amaya shuffled in her seat as she poised herself to continue the story.

"The sum of the story is that he spends his money on alcohol. You see he is a musician that used to play for the traveling circus. He cannot stop drinking except when he is on the road, with the circus, and surrounded by people he has known all his life. They take care of him, so he stops drinking. He gave up the circus and his friends to accept and take care of her. Staying in one location was one of the conditions of the adoption because she needed a stable home since her family died in that terrible traffic accident and he is the only blood relative she has, so he accepted the responsibility. But, between you and I, she's sacrificed much more than he has."

Thomas moved uncomfortably. "I didn't know any of this."

"Like I said before, she will be coming home soon, and you can see her."

"Sure, but you don't understand. At my parish, San Juan Bosco, the priest, Father Amos, corresponded with Father Pedro here about Enara and about four months ago, the letters stopped."

"That's because Father Pedro's sister got sick and he requested to move to the south of Spain, to Granada."

"Never been," admitted Thomas, "we've gone as far south as Toledo, but I've never made it to Granada."

"Beautiful city, Granada; the Alhambra especially, and the Albaicin too."

"How did she end up leaving her uncle and moving in here?" asked Laura, bringing the conversation back to Enara.

"She did not leave her uncle. She would never have done that. She came back on Thursday and asked me if I would give her a job after school in exchange for dinner and breakfast. She was twelve and I could have given her the food without work, but I understood that her pride would not have let me. So, I made the deal, as you Americans say," she said with a smile.

A questioning look from Thomas made her go on.

"Well not having her home gave Eneko the chance to drink a little more and a little more until it was hard for her to go home because of what their little place had turned into. She was also afraid he would hurt himself when she wasn't there. One night one of his circus friends came into town and saw his condition.."

Laura quickly thought in Spanish, "Borrachera," she said in Spanish.

"Yes, he was so drunk that he didn't even recognize his friend. The friend, I think his name was Ibai, came into the restaurant the next morning and spoke to me first, to find out why she was there, and then he spoke to Enara. At first, she could not break her attachment to Eneko, but then she finally understood that if her uncle kept drinking like he was, he would die. The friend stayed several days while we made papers and then Eneko gave me papers saying I could take care of her and put her in school and go everywhere with her in his name."

"Powers of attorney," said Thomas, affirming the story.

"Yes, that!" she responded.

Laura turned to Amaya, "You have made a nice home for her."

"I have tried."

The chef came in with the food and placed it on the table. As he left the room, she turned to them and said, "Obviously, Enara has grown up since you last saw her."

Laura and Thomas had inquiring looks, but she smiled.

"Father Pedro was a terrible detective, so it took him forever to discover where Enara and Eneko had gone to, but then, he was a worse secret keeper once he finally finds out whatever he is trying to find out."

"So, you knew who we were as soon as you opened the door?"

"You see tourists do not come to this part of town to have lunch, and when I went on and on about Enara without either of you changing the subject, well that confirmed it. The fact that Mrs. Esposito from the building called me to tell me she had sent you over here after you spoke to her did not hurt.

"Wow, are we that bad at being sneaky?"

"No, you are that bad at being dishonest." She responded with a chuckle. "So, do we tell her who you really are?"

"Who's that?"

"The Americans that wanted to adopt her. The people who took care of her night and day after the accident and the man and woman that gave her love every day until she recovered."

"Father Pedro does have a big mouth!" said Laura laughing.

"He is a kind soul without any malice. I do not know what life would have made of him if he had not been a priest," said Amaya shrugging her shoulders.

Thomas heard the door open behind him and before he knew it there was a uniformed dark-haired young woman kissing Amaya on the cheek.

"Tourists?" she asked. Her eyes circled the table and for the first time she noticed Laura and Thomas.

"I am so sorry," she said in accented English. "I'm so happy you are here; I get to practice my English. I do not practice enough in school and Mamá, and I do not have time while we work because everything moves so fast."

"We can speak in English if you'd like, but we can also speak in Spanish," said Laura in Spanish, smiling.

"Oh, are you Spanish?" asked the young woman.

"I am American, like my husband, but I was born in Spain."

"Oh, how cool," she said with teen enthusiasm. "How did you meet?"

"My parents moved from Asturias in Spain to Miami, Florida and I met my husband when I graduated from the College, and he had just begun practicing law in Miami.

"I lived in Miami, with my parents. We were going to make it our home. My Father worked for an American Airline company. My parents even took my brother and me to church as little kids."

"We know, Enara," said Thomas, removing his glasses to clean them.

Questions circled Enara's mind, and her face bore a bewildered expression.

"Why did you say my name, like you've always known it?"

"Sit," offered Amaya, grabbing a chair and pulling it over.

Thomas cleared his throat and looked at Laura before fixing his eyes on Enara's dark ones.

"I've known you for sixteen years," he said, pulling the photo of Enara and her family outside of San Juan Bosco in Miami and showing it to her.

Enara's eyes widened and grew upon seeing her past life.

"We've met but you won't remember when or how," responded Laura.

"When?"

"We were friends of your parents during your time in Miami."

Enara studied both Laura and Thomas, but she was very quiet.

"Your mother and I became good friends during the year that you lived in Miami."

"When your family died in the crash, the church asked us and three other families if we wanted to adopt you. No one knew about your uncle until the news reached the parish here and they told us about him, but for a month, you were in the care of the church and, by extension, us."

"The church chose you?"

"Yes," answered Laura, reaching for Enara's hand, "I was the closest with your mother and since she and I were both Spanish from the north, the church thought that it was best that you come and stay with us until everything was formalized."

Enara's eyes watered at the revelation. Amaya sniffled and reached for a napkin to blow her nose. Enara wiped her eyes with her arm choked on her tears.

"You look so familiar. I knew that from the moment I saw you through the window that there was something about you, but I couldn't tell from where."

Thomas retrieved another photo from his coat pocket. In the photo was a little boy and a younger girl.

"This is our son, Gabriel. You played together for that month that you stayed with us. You used to say your prayers at night thanking God that you had a brother again."

A tear escaped Thomas's eyes, and he inhaled deeply, fighting to hold them back.

They all cried for a few moments, allowing the grief to run its course while the relief of finding each other again set it.

"You came all this way for me?"

"Yes," answered Laura, "we stopped hearing from Father Pedro a few months ago and Father Amos at our parish told us that he wasn't sure why. So, when we didn't hear anything about you, we decided to come as soon as we could and since we go to Asturias every summer, we figured that we would come here to check on you."

"And luckily, it looks like you've got a family of your own," said Thomas, nodding to Amaya.

"I do," affirmed Enara through the tears. "Are you in town for long?"

"We'll be here for a few days," answered Laura.

"Can we talk for longer or do you have to go?"

"We have all night, Enara. Don't worry, we're not going anywhere."

Enara smiled and choked on more tears but didn't care. They spent the whole of dinner and dessert talking as Enara told them about her life without them and they enjoyed the daughter they never had.

Chapter 33: The Suits and Ties

Miami, Florida: June 1982

Sarah sat on the sofa admiring the sun on the wall.

"How do eggs and chorizo for breakfast sound?" he asked, from the kitchen. Sarah agreed and he made his way to the stove.

As they finished the breakfast dishes Sarah asked, "Are we going to get those suits you wanted?"

"If you don't mind," said Gabriel, running water over the used dishes.

"I'd love to. Where are we going, Saks, Brooks Brothers?"

"I usually go to Schein and Sons, so I was wondering if you wanted to go with me?"

"I would love that."

"Let me finish these and we'll go," he said, gesturing to the dishes.

A half hour later, they jumped into the car. He turned the key on the Ford, and it coughed. Ticked, and finally caught as the motor came to life. "You keep saying my bug is ten years older than your Mustang, but my bug doesn't do that when you start it, she said as they stood in front of a men's clothing store three blocks from the expressway in the garment district. "When are you going to either get a new car or a classic in decent shape?" To change the subject, Gabriel pointed at the door. "This is where you are buying the suits?" asked Sarah, eyeing the building from the door to the roof.

"The suits are good."

"I like that it's tucked away," admitted Sarah as they moved toward the building.

A short balding man greeted them when they entered.

"Mr. and Mrs. Lock, so good to see you."

Sarah giggled and Gabriel thought to correct him, but Sarah waved him off.

"Mr. Lock, your suits are ready if you would like for me to retrieve them."

As he walked away to get the suits, Sarah whispered to him.

"No need to embarrass him."

"That is Aaron Schein, the owner."

Schein came back walking quickly towards them with two suits in hand. One was a royal blue three-piece suit and the second, a double-breasted bone colored linen suit with no vest. He hung them up near the three-part mirror. He took the blue jacket off the hanger and draped it around Gabriel's shoulders.

"That color really does match your eyes," said Sarah, eyeing the jacket. She moved and grabbed the linen suit, feeling the material in her fingers. "This linen is wonderful. Now I see why you came here."

Schein smiled at her. Gabriel, stretching his arms out and allowing the jacket to settle, stepped toward the mirror. Sarah looked at his reflection and the coat fit beautifully. Out of the corner of her eye she saw Schein pulling slightly at the suit causing her to giggle. Sarah decided to be playful.

"Why don't you try on the vest and pants to the suit? The jacket looks very nice."

Schein turned his head to her slightly, realizing that she had noticed. Sweat broke out on his balding head, running down to the hair on his sides in the shape of a horseshoe.

"I don't think it's really necessary, Madam."

"Oh, I won't have it any other way. I want to see my husband dressed to the nines."

Gabriel's upper lip curled, and his eyebrows dropped as he squinted his eyes. He tried to ask her what she was doing, but her bemused smile was too hard to read.

"If you insist, Mrs. Lock," surrendered Schein.

Gabriel stepped back from the mirror, allowed Schein to remove the jacket, and took the pants and vest that Schein held outstretched in his hands. When he returned, the pants felt a bit loose around his waist.

"You look like you've lost weight, sir," added Schein as Gabriel stared down at the drooping waistline.

"Yes, I've convinced him to work out a lot lately. It's done wonders for his constitution," joked Sarah.

Schein handed him the vest, going so far as to help him put it on before standing right behind him again. When Gabriel shifted to his side, Schein moved with him, making observations about how impressive the color looked on him.

"Let's put the jacket on now so we can see the whole thing," pressed Sarah. Gabriel moved to reach for the jacket, but Sarah stopped him. "No dear, I really liked it when Mr. Schein put it on you. Let him do it again."

Schein lowered his head. He unclasped the fabric in his hands and crossed over, reaching for the jacket. Gabriel felt the vest and pants immediately expand but chose to say nothing. Schein dressed Gabriel in the jacket and, taking a step backward, allowed it to fall into its natural position. Everything looked bigger and looser.

"What happened?" asked Gabriel, "why doesn't it doesn't look the same?"

"Further adjustments need to be made; I think." she said, raising her eyebrows at Schein. Sweat beads slid down Schein's face and pooled on his balding head.

"Yes…of course."

"Why don't we take off his jacket and start with the pants?"

"As you wish, Mrs. Lock."

Sarah walked over to the linen suit from earlier as Gabriel made his way to the changing room.

"Mr. Schein," began Sarah pointing at the linen suit, "was this suit finished properly?"

"It was," admitted Schein, raising his head.

"Darling, will you try this one on before you put your normal clothes on?"

Once they were done redoing the fitting, and Gabriel had gone to change into the linen pants, Sarah stared at Schein, raising her eyebrows, and flaring her nostrils.

"My tailor quit a few days ago because a place down the street offered him better pay. My main tailor, who is my partner, and nephew, is out of town and won't be back until tomorrow. Your husband called yesterday to say that he needed the suits by today and I had no choice but to try to fix them myself. I used to be a very good tailor, but it's been years since I've done the work, and it was harder than I thought. Times have been tough, and I needed this sale. Thank you for not giving me away. I promise I will wait until my nephew comes back to make the new adjustments and I won't charge for them."

Sarah looked at the man's expression, searching for sincerity.

"I would like to pick out two ties, one for each suit to give to him as a present, can you help me with that?"

"Certainly," answered Schein, bowing his head. At that moment Gabriel came out wearing the linen suit. It looked like it was made for him.

"What do you think?" he asked.

"Incredible." When Gabriel went in to change, Sarah walked to the tie racks and picked out two ties, giving them to the owner and asking him to ring them up before Gabriel returned.

"No, no charge."

"If I don't pay for them, then they are not my gift, they would be yours." she said as she handed him her credit card. Schein walked to the register, rang the order, and returned, ties in hand.

"I'm sorry, Mrs. Lock."

"For?" asked Sarah, unsure of what he meant.

"The suits."

"Deceit is not a strong color on you, Mr. Schein, but I must admit that the linen suit looked made for him. I'll give you the benefit of your situation, but you'll lose clients if you misuse their trust." Sarah raised her head and glanced around the store, nodding and gesturing to the inventory. "You have a good selection and a lot of variety, so don't waste it. Do that and you'll do well again."

"Thank you, Mrs. Lock."

"My great-great-grandfather, Johannes, who my grandfather called Bestevaer, began as a tailor in New York City. He had a small shop but worked with pride and always did fine work. When he was thirty or so, a wealthy man needed to replace a jacket after someone had ruined it. Bestevaer tended to him immediately and earned his trust and formed a friendship. Realizing the quality of his work, the man invested in Bestevaer's store. In a few years, Bestevaer had more than five locations and money to spare. I would recommend that you rely on the same principle of trust, Mr. Schein. Trust goes the furthest."

"Yes, Mrs. Lock."

Gabriel came out wearing his clothes and carrying the linen suit over his left arm. Sarah turned to the owner. "When can we return for the other suit?"

"I'll have it delivered to Mr. Lock's office."

"That would be fine," said Gabriel.

"Would you like the ties now, Mrs. Lock?"

"What ties?" asked Gabriel, shifting his attention from Schein to Sarah.

"The ones I am giving you," she shot back.

"But…"

"They are my present to you, and you will accept them, or I will be offended. After all, I am your wife."

"Yes, God forbid the children see you in such a foul mood," he whispered.

"That is very wise, Mr. Lock. No child should ever have to see a mother in anger!" agreed Schein.

"If you ever forget again, I will leave you with our four kids and have a girls' night."

"That could be a lot of trouble, Mr. Lock."

"The trouble would be so bad, you'd swear someone imagined it, Mr. Schein."

Sarah giggled and Schein nodded. Offering his arm, Sarah took it, and they exited Baranson's, both trying their best not to laugh.

Sarah excused herself to use the ladies' room. Gabriel placed the receipt inside his wallet. He glanced at the picture and decided if it might be time to take it out. He heard her coming back and quickly closed his wallet.

They rounded the corner and crossed the street before entering the car.

"I've never had an experience like that," said Sarah, buckling her seatbelt.

"Quite a place, isn't it?"

"It's quaint for such a large inventory."

"The design is pretty bare and to the point, definitely a men's clothing store instead of a women's clothing store."

"Yeah, women wouldn't stay based on that interior."

"I loved watching him pull the fabric to make it seem right."

"He would have had me had it not been for you."

"You would have spotted it sooner or later."

"Maybe." Gabriel accelerated onto the highway heading back to his apartment. Wind blew from the east, and he decided to lower the windows of the Mustang, allowing the cooler air to filter through. "You know, Sarah…"

She stared at him, waiting for him to continue.

"Thank you for the ties, but you didn't have to get them for me." He glanced at her for a moment before returning his eyes to the road.

A sly smile escaped Sarah's face.

"Thank you, Gabriel. That's very thoughtful of you but don't worry they are just ties."

"What do you mean?"

"They are not an engagement ring. They are just ties."

"I didn't mean it that way." He blustered

Sarah's face brightened as she laughed. Her freckles became the backdrop of blood flushing her skin. Anger tinged her voice and Gabriel kept silent. "I can afford the ties, Gabriel. They are no big deal. I could have bought your suits and paid for the tailoring one hundred times and not noticed a dent in my accounts. The number of spaces before the period wouldn't have changed. Please, don't treat me like I'm some young lawyer who works at a small firm to make ends meet. That's not the world that I come from."

"I was just trying to be nice."

"You were, but I can handle my finances, Gabriel, I have a trust from my grandmother which permits me to live in Miami, work wherever I want, and rent a nice house in Coral Gables, fresh out of law school,." She paused and neither of them spoke for a few moments. Sirens and horns sounded from beyond the chassis, but silence filled the interior. "My father runs a Hedge Fund. With my grades and his influence I could have joined any firm in the country, but I chose to work at a small general practice firm to stay connected with people and to find a little more meaning in my day. I don't want to be the chief legal counsel of a fortune five hundred company, the head of a large law firm, or even a renowned litigator. That was a gift of freedom my grandmother gave me. I have always wanted to work for disadvantaged people in a legal aid society or something of that kind. It's what makes me happy. I look at my profession as a tool to serve others."

"So do I,"

"I know and that's one of the things I like the most about you."

Chapter 34: The Nocturno Cabaret and Cigar Bar

Miami, Florida: June 1982

The music boomed as the partiers swayed and danced under the disco lights in El Nocturno. Pierre Cardin, Versace, Yves Saint Laurent, and Louis Vuitton did little to improve the class of those who sported them. Otoniel Prío shifted his eyes around his nightclub, watching women throw themselves at lowlifes for the promise of a good time and Marimberos sizing each other up from their shoes to their watches. As he watched the filth around his nightclub, he shuddered as it reminded him of how different El Nocturno was from what he envisioned it to be. To his right, an obese Marimbero sat in the middle of a couch in the shadows along the back wall with two brunettes half his age. As they sat fake laughing at his shit jokes, he ran a free hand down a backside as the other pulled the closer brunette in for an unwanted kiss. To his left, a table of well-dressed shitheads toasted to a night out and a new big deal closed. In this joint, big deals were the chance for some of these drug runners and criminals to live it up before they died or got locked up in jail.

He interrupted his musings, saying hello to a group of ladies who come to the club at least once a month. They always came together and never danced with any of the men that always begged them to. *They're probably the only smart women here*, he thought. Walking over to their table, he greeted them and thanked them for coming. "Are we treating you well?"

"Yes, like always. You serve the best Mojitos in town," said a dark-haired woman with light eyes.

"Thank you very much. Please enjoy your night and if there is anything that I or my staff can do for you, just let us know."

"Thank you," they said in unison.

As Otoniel returned to his post and watched the packed crowd, his lead bouncer José Carlos nodded at him from the far wall before continuing to make his rounds. Six bouncers under José Carlos's command worked tirelessly to keep drugs out of El Nocturno. It was Otoniel's number one rule, but for a man who hated drugs, all the biggest drug dealers in Miami seemed to love him and his nightclub. He lowered his head and let it hang as he leaned against the counter of the bar, massaging his temples and trying to keep the exhaustion at bay.

"Jefe," came a voice from behind him. He recognized it as Calixto, his lead server.

"Dígame," answered Otoniel, commanding his employee to speak.

"Those two in the corner don't dance and don't drink; they're selling." Otoniel raised his head and looked through the sea of people to the opposite corner, to where Calixto instructed. Two men conversed. Neither had a drink in front of them.

"How long?" asked Otoniel, pressing Calixto for how long they'd been there.

"More than one hour, boss. They reject even water."

Otoniel snickered to himself, shaking his head.

Shitheads will always be shitheads, he thought to himself. Turning back to Calixto, he met the dark eyes and noticed the tilted bowtie on his tuxedo.

"Busca a José Carlos y sácalos por favor. Calladito y sin escándalo por favor," he ordered, making sure to avoid a scandal when throwing them out. Calixto bowed his head slightly. As he turned to find José Carlos, Otoniel stopped him.

"And Calixto, that tuxedo looks perfect on you, but fix your bowtie, it's crooked," he said in Spanish, complimenting Calixto's tuxedo and reaching over to fix his bowtie. "Perfect." Calixto nodded his approval at the perfected bowtie and set off to find José Carlos.

The lights shone as the music blared, and Otoniel found himself crossing the dance floor. Women eyed him up and down, groping him occasionally as he passed. He was handsome, and aged well as he approached his sixties, but while he didn't mind the passes, he loathed the drugs and the people who used them. He did not permit people selling drugs in his place and these two had to go. As he approached the corner, he saw the two shitheads rise from their table as José Carlos and two more bouncers guide them toward the exit. A few moments later, José Carlos came and stood by Otoniel.

"Nothing happened," said José Carlos, referring to the men who gave him no trouble.

"I'm glad. What did they have?" he asked, curious to know what they had.

"Cocaine, I made them throw it out in the grass," he said, as he moved his hands like he was throwing out the drugs.

"Why not in the river?"

"Because my son likes to fish, and I don't want that shit in the water." Both men laughed.

"Did you recognize those guys?"

"No, they must be new or must not know about this place. With how many drug dealers we have here, you'd think that if they would know, at least, some of these people's men, so they'd be a little more careful or stay out of my place all together." As he finished, he looked around from table to table, noting which ones had the drugs dealers that they knew about. Otoniel coughed into his hand, clearing his throat.

"Honor is a word dealers ignore, but class is something they know nothing about. Don't forget that."

"I won't. I can promise you that."

"Good. Do me a favor, walk with me."

"Sure, one second."

José Carlos looked up at his second in command, Salvador, who stood near the entrance. He gestured with his head toward Otoniel and then motioned with his hand that he would be speaking with the boss in private. Salvador understood and signaled for one of the other bouncers to take his place while he moved to where José Carlos and Otoniel were now.

In the background, Otoniel heard the music shift from Salsa to Merengue as he and José Carlos made their way to his office in the back. Closing the door behind them, he offered José Carlos a seat before taking one for himself behind the desk.

"You've downgraded," joked José Carlos, looking up and around the office.

"I had no choice. I took the real office and had to turn it into a bedroom for when I have to sleep here."

"Yeah, I know. We're doing the best that we can."

"I know that you are. It's not your fault. I had envisioned this place to be like what my family had in Cuba before Castro. Nocturno in Havana was a classy place. Nocturno in Miami has become the place for drug dealers and lowlifes."

"No everyone that comes here is bad. There's been less drug deals in the club lately." Otoniel smiled wide.

"No, the drugs are the same, they've just gotten better at hiding it."

"A few years ago, just the price of a single drink would have kept this riffraff out of this club, but times have changed. Day by day the drug trade increased in this town and the classy club by the river became the perfect place for the dealers to wait for their supplies." As Otoniel spoke, he pulled a thin, gold-plated box from the breast pocket of his tuxedo. Opening it to retrieve a cigarette, he offered one to José Carlos, who declined. Shrugging it off, he raised a lone cigarette to his mouth and steadied it with his lips as he lit it and began to smoke. He exhaled with relief and closed his eyes for a moment, enjoying the buzz that came from the nicotine as it clouded his lungs.

"That's going to kill you someday."

"JC, please. I'll bet you a gentleman's bet that one of these lowlifes shoots me first."

"I'll take your wager."

"Just remember that you've got a kid. Don't take a bullet for me just for a dollar."

"Oh, don't worry. I won't." They both smiled at each other.

"Seriously though, I need to know if you've heard anything from anyone that you've thrown out about things getting more serious with drugs in this club?"

"I haven't. Why? What's going on? – Is it the police again?"

"Something like that. They want me to inform for them." Otoniel blew a large puff of smoke out. As it rose from his lips, José Carlos waved it away. "Sorry."

"Not a problem. As for the police, if you inform for them, these monsters out here will kill you."

"Yeah, don't remind me. I think that my days are numbered."

"Don't say that."

"Just wait until you're my age, you'll see things a hell of a lot clearer." As he finished his sentence the lights came on and the music stopped. "¿Quién encendió las luces?"

Both men rose and bolted through the door. As they did, A rush of blue uniforms burst through the front door into the club, marching straight towards a table in the back. Otoniel looked over to José Carlos, "Do what you have to do." José Carlos signaled to the other bouncers who moved to the middle of the dance floor, separating the crowd. It parted, knocking over tables and glasses. Glass shattered and women screamed as they surrounded a table with three men. Two men dressed in street clothes lifted a short slight man with olive skin from his seat. Placing his arms behind him and crossing his wrists they placed handcuffs on him. and immediately began to drag him away. Otoniel noticed one of the patrons near him make a move towards his hip but before he could, Otoniel stepped in front of him and gave him a glance that was so penetrating that he immediately stopped, turned around, and began looking for an exit like everyone else. "I thought so," he said aloud.

As the police dragged their man out, Enrico Igaravídez and Román Escalona walked towards him. "To what do I owe the pleasure of your visits, Captain and Chief Inspector?" On the inside, Otoniel was screaming "Fuck," as they stood, but kept his cool.

"Mister Prío," said the Chief Inspector, "Nocturno is hereby closed."

"Gentlemen, we can meet anytime tomorrow to straighten out whatever issues are in violation before we reopen."

"Mr. Prío, it is closed until further notice by order of the city," continued Escalona.

"Based on what?"

"Building code violations, to say the least. The list is long."

Before Otoniel could utter another word, Captain Igaravídez pressed him.

"Here is a warrant to search the premises. If there's nothing here, my officers should be in and out in no time."

"I have personnel placed everywhere to try to control the sale and use of the drugs but I, like you, Captain, am not always successful."

"I'd hold that tongue of yours, Prío, if you know what's good for you."

"Or you'll do what, Captain?" Igaravídez smiled to himself as he moved closer to Otoniel.

"You know, you have a lot of bad people that come into this place. A lot of bad people that we're interested in. If you really cared about your establishment, your staff, and your livelihood, you'd help us catch some of those people. This isn't the first time that we've had this conversation." Otoniel leaned forward and, choosing his words carefully, spoke.

"You know Captain, you have a lot of citizens to protect, a lot of people that look to you as a beacon of hope. If you really cared about the uniform that you put on and what it means to find justice, you'd have caught them already, but you like the power that you have, and you'll use it on everyone." Otoniel pulled back as the captain's face burst red. "Search my place, but you'll find nothing, just as you've found nothing before." Igaravídez raised his chin.

"Search the whole place from top to bottom. Examine everything," he shouted to his men. "I know that you'll do whatever voodoo you do with the county, and you'll get whatever permits you need, but so help me God, if you don't inform for us, I'm pulling the concealed carry permits of every single one of your bouncers and then this place, your good patrons, and your employees will have no one to protect them. Test me, Prío. Test me." Igaravídez turned and walked away. Otoniel looked over at José Carlos who processed what he heard.

"Everybody, go home. I'll take care of this," he shouted to his staff. José Carlos came up to him.

"Do you want me to stay?" he asked. Otoniel shook his head.

"No, go home to your wife and son, I'll handle this."

"What are you going to do?"

"I'm going to make a phone call to an old friend of mine."

Chapter 35: The Impasse

It was early morning, and he had a day off from court. As he entered his office, Thomas called him.

"Son, come to my office as soon as you get a minute." Gabriel turned on his heel and sauntered over to his father's office.

"Close the door," ordered Thomas, glancing up at his son from his papers. The door clicked behind him and Thomas stared at him from behind his thick glasses. "What is on your calendar today?"

"I was handling a matter with the Ménéz case."

"Jérôme or Hervé?"

"Jérôme," affirmed Gabriel.

"What happened?"

"He had second thoughts about settling the dispute and wanted to litigate."

"To which?"

"To which Hervé intervened and explained that it wasn't in their best interest to go to court."

"Hervé's always been a bright man," complimented Thomas, smiling. "So, what else happened?"

"I explained that court could make it worse and they could end up losing a lot more than the settlement is offering." Thomas tilted his chin upward, inviting Gabriel to continue. "After a while, Hervé and I got his son to agree."

Thomas nodded his head.

"Well, I'm glad that you resolved that. Well done. Can you join me in an hour and clear up your schedule?

"I'm free already, so yes, what do you need?"

"Do you remember Otoniel Prío?"

"The nightclub owner?"

"Yes, him."

"Yeah, what about him?"

"He needs our help."

"Alright, what time do we need to be there?"

"The sooner the better."

"Alright, let me grab my jacket."

"Great, I'll drive."

Gabriel and Thomas arrived at *El Nocturno*, a few minutes earlier than the scheduled time. As they pulled up to the lot, there were six cars already there. They looked up to see a white-haired man in his mid-fifties with a humble gut and light brown eyes standing outside the club, waiting for them.

"Still have the boat?" asked Otoniel, pointing at the 76 Cadillac. Thomas looked back at the El Dorado, eyeing the burnt burgundy exterior and its white vinyl covered landau roof.

"You, more than anyone else should know that you don't throw out gold." Gabriel facepalmed upon hearing the pun in Thomas's reply. Otoniel showed his teeth as he sported a wide smile and stretched out his hand. Thomas rejected it and instead embraced him. Otoniel embraced as well.

"What a pleasure to see you again," said Otoniel, grateful upon seeing his old friend again.

Taking a moment to straighten his tie and remove some of the wrinkles from his suit jacket, Gabriel waited for an introduction. "¿Tu hijo, no?" he asked Thomas, observing the young man to his side. Gabriel met him square in the eyes.

"Yes, this is my son," confirmed Thomas, opening himself up to introduce Gabriel. Otoniel offered his bear-like hand. Gabriel took his and shook. The man's grip bore unusual strength, and Gabriel could tell that those hands belonged to a man who used to work the fields.

"It's a pleasure," said Gabriel, addressing him formally.

"Welcome to Nocturno. Please come in," affirmed Otoniel, moving to the side and allowing the lawyers entry to the club. The three men journeyed together toward the middle of the club. "Would you like any refreshments?" Gabriel shook his head, declining the offer for refreshments and instead asked if there was a restroom. Otoniel pointed to a small hallway to their right and Gabriel departed down the corridor.

A few moments later, Gabriel found his father seated on a Plexiglas and leather chair looking rather uncomfortable. "It turns out that in a few minutes we will be joined by both Police Captain Igaravídez and Chief Building Inspector Escalona. They will discuss the situation with us and there may be an assistant city attorney with them when they arrive." The switch to English caught Gabriel off guard.

"Noted," said Gabriel, looking around the small office, searching for a comfortable place to sit. Finding nothing except for the chairs in front of the desk, he asked if Otoniel had a good relationship with either Igaravídez or Escalona. "No?" checked Gabriel as Otoniel shook his head. "–They can stand then." He moved to one of the open seats in front of the desk. Thomas gave his son a disappointed look as he shifted in his seat. The alteration brought a grimace that Gabriel tried not to laugh at.

"I've known the chief inspector since he began at the city and have had matters with him through the years for various clients," began Thomas, turning to Otoniel and continuing in English. "Would you mind showing us some of the construction that was done without a plan or permit?"

"Yes, of course. It's just through here," he answered in accented English. He rose from the seat and the three of them left in a single file toward a room on the other side of the wall. Next to the office was a spacious bedroom with a king-size bed, dresser and two nightstands. Gabriel observed an extra door that led to a full bathroom with a shower. "This is illegal construction," said Otoniel, waving a finger from side to side, indicating the entire bedroom.

"I see," said Thomas, making a mental note of it. All of it, or just the purpose of the room?"

"The purpose. This was originally a storage area where we put the extra bottles, tables, chairs, and everything else. That use was approved when we built the building."

"That's good to know." Otoniel held the door open for them as they exited, going through the outer office before heading outside. They stopped in front of a storage space that had been connected to the building in back. "I take it that this is illegal construction?"

"Absolutely. No doubt about it." Thomas and Gabriel chuckled at the man's conviction.

"Ah, Otoniel, what am I going to do with you?" joked Thomas.

"What you always do when I call you, just shake your head." Thomas shook his head and half-grinned.

"Alright, can this storage unit be legalized and permitted or is there no shot?"

"If I remove two feet off the storage space and reinforce the structure a little it will meet the setback requirements as well as the code for storage space."

"That's what I figured," answered Thomas, moving around the exterior of the space, inspecting it bit by bit and moving his eyes from the top to the bottom. "Any chance that you can put a window in your bedroom?"

"No, there's nowhere to put it."

"Do you need to have a bedroom in the club?" asked Gabriel, shooting Otoniel an inquisitive look.

"Son, if you ever own a nightclub like mine, you'll see why I have a bedroom here, and it's not because it's that kind of nightclub."

"I was about to ask if you rented by the hour."

"Why? –Looking to use it?" inquired Thomas, chuckling as Gabriel formulated his response.

"No, I don't pay for my nocturnal activities."

"You should try it sometime; it's like having a girlfriend that actually does what you want for the money you spend on her."

"Gentlemen, please let's stay focused. Gabriel, mind your elders. Otoniel quit giving my kid a hard time. Look, a building like this cannot have a bedroom because that makes it mixed use. There is no mixed-use residential commercial in this area so I would need a variance, and the city would never grant that. So, you can set up an office with a sleeper sofa and alter the interior of the office credenza and a filing cabinet so you can store clothes in them. That would solve your permit issue. Are you okay with that, Otoniel?"

"I can become okay with that."

"Good. That solves one problem, but let's talk about the monkey that you've got on your back."

"What about it?"

"I know that the city probably doesn't care about the permit violations about a club on the river, so clearly Igaravídez is harassing you for another reason. What does he want from you?"

"The same thing that the police want from every nightclub owner."

"Yeah, I figured as much," answered Thomas shaking his head. Gabriel felt like something was missing and didn't click into place.

"Forgive me, it's still a little early for me. What do they want?"

"They want him to be an informant for them. They want him to rat on the lowlifes that frequent his nightclub as if throwing them out regularly wasn't enough impetus to leave him alone." Otoniel stared down at the floor below them.

"Because of the people that come here. My beautiful dream has become the place for all the Marimberos that are a plague on this town. The police know that these animals bring in their drugs through the river but can't seem to catch them. So, the Jefes congregate here, near the river, where they wait, drinking expensive champagne to get the good news that their shipment made it in. They are so close to the river that they get the news almost immediately after it happens. I look at all the groups that congregate here on any given night and wonder when the rivals will end the truce. Some time ago, they all agreed that this club was a safe place for all of them to come. If that truce ends, it will be a shootout. If it comes to that, then a lot of my employees and the honest patrons would die and if that happens, I wouldn't be able to live with myself."

"That's why you closed down once before, right?" asked Thomas, still pensive about the options.

"Yes, but there were no face lifts or repairs when we closed the first time, and it didn't work. I can't kick them out of here because if they decide I have disrespected them, they may shoot me or worse, shoot some of my people. If I co-operate with the police, the same. I was afraid these macho guys would get into in one night and it would be a disaster, so I closed hoping they would find another place. It didn't work because as soon as I reopened, they came running back. Not only back but celebrating the reopening as if the place were theirs. They were buying each other drinks for God's sake. I'm out of ideas. I think I will have to close and any possibility of achieving my dream will be gone."

"Before we reach any of those conclusions, we need to hear what the people from the city have to say. Maybe I will find a way to satisfy them and gain time for the drug pestilence to be over. Then, you will be able to bring back your dream," said Thomas very seriously. Gabriel and Otoniel stared at him, surprised at the weight of his stance. "But first, the police will probably get here soon so we should return to your office."

A few moments later, there was a knock on the office door. Otoniel looked at Gabriel who reached for the door and opened it. A short woman in her late forties entered.

"Los señores que usted espera ya están aquí. ¿Los hago pasar?"

"Of course. Have them come in." Otoniel crossed the small room and greeted the two public officials immediately. Captain Igaravídez and Chief Inspector Escalona entered the small office and shook hands with both Thomas and Gabriel.

"Lock and Lock. Good to see you again, Gabriel, Thomas," said Igaravídez with a stern look.

"Nice to see you again, Captain," said Gabriel, "Chief Inspector Escalona, it's a pleasure." Thomas gave a disinterested look to both public officials and smiled to himself. Igaravídez noted it but said nothing.

"Gentlemen, let us not meet in this office, but in the conference room that I have in the back."

"Is that new construction too?" asked Escalona in smartass tone.

"No, that room is from the original plans that you approved of. I can assure you of that." The five of them exited the small office and walked over to a room on the opposite side of the bar, crossing the main hall and past the seating area where the dinnerr tables were. They stepped through the doors of a room that harbored a long wooden conference table surrounded by six armchairs on the other side of it. "I want to thank you for responding to my invitation to meet so quickly. Would you like something to drink, Perrier, soda, or water?"

"No, we are all fine, Prío, thank you. Let's cut to the chase," barked Igaravídez.

"What's the matter, Captain? –Upset that you couldn't get the fat cats last night?" prodded Thomas.

"I will do whatever is required of me to cooperate with you. I do not want these people in my club either," interjected Otoniel, attempting to cut the tension in the room. Thomas stared Captain Igaravídez down, not blinking, or breaking concentration once. Igaravídez's face became tinged with red, his eyes focused, and he did not blink either. The two men stared each other down. "However, I will not cooperate with you by giving you information, it would be obvious if I did that and I am afraid they will take it out on my people, and they will be hurt too in order to show me lessons, and I will not shut down permanently. So, tell me what it is you would like this business to do."

"Ideally," said Igaravídez, not moving his eyes from Thomas's, "we want to shut all these guys down. To do that, we would like information on them which we believe that you have or could have. That information would be crucial for us, as officers, in carrying out our duties and protecting the great people of this great city. Our city."

"I understand that, and if I were in your position, I would want exactly what you have laid out," responded Thomas, "but, as you just heard from my client's mouth, that is not going to happen. My client is concerned about his people, all of which are young and inexperienced. The wellbeing of the innocent citizens of Miami should take priority over a practice that may put them in harm's way." Igaravídez scoffed.

"I've seen them handle themselves, and they are professionals. The other night, before the arrest, they escorted two guys we had our eyes on and, well they were very quick and efficient in escorting the two guys out of the premises." He closed his hands in front of himself and intertwined the fingers of both hands.

"Still, they missed the guy who you arrested only minutes later," countered Otoniel, also turning to look fully at the captain,

"He wasn't selling in your club," responded the captain, "He was doing a deal with several undercovers and changed the deal to this location at the last moment. We did not like it, but we had no choice but to comply or lose a year of work."

Otoniel rose from the table and began to pace in the middle of the room. "You endangered the patrons and my people. You did not even warn us that you were coming to take measures," he erupted in a low growl. "I had to stare one of them down as he made a move towards his holster. Another one of my guys had to grab another guy's hand and whisper, if you do, they will kill us all. Both stopped, but they could have just as easily continued and then what? How many patrons would have died?"

"I noticed you did not mention officers," said the captain intensely, now glaring at the Otoniel. Gabriel went to intervene but caught Thomas slowly shaking his head.

"I did not mention Marimberos either. Both groups know what they are doing and even the drug runners, in a manner of speaking, are professionals. They know the risks. The Marimberos know that in five years they will probably be dead or in prison. Your guys know that there is always the possibility that one of these people may shoot them. The public is not any of this."

"Yes, but the people that come here know the type of club you run here, and they are aware of the risk. They know that a shootout can happen at any time."

"No, they don't really know," said Otoniel, a tone of defiance echoing in his words, "But I do, and it worries me. It keeps me up at night. I don't sleep and when I do it turns into a nightmare featuring people lying on the ground shot dead all over my club. I am perpetually tired and run down."

"Close it," volunteered the Chief Inspector.

"I did, but I found that my other businesses could not pay the debt on the club, and I was going to lose everything and put seventy families out on the street without jobs. So, I did a light remodel and tried to reopen as a different club so these lowlifes would stay away from here, but they didn't. It didn't work."

"So, inform on them, Prío, it's your best option," barked Igaravídez.

"Absolutely not, Captain. I am not going to risk my life or the lives of my people."

"Then it seems that we are at an impasse." The red tinge in his face turned scarlet.

"I'm afraid, Mr. Prío, that if you don't inform for the police, then we are going to have to do everything we can to keep you closed," said the inspector pointing at Otoniel. Thomas slammed on the table with both fists as he rose, knocking the chair backwards and crashing it against the wall.

"No, you are not, Chief Inspector. No one threatens my clients that way. You have no right, and you know it. You will not bully and harass my client to serve your gain at his expense. You will not abuse the power bestowed upon you by the badge that you represent and the citizens you swear to protect. I'll go to every paper in this town and tell them about what you've said here today. You will not close this place down because you both are incompetent at doing your jobs, and I will make sure there is plenty of information to back me up. Have I been unpleasant enough?" The two men glared at Thomas. Rage emanated from his cerulean eyes. "Now, let's turn the page, become collaborators again, and get back to solving the problem because we will not accomplish a thing unless we do so together!" "Captain, Chief Inspector, let it be the last time that I ever hear you threaten one of my clients. So help me God, this had better be the first and only time." No one dared to speak, and a few moments passed before the tension eased. Thomas's glare dissolved into a slight smile, but no one moved. Igaravídez's scarlet face looked pale compared to Thomas's. The grayed lawyer collected himself before speaking in a more polite tone. "What is it that you would like here other than closing this place down?" The captain leaned toward Thomas.

"We would like the Marimberos to stop using this club as their communications center. This place gives them an excuse to be close to their shipments without running the risk of getting caught. It's the perfect cover and it needs to stop."

"We'll, we are all on the same side then," Thomas concluded the other man's comments.

"What we need is a successful club that they won't want to come to under any circumstances," said Otoniel.

"Yes, but other people don't drive these guys out, these guys drive other people out," observed Gabriel.

"That would be the formula, but how do we accomplish it is the question," mumbled Escalona.

"I want out of this problem, for the sake of my people and my business I need to finish this just like you do."

"I just gave you the solution. You follow this, and I could get behind that. You do that, and I'm willing to be very flexible," offered the captain.

"I'm not going with your plan, but I need to find a way."

Chapter 36: The Propositions

Miami, Florida: July 1982

A short while later the meeting was over and the two city officials made their way to the exit, followed by Gabriel, Thomas, and Otoniel. As they watched the uniformed men part, Otoniel noticed a tall thin woman with olive skin, midnight hair, and deep black eyes leaning against her car on the outside. He delayed a few moments in recognizing her as one of the ladies that came in together once a month.

"Olá, tudo bem?" she asked him.

Otoniel smiled.

"My Portuguese is not the best, so let me not embarrass myself. You are Rafaela, right? – You come in with the same group of girls once a month, right?"

"Yes, I am Rafaela and yes, we come in once a month. I see that you're closed?" she said eyeing the club up and down and hinting at the closed sign.

"Yes, for repairs and to upgrade the building to code."

"Is that what you're going to tell people?"

"Yes, think that they'll believe it?"

"Not a chance, but it's a better excuse than most."

"I see," said Otoniel, looking from the closed sign to Thomas and Gabriel and then back to her.

"Is this a bad time," she asked, raising her head toward Thomas and Gabriel.

"Not at all," said Thomas, "we we're just leaving."

"That's a shame. I had a proposition that I wanted to share with you."

"Oh yeah?" asked Thomas, amused, "Well, so long as neither of you mind, I'd like to hear it." Rafaela grinned.

Gabriel interrupted, "I am expected at the office for a meeting with a client, so I'll leave you in better hands than mine" he said to Otoniel and the rest. The group watched him walk away and out the door, each of them contemplating their own thoughts.

"May we talk about it over a drink?" Otoniel smiled.

"Sure, let's all go inside. I've got just the drink for the occasion." They returned to the conference room except this time, Otoniel brought a bottle of Bacardí, four cans of Coca-Cola and four lime wedges. After making four Cuba Libres, he passed them to Rafaela, Gabriel, and Thomas before taking a sip.

"So, Mr. Prío, I have a proposition for you that will eliminate your problem with the Marimberos, solve whatever issues you have with the police and city, and at the same time, cut out all of your competition in one go." Gabriel and Otoniel gave very confused looks while Thomas gave a sly smile.

"How do you plan to do that?" asked Gabriel, still confused.

"Yes, Rafaela, how do you plan to do that?" asked Otoniel, running a hand through his grayed hair. Rafaela glanced over at Thomas who still smiled slyly.

"You seem to know what my plan is, Mr…"

"Lock, Thomas Lock. The young man here is my son, Gabriel, and we are the attorneys for Mr. Prío. I have an idea as to what you are proposing, but I'll let you tell it. It's your idea."

Rafaela grinned, then turned back to Otoniel.

"Your problem is not the club itself, but the people in it, as you know. I have overheard you telling José Carlos that this club is not what you wanted it to be and it's because of the Marimberos. They have created problems for you with the police and have made you violate building codes, but we know that those changes you made were because you need to protect your people and so you even sleep here when things get crazy, right?" Otoniel nodded but kept silent. "The only way that you can get rid of everybody is to change the nature of the club."

"What do you mean?"

"I'll tell you, but you have to agree to my terms." Otoniel smiled, intrigued by her assertiveness. He reached for a Cuban cigar from his breast pocket and a lighter from behind the bar. He brought the flame to the cigar, inhaled a bit, and blew a puff of smoke into the air next to him.

"I'm listening."

Chapter 37: The Chalk Line

Miami, Florida: July 1982

Gabriel stared at the chalk drawing on the pavement. The drawing, and the darker spot inside of it, were the only remnants of the violence. Above him, the metal roof of the gas station shielded him from the sun that beat down onto the asphalt and chalk. He looked up, taking in the two squad cars and officers still on the scene. Gabriel turned and saw a short brunette, with tan skin and inviting eyes, emerge from a red Honda Civic hatchback just beyond the police tape. As she made her way to the edge of the border, he noticed a small clipboard in one hand and a pen in the other. *Insurance adjuster for workman's comp and right on time. Santiago's going to love this negotiation*, he thought. She looked at him from across the police tape, and he strode over to meet her.

"I am Clarissa Berkley from Simpson's Adjusters out of Fort Lauderdale, nice to meet you, Mr…"

"Lock, but please call me Gabriel. I represent the owner, Mr. Santiago Alemán." Gabriel stretched out his hand, and she took it. The warmth of her hand lessened the firmness of her grip. *Assertive. This should be fun*, he thought.

"So, would you mind filling me in on what happened here, counselor?"

"Given that this is an ongoing investigation, I have no real results to offer except that an individual that worked for my client is deceased from a gunshot wound, there is a police representative, Sergeant González, that you are more than welcome to speak with when he frees up." Gabriel pointed over to González and Clarissa gave him a trying look forcing Gabriel to counter with a slight grin. Studying him, she sized him up from head to toe and prodded again.

"So, when may I speak with the corporate representative?"

"You already are."

"Don't tell me that we are going to play games here, Mr. Lock."

Gabriel continued with his grin but treaded delicately.

"The officers of the company know no more than I do. I have been asked to gather as much information as I can and relay it to you. No other employee, shareholder, or member of the company or any of its agents was present when this happened except the deceased. As you can understand, we do not know what the outcome of your investigations will be, but we advised you immediately as is our duty under the policy."

"I understand but I will have to take a sworn statement at some point."

"If it comes to that, you will but remember this is also a murder scene and both the police and the prosecutor may not want statements taken just yet by people who are not cleared to do so."

Gabriel and Clarissa walked around the small property together and Gabriel patiently waited as she took pictures of everything relevant to her work.

"You are very thorough, Miss Berkley."

"And you are very sharp, Mr. Lock. I think that you are the first man that I've met who has noticed that I'm not yet married." She held her left hand up, showing off the enormous diamond on her lone engagement band.

"Well, that stone pretty much seals the vows. It should ward off most men."

"Just not the cunning ones, right Gabriel?"

"Merely an observation, Miss Berkley, nothing more."

"And my observations tell me that you are not going to give me anything that would let me handle this claim for Mr. Alemán any faster. Am I right in my calculations?" She asked as they walked toward the Civic.

"If you were handling it for Mr. Alemán, I would be more forthcoming, but you are handling it for the insurance company instead."

She laughed.

"I always walk a thin line."

Gabriel did not break his gaze as she sized him up.

"Integrity is a hard thing to find and harder to keep," he said, keeping his sight on her eyes.

"No, Gabriel. Integrity is like a good man, hard to find and when you do, it's only a matter of time before he lets you down."

"Metaphor or personal experience?"

"Both."

"Sounds like Shakespeare at his finest, though I prefer Molière myself."

"I'm sure that our John Doe would have too." She opened the door and just before she got in, she turned back to him. "I don't think that you and I will be sitting across the table in a dispute. I will tell you that this isn't the only claim that has been filed against this insurer for an incident where the clerk came outside in the middle of the night for no apparent reason. There was one about a mile down. Luckily, the shot did not hit the young clerk but instead shattered the plate glass window which was not bulletproof. Now, it's a criminal case with no insurance proceeds and the clerk won't talk." She crooked her head back toward the chalk outline. "How old was the deceased?"

"Forty-two as of last month."

"Can you give me a name?"

The small lines in Gabriel's face folded, exposing a small set of wrinkles as he raised his eyebrows with a playful look.

"I don't have his full legal name. I can get you that information once I return to my office and receive the records from my client. I understand that you have reports to complete so I will get that information to you as soon as possible.

"Just call me when you get the information."

Acknowledging defeat, she lowered herself into the seat, fired the engine into life, and waited until Gabriel closed the door. She nodded and Gabriel smiled his goodbye as she pulled back onto the street and left. Turning back to the scene, the attorney shifted his cerulean eyes to Detective Sergeant González who waited for him.

"Friend of yours, Lock?" joked González, pointing with his chin to Clarissa.

"Could be, we'll see. Anything that you need from me?"

González shook his head.

"Just thank you for not giving her anything."

González stroked his five o'clock shadow on his freshly shaven face.

"Ya know, you really would have made a hell of a prosecutor. You really could help us clean up the lowlifes like the guys who cleaned his clock," he said, gesturing down toward the chalk outline. Gabriel glanced at it for a moment before returning to González.

"I have enough work as it is defending my clients from the parasites that want to ruin them." González snickered.

"Seems like this town is full of them."

Gabriel jilted his head.

"That's why you drive a classic Mustang, and I drive a Chevy Caprice."

"But in your world, you can tell who the bad guy is. It's not so easy in mine."

"So," exhaled González, "where're you off to now?"

"Back to the office. It's the beginning of a long day."

"Tell me about it."

"Well, it's time to go defend my client from the parasites that want to ruin him," said Gabriel, raising his eyes and referring to the insurance agent. González laughed.

"No rest from the wicked is there?"

"Nope, why do you think that only the good die young?" González and Gabriel shared a set of laughs before Gabriel headed back to his Buick. Before he opened the door, he paused, thought for a moment, and walked back to González. "Hey, has this neighborhood gotten rougher lately?"

"Like many others in this part of town."

"What do you think happened here?"

"You've got a hunch?"

"First guess from the neighborhood, drugs, but there's none on the body or even close to the scene, so I'm not so sure."

"Could have cleaned it up. It was still dark out," said González, looking at his watch, "it's only just after eight now."

"After killing a guy? The bullet wound was clean, which means that it was close and since there are no defensive wounds on the body, there was probably no struggle."

"After asking around, those who may have heard or seen something claim not to. Anyway, people on this street at that time of night are the type that don't see anything, don't hear anything, and disappear at the first sign of trouble."

"No witnesses?"

"No."

Gabriel scanned around the scene. He walked over to the chalk outline and González followed.

"Okay, so it was impassionate, nothing messy between the two men, but what I can't figure out is that if it's a deal, then why would he kill the guy if it went through?"

"A disagreement on price or supply, you think?"

González and Gabriel looked around the scene. After a moment, Gabriel decided against his earlier thoughts.

"If he knows the guy, then he comes out of the gas station. If he doesn't know him, then he stays inside behind the glass and has no issues. So, the guy on the outside was either under duress, had an issue with the pump, or was someone that the victim had seen before."

"There were no issues with the pumps, the techs checked. I'm going to concur with option three, Gabriel. He must have seen this guy before."

"Yeah, that's what I was afraid of."

Chapter 38: The Decision

Miami, Florida: July 1982

Gabriel arrived at the office by half-past ten. Closing the entrance door behind him, he was halfway across the waiting room when Susana pulled the sliding glass and peered at him.

"Mr. Santiago Alemán is here."

Gabriel checked over her shoulder to see if Santiago was behind her.

"He's in the main conference room speaking with your father."

"Would you mind making us some coffee?"

"It's right here." She held up a small glass so that Gabriel could see it.

"Let me put my things up and I'll be in shortly."

"The coffee will be right here." Susana placed the small cup on the corner of her desk.

"Gabriel, good to see you. How are you?" asked Santiago as Gabriel entered the conference room.

"Morning, Santiago. I'm doing well. How are you?"

"I would like to say that I am doing better, but as you know, I am not." "What did you find at the scene?"

Gabriel went through the basics at the scene.

"I suspect that we will have a police report in two days which would follow suit. As for the repercussions, the insurance adjuster and I spoke briefly."

Gabriel turned to his father after addressing Santiago's question.

"Hey Dad, how are you?"

"Fine Son, thanks," answered Thomas, placing the pen in his hand onto his legal pad.

"Did you give them anything?" asked Santiago.

"No, but I contacted her after she drove out. I just didn't expect her to be there as quickly as she was."

"You know insurance, charge as much as they can, pay as little as possible or not at all, and slowly bleed the client to death."

"Well neither of us want you to die and to prevent that, we need to figure out exactly what happened."

"I already told you everything that I know. I was there before the sun even rose. I don't understand why Jean Robert was outside. Besides all the exterior doors being locked all night, the station has an impenetrable area within it in case an attacker tries to get in. It has bullet proof glass, an incredible lock, and virtually no way to get to him. The rules are that, at night, my people do not come out of the store for any reason. We do restock at night but move the merchandise into the store before it gets dark because the little storehouse area is not as secure. If we are out of a product, we don't sell it, but no one comes out of the store; no one!" Santiago stood up from his seat at the table and stared out the window, racking his mind for additional details. "There is even a bathroom inside the secure area, so they have no cause to come out if there is danger. There is no reason for this." He finished quietly but with palpable anger in his voice. "I have been racking my brain to figure out what could have drawn him out."

"How long had Jean Robert been working for you?"

"A little over two years. He's got a wife and two kids that just arrived from Haiti six months ago. I can't even imagine how they are feeling right now."

Gabriel shuddered.

"Santiago, what else can you tell us about Jean?" asked Thomas, taking a pen to his notepad.

"Oh, well, he was a hard worker and was meant to replace Pepe when he retired."

"Who is Pepe?"

"Pepe is the gentleman who works the other night shift like Jean Robert."

"They work together?"

"Pepe works the alternating shift to Jean Robert and is a kind of manager of the store keeping an eye on the operation, like making sure that we order the right products, the correct amounts, and making sure the displays are well placed. You know, things like that and the physical part of the store. Claudio does the numbers while Lázaro and Baltasar also work at the station. I'll give you a schedule of their hours."

"Does Claudio only work one day?"

"Claudio works every day, but I have a lot of gas stations so he, along with a few other employees of mine, work one day at different locations. I have over twenty gas stations and five employees that roam and supervise. Claudio is one of them just as Jean Robert, Pepe, and Lázaro, and Baltasar have their copies at other locations."

Thomas nodded and continued jotting down notes. Gabriel kept silent, allowing his father to press the questioning.

"Do they overlap?"

"Shifts? For one hour at a time."

"I see, so Thursday night was Jean Robert's shift?"

"He was covering."

Thomas lowered his spectacles to the tip of his nose.

"What do you mean he was covering?"

"He and Pepe traded so that Pepe could see his granddaughter's play."

Thomas and Gabriel looked at each other.

"Is this the first time that they had traded shifts?" asked Gabriel.

"They had traded shifts a couple of times before. Pepe had made requests of Jean Robert and Jean Robert had made requests of Pepe, especially when his family arrived from Haiti."

Thomas interjected before Gabriel could speak.

"Understandable with his newly arrived family. What else can you tell us about their shifts?"

"Nothing really."

"Can you write out what their schedules are on this piece of paper, please?" asked Thomas, sliding a torn sheet from his notepad over to Santiago.

"Sure." Santiago borrowed a pen and began jotting the schedules. When he finished, he handed it back to the attorneys.

	L	M	Miér	J	V	S	D
23:00 – 7:00	Jean R.	Jean R.	Jean R.	Jean R.	Pepe	Pepe	Pepe
7:00 – 15:00	Pepe	Lázaro	Lázaro	Lázaro	Lázaro	Lázaro	Lázaro
15:00 – 23:00	Baltasar	Baltasar	Baltasar	Baltasar	Jean R.	Jean R.	Jean R.

"Thank you, Santiago. Would you mind giving us a list of the days that were changed for all their shifts?"

"From how far back?"

"The last three months should suffice."

"I can ask Claudio to give it to you. He's covering Pepe's shift while he runs the books today."

"The one that Jean Robert was supposed to cover."

"Yes."

"Santiago," began Gabriel. Thomas looked up at him, and Gabriel waited for his approval. Thomas gestured toward his son, giving the green light and Gabriel proceeded. "The insurance adjuster said something to me this morning that seemed very curious."

"What did she say?"

"She said that this was not the first shooting where a clerk had come out of the station in the middle of the night. She said that a previous one had happened a month before, but no one had died."

"I heard about this, but don't know too much more."

"How did you hear about this?"

"At the Ayesterán Bar."

"The owner?"

"The patrons," corrected Thomas before Santiago could react.

"The old dog's still got it," joked Santiago. "A group of us meet twice a week in the bar, have some drinks, talk business, and of course, politics and the liberation of Cuba."

Thomas grinned while Santiago's thoughts drifted.

"Think that we've got a lead?" asked Gabriel.

"I do," admitted Santiago, returning to the business at hand, "Thomas, what's your schedule for lunch today? Want to join me in finding out more?"

Thomas looked down at his watch.

"What time?"

"As soon as we're finished here."

"I've got a lot of work that needs to be done. I don't know if I can spare lunch."

"Come with me and I'll introduce you to a few people who are shopping for a new lawyer."

"You do that anyway," explained Thomas with a grin. Santiago looked up at him. "Yes, I'll come to lunch with you. I know that you don't want to be poking around the restaurant asking questions about the shooting because you don't want people to pepper you about the gas station. I'll take care of that for you. I'll be your shield." He picked up the phone on his desk, hit the clear button at the bottom of the receiver and, after a moment, said, "Susana, please change my afternoon appointment for tomorrow."

He hung up the phone and turned his attention back to Santiago and Gabriel.

"Okay then. Find out what information you can about this incident. I'll need to sit down with Jean Robert's family and ask them about it. I'll see if I can get to Pepe and the others too," said Gabriel.

"That sounds like a good idea, son. Let me know what you find. I expect that I won't see you until tomorrow."

"Probably not, but being that this is urgent, Santiago, can you meet us back here on Thursday?"

"Yes, I can, and I will."

Gabriel asked Susana to clear the rest of his afternoon before leaving the office to return to the Station.

Chapter 39: The Station

Miami, Florida: July 1982

The police tape still encircled the crime scene but didn't interfere with the other gas pumps. Seeing the exterior empty, Gabriel parked and entered the station to find Claudio seated in his chair, distraught, and motionless.

"Good morning, Claudio."

"Good morning," responded Claudio in accented English.

"Do you speak Spanish?" asked Gabriel. Claudio shook his head.

"I speak Portuguese."

Gabriel sighed, knowing that his Portuguese was not sharp enough to carry the conversation.

"Don't worry, I speak basic English good."

Gabriel nodded and reached inside his suit jacket. Claudio flinched and moved backward. Gabriel removed his hand from his interior pocket slowly, retrieving his business card and showing Claudio that he wasn't a threat. Claudio sighed and eased up as Gabriel handed the card to him.

"I am Gabriel Lock. I work for Mr. Santiago Alemán. I wanted to ask you a couple of questions about Jean Robert. Is that okay?" Claudio nodded and sat down in his chair. "Claudio, can you tell me what the procedures are for the store after dark?"

Claudio began explaining the nighttime protocol. He pointed up at the bulletproof glass and the other measures within the station that protected the employees.

"So, the inside is basically impenetrable, right?"

"Yes, the only way in is if the employee voluntarily opens the door or walks out."

"How many violent instances have you had here before?"

"None. At least, not since I started working with Mr. Alemán, but the threat is always present, especially at night."

Gabriel looked around the station to see all the food, alcohol, and other goods within the store.

"How much value do you think the merchandise in here has?"

"The goods are not that much because this is a smaller store, but about twenty thousand in merchandise."

"So why is the gas station open twenty-four hours if the merchandise isn't of high value and the neighborhood isn't so bad?"

Claudio smiled slightly and exited his post after looking outside to make sure that no one was around. He gestured to Gabriel to follow him and began showing him to different sections inside.

"You see these coolers? You see these pipes? These aluminum and copper wires over here?" he asked as he pointed to various places within the interior.

"What about them?"

"If nobody watches the place for two hours, all of this is gone."

"You can't be serious."

"This is Miami, Mr. Lock. Would you leave your briefcase anywhere unattended for five minutes?"

"A briefcase is much easier to steal than piping, wires, and merchandise from a gas station."

"Not for professionals."

Gabriel nodded. He knew that Claudio was right and began to question why Jean Robert left the store when the policy stated not to leave under any circumstances. He turned back toward the view from the pumps, analyzing the entrance points to the station.

"Claudio, was there any indication of things being stolen in the last six months?" Claudio shook his head. "Have you ever broken policy and left during a night shift?"

"Once, I saw a man collapse outside the Flagler station and I ran out to help him, but that was different."

"Why was it different?"

"Because the sun was rising and there were people walking around on the opposite side of the street. Not many, but enough. I called the police immediately when it happened and made sure to lock the store, but again, there were many people around and cars on the street. There is a great difference between day and night at this location, during the day you have traffic and people going into the grove area for work and other activities but at night there is nothing."

"What can you tell me about Jean Robert?"

"I didn't really know him well. Santiago can probably tell you more and so can Pepe. Lázaro and Baltasar could too. They worked with him a lot more than I did."

"Anything at all that you can tell me?"

"Jean Robert mentioned that there were two men who would occasionally come to the station and watch from afar, like they were surveying the place. He was always suspicious of it."

"Do you think that they were checking out the station to try and steal from it?"

"Possibly, it may have been their place of nocturnal business. About two weeks ago, he said that he hadn't seen them for a while."

"Any descriptions of these individuals?"

"No, it was dark. And these men never showed their faces. When Santiago and I asked him about it, Jean Robert couldn't confirm if they were black or white, purple or green. This neighborhood has people from everywhere, so everyone blends in by appearance."

"Understood," spoke Gabriel, nodding and making a mental note, "do you know where Jean Robert lived?"

"Yes, I have his and all of this station's employees addresses here in my notes."

"These stay in the store?"

"These are always with me and only in relevance to the station that I am working from that day. Personal and financial information does not stay here or at any store. No one's going to steal that." Claudio looked up at Gabriel. "You really don't know your hometown do you, Mr. Lock?"

"What do you mean?"

"Santiago has a walk in safe at the main office and everyone knows he's a rich man. The thick steel door has an impenetrable lock. Two years ago, they tried to rob it. They could not get in through the safe door so they drove a forklift through the wall, and they rammed the wall with the lift until they finally created an opening and then they widened the hole until they could get through. We had another station that was being remodeled, and we thought it was secure, but the thieves opened a hole through the roof and ceiling and striped the place of all copper, aluminum, and small equipment. The construction workers found the remnants of ropes and pulleys the next day and found one of their ladders leaning on the back outside wall."

"I guess I don't," joked Gabriel. Claudio retrieved the address from the files and gave it to Gabriel. "Thank you,

Claudio. I am going to see Mrs. Marchant. Lázaro works here tomorrow, right?"

"I'll let him know to expect you."

"And I should be able to see Pepe tonight, right?"

"Not tonight, tomorrow afternoon. Baltasar is going to cover the night shift tonight. Pepe and Lázaro will be there according to his schedule. Some of the employees from our other locations will help until we can hire a new person."

"What time would be the best for me to come by the station in the afternoon?"

"Three. They overlap for two hours in the afternoon.

"I thought that it was only one hour?"

"Not with the mess from the weekend. There are many things to do now that all of this has happened."

Chapter 40: The Collection Process

Miami, Florida: August 1970

Thomas opened the litigation file and saw the judgement at the very top. He smiled and read it slowly. *A final Judgment is entered in favor of the Plaintiff, Raúl Morales and against Defendant Cuesta. Plaintiff is due $197, 258.00 as principal, $ 7,334.00 as interest to date of this Judgment, with $481.00 for Court cost now taxed and that shall bear interest at the rate of 7% a year.* The victory had been sweet and the judge kind. He turned in his chair and reached for the phone.

"Good morning, Raymond, how are you?"

"Not as well as you are, I'm sure. I just got the judgement in the mail."

"No, probably not, but I didn't call you to rub salt on the wounds, I called you to see about payment of the judgement. When can we expect the money?" asked Thomas in an empathetic tone.

"Actually, not any time soon," admitted Raymond. A long silence filled both sides on the line.

"Why is that?"

"Well, in his last purchase my guy really overextended himself. That's why he couldn't come up with the money necessary to correctly repair the building."

"He went all the way through litigation and a trial. That would cost him more than simply having fixed it."

"No, that is not the case. The building's problems go deeper than what the inspector saw that day. The problems are in the foundation which is tilting the building and causing cracks both in the wall and in the roof. If he would have pulled a permit to fix the wall and the roof the inspector would have seen the real problems and those might cause a little over Two-hundred thousand.”

Thomas counted to three before answering, calculating his response, and selecting which strategy to take. He kept his composure, lowered his tone, and measured his diction.

“Now he owes my client a little over two hundred thousand and he is not collecting rent every month from his biggest space in that shopping center and his only stand-alone building on that property. With no tenant, how will he collect any money?”

The question hit Raymond hard, forcing him to pause and measure. “Thomas, we need to work out a payment plan.”

“My client needs the money now, not later. He’s signed a lease for the daycare at a different location, and he needs the money from the judgment for the build out.”

“My client doesn’t have the money, so he can’t pay.”

Thomas knew what Raymond said was true. He felt it from Raymond’s tone, but also from the client’s behaviors and the way the proceedings played out. Still, he had to investigate Cuesta’s financials before agreeing to any payment plan.

“Tell you what, Raymond. Get the financials I requested by the end of the week for me to review and then, if everything is Kosher, we can come up with a plan.”

“I will, Lock. I’ll have the financials to you by Thursday afternoon.”

Chapter 41: The Details

Miami, Florida: September 1970

Rain beat down on the tiles on the roof of the small building and Thomas found himself watching the clicks of his watch as the second hand continued its marathon around time. He cleared his throat, allowing a small cough to escape as he tried to trap it with his hand. Raymond Levine offered him water, but Thomas declined. As he reviewed the questions in front of him, a small knock came at the door. Raymond rose from his chair at the conference table and walked over.

"I'm sorry that I'm late, Raymond. The weather outside is horrible," said Cuesta as he walked through the frame.

"I can see that," joked Morris, pointing at the water marks on Cuesta. He greeted Thomas who nodded in turn.

"Give me just a second," requested Cuesta as he disappeared behind the door. Cuesta re-emerged holding a large banker's box and hoisted it onto the table opposite Thomas before sitting down next to Morris.

Morty, the court reporter, straightened the paper in his stenotype. His dark eyes focused beneath his bushy eyebrows and from behind his glasses as he took a sip of water.

"I'm ready to begin when you are, gentlemen."

"Raymond, let's get started."

"Okay," said Raymond, "Morty, please swear the witness in."

Cuesta raised his right hand in the air and Morty swore him in. Thomas began proceedings and asked Cuesta for his name and address, explained the format of the questioning, and then began the direct questioning.

Cuesta leaned backward in his chair and seemed to be listening for something as Thomas spoke.

"Is everything alright, Mr. Cuesta?"

Cuesta straightened himself up in his chair.

"Yes, sorry. I thought that I heard something. Please continue."

"I take it that the box next to you is a collection of all of your documents concerning your financials and other materials concerning the lawsuit with my client, Mr. Morales, correct?"

Cuesta nodded. Thomas flipped the pages in his yellow pad to read his questions.

"Mr. Cuesta, you have filled out the written questions I sent to your lawyer, and you reflected in them that the company has three multimillion-dollar properties, is that correct?"

"We do, but they are highly leveraged. We should not have bought the last one, but I felt that the value of the property was too good to pass up."

Thomas spread three documents on the table before Cuesta.

"I am showing you a series of deeds which were included in the documents your lawyer sent pursuant to my request for post judgement documentation. Are these the deeds for all the properties owned by your company?"

"Yes."

"Any other real property owned by this company?"

"No."

He picked up the deeds and spread new documents before Cuesta.

"I am showing you a series of bank statements from an account ending in 4387. Do these statements represent true and accurate copies of the last twenty months of statements for those accounts?"

He looked over the papers quickly.

"They do."

"Is there anything that I should know about this account?" asked Thomas, waving his hand over the papers.

"Not really, this one is our payroll account."

"Thank you for confirming that, Mr. Cuesta." Thomas picked up the papers before spreading another series of documents from his file. "I have a series of statements for a bank account also with Sunrise bank for an account ending in 0903. Is that a corporate account?"

"It's our general ledger account."

"Is there anything that I should know about this account?"

"All monies from rent and other income go into that account and payments are made to our creditors. At the end of the year, if there is money left over, we report it to the IRS. Nothing more than that.

"Okay," mused Thomas, nodding. "I would like to bring a series of cheques to your attention. They are made out to Julio Landscaping."

Thomas quickly selected nine checks from the ones arrayed on the table and handed them over to Raymond, who inspected them and nodded his approval as he returned them to Thomas.

"What does Julio Landscaping do for you?"

"They do our landscaping for all of our buildings."

"How long have they been doing your landscaping?" Thomas brought his hand to his chin.

"For a while now, possibly a couple of years. Why do you ask?"

"Has this always been their name, Julio Landscaping?"

"That I can remember."

Thomas removed another set of cheques from his files and handed them to Raymond as he had done with the previous group. Raymond examined them and returned them, nodding his approval for the second time.

"I am placing nine documents before you. Do you recognize these?"

"Yes, these are checks from the same account as before, made out to Acosta Construction."

"What were they for?"

"We are making major repairs to two of the buildings."

"How long have they been doing your construction?"

"I'm not exactly sure, but at least a year and a half."

"When did you decide to use this company on the building?"

"About a year ago, when they finished another job for us."

Thomas rose from the chair and walked over to the window behind him, glanced toward the street, and turning back to the table, he lowered himself to point at the cheques, a flash of blue and gray caught his attention, and he found himself focusing on the doorframe. Thomas tilted his head to see better, but finding nothing, he brushed it off.

"Is something wrong, Mr. Lock?" asked Cuesta.

Lock gave him an intrigued stare. Squinting his eyes slightly.

"Never mind, I thought that I saw something outside of the door."

Cuesta rose from his chair, walked out to the hallway beyond the doorframe, looked to his left, then right. Thomas saw Cuesta's eyes lower for a moment before turning around and returning.

"No one's out there."

"Probably just my secretary passing by," said Raymond, bringing the attention back to the business at hand and gesturing at the documents. "Anyway, as you were saying?"

Thomas lingered for a second before resuming his train of thought. He cleared his throat and pressed on.

"Here's my problem with this. All the cheques to these two companies started a week after our trial. While it is true that you did not know if my client was going to win until a full twenty-five days after the trial, both creditors popped up between the time of trial and the issuance of the final judgement." Thomas opened his arms questioningly. "Additionally, Julio's Landscaping has no trucks, no equipment, and no occupational license in either Dade, Broward, or Palm Beach Counties."

"Objection to the form of the question," opposed Raymond.

"Let me take this a little further. No construction permit has been pulled on any of your properties in the last two years."

Raymond objected again.

"Lock, you are not asking my client questions, if you continue, we'll stop the deposition."

"I don't understand how that can be, I told them to pull permits for everything," blurted Cuesta.

"They probably would if there was something to pull a permit for, isn't that right, Mr. Cuesta?" Thomas commented but asked no real question. "Lastly, can you explain why, in checking the Florida workman's compensation records, none of these companies have employees?"

Cuesta kept silent.

"Have you told your counsel that you were committing fraud by hiding corporate funds from a judgement creditor by paying large sums to companies that you control for work not done?"

Raymond sprang from his chair.

"This deposition is over!" shouted Raymond, anger fuming from behind his eyes.

"Well?" asked Thomas, ignoring Raymond and glaring at Cuesta.

"Raymond knew nothing."

Silence befell all of them. Cuesta sighed and Raymond turned to him in disbelief. Thomas sensed the moment and spoke.

"Morty, we are off the record."

Morty stopped typing and gave Thomas a blank stare.

"See Raymond, now you are in the clear," said Thomas, turning back to Raymond, "he can't turn around and blame you, when in desperation he gets other counsel, and they allege that he opened these companies moved the money into them under your advice."

"I would never have done that to you, Raymond."

"No, but your next attorney might not have a problem making that accusation," retorted Thomas.

Raymond held his smile.

"What are you looking for, Lock?

"The two straw entities created by your client to hide company funds so that my client cannot get to them. By tomorrow I will have the information on the owners of each DBA from the county, and I will move against those funds and have your client go before the court on charges of defrauding the court and perhaps lying under oath.”

Cuesta looked at Thomas with a strange expression and speaking almost inaudibly confessed.

“Alright Mr. Lock, you win. There will be a cheque for the complete amount of the judgement at your office next week by Thursday,” said Cuesta.

“Can you see your way to waiving the interest?” asked Raymond.

“Yes, if a cashier’s cheque for the remainder is on my desk by next week, Wednesday at noon.”

Thomas collected his things, stuck them in his briefcase, and left. When he exited, he heard the soft sobbing of a black-haired girl he found in the corner of the hallway. Before he could say anything to comfort her, Raymond caught his attention.

“Lock! I know what you did there, but I don’t appreciate the way that you did it. Let’s step outside.”

Thomas followed Raymond down the hall, passing the young girl and seeing the slash of black hair whipped as she turned away from him. Thomas refocused his attention on Raymond and the two men exited the building.

Chapter 42: The Payment

Miami, Florida: September 1970

The phone rang. His new secretary, Susana, had gone to the corner for their lunch, leaving him to cover the phones until she returned. Thomas picked up the phone.

"Law Offices of Thomas Lock."

"That you, Lock? Do you need me to lend you money to hire a receptionist or are you waiting for my client's money to be able to afford one?"

"Funny, Raymond. What can I do for you?"

"I got the copy of your pleading accusing my client of a fraudulent transaction, you are really coming down on my client."

"Look, I am not doing that, Raymond, that is what you call the action that I have filed. You know that. He was hiding the company money to avoid paying my client and dressing it up as though a real transaction had occurred. Anyway, I sent it to you first to see if I could get a reaction from you before filing it."

"Well, you got it. The reason my client needed the money was to pay off a balloon mortgage coming due on one of the properties. The payoff is almost \$500,000.00 and since he is so leveraged, he was having trouble getting a new loan to pay off the old one. Someone from a bank in Puerto Rico has now stepped in and though the interest rates are a little steep, my guy can make the payments with the rent and borrow from some of the more lucrative buildings to make overdue repairs on the others. You will be getting a cheque by the day after tomorrow. I give you my word, please don't file that action, it might frighten away this lender and all others in the future."

"No problem. Consider it held. If you have any delay though, please let me know."

The next morning Thomas arrived at work and got busy going over a long contract for the purchase of a cigar rolling factory in Hialeah. Laura walked into the room with an envelope in one hand and a file in the other.

"This just arrived, hand-delivered for you."

She put the file down and the envelope on top. Thomas looked at his watch. It was 5 minutes till noon. He watched his wife gracefully walk out of the room.

He turned his attention to the envelope. He ripped the top and opened it. He drew the contents out. There was a cheque for the complete amount including interest. *I must call Morales.* Then he realized there was a note with the cheque in the envelope. He unfolded the paper and in a stylized handwriting it read:

You won and I am an honorable man. I would not have done everything I did if I were not in such a difficult position. I hope you will forgive a desperate man. The last couple of days have brought me a moral and practical solution. Thank you and please accept my apologies.

Thomas sat and wondered if before the litigation got started, Cuesta's pride had also prevented him from confessing to Morales that he did not have the money to do the needed outside repairs. *Had it been pride or greed? Hard to tell,* contemplated Thomas. He was still glad to have aided the man to solve his problem. It only took one call and the right documentation. It helped that he knew Feliciano Torres from way back when he was at Banco Internacional. Besides, in the process he got his own client paid, so he picked up the phone and dialed Raúl's number.

Chapter 43: The Minuta and The Hotdog

Miami, Florida: August 1982

Gabriel parked the Mustang and let the radio finish its song. As he listened to the music, he reflected on all that had transpired. In December, he had helped Joaquín become a free man, he had delivered a check that changed Katerina and her parents' lives, and he had received a gift that would stick with him forever, but now work buried him beneath a mountain, and he felt like he was just going through the motions trying keep up with life around him as days faded into each other. He looked in the back seat to grab his jacket and saw the gym bag with the boxing gloves he now seldom used. A pang of guilt and remorse filled him. Grabbing the jacket, he turned off the car and dismissed his thoughts, choosing to focus on the next task at hand. He exited the car, brushed the wrinkles off his jacket as he put it on, and entered the building, leaving everything else behind.

Susana looked up as Gabriel closed the door behind him.

"Good morning, Gabriel."

"Do you have my calendar handy or is it in my office?"

"No, I have it."

"How does my day look between eleven and one?"

"Clear."

"I am going to meet Detective Sargent González. Mark it in the calendar so I can bill Santiago, please."

"No problem."

"I will see him at the criminal courthouse and if Rodrigo is around, we'll go to lunch. I have some things to talk to him about in a case."

"Do you want me to call Mr. Vivar's office and set it up?"

"Please, if you would."

"Sure."

Gabriel went into his office and just as he sat down the intercom buzzed. Picking up the receiver he said, "Am I confirmed with Viviar?"

"Not yet but you have Sarah on the line."

"Thanks." Gabriel looked down and only line two was blinking.

He waited a moment until he was relaxed and picked up.

"Hey, how are you? How is that trial prep going?" said Sarah from the other side of the line.

"Doing well and the trial prep was going so well that I settled it."

"Already?" she questioned, surprise echoing through the line.

"Yeah, luckily."

"Did you like the settlement?"

"It was the best I could get."

"Well, I'm happy to hear that. I haven't seen you since last week. When do I get to see you again? I was calling to take you to lunch if you have the time."

"I'd love to, but I can't; I'm slammed."

"Paperwork?"

"No, I'm meeting Detective Sargent González for a talk, and then Rodrigo for lunch."

"Well, I need some good news from the Sargent so please go ahead and meet with him. Mrs. Marchant is getting desperate to clear up this matter."

"I understand."

"Maybe a movie tonight?

"Yeah, that sounds great. Any ideas?

"I'm in a sci-fi mood so it's Star Trek: The Wrath of Khan, Road Warrior, or ET."

"I'm game for any of the three."

"Okay, just remember to bring along a report."

"From González?"

"Well, I like Rodrigo, but I am not waiting for news from him."

"Right. See you tonight," he said as he began to review all the correspondence on his desk.

What seemed like a minute later, thc phone buzzed again.

"Yes?"

"If you don't leave now, you'll be late for your meeting with González."

"Leaving now."

Gabriel glanced down at his watch and turned into the large parking lot in front of the criminal courthouse. As he neared the brown granite stairs, he saw the Detective Sargent at the hot dog cart standing in line. Gabriel stood beside him and whispered, "I thought you were going to stay away from those things after your last checkup."

"I allow myself one every second Tuesday and one on special occasions."

"But today is Wednesday."

"Yes, but I'm meeting you,"

"Meeting me is a special occasion?"

"Well, pretty much anything is a special occasion."

"Funny man."

"No actually, I think we have the shooter in the gas station shooting. We have confirmed that someone at the station was in on it but from what we know, we do not believe it was Jean Robert."

"How did you get the information?"

Sergeant González gave Gabriel a withering look.

"Sorry, the enthusiasm got the best of me."

"Gabriel, I may need your client's co-operation to flush out who it is that was in on the trafficking."

"Can you clear Jean Robert?"

"Not yet and that is why we may need your client's cooperation. Tell me, is there always an employee on the premises?

"Yes, they are open 24/7."

"Can your client cover for anyone?

"What for?"

"So, we can conduct a search with a dog or two without any employee being present to spill the beans and get taken out of the country or simply taken out. Maybe we can find out where the drugs are or were being stashed. That could lead us to discover the person that cost Jean Robert his life."

"We must find another way because my client hasn't worked hours behind the counter at the stations in years and if your intent is to surprise someone, Santiago working the register is the reddest of flags. Let me talk to him and see what we come up with."

"You know your client, Santiago, is not out of the woods either."

Gabriel gave his friend a sharp look.

"Well, I have no evidence that he is not involved in some manner," pressed González.

"Subtle pressure to cooperate Detective Sergeant."

"Just doing my job."

"I get it, so we will find a way."

González saw Rodrigo approaching over Gabriel's shoulder.

"Here comes one of the few Defense attorneys, I like."

Gabriel turned just in time to hear Rodrigo say, "I thought you were going to quit eating those."

"Is everyone my mother now?" he asked with a grin.

"If you die my friend, I'll be down to zero," admitted Rodrigo.

"There are no cops that like you. Hmm. I wonder why," joked González.

Gabriel laughed and looked at his two friends.

"I am going to be deposed in a case, so I need to get going. You guys take care." Gabriel and Rodrigo laughed as they watched the cop walk off, climb the stairs, and go into the building.

"Let's go to Joe's on the river."

"Don't have time for that," said Rodrigo, "But how about La Camaronera?"

"I can do that."

They parked Rodrigo's car in the small strip shopping center.

"Dos minutas por favor y una orden de tostones," said Rodrigo to waiter eager to take his order. He wrote it down in a notebook before realizing that there was something missing.

"Pa tomar?" he asked as he looked up from his notebook at Gabriel.

"Dos Millers," responded Rodrigo as he looked at the people standing next to the snake-like bar. "My favorite part of the experience is the fact that the food is so good that people don't mind standing up while they eat."

"Yeah," said Gabriel looking at the plate of tostones. "I haven't managed to figure out how to get to the truth in the problems at the daycare, but I keep going back to my father's old case. There is something that was going on that we don't know about. I think I know who this person is trying to create a problem for the client. They are good people. Doing the right thing so why attack them?"

"Maybe starting with any case filed against your client and going backwards. Sorry man, I have a lot on my plate today. Including the one in front of me." Maybe next week we can take time out and do just that, and with that Rodrigo picked up his hot Minuta sandwich, surrounded it with tostones from the bigger plate and spoke no more.

Chapter 44: The Grand Reopening

Miami, Florida: August 1982

A week later, Gabriel entered Thomas's office and found a seat in front of his father's desk. "The Bald Wood Furniture case was settled this morning, so I am free to go wherever you need me tonight."

"Good. I was going to run from the gala with your mother to Otoniel's grand reopening, but now you can go."

"Do I have a choice?"

"Absolutely. You can either go to the Latin Chamber of Commerce Dinner or to Nocturno," said Thomas nonchalantly. "I understand it's going to be filled with many high-powered people we could use as clients. You don't need to meet them all, but it is important that you are seen, at this type of event."

"Wouldn't the Chamber be the same?"

"No, not even close."

"What?" inquired Gabriel, not seeing how the Chamber could be less valuable than a night at a nightclub.

Thomas, sensing his son's confusion, explained. "Son, the Chamber is straightforward. More or less the same people and it's more of a formality and requirement than anything else. I need to go too because I'm the old man, but the night club is going to have wealthy people from all over the world."

"Do you prefer to go to the nightclub then?"

"I would prefer to go there than the Chamber. But honestly, that's more your speed." said Thomas, and Gabriel responded with a very serious look. "Seriously though, you need to go. It has been over sixty days since they shut him down, but he and Rafaela have worked hard to change the place and get it to where it needs to be. Not to mention setting up the new membership and recruiting patrons. What they have accomplished is spectacular. I think that you'll have a lot of fun."

"I see. But I am going out with Sarah and how I'm I supposed to pay attention to her and network at the same time? More importantly, how is she going to feel about that?"

"Well, it's going to be an interesting night for you then."

"Yeah, it will.

"So, I decided to give you the day off tomorrow," continued Thomas.

"Tomorrow's Saturday, Dad. It's not really a day off."

"Monday, I mean. You've been working hard in the past few weeks so I figured that Monday would reward your work and make up for going to Nocturno with me last time."

"Thanks, Dad. I appreciate that. So, do we know if Nocturno is a black-tie event?"

"Yes, it is. I expect you to be there for dinner and stay until it turns into a full-fledged club at half past ten."

"You're joking?"

"No, part of the deal that he and Rafaela made with the city to get it opened on time was that if it served food, then they would be willing to fast track it. That's why he was able to get the permits so quickly. Your tux is already at your apartment; Otoniel requested your measurements and wanted to get this for you personally as a thank you." Gabriel nodded with approval. He got a special gown for

Sarah which was delivered this morning by the designer herself.

"Okay then, I'll be there, tonight." Gabriel looked down at his watch; oh I need to call Sarah.

"Alright. Get there just after eight. He's expecting you by no later than half past eight."

At quarter past eight, Gabriel and Sarah drove into the club parking lot. They struggled to find a spot but found one after waiting for a little under twenty minutes. Turning off the car and taking one last look in the mirror before exiting, they walked toward the building. "Thanks for accompanying me tonight," said Gabriel,

"You, Mr. Stiff, dancing at this nightclub?! Wouldn't miss it for the world."

He grinned. As they drew closer to the building Gabriel noticed that the neon sign had changed. It was no longer flashing and had gone from red to a light magenta while faint aqua stars surrounded the name. Though trendy, it looked much classier than the previous one.

Gabriel approached the front door when two of the staff cut him off. Realizing who he was, and seeing he was accompanied by a woman, they stepped aside and let them pass. "Sorry to have stopped you; new club rules."

"No problem," said Gabriel, moving to the side and letting Sarah in first. "Is Mr. Prío inside?"

"Yes, you'll find him next to the bar on the far side once you enter the main room."

Gabriel walked through the new entrance way and looked toward the bar. Otoniel leaned against the bar and beside him was Rafaela, the woman Gabriel had met at the previous meeting.

"Gabriel! Good to see you," said Otoniel, stretching his arms and giving Gabriel a warm hug. Looking at Sarah, he greeted her with a handshake that turned into another warm hug., "You must be Sarah."

"Did you recognize me by the lovely dress?" she asked, smiling.

Otoniel laughed and turned to the woman Sarah didn't know.

"This is my new manager, Rafaela Aldo. Rafaela, these are my esteemed guests, Gabriel Lock and Sarah Jensen. You remember each other from the meeting, right?" he said pointing from Gabriel to Rafaela, and she giggled in response.

"Yes, I remember you. Where is your father?"

Otoniel answered before Gabriel could.

"Thomas couldn't make it, Rafaela. Gabriel came in his stead to show his support."

"What a pity that he couldn't make it. I liked his style," she stated, smiling. "Regardless, I'm glad to meet you again. So, do you like the club?"

Gabriel looked around and took in the surroundings. The furniture had changed from dark faux leather black couches to genuine leather brown ones. There was a small stage where the original elevated platform had been. The raised section now harbored white wooden tables and matching chairs. The small Plexiglas tables from earlier had been repaired and better maintained, reflecting the new lights and created a subtle light show. All the previous black tuxedos had changed to ones with tropical white dinner jackets and in the corner of the bar there was a small jazz band playing Garota de Ipanema.

"I do. I can see a lot of changes in the details of the decoration and the table placement, but I can't see a significant change in any other aspect of the club."

"I'm surprised Counselor. You, who are famous for noticing the most minor details, missed such a major one."

Gabriel looked again and grinned at Rafaela.

"Well of course, there are no marimberos," he said in a joking tone.

"Yes, it's an invitation club only, unique and the one of its kind in town and maybe in the country."

"In order to avoid discrimination suits we created very strict guidelines for membership. You can only be a member of this club provided you have been a member of one of a number of exclusive clubs from around the world. Naturally, the clubs on the list are some of the most select clubs in the world.

"For instance, the New York Yacht Club, or El Real Automobile Club de Madrid, and a one or two from each of the countries in South America, Mexico, Europe and Asia."

"And you had no problem recruiting?" asked Sarah.

"Not really," began Otoniel, "you see Rafaela, or members of her family, knows many of these people. Many of them come to Miami occasionally for business or vacation and so they come here not only for dinner but during the day for meetings and lunch. For most of these people $3,000.00 a year is a pittance."

"But many people can pay that."

"The old crowed *could* have paid that," answered Rafaela, "so, the key was to create another type of selection of members. Yearly fees have not been enough to keep undesirables out of the other clubs in the city. They still get groups they don't really want, so we had to come up with something different, and we could do this because of my contacts, but the good news is that when they come, they spend and, occasionally, they'll bring us new members. The real adjustment is in the patrons, the foods we serve, and the music we play."

"When we announced the grand reopening, the regulars thought they were coming back to their old haunts, but Rafaela handled it well." interjected Otoniel.

"I can imagine," said Gabriel.

"I spent the whole beginning of the night telling them they were not allowed in," explained Rafaela. "Some of them did not understand at first but they slowly caught on.

Some were not too happy with me, but I told them there were new owners from London and those were their orders not mine."

"When they came to me for help, I told them that I sold the place and that this was now part of an international chain with very particular clientele that go to this chain's places when they travel all over the world," said Otoniel.

"The business will not be as good economically, but it will be steady and without problems," added Rafaela. "Once the Marimberos move somewhere else permanently or they are wiped out by the authorities, then he will reopen his dream place," she said pointing to Otoniel, "and I will have sufficient capital to open my own place if I choose to."

"So, the rampant Marimbero night club became one of the most exclusive places in town," joked Gabriel.

"All thanks to Rafaela," confirmed Otoniel, "and now I have a life and even an apartment outside of this place."

He hugged her and Rafaela blushed. Gabriel looked around the club once more; circular booths surrounded the array of tables on the main floor where the stage was. The booths had been raised on platforms so that they could see the performers.

"So, fine dinner and dancing too?" asked Gabriel as waiters with trays of exquisite food went by.

"Yes, tonight is Brazilian Jazz night. We have a Brazilian Jazz band that comes every Friday night for the dinner portion before we turn the club into a discotheque," explained Rafaela, "by the way, we have a table over there in the center for all of us. Would you like to join us for dinner?" she looked from Gabriel to Sarah, who nodded.

"Sure thing," answered Gabriel. They moved to the center table and settled in. A waiter came to them, offering the special of the evening which they all accepted. Gabriel glanced from side to side, taking in all the changes that made El Nocturno what Otoniel had always wanted, a classy up-scale nightclub. The food was delayed no more than a few minutes in arriving from the time they ordered and after another half an hour or so, Gabriel returned to business.

"And my father has been in on this plan?"

"Yes, of course, he negotiated out the details between us, drew up the contracts, and settled the details with the police and the inspectors."

"Well, I have to hand it to you, Rafaela, you managed to outsmart the police, the dealers, and even two of Miami's best lawyers."

"Well, one of them."

Gabriel gave her a puzzled look.

"Your father guessed it when I said that there would be no competition, and the Dealers would not be back. I could see it in his face."

"Always one step ahead."

"No, Gabriel. Your father might still be one step ahead of you, but he's like ten on the rest of us. When you're my age and have a little less gray than I do now, you'll be wiser. He tells me all the time."

Gabriel nodded. Rotating he looked to Sarah, and, offering his arm, asked, "Well, shall we dance?"

Sarah smiled warmly.

"I'd love to, Counselor."

Gabriel nodded and raised his eyebrows.

"Well then, let's go!"

He led her onto the dance floor as the next song began. As they walked toward the main part of the room, the trumpets and bongos from the band sounded the iconic rhythm of Llorarás by Oscar D'León.

"I LOVE this song!" yelled Sarah.

"You know this?" asked Gabriel, a combination of excitement and surprise showing in his face.

"Who doesn't know this song?!"

"I'm impressed."

"Take my hand and I'll impress you some more."

He stretched out his hand, and she placed hers in his as he placed his right hand on her back, holding her slightly off center and close. The music blared and the words set them off with Gabriel stepping forward as Sarah stepped back to the Salsa rhythm. They moved to the beat with Gabriel spinning Sarah, whose dress flowed and fell, breaking to the commands her feet gave.

"You know, for a Spanish American, he moves like a Cuban," joked Rafaela with Otoniel in Gabriel's earshot.

"We adopted him," fired back Otoniel.

Sarah and Gabriel burst into laughter as they danced.

"You should see his father move," continued Otoniel, commending the familial talent.

"You will again soon!" yelled Gabriel as he spun Sarah before dipping her low, her hair almost touching the floor. He pulled her back up, moving back to the step before completing *el ocho*.

"Look at you go, Church boy," quipped Sarah.

"It's a gift of the Spirit," said Gabriel as the music lit the club up.

"I can see that, Counselor," said Sarah as the song faded to its end. When it finished, he led her to the bar where they grabbed drinks, readying themselves to dance all night long.

Chapter 45: The Widow

Miami, Florida: August 1982

The Cathedral of St. Mary on his left noticing dominated the multicolored houses lining either side of the road. As he came to a stop at the intersection, he checked the street signs and confirmed that he was only a few blocks from the Marchant household. Staring up at the light, he glanced down the street to see the little Haitian market lined with shoppers and old men hanging around outside trading jokes, smokes, and smiles. Turning left, Gabriel located the address in the form of a quaint home on the corner. He parked on the edge of the street and made his way to the front door. He knocked three times before hearing light footsteps.

Mrs. Marchant opened the front door slowly, holding it with a trembling hand and using her foot to allow only the slightest amount of space from the frame. Gabriel met her dark and swollen eyes. She stared back with a cold and worn face.

"Mrs. Marchant," he began in English. Her face made no expression. "Mrs. Marchant, I am Gabriel Lock. I work for Mr. Alemán, Jean Robert's boss. I'm a lawyer and I was hoping to ask you a couple of questions about your husband if that's okay?"

Her eyes widened as he spoke Jean Robert's name, but she said nothing. Gabriel moved to say something more, but Mrs. Marchant interjected.

"My English is no good." Haitian Creole carried her accent as she spoke, and Gabriel could see that the language barrier would be more for her to handle. He inhaled deeply and did his best to remember his French from college and high school. "Sarah said to expect you." She said in French.

"I am sorry, Madame Marchant. I imagine you prefer French?" he responded in broken High School French.

A small smile escaped her, and her cheeks reddened as her lips parted to speak.

"Oui, monsieur. You do not speak Creole?" Gabriel shook his head but was relieved that she spoke French and not just creole. She looked at him, waiting for him to respond and he realized that he had forgotten to answer.

"Non, Madame, I don't. English and Spanish and a little French."

"Where did you learn French and Spanish?" she interrogated, in French with a mixture of intrigue and caution in her voice. Gabriel opened his palms and shrugged.

"French in High School and Spanish from my mother, madame, who was born in Spain more years ago than she would admit."

Suddenly her face lit up with a wide smile.

"No woman cares to admit her age, *évidemment*."

Gabriel, sensing the sudden connection, continued.

"She taught me her native language because all her family is Spanish, and she wanted me to be able to speak to them well. My father, who is American born, learned it to be able to romance her in her mother tongue. Now, that is what we speak at the house to be able to practice."

"A smart man," she responded in French.

"Sadly, I have no one to practice French with except an occasional client." He finished with the most flair he could muster in his rusty French.

Mrs. Marchant's face relaxed increasingly as they continued in French. "Your French is not so bad," she admitted, while opening the door wider and adjusting her position, "Vraiment, really."

"As I said before, I am Gabriel Lock, I work with Mr. Alemán,"

Mrs. Marchant nodded. "Sarah told me all of that."

"I need to ask you some questions about your husband, Jean Robert. I need to know a little more about the situation to better understand your husband's case."

Mrs. Marchant brought her hand to her chest as Gabriel mentioned her husband. Trembling slightly and widening her eyes, she stared at the briefcase in Gabriel's hand, examined his suit, and remembered all that Sarah had told her about this interview.

"I don't wish to be dramatic, Mrs. Marchant, but your future and that of your children depends on how you help me. Based on what I've seen so far, I believe Jean Robert was innocent of any wrongdoing."

"Okay," she whispered under her breath as she opened the door, and allowed him in. Gabriel thanked her and entered the home. White walls contrasted the terracotta-colored tiles. There was a small iron stove in the corner along with an older couch and matching love seat.

"Please sit," she commanded, this time in English, while gathering fortitude, and pointing over to the couch. He turned his head and acknowledged her order. He sat down on the cushion and placed his briefcase next to him, resting it against the side of the couch. Mrs. Marchant returned after a few moments with two glasses of water. She handed one to Gabriel, placed two dish towels on the coffee table as coasters, and waited for him to drink before taking a sip. They gulped down some of the water before refocusing on the reason for his visit.

"What brings you here, sir? We are not important here like other people are in Miami. I am careful, because when they care about us, it causes us more problems. We prefer to go unnoticed. Someone must have noticed Jean Robert and now he is dead."

Her assertion caught him off guard. He expected a widow in mourning, distraught and confused, but instead, Mrs. Marchant met him with strength and composure.

"Mr. Alemán is a good man, madame. He takes care of all his employees," he articulated. Mrs. Marchant raised an eyebrow.

"All men are good until they are not. You should know, you are a lawyer." She shuffled in place and began. "My husband was also a good man, and he was murdered at work. Right now, I have two sons who have lost their father and stopped talking. The only noise I hear is my children crying when they fall asleep." Anger perforated her voice as she explained all that she and her sons had lost.

"Sorry, madame. I'm sorry, but all the things you can tell me will help me discover the reason for his death, and this is important because, the police consider that your husband's death may be related to drugs."

Mrs. Marchant gave a horrified look as he said the word drugs.

"My *husband* did not do *drogues, no vend drogues*, Monsieur Lock!" she pleaded in a mixture of outraged French and her accented English. Mrs. Marchant began moaning with cries of anguish. Tears erupted from her eyes, and she did her best to rid her cheeks of them.

"The police think he may have died because he had an argument with the people that may have supplied him with the drugs he may have sold. Today in Miami, police always ask drug-related questions in a death like this. I don't believe that he sold drugs." said Gabriel, trying his best to explain that this was a standard procedure.

She squealed at the thought of her husband's murder being in cold blood. Taking a moment, she took another sip of her water and began recounting everything that she had learned about Jean Robert and his work. She told Gabriel all she could remember about his life; about the long nights and early mornings, the letters he wrote to her when she and their kids were still in Haiti praying every day to join him. She even went so far as to tell him that Jean Robert got along with all his coworkers and felt safe with them, but worried about eyes that watched the station after hours, unwanted eyes. As she spoke, Gabriel examined his surroundings.

"He was not supposed to work that night. The bullet was not for him, *je crois*. If my husband were involved, do you think we would live here?"

As Gabriel shook his head, he saw a small pair of eyes behind Mrs. Marchant. He made eye contact with them for a moment and found nothing but emptiness and sorrow. Before he could say anything more, the eyes left, leaving Gabriel and Mrs. Marchant to finish their conversation.

"Forgive me, but I have two children to take care of." she said, raising herself from her seat.

"Take care of your children, Mrs. Marchant. I am done. Please call Sarah should anything more come to mind. She and I will continue to find the answer to all your questions."

Mrs. Marchant nodded, Gabriel collected his briefcase, and Mrs. Marchant saw him out.

As he entered the Mustang, he rolled the window up and fired the engine. As the car moved down the street and onto the highway, Mrs. Marchant and her two sons lingered on his mind. The squalor of the apartment was incongruous with a man selling enough drugs to get shot over. *I have two sons who lost their father and who have chosen not to speak, the only noise that I hear is when they cry themselves to sleep.* He fixated on her translated words. Gabriel ran through all the facts that she gave him, and Mrs. Marchant confirmed all of Claudio's statements concerning the figures watching the station. She went so far as to explain that her husband got along with all his coworkers and enjoyed working with them, even learning bits of Spanish from Pepe and Lázaro to feel more at home in Miami. As Gabriel passed the colorful Little Haiti homes and stores, he recognized the need to confirm, with both Lázaro and Pepe, what he had just learned. *All the cultures that meet in this town,* he thought, just before his mind turned to the two little boys and Mrs.

Marchant. "Why? Why them just as they were headed for a better life?" he asked God aloud. Receiving no answer, he shook his head, slammed his fist onto the dash, and accelerated as he merged onto the highway, and headed home.

Chapter 46: The Night at Monty's

Miami, Florida: August 1982

The sun filtered through the jalousie windows and transformed the white walls of the bedroom in his apartment into a weird mix of light yellow and pale grey colors. As he lay in bed, he thought about the night he and Sarah had at the nightclub on Friday.

He rose from the bed and moved over to the kitchen hoping to find something in his fridge. He was so tired from the night before that, after taking Sarah back home from Nocturno, he made it home, showered, and collapsed, going so far as to sleep well past noon. He yawned as he opened the fridge and, to his dismay, found nothing of interest. He tried the cupboards, and the story repeated itself. Hearing his stomach grumble, he decided he wanted something more appetizing and decided to call Sarah to see what she was up to. The phone rang for a few moments before the soft voice on the other side answered. He asked if she wanted to join him for dinner and after she agreed, he informed her that he would also invite Rodrigo and Arlene.

They arrived at the entrance to the outside raw bar adjacent to the restaurant. Gabriel saw that it was only half full and they would have their pick of places to sit. As they approached, the hostess called to them.

"Just the two of you, this evening?" she asked.

"No, we are waiting for another couple," answered Sarah. "They should be arriving soon. Can you please sit us now before all the tables by the water are taken?"

"Of course. Follow me, please," she said as she walked toward the picnic tables scattered on the wooden deck.

Next to the restaurant deck, boats and yachts lined the piers that formed the Marina. Hundreds of mostly white vessels that bobbed in the water, waiting for their owners to free them for afternoons around Biscayne Bay and even fishing in the Bahamas. *This is a much better way to enjoy dinner than the one can of soup that I found*, thought Gabriel.

She found a table, facing east, next to the wooden railing that separated the raw bar deck from the marina.

"Is this, okay?" she asked them.

"Wonderful, thanks," he said as he gave her his best smile.

Gabriel let Sarah sit facing the setting sun as he sat across from her facing the ocean.

"Thanks for inviting me out. I really needed this because I have been working since early this morning," said Sarah after a minute. "I have a stack of cases sitting on my bed that I need to review for court tomorrow."

"Do you have time for this? Would you prefer to order and go?"

"Are you kidding? Absolutely not."

"You know, Rodrigo says the same thing you do about his work. He claims it's all the same and his clients are all the same," commented Gabriel, trying to make her feel better. "Think about it; his work deals with people's liberty, and mine with people's way of life in many ways, and you, freeing people from failed marriages or obtaining legal entry into this country both of which they think will result in the pursuit of happiness. So, among the three of us we have the Declaration of Independence covered.

"Funny Gabriel, you do more serious cases than you let on, even violent ones, I know you do."

"Yeah, I do. I just had one. My client, the husband, broke down the door of his house because his wife changed the lock, except he found her on the other side with a gun pointed to his head," he said, chuckling. "His kids saw the whole thing."

"Wow, what happened?"

"She shot him in the leg and then put the tip of the warm barrel on his forehead and said, 'I won't shoot you again because the kids are here, and I don't want them to see that, but if they weren't here, I would have put you out of your misery.'"

"Why did she shoot him?" inquired Sarah, confused.

"Well, she didn't know it was him. He didn't announce his intentions; he just broke it down and she shot the first thing that came through the door, or in this case, over it."

"So how were the kids there?"

"He looked to the side and sitting on the sofa were his two kids looking at the scene between their father and mother as it was playing out."

"Was there a court decree giving her possession of the house?"

"He had not been served with it."

Sarah could see the waitress heading toward them with a pad in hand.

"Okay enough law. Let's order a drink and spend a lawless evening."

The waitress passed by another table, and as she did, Gabriel called to her.

"We are waiting for another couple, so please bring us just the fish dip for now. Also, would you mind if we ordered drinks?" requested Gabriel.

She nodded to them and pulled a small notebook from her pocket.

"A Mojito, please," ordered Sarah.

"Make that two."

The server left and he continued their discussion.

"She was perfectly in her rights to shoot him."

Despite her previous statement, for the first time Sarah seemed interested in the case. "Of course, she was, but think of the kids," responded Sarah, leaning forward and rearranging her plastic silverware with a touch of impatience. "I'm not sure there is enough therapy to fix what they saw: a father bursting through their door violently and the mother shooting him in the leg and holding him at gun point, is not an easy image to erase. It's not something you put in the family photo album," she added, shaking her head.

"No, absolutely not," agreed Gabriel.

Rodrigo and Arlene appeared from the entrance and began walking towards them after the server pointed out their table.

The pair walked through the crowded dance floor and finally reached the table.

"Buenas noches," said Arlene. "You guys look happy and cozy,"

"And we are happy to see you guys," added Sarah.

They all exchanged hugs before the waitress showed up and took their order.

"What were you talking about?" asked Arlene. "I saw your intensity all the way across the dance floor."

"A shooting"

"You're kidding, where?" inquired Rodrigo.

"At my client's house," answered Gabriel.

"What happened?" pressed Rodrigo.

"Hold on," interrupted Arlene. "You never talk to me about your cases because you don't want to talk law after hours and now you want to hear about his case?"

Gabriel looked down and saw Arlene's finger pointing at him.

"I've told you about a case before," answered Rodrigo defensively.

"Yeah, but only because you wanted to prove *how much you love me*" she said in a singsong voice.

"Is there a better reason?" asked Sarah.

"More like is there another alternative?" pipped Rodrigo.

Everyone laughed.

"Hey, I haven't heard that one." declared Gabriel.

"Well, I'm not in love with you, Lock."

"Trying to get on my sweet side, huh?"

"Every day, Arlene." grinned Rodrigo.

"So, what happened? asked Sarah.

"Okay, okay." Rod looked around and started, "I had a case in Broward County, an armed robbery. I filed a motion for a change of venue due to the extraordinary publicity generated in the county and a motion to suppress evidence for improper search during a traffic stop. The motion to suppress didn't pan out but the motion for change of venue was granted and the trial was moved to Manatee County. So, I thought, well, I have a shot at winning but if not, I'll get a good plea for my client. The morning of the trial one of the co-defendants, the driver of the getaway car, pled guilty to a much smaller crime and agreed to testify for the prosecution, the other attorney moved to have a separate trial and was granted the motion by the judge. At that point, my client decided to accept the plea." Rod began to speak a little faster. "It was Friday afternoon, so I thought the Judge would take a plea, and we would all go home. I had just met Arlene, and I was well, enthusiastic to say the least. So, I called Arlene and said that I would be coming home late, but I would be back Friday and asked if we could go out."

"And I said yes," she blurted.

"When we go into chambers," continued Rod, "the judge says, 'Gentlemen, we will pick a jury this afternoon and Monday I will take the plea, the other defendant will think about his predicament all weekend and maybe both will take a plea on Monday.'"

"This judge was single-handedly destroying his romantic life," giggled Arlene.

"I looked at my watch, and it was two o'clock. A few minutes later, we went into the courtroom and a few times after that they brought the jury in. The judge seated the first six, jurors and the prosecutor asked his questions until he was satisfied. He accepted the jury and sat down. I looked at my watch, and it was only 2:30 so I thought that I still had time to make it back to Miami for my date with Arlene, so I got up walked to the jury and said, 'please raise your hand if you believe in truth, justice, and the American way.' They all raised their hands and out of the corner of my eye I could see the penetrating look on the judge's face. Then I commanded, raise your hand if you will make a good faith effort to render the right verdict in this case.' They all raised their hands, so I turned to the judge and said very solemnly, 'I accept the jury, Judge.' Well, if looks could kill, I had just been murdered."

Gabriel grinned and Sarah had a look of wonder.

"Later I found out that the judge had planned a getaway with his wife on the county's dime, and I had just ruined it."

"Really?"

"Oh yeah," chuckled Rodrigo, "I completely ruined it."

"What happened the next time you were before that judge?" asked Sarah.

"I haven't been. Before the trial I learned that he had been rotated to civil division, so I didn't see him again for years."

Sarah almost spit up her drink.

"Well played, buddy, well played." joked Gabriel.

"That was a great story Rod, why don't you ever talk about your cases?" asked Sarah.

Rodrigo's laughter lessened.

"You know Arlene is a trauma nurse. She sees gunshots and car accidents, people who have fallen from roofs, or kids from monkey bars, so I don't want to burden her with more gruesome things than she already must deal with. I don't want to bring what I see home, so it stays at the office. One day maybe, when I do other types of work, then maybe I'll talk about it, but not until then."

"But you can't carry that around with you, can you?" asked Sarah as she put her glass down.

"I don't. Once or twice a month I speak with a good friend of mine, who is a priest at Saints Peter and Paul church. We blend it in with confession in his office and I get it all out, including my doubts about my actions, my clients and my defending them."

"Do you ever have doubts about defending people that you know are guilty."

"Not anymore. He told me once that I fulfill a sacred obligation under the constitution which is to make sure that everyone gets a competent defense no matter what he or she has done, and he fulfills a sacred obligation under our faith, which is to carry with him everyone's confessed sins no matter what he or she has done, and give absolution if he or she repents and fulfills the penance."

"You know," said Gabriel, "that's not a bad idea."

"But you go to confession often,"

"I do, but I just forgot that what is said under the seal of confession is sealed forever, but my clients aren't up for jail time in their cases."

"That's true," admitted Rodrigo.

The waitress returned with their orders and the four of them began to eat. After a little while, Arlene's curiosity perked up.

"Where are you from, Sarah? asked Arlene, turning to her.

"Upstate New York, near Rochester. I went to college at Iona and then came down to Miami for law school."

Rodrigo looked up from his plate of food.

"Hey Lock, you didn't tell me you were dating the enemy."

Sarah gave an offended look, but Rodrigo finished his sentence.

"I am still carrying that loss to UM in my heart."

"And your pocket if I remember correctly. You lost the bet with your cousin, right?" smirked Gabriel.

"Misery, pure misery. What's worse is that I have never heard the end of it."

They all laughed and spent the rest of the meal talking and sharing stories. After they finished their meals, they ordered an after-dinner drink and Arlene reminded them of her early morning tomorrow. As they bid farewell, Sarah extended her hand, inviting Gabriel to take it. He did and apologized for talking about work earlier.

"I'll forgive it this time, Counselor, but there's more to life than work."

"I know there is," he replied, "it's just been so much lately."

"I know. I still have a stack of files on my bed to review, but I needed this break and it's still early enough where I won't lose too much sleep."

"Then I'll try to get you there quickly," said Gabriel, opening the door to the Mustang for her.

"Always the gentleman," she said, smiling.

He entered the car, fired the engine, and lowered the windows, blasting the music as the car exited the parking lot and took off down the street.

Chapter 47: The Mother

Miami, Florida: September 1982

When Gabriel was getting ready to leave the office for this five o'clock meeting, he debated with himself over the merit of taking the files or of taking his father. He took the first and the last files from the stack and placed them in the briefcase. He walked out the door and exited the office out to his car parked on the curb in front of the office. As they drove through the streets of little Havana, Gabriel thought about the changing neighborhood.

"You know, this part of town was the center of Cuban immigration, where your grandparents made some of their closest friends," said Thomas, surveying the changing neighborhood. "Now, you barely have any Cubans."

"Nicaraguans, Guatemalans, and Hondurans are replacing them. Go figure, the Cubans that have been here long enough are moving to the suburbs. The whole city is changing."

Thomas observed the change in colors, the difference in paint and art that covered the walls of Little Havana. He lowered the window and the aromas of street vendors, restaurants, and tourists filtered through him. Music played from open windows and in the corner of his eye, Thomas saw a set of tables and chairs where the old guard played dominoes, wearing their authentic Yarey hats and smoking cigars. As the smell of cigar smoke grew, the car slowed, and Thomas realized that they were close.

"Which apartment is it?" asked Thomas, scanning the buildings from top to bottom.

"Across the street," he answered. "Bottom Floor, far right, apartment 1. I came to see Graciela earlier today so she's expecting us."

Thomas and Gabriel exited the sedan and crossed the street toward the opposite sidewalk. They walked up the cement pathway past the metal mailboxes and reached the cement walkway, taking refuge from the sun. They strode towards the apartment and knocked on the last door. A woman came to the door. When she saw Thomas, she stiffened.

"I did not expect to see *you* here."

"María Elena, I believe the last time I saw you was in at your husband's funeral."

"We have seen each other two times, the trial and my husband's funeral Mr. Lock. I did not go to my husband's depositions afterward, though I did hear about them as you can imagine. And now I understand you are after my daughter."

Thomas did not respond.

"May we come in?" asked Gabriel, trying to keep the encounter civil.

"Please do," she said with a slight Spanish accent and a graceful movement of her left hand.

The elegant gray-haired woman moved to one side and both Gabriel and Thomas entered the apartment. Graciela nodded her head and pointed toward the brown sofa. Both men took a seat. María Elena began to pace.

"I understand that you have information about my daughter."

"Yes, we do, but what makes you so sure?" asked Gabriel, pondering how much Graciela had warned her.

"Because there are only two Cuesta's left and seeing how I didn't call you, it must be about my daughter.

"I'm afraid that your daughter has gotten into some trouble."

"How do I know that what you are saying is true? Are you sure that it's my daughter?" The lines in her face intensified as the focus in her eyes shifted from Gabriel to Thomas and back.

"Mrs. Cuesta," said Gabriel. "Graciela identified her as being the only person other than you that would have access to her documentation and license. But, if you still have doubts, I have a video tape of Eleonor's alleged involvement. Do you have a VCR where I may play the tape?"

María Elena raised a trembling finger and pointed toward the small entertainment center behind him. He turned and stepped over to it. He popped in the tape and turned on the television set.

María Elena moved to where Graciela sat while Thomas remained in his seat. As the tape played, her face moved from shock to horror before releasing streams of tears. She sobbed for a moment, and Thomas kept silent as Gabriel gave her a moment to collect herself.

"Did anything happen to that child?"

"As you saw, a family arrived while picking up their own child and brought him inside. No harm came to him, but he was a little shaken up."

"Oh God," she cried. Gabriel tried to be delicate, but Thomas had none of it.

"We believe that Eleonor knew about the early arrival and timed the incident to coincide with harming the daycare, but not the child," said Thomas in a low, assertive tone.

"You think that she planned this?" fired back María Elena, breaking her sobs, fury raging through her firm voice.

"We know that she did, María Elena. You can't refute this footage, but rather than fight us, you can help us. We need to know why she would do this and until we know what's at play, we can't help her."

Maria Elena's fumes subsided as Thomas kept his low voice and calm demeanor.

Appreciating his father's composure, Gabriel let him take the lead.

"To whom does the daycare belong?"

"Morales, Raúl Morales, my long-time client, and the man that your husband had a legal dispute against. The daycare is no longer his, but his daughter's, Mirella."

"Do you know how much pain Morales caused my family?" hissed María Elena.

"Luis was a good man who was over-extended, María Elena. You know that I know that, and Raúl came to know that, but Luis almost caused the same pain that you feel to my client. One side was bound to lose the lawsuit. Both men were overextended. The country was in a recession and there were losses everywhere. Morales was, and is, a good and decent man and, does not deserve this. If you won't do it because of Raúl, do it for your child. Do it for the good of that child that Eleonor put in danger or the next child. If you tell us where she is, I promise you that I will make sure that the prosecutor is lenient."

María Elena stared at the screen as if looking at it long enough would change what she saw. After a few seconds she spoke, allowing herself to tell the story of her husband's untimely end and his funeral.

Chapter 48: The Untimely End

Miami, Florida: September 1970

Luis Cuesta sat in the waiting room in front of Feliciano Torres' office. The door opened and Feliciano came out, stretching his hand toward him. Cuesta stood up and shook the banker's hand. Feliciano welcomed him into his office, and they both sat in the chairs with the banker opening the files on his desk.

"I have great news for you, Luis; your loan package has been approved. It will require your personal guarantee, but the loan committee understood the vision for the properties and the development of the area, so they agreed with the logic of the numbers and the projection as well as the necessary investment to make them come to fruition. The present loans will be paid off immediately, but the construction money will need to remain in a special account with the bank so you and your general contractor can draw from it for the amounts the bank inspector may authorize as the remodeling progresses."

Cuesta's smile broadened, "I can't believe this is happening."

"Thomas Lock recommended you and your project. He has a very good eye for these things. If he didn't like what he does so much, he would have made an incredible land developer. He has an amazing imagination on how to proceed with making the best use of property. He claims that he has learned it from his clients over the years because he has been able to see all of them develop their investments in profitable ways and he said that he saw the same potential in your plans. It's still up for final processing, but if you can guarantee everything personally, then we can sign next week. Advise your attorney."

"I can do that. Honestly, I am just happy that he took an interest in my project," said Cuesta. "Did he ever tell you how that came about?"

"Yes, after you paid off what you owed his client, your attorney mentioned that you could use financing and that the lack of it had caused the litigation, so he began to think and came to me with the recommendation. Sometimes our adversary can become our friend or benefactor."

"I wouldn't have guessed it since he was on the opposing side, but when we met before, he struck me as a man of honor."

"One of the few still left in this town." affirmed Feliciano.

The men shook and Cuesta hurried off to the nearest elevator. As he walked away, Feliciano thought. *The bank will make a great deal of money off this project, and I will get all the glory for it. I must send more work Thomas' way. As they say, one hand washes the other and both wash your face.*

Cuesta reached his car and sped out of the bird road exit of the bank parking lot. He headed toward little Gables to pick up Eleonor. By now the little girl would be sitting outside waiting and only she and a couple of other children would still be waiting. He was very sorry, but he could not cut Torres off in the middle of their conversation. He approached the entrance way slowing down quickly and there she was, waiting for him with a smile. She was truly his little angel. He came to a smooth stop. She bolted to the front door and grabbed the handle.

"In the back sweetheart. You know the rules."

"Papa!"

"No exceptions. Not even today."

"What's so special about today, Daddy?"

"I will tell you but right now we have to go, or you will be late for ballet."

"Do I have to go? Can't we go to the mall or the movies?"

A laugh escaped from his chest. "Nice try, but no we can't."

She sat in the back passenger side and buckled her seat belt.

"Good," he said.

She felt him pull the car out of the parking lot and move onto the four-lane avenue. As they drove, she looked out the window, watching the sun's rays dance between the leaves of the oak trees that lined Coral Gables. As they passed the Biltmore, she looked to the front of the car, staring at her father's gleeful eyes in the rearview mirror. He peeked back at her for a second, smiled, and then the world went dark as the car jerked left and the sound of metal bending, scraping, and breaking filled the air.

Eleonor woke up a few moments later, searching for her father and yelling his name. In the chaos of the crash, the silence of her father's voice deafened the rest of the world. She wiped her eyes with her little hand and searched for her father. She saw his head covered in red and fought to stay awake as the shock hit her and everything went dark again.

Later she woke up to the bumpy ride, the siren coming from without and a pair of reassuring hands on her right arm.

"We'll be there soon, close your eyes and try to sleep." said a voice without a mouth or face. She tried to look toward the voice but found it hard to move her neck as there was something hard around it and someone had taped her down to a hard surface. She closed her eyes and had the nightmare for the first time.

She heard the voice again but slowly the reassuring voice became her mother's voice.

"Wake up, my love, I need to give you some apple juice. You need to eat something too."

"Am I getting my appendix out again?"

"No, my love, you did that two years ago, but you got hurt today, so you had to visit the hospital again."

She opened her eyes and looked around the room.

"Mamá, this is not the same hospital."

"No, this time we decided to try a new hospital," declared Eleonor. Then it all came rushing back.

"Where is Papá? I saw blood on his head. Where is Papá?"

"He is asleep and cannot wake up now." She told the half-truth she had prepared knowing she would ask.

"Oh Mama, I saw red stain on his head." She started getting agitated, "It was blood, I think, is he okay?"

"I told you he is asleep now."

"But I can see him, can't I?"

"No, the doctors say you can't get up from bed and will have to stay here for a few days. Then we will see what happens."

"But I have to make sure he's Okay."

She swallowed hard and answered.

"The last time I spoke to your father he asked me to take care of you and make you well, and I promised him I would, so go back to sleep and rest. We'll talk later."

Eleonor gave her mother a little smile.

"Okay, Mama," she said, and slowly closed her eyes.

Chapter 49: The Funeral

Miami, Florida: September 1970

Eleonor touched the surface of her white dress. It was very smooth and cool. Her grandmother, Herminia, called it silk, but the dress had little pink adornments of pearls and lace on her chest and sleeves. It was very pretty, but she didn't feel so. She would have preferred to wear black like her mother. She could see her, with a brave face, hair in a bun and the grey hair at her temples which she refused to dye for the funeral.

Eleonor had been sitting there for hours in a wheelchair, not because she needed to use it, but as a precaution due to the long hours the funeral would last. She was a few days from becoming a teenager. There would be no celebration this year, not without Papá. She refused everything including a cake and candles. The doctors had not wanted her to come today, but she had insisted, and her grandmother had promised to stay with her in this corner of the lobby, just outside the viewing area where her father lay in his casket, in eternal sleep. Her mother had explained that she had told her that lie on the doctor's advice. They had informed her that the news of Eleonor's father's death in her condition at that time, was not a good idea. Her mother had agreed, but to Eleonor the lie was unforgiveable. She wanted to see her father as he was when he died, not like now when the funeral people put make up on him. *Papá would have never agreed to wear makeup,* she thought, *but of course, they do not ask a dead man for permission.*

Her cousins, and aunts were all here from Colombia. She had heard them say that they had asked her father to sell everything and come back to Colombia, but he had said no. He liked Miami very much. Now all her father's family sat around lamenting that he did not go home when they asked. She turned her head and looked at the older lady with deep smooth white hair in the black maxi-dress. Like her mother she wore no makeup but did put on a smile whenever she looked at her granddaughter. Eleonor smiled to herself as she felt the warmth emanating from the older woman. After her father's death, when his family showed up at their house and turned on her mother, it was she that protected her mother fiercely and shut down the talk.

Her eyes searched again for her mother and found her still bravely shaking hands, giving kisses, and occasionally, hugging and sharing a tear with someone who cared. She looked around at all the people who cared for her father and the rows of flowers tied in wreaths with two metal legs resting against the far wall. Most had ribbons with words written on them of peace and eternal sleep, but there would be no peace in their lives anymore. How do I live without Papá? she thought. As she was turning her attention back to her grandmother, she glanced at the double door entrance, and she felt herself grow cold. There he was, the tall man with the bright eyes and thick glasses, who had raised his voice at her father that day at the lawyer's office walking in to disturb her father in his death sleep. How could he dare do that? She remembered that her father had been so sad and silent in the car on the way home. She had asked, "Papa, why did that man raise his voice at you?"

"Did you hear that?"

"Not the words, I could not understand the words, but I heard his raised voice. He was ugly to you."

"Your father made a mistake, and he was reminding me."

"We all make mistakes daddy. You have told me many times."

"Yes, but your father did something bad." He had said that, but she knew her father was just being kind to the tall man. She looked back at her mother and to her shock her mother was hugging this tall man. "How could that be?

Didn't she know how mean he had been and what a bad man he is?"

"How do you know he's bad?" asked her grandmother.

Eleonor watched her mother, and the tall man speak. They talked for a while, and then the man made his way toward her.

"Abuela, please don't let anyone bother me, I am really tired, and I need to sleep for a little while."

"Do you want to go home?" asked her grandmother.

"Yes, I just want to rest for a little while."

"Okay, I'll ask my brother to take you home," said Herminia," she explained before leaning back in the chair and closing her eyes.

She heard her grandmother get up and she heard her voice and the voice of the tall man which she recognized from that day.

"Hello, my name is Thomas Lock, I knew your son-in-law only briefly, but enough to know he was a good man. I am so sorry to meet you under these circumstances. I wanted to give my condolences to his wife and now his daughter."

"As you can see, she's not here, she's leaving for home now to sleep, but I'll tell her. She is still in recovery from the accident, and she is so tired from participating in all of this. She came because her Papá was the love of her life."

"Yes, fathers are always special in the lives of their little girls."

"Yes, especially this father and this little girl."

After that, the voices did not speak and no one bothered her. After a long time, she opened her eyes and looked around. The tall man was nowhere to be seen.

Chapter 50: The Arrangements

Miami, Florida: September 1982

She finished her story and looked at Thomas with sad eyes. "Since that day her need for rebellion grew. First it was against what happened, next against me, and then against the world. She finally rebelled against herself and embarked on a path of self-destruction which I have been unable to persuade her to leave. She has consumed thousands of dollars in all types of drugs, natural and synthetic, from daily doses of marijuana to strong doses of LSD and everything in between. She has been in rehab more times than I can count. Torres, who did show up a year later, could not stay with me because he was afraid his kids would begin to indulge."

"I am so sorry," said Thomas. "If I would have known, I might have been able to help."

"Don't beat yourself up Mr. Lock. It was meant to be. That's all."

"Sorry to be so business like" interrupted Gabriel, "but we need to get to the problem at hand. Right now, the authorities are looking for Eleonor. If they find her, they will jail her and prosecute her. I would like to soften the blow, if possible. I have already spoken to a colleague at the state attorney's office, and he is looking into the matter. Once I give him a little background on her he will be a lot more lenient. Has she had psychiatric treatment and psychological therapy?"

"Yes, plenty of both, and she was Baker Acted when she tried to kill herself by cutting her wrists."

"Would you put all those records together for me?"

"Of course."

"Do you have any writings by her, paintings or drawings she may have made or attempted, or any other such material stored at your house?"

"I do."

"Can I come see you in a couple of days to pick those up."

"Name the time."

"I will call you. May I have your telephone number and your address? She immediately took a card and gave it to him. The card said Adult Care specialist. "Last two items" finished Gabriel, "do you know where Eleonor may be now and the address?"

"Yes."

"Where can we find her?"

"San Juan Bosco."

"She goes to Father Amos Mulroney?" asked Thomas, realizing the coincidence.

"Yes, though one of the sisters takes care of her. The church contacted me when she wanted to go through rehab and have helped her a lot."

"May I use your phone?" asked Gabriel, directing himself to Graciela.

"Be careful when you put it back in the cradle, sometimes the handset slips."

Gabriel walked over to the phone and dialed.

"Father Mulroney, please. Oh, hello sister...I am well, thank you and you?" Silence followed then, "I'm wondering if there is a young girl there by the name of Eleonor Cuesta."

The line became silent again for a moment before muffled sounds gave Gabriel the information that he had sought. "Do you know if she is working here or is in one of our programs?"

"Yes, she is in your program and doing voluntary community work? Please look for a way for her to stay for a few days until I prepare the situation to help her with the authorities. It's not good Sister but there are solutions to everything, and your church hopefully will be a great part of that solution."

He placed his index finger on the button and then put the receiver back to his ear listening for a dial tone. He dialed again.

"Yes, good afternoon. May I speak with Moses Akouala, please?" Background noises answered. "Yes, it's Gabriel Lock. Thank you." He waited a while. "Mo, how did the trial go?"

Moses made noises on the other side of the receiver.

"I'm glad that he pled before you got started. So, I assume you are free?" After a moment of silence, Gabriel continued. "Have you seen the video, and have you made a decision?" After a longer interval with Gabriel nodding periodically, he spoke again. "Listen, she has a serious psychological imbalance and a drug problem." Gabriel became silent as Moses spoke. "That would be great, Mo. I may have located her, and I will have all the material for you to consider together with an attorney to be able to cut a deal soon." Gabriel listened as Moses responded. "Great, I'll let you know when I've got her location confirmed." Gabriel put the receiver back carefully into the cradle and, looking at Graciela, said, "Can I have the number here so I can call you when we are done?"

"Yes," responded Graciela, "264-6552."

"Thank you," said Gabriel picking up his briefcase and signaling to Thomas who stood up and thanked Graciela but when he turned to María Elena to say goodbye, she hugged him.

"Please help my little girl. She is everything to me."

"We will," answered Thomas" Gabriel opened the door, he followed, and María Elena buried her face in her hands. After a while of standing and trembling before the closed door, she walked over to the armchair, sat, and began to think.

Chapter 51: The Intercession

San Sebastián, Spain: August 1977

Thomas and Laura sat on the train, watching the emerald rolling hills and mix of elms, oaks, and ash trees as they passed by. They sat together; Laura read her book while Thomas read through the notes he had made in his notebook about the journey. The flight from Miami to Madrid lasted more hours than they cared, so they always spent at least one night in the city to rest before heading to Northern Spain.

As the train made its way through the small towns and countryside, the passengers occupied themselves with cards or games, books or magazines, and even a few drinks from the dining car when the moment suited them and grew tired of talking.

They hadn't heard from Enara in over a year and the letters from the new priest had only brought tough news.

"Are you okay?" asked Laura in Spanish, sensing his discomfort.

"No," admitted Thomas. "Amaya having a stroke wasn't the news that I expected to get, and I guess not hearing from Enara directly in over a year didn't make it easier."

Laura turned in her seat to face her husband and brushed her fingers over his face before adjusting his glasses back in place.

"Thanks," he said, "I thought they had slid a little far down my nose."

"Anytime, Love. I must admit that it's been hard not getting mail from her. We never expected it to be every day, but at least every new season or even every six months. Over a year is a long time."

"It still bites at me, you know."

"The guilt?"

Thomas nodded and Laura adjusted, leaning on her husband from her chair. He put his arm around her and held her, smelling the perfume on her hair from this morning and taking a hold of her hand.

"She found Amaya and Amaya found her. She got the mother she always wanted, and Amaya got the daughter she could never have."

"I know," confessed Thomas, breathing deeply before letting it out with a sigh, "I just feel like her life has had tragedy after tragedy."

"Maybe," answered Laura, nodding. "Or maybe San Sebastián is home, and she was always meant to live at home."

Thomas considered his wife's words and realized that he had never thought about it that way.

"Maybe," he said, "I still feel the guilt though."

"There's no need, Honey. She's doing fine, you'll see, and that's all that matters. You need to let it go."

"We'll see," he said, squeezing Laura tighter, "maybe I can."

Laura giggled and Thomas held her as the train journeyed northward, and the light of the moon began to light their way.

The train arrived in San Sebastián early in the morning and, after a brief stop at their hotel, Laura and Thomas were in the cab, making their way back to The Cepa, hoping to visit Enara.

"It's a shame that Gabriel is in Mexico in that program, he could have come with us. He will miss the chance to meet Enara," commented Laura.

"The classes and the internship are a great chance for him to learn a lot of law in areas he would not otherwise see, as well as develop a set of skills that might come in handy especially in Miami, where so much is international in nature. I think this program was a fantastic opportunity," said Thomas.

"I agree, but he would have enjoyed this very much. He would have fallen in love with San Sebastián."."

"Granted, but he is seeing the real Mexico and getting an education. Besides, at the time when he signed up, we didn't know that'd we'd be coming back here, especially in these circumstances, but I am not complaining. From here we're going to Asturias to say hello to the family. I love Oviedo and going to Salinas surrounded by mountains for a walk on the beach. It will be like…" he counted on his fingers, "a ninth honeymoon."

"Sweetheart, you are so cheesy."

"But I'm your cheesy, and that's what counts."

"What did I get myself into?"

The cab pulled up in front of the restaurant. Laura had the money ready, and, in a flash, they were out of the car and onto the sidewalk. They looked through the window where they had sat the last time and reflected on the place where Enara and Amaya spent most of their lives.

At the edge of the bar on the far side sat Amaya. Thomas noticed a cane by her chair and understood that the stroke had left her with limited mobility.

The door swung open, and a waitress stepped out. She asked Thomas and Laura if they needed anything as they had been standing there for a while.

"We were hoping to speak to Amaya," said Laura in Spanish.

The waitress nodded and asked them to follow her.

As they approached Amaya, she turned to them and gave a broad half-smile, showing the effects of the stroke. Laura rushed to hug and kiss her on both cheeks. Amaya moved to rise from her seat, but Laura stopped her.

"I had a stroke, I didn't die," fired Amaya, laughing with a small wheeze. Grabbing her cane, she walked toward Thomas and hugged him. "You brought the handsome man with you again, Laura."

Thomas grinned and squeezed Amaya in his hug. They sat at a table in the back of the room and Amaya signaled for three glasses of water and some tapas to start. "Enara will be here later, she's been busy."

"Busy with what?" asked Laura.

"The wedding."

"Wedding? Whose wedding?" asked Thomas, bewilderment gnawing at his face.

"When was the last time Enara wrote to you?" Inquired Amaya.

"Over a year ago," answered Laura.

Amaya leaned back in her chair and started recalling what had transpired in the last year.

After adding it all up, she sighed and slumped in her chair.

"Yes?" asked Laura.

"Amaya moved out of my house a little over a year ago to her own place when she became the general manager of the restaurant.

"When did that happen? – That's excellent news," began Thomas.

"A little over a year ago. Anyway, when she moved into her new place, she met a new man in her life, and they've spent all their time together."

Laura's face perked into a smile and Amaya's joy matched hers.

"He's a very good man, Laura, very good. He helped her move in and when he said that he had to go, she asked where and when he said that he was going to the Basilica for mass, she knew he was special. Well, they got to know each other and then started dating and he proposed two months ago."

"She's a little young, no?" asked Thomas, expressing concern.

Disappointment and shock competed for Laura's outward expression.

"How old were you when you got married?" asked Amaya, unsettled by Thomas' question.

"Twenty-five," answered Thomas, flatly.

"She's twenty-two, and Álvaro is twenty-seven. The wedding isn't even until next year."

Thomas appeared to sink in his chair as he surrendered to their protests.

"Never mind that I asked."

Laura and Amaya took off on their own conversation, trading questions and answers about wedding details as the morning went on. Somewhere in the conversation, the tapas and water came followed by orders for breakfast and even a bottle of champagne. Thomas sat, reflecting on how Enara's life had turned out, how she had gone from the orphan girl that could have been his daughter to the engaged woman who had made a family and became their friend. She may be all grown up now, but she'll always be a little girl to me, he thought. As he sat, he thanked God for the chance to see what he always hoped would come true, and as he finished his praise, he heard a commotion from the women.

Enara had just entered through the front door and not a second later Laura ambushed her, squeezing her firmly and giving congratulations. When the greetings and commotion ended, Thomas rose, and they embraced with Thomas kissing her head while she hugged him a little tighter.

As Laura and Amaya chattered away at the table, Enara took Thomas for a moment to herself.

"I'm so glad that you're here," she began, "I'm sorry that I didn't write to you for so long, it's been a little crazy."

"I know," answered Thomas, "Is he a good man?"

"The best," she replied.

"Then that's all I ever needed to know."

"You'll get to meet him."

"Is he coming by?" asked Thomas puzzled and looking up.

Enara giggled.

"I meant at the wedding."

"We're invited?"

Enara raised her eyebrows and tilted her head playfully.

"Always, Thomas. My mother entrusted you with my life and even when it wasn't yours to care for, you still did. It would honor her to invite you and Laura to my wedding, and Gabriel too. I can't wait to meet the boy that could have been my brother…again."

Thomas laughed and Enara giggled. He gave her another embrace and looked down at her.

"We'll be there and wouldn't miss it for the world."

Enara smiled and, as they broke their embrace, Amaya and Laura pulled her into their conversation. Thomas saw the three of them lost in the details of their chat and told them that he was going to get some air and would return shortly. Acknowledging him and letting him go, he slipped out of the restaurant and walked down the streets of Old San Sebastián, making his way through the life that busied the city. As he wandered down the block, he stepped into shops, taverns, bars, and plazas, making his way back around to The Cepa. As he neared the Basilica, he stopped for a moment to venerate the statue of Mother Mary above the door. He met her eyes and remembered the words of the old priest from his confession all those years ago. A tear left his eye, grateful for her intercession, and the life he cared for. "Thank you for interceding for me so that I could see this and thank you for your love." He lingered a moment longer before walking back toward The Cepa, eager to see his family and free of the guilt that he once knew.

Chapter 52: The Missing Piece

Miami, Florida: October 1982

The workday seemed like an eternity as Gabriel labored through his day waiting for three o'clock. He had asked Susana to clear his afternoon which forced his thoughts to turn to Jean Robert and his family as he prepared his questions for the men. The weight of his conscience bore down on him from the previous evening and through the night, where the sleep he desperately needed eluded him.

As Gabriel prepared to leave the office, he grabbed a few files and an expandable on the credenza behind his desk and placed the yellow pad with the questions inside. Standing with his back to the door, he heard his father's voice from behind him.

"I know that you have to go, but I wanted to let you know that if you need anything, I'm here to talk," said Thomas, lowering his spectacles and tilting his head forward to look at his son through his own eyes.

Gabriel kept silent.

"It's tough speaking with someone who's going through what they are going through. I've been there. I've had to deliver bad news before too, so if you need anything, I'm here, Son."

"Thanks, Dad, but right now, I'm more focused on finding out what happened. My feelings and reactions will come later," said Gabriel, exhaling. He turned from the credenza to his father who leaned on the doorway using his forearm to hold himself up.

"Santiago is going to take care of Jean Robert's family, at least as much as he can. You just focus on doing your job. That's the best way to help Mrs. Marchant and the boys. Trust me on this one."

"Yeah, that's what I keep thinking," affirmed Gabriel as he moved from behind his desk. Thomas's voice became very stern.

"You should know that Santiago and I found out some very curious information from the Ayesterán when we had lunch."

"Oh yeah, what's that?"

"Do you remember the clerk that was almost shot at the other gas station?"

"Of course, I do."

"Well, they were trying to scare him."

"For?"

"Drugs. They were going to pick up drugs from the station."

"How do we know?"

"The clerk said something to the owners about the men yelling at him about a pickup. Apparently, they got him confused with another one of the employees. When he didn't know about it, for some reason they shot at him. Luckily for him, he stayed in the station and didn't let them in, so when the gunshots went off, they brought a lot of attention, and they didn't stick around. The owners tore the place apart and found a compartment in the gas station. Word on the street is that maybe the same thing has happened with Jean Robert."

"So, you think that someone else at the station was in on this drug ring?"

"It's a possibility. So, as it stands, if it was a drug deal gone south perpetrated by an employee and caused his death, then the insurance pays nothing. If it wasn't by his design, then someone else must be in on it and Jean Robert will receive workman's comp."

"Well then, I need to make a phone call."

"To whom?"

"I need to call González again. I'm going to need to speak to that victim."

"You had better be careful with this one, Son."

Gabriel chuckled and Thomas raised his eyebrows in surprise.

"Aren't I always, Dad?" he joked, dialing the phone.

Chapter 53: The Glass Box
Miami, Florida: October 1982

Pepe placed the three cigarettes on the counter. Gordito contributed the oversized bottle of beer together with some coins and Pepe stared at the coins before him next to the merchandise. He spoke a little louder than usual so his voice could be heard through the little rectangle cut into the bullet proof glass between him and Gordito. "You're short. Put some more money on the counter and then I will give you the merchandise back," he said holding on to the cigarettes and picking up the beer. The overgrown man frowned, put his fat hand in his pocket, and took out a dollar bill.

"Here," said Gordito, handing the cash to Pepe.

"Why do you play these games man?"

"What games?"

"Doesn't matter," Pepe said in disgust. Leaving the goods on his side of the glass, he picked up the money and counted it once again. Finding that it was all there he pushed the merchandise toward the big man who grabbed the stuff, turned, and walked out of the store.

Pepe welcomed the exchange with Gordito, as unpleasant as it always was, simply because it broke the monotony of the Tuesday afternoon. For some reason, Tuesdays were always slow at this station, but it was alright because it gave him time to do all the paperwork for the seven stations he helped manage. The busy days would not let him do that. Sundays were a nightmare; not only were there more sales than usual because everyone came in for something they needed to buy for the week, but the propane gas jugs, the extra ice, the beer, the last-minute chips before the Dolphins' games, and the customers fill ups for the week would exhaust him. He went back to the numbers on the white pages before him. *Things have slowed down quite a bit at the station since Jean Robert's death, an unavoidable consequence. People who had looked at the place as their neighborhood store were now afraid it had become dangerous to come here. One bad night changed the neighborhood, but they'll get used to it in time,* he thought.

Only the guys that played dice on the side of the station at dusk still came back. The group that sat on the upside-down wooden boxes and drank beer all day, had not. *None of them purchased a lot but they did give a strange sense of safety and continuity to the station,* he thought. *Maybe the fact that Jean Robert's lifeless body was found a few feet away from their boxes contributed to their fear.* He remembered his co-worker's dark black skin with that pale sheen of death and his grimaced expression frozen in time. A call from a neighbor had brought Pepe to the station before the yellow tape and the removal of the body. Jean Robert's widow had arrived as the EMTs loaded him into the ambulance and the firemen were pulling away. When all the others left, only the patrol car and the forensics team remained, one making sure the scene was not disturbed while the other collected evidence. He had called Santiago to give him the news, and his boss had been strangely quiet, until he said that they must do all they could for the widow and her children.

Pepe remained silent in turn. He had thought of his own wife lying on a hospital bed in the middle of their family room together with the cot he had slept in for three years. She painfully battled the breast cancer that had migrated into her bones and finally all over her body. Her pain had been overwhelming and debilitating. At the end, the pastiness of slow death had been much like Jean Robert's body. He had tried everything to ease her pain and when the legal drugs were not enough to calm her, he bought illegal ones. She had been the love, friend, and companion of his life. They had been together since high school in their small town in Cuba and he refused to see her suffer more than she had to, but she did and when she passed, he passed judgement on himself.

If I had been a braver man, I might have ended her stay on this earth and not let her suffer. But I couldn't take that step. I knew God would have understood, but I couldn't let her go, he thought. A pang of guilt entered him and touched the thick glass of the protective box. *What could have made Jean Robert leave this glass box? Now his wife suffers needlessly, and his kids have no father.*

His mind flashed to his own daughter and grandchildren, then he broke away from his thoughts with a shake of his head and went back to the white pages. He worked, barely interrupted, until Claudio arrived for the next shift.

Chapter 54: The Breakfast

Miami, Florida: October 1982

They sat near the window and ate their breakfast as the morning sun smothered their food when Gabriel saw Detective González come in through the side door. He stood up and waved through the servers and busboys. Looking over the patrons, González located them and smiled, making his way around the tables to them. Gabriel remained standing and once his friend reached them, he introduced his companion.

"Sarah Jensen, this is Detective Sargent González."

She smiled and stuck out her hand which he took firmly and shook. Everyone took a seat, and their server approached the table. González looked up and smiled.

"Café con leche y tostadas Cubanas."

The chit chat that followed included: how are the kids, how did a guy like you get lucky enough to have breakfast with her and the obligatory, the Dolphins are looking good this year, but not good enough to win another Super Bowl. After a few minutes Gabriel moved the conversation on to the topic of the day. "Did you speak with the witness?

"I did. It was just as you suggested."

"What did he say?" interrupted Sarah. González smiled at her impatience. She realized how rude she had been and apologized. "I'm sorry I have a family without a father waiting for the answer you are about to give. Their future depends on your next words, and I get impatient for them.

"Don't worry, I admire your passion. Please remember that what I tell you must not be repeated because the investigation is still ongoing." he said smiling and continued. "He informed us of many things we already knew but it confirmed them and there was useful information as to your case."

"Like?"

"He told us the guys who shot at him are Colombian. The Colombians are now penetrating the street level market in this area and are using Gas stations as a place to stash their stuff because it's convenient since these establishments are opened 24 hours a day and with simply keeping in mind the work schedule of their people employed at each station, they have instant access to their stuff in a cost-free distribution system. They take the stuff to the stations at peak traffic hours when no one has time to look out for them and retrieve it when needed. The only catch is that if they show up to pick up the cocaine on the appointed day and time, the individual who is present needs to be ready to hand the merchandise over immediately."

"So, when Jean Robert did not know what they were asking for they thought he was holding out on them, and they shot him." She speculated.

"Maybe." Said the Detective, "because that would not explain why he was out of his protective enclosure."

"On the other hand," commented Gabriel, "if he was going to rip them off or break his deal, he would have stayed inside the enclosure in order to stay protected and not expose himself by going out to talk to them."

"True. We also considered that."

"So, what led him out there?" asked Gabriel, almost to himself.

"The other thing that he said was that the people doing the pickup and delivery become customers of the stations they will be keeping the stashes in so the staff is familiar with them and their presence at the station is never questioned and in case of a bust the staff can say that they are regulars and justify their presence that way."

"Well thought out." commented Sarah and in the same breath she said excitedly, "Wait that means that Jean Robert knew them and may well have gone out to them if they called him thinking they were regular customers and nothing else."

"Assuming you are right," added the cop, "how are we going to find that out."

"I can do that."

"You can?"

"Sure, I can question all of them as to their times, their routine and all the information you need without suspicion because they all know I am doing it on behalf of the Santiago, the owner. As his attorney, it is my job to handle any claim for, and against, the station."

"When can you do this?" I am meeting the employee that keeps track of all the information as to employee hours, paychecks, schedules, and responsibilities the day after tomorrow."

"He is their inside bookkeeper?"

"Yeah, basically. Santiago has quite a few businesses, so he delegates the routine station stuff to this gentleman and the day to day of a group of stations, including this one, to a guy named Pepe."

"Makes sense. Okay, Lock, let me know when you have some answers."

"I will."

González swallowed the last gulp of café con leche and he rose to go. "I need to run, I am testifying in a suppression hearing today and Beckett, wants me there early to prepare."

"She is a pain, but she is good. She gets narcotics convictions where people think it can't be done."

"Yeah, but in the meantime, I have to be there two hours earlier than I need to be."

"Don't cry, it's all overtime for your pocket."

"And stress for my life."

"Okay, enough crying."

"Call me" he said, turning to leave.

"I will and take care."

"Nice meeting you," Sarah called after him.

"You, too."

Chapter 55: The New Partners

Miami, Florida: October 1982

Santiago played with his pencil. The grid paper sat blank on his desk. He had been unable to perform any of the work he had planned and was lost in his feelings. *Life has shown me that betrayal comes in strange forms and from unexpected places, but this one was not a surprising discovery, it was a shocking one.* The man that managed almost half of his stations had abused his position costing a coworker and family man his life. *What remains is a husbandless wife and fatherless children that must find their way in a new country without his help and guidance.* He looked around as though the walls would give him the answer he had been looking for since he, Gabriel and Thomas had heard the report from Detective Sargeant González and the two detectives. His mind had frozen in place even though the gears that moved his thoughts kept going in circles.

"Are you alright, Santiago?" He looked at the open door to see Alfonso staring at him, unease appearing on his face. He saw Franco behind him.

"Come in. I know we had a meeting planned to talk about the new look remodel of the common areas of our building, but I have an emergency, so I need to postpone it for Friday."

"Not a problem," said Alfonso, his white hair brighter in the lights of the hallway. "Anyway, how we can help?"

"The problem, unfortunately, has a personal and a professional aspect. I can't do anything about the personal one, but Alfonso do you know a bookkeeper that you trust?"

"I can ask around, but don't you have anyone, Santiago?"

"I had one but not anymore. I have a nephew that I trust but he doesn't know enough accounting yet to be left on his own."

"That solves the problem. Franco has been very busy with the gym and the interior design business and really has no time to help me manage the store, so my daughter is coming on board to help with that. That is happening next Monday and, if you want, I will have time to oversee your nephew's work and teach him the ropes until he catches on. If he is anything like you, that won't take long."

Santiago considered the offer. *One door closes and another one opens.*

"I could pay you for the help," he began to say but he cut his statement short when he saw his partner's reaction.

Alfonso smiled.

"Just returning a favor."

Santiago smiled back and nodded his head.

"Meeting adjourned," said Franco from behind Alfonso. All three men chuckled.

When his partners were gone, Santiago picked up the phone and hit his nephew's number. "Benjamin, tomorrow morning please report to my offices in the morning instead of the distribution center. At seven, please; the office opens at eight. Pay attention in class tonight, you will need to know as much as possible."

He hung up the phone, sat back in his big leather chair, and thought, *Life has been kind to me. It always sends the solution with the problem. Sometimes I don't see that right away but it's always there. The pain of betrayal may not be as easy to handle but time will take care of that.* In the next half an hour the empty grid paper was full of numbers.

Chapter 56: The Retirement Plan

Miami, Florida: October 1982

When Gabriel arrived at the station, he knew that he had just an hour to speak with Lázaro and Pepe before González and the canine unit would arrive in the unmarked cars. Though he knew that there was always the chance of danger, he wanted to get the truth about Jean Robert from them without the police. Finding both Lázaro and Pepe behind the counter, he introduced himself. Lázaro was tall and broad with salt and pepper hair, clean shaven and well-groomed with caramel eyes and pale skin. Pepe was also broad, but short and one could tell that he never lacked for food. His eyes were dark, but his hair was gray and nearing white. As Gabriel shook their hands, they offered him a stool that they had just behind the counter. He passed on it, thanking them and withdrew a small notepad and a pen from his briefcase.

"I'm sure that Santiago briefed you on why I'm here, correct?" asked Gabriel in Spanish. Lázaro and Pepe both nodded before Lázaro answered.

"Yes, he explained that you would want to ask us questions about Jean Robert to see if there is anything that can help with all of this, but we've already spoken to the police so why do we need to speak to you?" The corners of Gabriel's mouth turned downward as he calculated how to respond. He didn't want to frighten them or scare them anymore than the situation and the police had, so he answered firmly but with as much grace as the situation allowed.

"The police questioned you to help them with their investigation in Jean Robert's death, so you have already been down to the station and so forth, but they asked you the questions that they did, because they need to concentrate on solving Jean Robert's murder. My purpose is different. I am here because, as it stands, it is alleged that Jean Robert participated in criminal activity. If that is true, workman's compensation will not cover this incident, and his family will receive no benefits for his passing. Santiago, on the other hand, will receive a notice from his carrier that he will no longer be insured. I am here because I need to make sure that those consequences do not happen. I want to help Santiago keep his policy so that his business can go on as it is and, most of all, to take care of Jean Robert's family. I am sure that both of you want to help me with that."

"What do you mean Jean Robert was involved in criminal activity?!" Shock rose through both of their voices as they processed Gabriel's words. "Why do they think that he was committing a crime?"

"According to my contacts with the police, the word on the street is that there is a serious cocaine ring making deliveries at gas stations in various parts of town and using the gas stations to hold the drugs. What the police don't know is where the drugs are hidden or how they are getting there, but a witness came forward and said that they saw Jean Robert hand a hooded man something before getting involved in an argument just before he was killed."

Neither man uttered a word. Silence befell them as Gabriel pressed on.

"It turns out that Jean Robert put up quite a fight despite being shot multiple times." Gabriel continued the well-studied script that he had noted in his yellow pad. Exhaling, he turned back to them. "He had seven bullet holes in him when the police finished examining his corpse. It was a slaughter."

"Seven?!" screamed Lázaro, his face turning a light shade of green.

"So, the reason why I am here is because I need to learn all that I can about Jean Robert. I spoke with Claudio yesterday and will speak with Baltasar soon. I know that he covered the night shift last night and there is some re-arranging in the shifts, but I'm sure that he'll just confirm what both of you have to say about Jean."

"Why would Jean Robert's family receive anything from Santiago if he was a criminal?" asked Pepe. The corners of Gabriel's mouth turned upward and his eyes gleamed.

"Because we all know that Jean Robert wasn't involved in criminal activity. Do you believe that he was involved in illegal things, Pepe?" "Do you, Lázaro?"

The attorney turned to the side, looking out the window for a moment before returning to his hosts.

"What we don't know is why he was killed. What I believe happened is that someone else who works here or in the company is in on the drug ring that is apparently operating from the gas stations in this area."

Both men's eyes widened and the wrinkles on their foreheads and around their eyelids grew as they processed the news.

"You think that Jean Robert was murdered because of a drug deal?" asked Lázaro, still wide-eyed and with streaks of panic in his voice.

"I believe that he was. I believe that Jean Robert was murdered as the police say, in cold blood." Gabriel examined both men's reactions, looking for anything to work from.

"What do you mean a drug ring?" asked Pepe, straightening himself up, "What have they been doing and why target Jean Robert?" Gabriel looked around trying to formulate his words. Calculating and piecing them together, he collected himself.

"There's a drug ring active in these areas. There shouldn't be much of a surprise as it's Miami, but Jean Robert is the piece that doesn't fit. You have a guy that leaves Haiti to come to the USA. He works and saves every penny that he can to bring his family out of the country that they call home. It takes him three years to raise the money to get them here and that's where I have a problem."

"What do you mean?" asked Lázaro.

"If he would have been selling drugs, he would have been able to bring them in three or four months, so he wasn't selling before they got here. Then they get here. He has two boys and wants to make them proud. He rents a little house so that they can live a little more comfortably because his boys need a neighborhood to run around in. They live happily enough for six months and then, suddenly, he is a drug dealer who gets into an argument with another drug dealer and dies during the night shift; the victim of seven bullets." Gabriel paused, shifting his eyes down toward the floor of the station. "It makes no sense to me." He inhaled deeply and exhaled, sighing and trying to relax himself as the muscles in his back tightened with the stress and nerves of what he was about to say. "Jean Robert didn't deal drugs. I went to his home, I spoke with his wife, I saw the squalor that he could barely afford to live in and saw the remains of a family that lost years of memories for the promise of a better tomorrow before losing him forever. He covered for both of you before. Lázaro, he covered for you when you needed to have your routine visits to the doctor for your daughter, and Pepe, he covered for you when you had your family needs, but we all know that Jean Robert was innocent of a drug deal, and he died because someone in this station is a part of that ring. It's not an accident that the deal happened. The accident is the mix-up in your schedules that could have led to this."

Gabriel looked up to see both men frozen. Neither dared to speak, nor utter a sound. Gabriel checked his watch and counted the seconds, waiting on the go time.

"If I am right, and Jean Robert is not their man, that means that they didn't get what they were promised, and they'll be back to find out why. When they do, it won't be at night when they can't penetrate the secure space. It will be during the day, and the station will be filled with clients and families. That is what I'm here to prevent. That is my job."

He gestured his eyes just beyond the glass and saw González and the rest of the police walking toward the door, canines leading them.

"Well, gentlemen, you can either confess now and aid with this investigation which will soften the blow in your plea deals, or you can forever hold your peace and pray that the court will be more merciful than God when they judge you."

As Gabriel finished, González and the other officers walked through the door. Behind them, he observed Santiago, who was there to give consent to the search if that became necessary. Lázaro looked from Gabriel to Pepe, to the dogs, to González, to Santiago, and back. Pepe did not move.

"Are we ready to begin?" asked González. Gabriel raised his fingers, signaling that he needed a moment. One of the dogs snarled and began barking. González glanced at it. "Something's here."

"Last chance, gentlemen. What's it going to be?"

Lázaro's face turned pale green and then flushed, but Pepe remained very still. Gabriel looked at Santiago who nodded with approval. Gabriel then signaled to González and the officer turned to his men behind him. Before he could issue a command, Pepe spoke.

"Jean Robert was a good man, Gabriel. He died because of me." Sweat slithered down Pepe's temples and Lázaro's pale green darkened. "It was my shift. At first, I needed the money when my wife got sick. She died of cancer, and I spent my whole retirement on trying to save her. I lost my wife and all my money and then some." Pepe exhaled and González raised his arm, making a fist, and signaling his men to stay still. Pepe shook his head and buried it in one of his large hands. "I couldn't afford to take my granddaughter to the movies or to lunch or to give her the things that any grandfather would. I was in debt to some bad people. They told me that if I helped one of their guys out, that I could pay them back in a year and then in five years, I could get my retirement back. I was going to quit after that. All I had to do was just give them a place to put their stuff so that they could lay low. I didn't mean for him to lose his life!" Pepe's face turned bright red. Agony and anguish surged through his veins and the guilt began to pour out of him like the sweat from his scalp and temples.

A young officer began to move forward with handcuffs, but González and Gabriel stared him down. Both experienced men knew that this had to be handled with care.

"Pepe, I can't speak for the police, but I believe that you are contrite and remorseful for what you did, and I believe that in a difficult moment the wrong people persuaded you, but a good man is dead. None of us can change that, but you can help us find the guy who killed him, and you can help us stop this drug ring. Will you show us where the drugs are?"

Pepe nodded.

"It's in the cooler," he said, sticking his arms out. González understood the gesture and grabbed the handcuffs.

"You have the right to remain silent," began González, patting Pepe down and reciting the Miranda rights, "anything you say or do may be used against you in a court of law…"

The drugs were behind a panel in the walk-in cooler hidden by the diet and sports drinks. The two packages weighed about two kilos. Pepe was led away to be placed in a patrol car. At the door of the store, he faced Santiago.

"You could have come to me for whatever you needed; you were always there when I needed you. Why wouldn't you expect the same from me?"

"I worked for you for years and when my wife got sick, I could barely make ends meet. She died because everything I had wasn't enough to save her. You cared so much to expand that the money went into new properties and not to your people. How many hours do we work just to make ends meet? Look at how Lázaro, Baltasar, and I live. Your lawyer saw the shithole where Jean Robert kept his family.

Were more gas stations worth more than paying your people better?"

Santiago gave Pepe a hard stare.

"I did everything that I could to help you and your wife. I paid for a good deal of the treatments that she received and did so anonymously telling the hospitals to inform you that you had qualified for a special program based on your income. Do you not remember that we've been in an oil crisis for three years?! You can blame the war between Iran and Iraq for your wages, but you can blame me that all of you still have a job. Not one person has been fired from this company and not one station has been sold even when some of them have been losing money for years because I knew that if I sold them, my employees would be fired and their families on the streets or in squalor. Jean Robert and I were working to get his family out of that house, but they enjoyed living in Little Haiti. As for you, if you had bothered to ask, I would have given you the down payment to buy your own station and co-signed the loan at the bank because you deserved it after twenty-five years of loyalty. I just couldn't do it right now. Instead, you forgot the man you were and cost an innocent man his life."

Santiago panted as he finished. Color flushed his tan face and the veins in his temples flared with outrage.

Pepe did not respond but signaled the officers and they walked out of the station without a word. Santiago's eyes followed them all the way to the car.

Lázaro moved to the phone behind the counter.

"Claudio, please come over right away, I am a little nervous and under the circumstances, I need a second person here."

After Lázaro was back behind the register, Gabriel called Thomas.

"The plan worked; I will be in the office later. First, I want to see Mrs. Marchant and tell her what happened. I will go to the office after that. Tomorrow, I will call the adjuster and move the case along. Also call Rodrigo to see if he will represent Mrs. Marchant in the claim, and if he will, have him call me tomorrow morning to make arrangements for him to meet with her." Gabriel listened and thought for a moment. "I'll see you later. Tell Abuela that it's been a long day and see if she'll make dinner."

Chapter 57: The Banyan Tree

Miami, Florida: October 1982

The sun shone closer to the west when he arrived. Five more minutes passed before he found himself near the Student Union center where the Banyan tree towered over a set of benches. From a distance he noticed Sarah with her brown hair and freckled face. He stopped, choosing to watch her for a moment. Her crossed leg bounced over her still one as she flipped to a new page. Choosing not to delay any further, Gabriel strolled over to her. She looked up when he came within a few yards and gave him a warm smile revealing a pair of dimples. "Hi," she said softly, raising an arm to welcome him.

"Hey," he greeted back, "want to work here or is the library still fine?"

"I need to do research, So, to the library. Come on let's go." Sarah uncrossed her legs and rose from the bench, placing a dog ear on her page as she closed the book.

"Ready?" he asked. Sarah nodded. "Then lead the way."

"What is your involvement in all this, Jean Robert wasn't getting divorced was he.?" he asked, turning his head slightly to face Sarah.

"No, he and his family were...well, are my client in their immigration process. The decisions taken by your client and his insurance company will not only determine what compensation they will get or not get, but it may well determine what country they live in and what their whole future looks like."

"I see. So, you are very intricately involved in the outcome of this case because you represent him and his heirs."

"Yes."

"There are three ways to go on this."

"Let's hear them, Gabriel."

"The first one is that he was out of his protected enclosure at that time of the night to sell drugs, buy stolen goods or something like that and his murder was a consequence of the deal going bad. The second is that there was a problem with the equipment, and he had to go out and fix something and was mugged on the way either in or out,"

"Lastly, he recognized a person he knew and went out to talk or do something not illegal but unrelated to his job and during that dereliction of duty, he was shot."

"That about sums up the ones you would think of with the facts you have."

"And what facts don't I have?"

"That wasn't his shift. He was subbing for another person, and he got shot."

"Why would he leave his safe space?"

"Your third hypothesis. He recognized the individual who came to see the other employee."

"Okay, I'll think about that, but I am not convinced yet."

Fifteen minutes passed before they found themselves crossing the entranceway of the law library. Sarah greeted one of the librarians before as they made their way to the second floor, trying to find a deserted spot where they could examine the cases and whisper.

They found the second floor deserted. Perusing through the stacks on the eastern side of the floor, an open table with empty chairs appeared tucked next to a set of windows.

"Is this fine?" asked Gabriel.

"Sure, this is great," answered Sarah.

They placed their belongings on the tabletop and Sarah opened her briefcase, flipped through a yellow pad, and began to look through some notes. "I had a chance to stop by the library in the Courthouse yesterday, I was able to do the research, but I did not have time to copy the cases I need."

"Can I help?"

"Here is the list of cases I need to copy; I'll take half the list and here is the other half."

"Meet you back here in a half an hour."

They both took off in different directions.

Half an hour later, she found him among the stacks on the second floor, flipping through the pages of a book, searching for anything relevant.

"I found all the ones that were on my list," said Sarah, carrying a stack of five books.

"I found several additional cases referenced in the Florida Jurisprudence, so I brought them along also. Where is the copy machine?"

"At the end of this hallway but you need dimes."

Sarah opened her briefcase and took a bag of dimes. "I came prepared." They began to deposit dimes and make copies. "So, what made you want to become a lawyer?"

"My dad. I mean, I didn't become a lawyer to be like him, but his passion for his work and using the law to help his clients is what inspired me. What about you?"

"I grew up surrounded by helpers and servants and I saw how they took care of me and my family, so I want to help people, like they helped me. They didn't care that I was a rich spoiled brat, they accepted me for who I was. When I got older, I did a lot of volunteer work. When I was in high school, I worked at centers for women and children doing errands or assisting clients in filling out simple forms. In college I participated in programs to help the needy on behalf of my family's companies and found that all the legal staff was overworked. Then, four years ago, I went to work in a small-town legal aid office, and it confirmed everything that I believed. The poor have very little access to legal assistance."

Gabriel nodded and took a deep breath. Sarah looked down at her hands for a moment before turning her eyes back to him.

"So, what is it that you're looking for in this research?"

"Cases saying that my clients can stay in this country even though the bread winner is gone. I have found some indication that if clients are witnesses to a crime and needed by the prosecution then they can at least stay until the conclusion of the case. But that is obvious. What I need is case law that enhances their chance to remain in this country because of what happened to Robert."

"That's a lot to take in," admitted Gabriel, looking down at his hands and realizing he had not written a single word of everything she had to say, "I understand what leads you to want to do this work. It's clearly in your heart but working with families and helping those in situations like these is going to. You must have seen that when you worked in the centers and at the law firm."

"Somewhat, but the difference is that I dealt with them after it had happened at the centers. I worked in relieving their pain, not advocating for their best interests, and avoiding the pain."

"Relieving pain is always in someone's best interest so don't beat yourself up. I look at what I do and most work is routine, but the routine cases are rarely the ones that make you lose sleep. It's the difficult ones that do; the demanding cases always take their toll, and the damage extends beyond collateral."

"I think this case qualifies as one that is definitely not routine."

"That is now, very clear."

"So, what do you propose that we do for my meeting with immigration?"

"I don't know exactly," answered Gabriel, "but the answers are in these books, so let's get to it."

Chapter 58: The Immigration Hearing

Miami, Florida: October 1982

The waiting room was a large boring rectangle with light green walls and an off-white drop ceiling. The lawyers sat in the metallic chairs that were placed all around the room dutifully waiting for their turn. Sarah played with the little ticket in her hand. Her number was not being called. Hopefully, she thought this would be the last lag in a long day of delays. In the first line by 5 o'clock in the morning to have the opportunity to obtain this entry ticket and wait all day. Only sixty numbers this morning were distributed to the waiting crowd of attorneys, and she was lucky to get one of them. Doing immigration law had become a contest of will between the lawyers who were ready to accept the abuse and those who, being overwhelmed themselves, had no choice but to be abused.

The hour hand on the standard white face black numbered government clock raced to three o'clock in the afternoon and she had accomplished very little. An officer stuck her head out the door and said in a loud clear voice, "Numbers 34 and 35 please come in." *I'm next.* She thought as she began to collect her papers and organize her ideas.

Sarah walked slowly toward the gray door, briefcase in hand, and as she got closer, to her surprise, it opened. "Number thirty-six please" she heard and simply continued walking through the door as though she had always expected the door to open. She turned and saw a black woman wearing the Service uniform with a name tag that read Georgina Jefferson. "Officer Jefferson, I am Sarah Jensen, and I represent the family of Jean Robert Marchant." She held out her hand containing ticket number 36. The officer held out her own hand, palm up and Sarah deposited her ticket in her grip. Officer Jefferson marched down the hall and Sarah followed. They both strode around a ninety degree turn and into the first door on the left. Officer Jefferson pointed towards the metallic gray chairs in front of a metallic grey desk and Sarah understood the rules of the meeting. For the moment she would comply with the unspoken rules, but only for the moment. Sarah approached the chair closest to her and in almost one movement she deposited herself in that chair and her briefcase in the far one.

The officer looked at the file that was lying on her desk, picked it up and looked through it briefly. "Your client received a winning immigration lottery ticket and moved to the US. He is therefore entitled to residency which he has applied for and will most probably receive, so why the appointment?"

"Because he is dead."

"Then I close the case and it's still not complicated. I repeat my question, what is the purpose of your visit?" She asked, lowering her head to try and look more intense. "Surely you did not wait all day just to tell me your client is deceased," she said, feeling her voice become harsh.

"No, I did not, but what we have to do is determine the status of his family."

"Since it was he who won the lottery and their status is derivative of his, once he is gone, they have no status and they have to return to Haiti," she said, "and please do not talk to me about how terrible and violent Haiti is right now because, legally, that does not matter unless you are claiming asylum for the wife."

"Not at this time, though she may be entitled to it as her husband was pursued for his statements against corruption which were called anti-government activity. He was a lawyer in Haiti, and he was a vocal critic of the stealing of funds from international organizations by government officials. He left in response to threats to himself but mostly his family."

"Can you prove that?" said the officer looking at the file in her hands.

"I will, but in the meantime, I have another petition."

"Yes?" she answered without looking up and Sarah, opening her briefcase, pulled out a file and handed the officer a small stack of papers.

"Jean Robert was a victim of a crime, and that is how he was shot and killed at his place of employment."

Officer Jefferson's head moved quickly, and her eyes fixed on Sarah.

"How did it happen?"

"You will see in the perp's A form which I have included with the petition, that a co-worker was storing drugs for a gang inside the gas-station where he worked. He and his co-worker, Jean Robert, switched shifts and the gang showed up unexpectedly to make a withdrawal from the stash, but Jean Robert did not know what they were talking about. Thinking he was holding out on them, they shot him, and he died instantly."

"He was not involved?" asked Jefferson.

"No, he was not. You will also find a letter from the employer's attorney, Gabriel Lock, which explains that both his investigation, as well as that of the police, established that Jean Robert was innocent of any wrongdoing. As it happens often in this town, he was in the wrong place at the wrong time and he paid the ultimate price, leaving a wife and children behind."

The officer's eyes softened.

"That still does not give me a basis for her and the kids to remain in the US."

"I have also included a letter from the state attorney's office stating that they will need the wife as a witness in the coming criminal trial to establish that her husband was not part of the gang if at trial the accused tries to wash his hands of the whole thing and blame Jean Robert for his own death."

Jefferson took the letter and skimmed it.

"Does she have a job, or will she be a charge on the state?"

"Behind the State Attorney's letter, you will find a letter from Attorney Rodrigo Vivar who is handling the workman's compensation case for the family stating that the matter has been settled, and they are now signing the final documentation for payment to the family of a substantial sum. Lastly, you will find an affidavit of support signed by Mr. Santiago Alemán, Jean Robert's employer, stating that, subject to the Service's approval of her petition, he has given the wife, Mrs. Marchant, a job with the company so she can support herself upon receiving the S 1 visa as a result of the application that I have presented today. This is the reason for my appointment. I need to fast track the application so that Mrs. Marchant can begin to work, and the family has financial support pending the payment of the compensation award. In that way, they can support themselves without being a burden on the state."

Officer Jefferson's hand stopped shuffling papers and stared down at the file. "What's this picture here at the end?" She turned the file and showed Sarah the picture of Mrs. Marchant and the children.

"I am sorry, I forgot to take that out. I always put a picture in my files of my clients, so I remember who I am fighting for when I go into a hearing. I should have taken it out. I apologize."

Officer Jefferson broke her stare from the image and smiled. She knew perfectly well why the picture of the deceased and that beautiful, neatly dressed family was there, and it had nothing to do with counsel, and all to do with her.

"No problem, Counsel." She reached for the picture and handed it to Sarah. "I have nothing else, do you?

"No," responded Sarah.

"Here is my card," said Jefferson reaching for one inside the cardholder on her desk. "Call me next week and by then I will have finished my investigation and have an answer for you."

"Thank you."

As Sarah walked toward the elevator, she recalled Jefferson's long stare at the photo, and she knew they would be allowed to stay.

Chapter 59: The Old House

Miami, Florida: April 1971

Eleonor gazed through her window into the blue green lake. The wind had begun to bend the trees under the deep grey sky, and it reflected her mood. The goodbye party for her and all her friends had been so carefully prepared by her mother, but it was not a happy occasion. The small moving truck would be there tomorrow. That was all they needed since most of the furniture had been sold to strangers that came and took their things away. They kept only what fit in their little two-bedroom home in Westchester. At least she could walk to Saint Brendan's where she had received a scholarship.

Her grandmother had left last week with a promise to return but Eleonor knew that would not happen. She had overheard the argument with her mother. Grandmother insisted they go back to Colombia and live with her. If not both, then at least Eleonor, but her mother would not hear of it. She refused to go back because she wanted to stay in the States. There were all kinds of things between them and Eleonor very quickly realized that none of those things could easily be taken back. Grandmother liked everyone doing was she said. The older woman was used to that. Her mother knew it and following her husband's footsteps, was, in her own way, refusing to surrender to it.

She might have liked living with her grandmother. She ran her fingers through her long black hair and thought of all the people who would have been pampering her and making sure she had everything she wanted. She would be going to the most exclusive schools and places. She did not mind getting away from the place where she saw her father die. Instead, she would have to see the corner every time she went from school to practically anywhere. Hopefully, her mother will take a detour around the place.

Jacinta and all the other girls had talked about getting together, going to the movies, or to the mall, and having sleepovers, but she knew those friends were now out of her life. Her mother would not be able to afford the same types of places she had gone to in the past. She might see them occasionally, if they went to the movies at the AMC on Coral Way and 87th Avenue, but that was about it. She got up from the comfy chair her father bought for her and, opening the bedroom door, walked down the hall into the family room. She walked to the bookcase and read the title of her favorite books she looked out the front window and saw a Toyota Corolla where her mother's Mercedes used to be. Life was changing but she would not forget the man who screamed at her father. She would say goodbye to everything else, but not to him. One day she would make him pay.

Chapter 60: The Paperwork

Miami, Florida: November 1982

The house was a late 1950's Miami house lifted on blocks two-and-one-half feet off the ground. It was located on a standard lot measuring 100 feet by 75 feet and surrounded by homes much larger and more modern than the Cuesta residence. Gabriel walked up the cement walkway and knocked on the door. María Elena answered with a smile this time and said hello.

"You came by yourself?" she asked.

"Yes, I thought it was best. I want to collect what I need as fast as I can and get in touch with the prosecutor as well as children's services if it comes to that. I want to present documented proof of Eleonor's problems and traumas before they begin to make up their minds with the case, so that we find a solution that works for everyone. I have already spoken to Mirella; the owner of the daycare center and she is on board so that is a positive, but to do the most of what I can for her, I need all the paperwork you have."

She looked at him intensely.

"Gabriel why are you doing this?"

"Because it's the right thing to do, especially because Eleonor was the victim of an unintended consequence of an unfortunate set of events. Not to mention that my father feels so guilty about something that didn't sleep for the last week."

She smiled at him.

"The world has enough heartache for all of us to get some. This was ours. For some of us it is our destiny."

"Fate and destiny are words that are a bit too big for me. They imply an unalterable path of life, and I have a hard time accepting that."

"I understand that at your age, it is difficult but sometimes there is no other explanation."

"Can we take a look at the information you have for me?"

"Of course." She walked to the dining room table and invited him to sit. "I have the paperwork supplied by her psychiatrist and her two therapists. She was in their care until she turned eighteen and she refused further care. She handed him a thick folder and reviewing it briefly Gabriel observed several reports that mentioned borderline personality disorder, "After that she was baker acted twice, both times for endangering herself." She finished and handed him a second file which Gabriel saw contained police reports, psychiatric determinations, and a judicial order among other documents. "Lastly, I have this for you. She gave him a notebook, Gabriel looked through it.

"What is it?"

"It is Eleonor's book of thoughts, poems, and musings."

Gabriel looked at her with a puzzled expression.

"It's a collection of writings containing her soul and innermost thoughts. When you review it, I think that you'll find that she is very deep and gentle and that life mistreated her badly on one occasion. You also find her description of the reason for the trauma in her life. I know you'll review it with love and compassion."

"I appreciate the fact that you have this confidence in me."

"I do, but I am sorry, today I have run out of options with her, and right now I would strike a deal with God if it would help get her out of the hole, she's put her life in."

"I understand. This hatred for my father, where does it come from? She blamed my father for all of it. Why?"

"On the day of that last deposition, my husband picked her up from school to leave her at home, but the traffic made them run late. Instead of taking her home, he took her to the deposition."

"He left her outside, but she overheard some of the interrogation. She heard the questioning and the ultimatum your father gave my husband," she said. "Since she thought her father could do no wrong, there had to be a different reason, so she began to think that he was not paying attention to traffic on the day of the accident because your dad's eminent threat distracted him. So, Mr. Morales was the cause, but your father was his weapon. Luis' death had to be avenged and nothing I ever said could convince her otherwise. She needed someone to blame, and Thomas and Morales were the only choices. So, my daughter not only lost her father, but her home, her friends, and everything she knew. Her obsession sent her over the edge and through years she turned to drugs as an escape. As the usage grew and as the years passed, we started to lose touch."

"My father caused his death?"

"No, he didn't and to say so would be unfair. You know the truth, but she wouldn't accept it. It's crazy, Paul Simon wrote a song with a line that comforts me from time to time: All lies and jests, still a man hears what he wants to hear and disregards the rest. She disregards everything but what she wants to believe. The fixation has destroyed her life."

Remorse, guilt, and pain emanated from her voice and Gabriel knew the years that added to the feelings and the regret that plagued her life.

Gabriel did his best to comfort her.

"Let's see what we can do for her, María Elena. Hope is all we can have now."

Chapter 61: The Final Pages

Miami, Florida: November 1982

Gabriel closed the last page and checked his watch, seeing that it was seven thirty. *I've still got some time before I need to meet Sarah*, he thought. He walked over to the table and retrieved Eleonor's diary. The writing impressed him as hope seemed to linger on almost every page she had written, despite the darkness they held. Her search for friends at the new school had been especially disheartening and no one could withstand her depression for very long except for others who, like her, carried their own. This led them all to the alcohol and the escapism of hard drugs. She documented her descent into a deeper and expansive gloom, going through a goth phase which made her feel comfortable and at home but even that was awkward after a while. Almost every moment of high school covered the pages as he read through Freshman, Sophomore, Junior, and almost Senior year. As he closed the notebook, he took a moment to think.

Gabriel began to realize that, until she came to grips with what really happened, she would never rest and would continue this downward spiral. He looked up and wondered, *will she ever be capable of accepting the truth?*

He grabbed an expandable file with divisions and filled each one with copies of reports, records, and judicial orders according to age and incident. In the last section he placed tabs on all the pages he thought were significant and revealing. He looked at the watch again and realized it was a quarter to eleven. *Shit,* he thought. *I missed my date with Sarah.* He picked up the phone and dialed immediately.

"Hi," he said, exhaustion seeping from his voice.

"Hi," answered Sarah with a tinge of sadness in hers.

"I'm sorry that I missed our date. Can we reschedule for tomorrow?"

"Why did you miss it?" she asked, the sadness turning to disappointment.

"I just finished the review I was doing on this case, and I lost track of time. I am sorry and, honestly, I'm beat."

"I am leaving on Wednesday, remember? –And today is Monday."

"I'm sorry Sarah, I will meet you now if you wish."

"No Gabriel, you are tired and so am I. I thought you would have called me earlier, but I understand."

"You're disappointed."

"Yeah, I am. I know that you're busy with work, but work can't be all that you do."

"It's not, Sarah," he began, defiance rampant in his tone. "That's unfair to me; it's been a lot, more than anything I've had this year. All my cases in the last few months have been bigger than I ever expected. I haven't even gone boxing, poker night, or been involved in anything else but work and you. Right now, that's been everything in my life."

"But it's not me and work, Gabriel; all we talk about lately is work and work is your life." Her tone was neither harsh nor unforgiving, but the words shredded his being. "Look, let's not speak any more about this, you've been busy, but I'm not sure that it's just work. Something's holding you back, Gabriel, something you've never let go of. Maybe this case is what you need to let that something go, so don't worry about tonight or meeting me tomorrow. I'll see you on Wednesday."

Gabriel couldn't speak; her words disarmed him as they unearthed the truth he struggled to face.

"Good night, Gabriel. I'll call you tomorrow night." Sarah hung up and Gabriel stood there, listening to the silence before returning the phone to its cradle. He wanted to bury himself in the sand. He knew what she meant, and he knew that even though Sarah had been the most important interest since she walked into his life, hers was not the photo he carried in his wallet. Sarah never knew about her, but she felt her presence, not in conversation, but in his lack of conviction, and it had been that way once the butterflies had worn off. He looked at his watch again, knowing that it wasn't the time he searched for, but confirmation that it was too late for him to do anything more. *I'm sorry, Sarah*, he thought, as he prepared for bed and the new day.

The next morning Gabriel parked the mustang in the lot and sat there, thinking about everything that Sarah had said and what he had done to try and make up for it. Waking up before dawn, Gabriel had driven to Hervé's art gallery where he had met Jérôme and the two of them had gone through all of paintings of their local artists, trying as a team to fix Gabriel's problem. Jérôme, having a girlfriend of his own, knew peace offerings better than anyone. Together they had chosen a piece that stood out to them because of the play of light and shadows. Gabriel had dropped it off in front of Sarah's front door along with a note saying that he was sorry. Checking his watch in his car, he knew that she was still sleeping, but hoped that when she woke up, he'd be forgiven. Brushing off the distress of last night's call, he left everything in the parking lot before he entered the office, heading straight over to speak with his father.

"Good morning, Dad," he said as his father looked up from the files on his desk and smiled. "I need to talk to you for a few minutes. Can we do that now?"

"Sure, Son," said Thomas, using his hand to gesture at the chairs in front of his desk. What's going on?"

Gabriel took a seat and leaned forward, keeping eye contact with his father as formulated what to say.

"Mrs. Cuesta collected all the records I wanted and more and I learned a lot about Eleonor and the trauma she went through."

"Tell me."

"She was in the car with her father when the accident happened and he passed. She became obsessed with the idea that losing the case made him distracted and that is why he wasn't paying attention as the other car came towards them, which is why they were T-boned, he blew right through the stoplight." Gabriel had been thinking all night about how to best soften the story for his father. Gabriel looked at his father and could tell that he fought back tears. Thomas's eyes puffed as the emotions fought within him.

"You know…"

I know, Dad," said Gabriel, cutting him off. "But she had to blame someone, and you and Morales were it, especially because of the deposition where Cuesta lied and tried to hide assets," said Gabriel, reminding his father of the situation.

"She was the black-haired girl. The one that I hit with the door by accident."

"Yes, she was," confirmed Gabriel.

Thomas opened his eyes wide.

"I never made the connection."

"She is entrenched in her mistake and that has led to her downward spiral. She refuses to admit her profound grief and finds revenge, the perfect excuse to wallow in sorrow. So, while we can't change the past, let's try to do something for the future."

"What do you have in mind, Son?" asked Thomas, focusing through the guilt.

"She is still in the Sister Carmela's program at San Juan Bosco. I called Mo last night and today he will meet me at the church and go over all the information I have on her mental state. I also called Rodrigo, and he promised to be there to represent her, if she wishes, and make sure we do everything by the book. We have agreed, that if the situation is as I have described to them, that she can be institutionalized and later be released into the custody of Sister Carmela and her program until she is fully stabilized."

"Okay. When do you plan to do all of this?"

"Now."

"Did you speak with Mirella and Raúl? Are they Okay with this? It was their childcare center after all."

"I did and they are fine with it. Mirella repeated that the way the child was left outside, it minimized the danger to him, and the parents are not going to press charges either. So, Mo has a free hand to act."

"Okay, Son. Looks like you've taken care of everything."

"Not everything. There is still the girl."

"I have been looking through the papers in the daycare case, and I would like to give you some additional documents. You need to look at these before you go." He handed Gabriel a manila envelope. He took the envelope from his father, went to his office to retrieve the expandable file, and within minutes he was gone. Thomas heard the door close and continued to gaze out the window for a long while.

Chapter 62: The Little Girl

Miami, Florida: November 1982

Gabriel turned the Mustang into the lot and parked in one of the empty spaces. As he parked, he turned off the ignition, Thomas unbuckled his seatbelt and reached for their coats and the expandable file in the backseat. "Ready?" asked Thomas, handing Gabriel the suit jacket and expandable.

"Yes, are you?"

"It's been a long-time coming."

As they exited the car, they saw the familiar face of Father Amos coming toward them in the distance. Adjusting the expandable in his hands, Gabriel put on his jacket one sleeve at a time as Thomas did the same, brushing off the wrinkles of his coat as well. As Father Amos drew nearer, Thomas turned to Gabriel and retrieved a thin file from the expandable.

"I know that I gave these pages to you earlier, but I'll need these for this conversation. You'll get them back after I'm done and you can give this to Mo and Rod."

Gabriel nodded and looked at his father's eyes, finding anguish.

"It'll be alright, Dad."

"I know it will, Son, but meetings like these are never enjoyable."

"Just like confession," joked Father Amos, reaching them. A grin escaped Thomas' face as he turned to Father

Amos and greeted him with a handshake. Gabriel did the same.

"Thomas, you got away from confession with me by moving to The Roads. You're at Saints Peter and Paul now, or is it Saint Augustine?"

"Saints Peter and Paul," affirmed Thomas, "Saint Augustine is beautiful, but I don't want to feel like too much of an old guy with all of the students."

"You'll always be the old guy," joked Father Amos. "You're an old soul."

"I'll remember that."

"Gabriel, I've not seen you for some time now, though I see that you take after your father well enough." "I'm doing well, Father, thank you, and I'm at Saint Hugh, just in case you wanted to know."

"I was just about to ask."

"And it's been one week since my last confession, so I'm not too tarnished."

The three men laughed.

"Anyway, I got your message from the secretary. Thank you for calling us earlier. Eleonor is with Sister Carmela and she's not expecting you though Sister Carmela is."

"Thank you, Father," said Thomas. "May I go in?"

"Sure. She's in Sister Carmela's office, third door on the right."

"Thanks. Do you have a room where Gabriel can meet with his colleagues?"

"I assume that it's in reference to Eleonor, right?" asked Father Amos.

"Yes, Father," answered Gabriel.

"Then you'll need privacy. Use my office; it's through here," said the priest, leading the way.

Thomas straightened his stance and walked through the doors heading to Sister Carmela's office. When he approached the door, he slowed down his pace and knocked on the wooden surface. He heard a voice he recognized as Sister Carmela's.

"Come in." He turned the handle and stepped into the office. Eleonor and Sister Carmela were seated at the desk, and they now stared at him.

"Thomas, nice to see you again," said the nun.

"Likewise, Sister Carmela." "You know each other?" inquired Eleonor, surprise riddling her defiant voice.

"For a long time," answered Sister Carmela, "longer than I've known you, actually." Eleonor's face reddened with anger as a feeling of betrayal settled into her mind.

"Eleonor, you and Thomas have a lot to talk about…"

"–No we don't," protested Eleonor, rising from her seat to leave.

"Yes, you do," fired Sister Carmela, taking a hand and grabbing Eleonor's wrist. "With what you did, you're lucky that the police aren't here taking you to jail. If it weren't for Thomas and the mercy that his client showed you, you'd be facing severe punishments. How could you even think to use a child for your sick revenge?"

Eleonor ripped her wrist away from Sister Carmela's hand and glared at her but dropped in her seat. Sister Carmela stared right back at her, unmoved by Eleonor's intensity.

"I've assisted with Exorcisms, sweetheart; you're fits of anger don't impress me."

Thomas suppressed his laughter and remained impassive.

Sister Carmela got up to leave, and as she did so, Eleonor huffed in anger.

"Now you listen to everything that he has to say!" fired the nun before closing the door behind her.

Thomas, allowing a moment to pass, held the file tightly in his hand.

"Hello, Eleonor," he began.

"Are you going to tell me the same lies my mother has told me all these years?" yelled Eleonor.

"Nobody's lied to you, Eleonor," said Thomas, keeping his tone level.

"Are you going to give me money and tell me to go away or are you going to put me in jail?"

Thomas did not answer. Instead, he walked to the desk, placed the file on it, and opened it in front of her.

"This is from the file that I carried the day I deposed your father. My partner has the complete file outside, and it has all of the collection information for the judgement the court awarded Mr. Morales at the trial." He held up the thin file. "Other documentation is in this one," he said, pointing to it. "I don't think we will be needing the fat one, but it's just outside in case you want to review it. I haven't come to defend my actions, but I'm here because you deserve the truth."

"And you're going to give it to me?!" she balked in misplaced outrage, "You took my dad from me. You aggravated him so much that he couldn't think straight when he drove. He wasn't looking anywhere. He was so distracted that I saw the truck coming before he did. I was in the car!" she screamed. Rage echoed through her voice as it emanated through her. Eleonor shook and the veins in her face pulsated as the anguish ruptured out of her. "I was in the car. I was twelve. and my dad was gone."

Thomas allowed the anger to fume out of her between her shortened breaths, keeping silent until the fury dissipated and her breathing normalized.

"Yes, Eleonor, he was distracted, but not because of desperation," said Thomas softly. "You have built your life on that desperation and refused to believe that it wasn't there. But many things happened after the deposition that you you've heard but failed to understand."

"Yes, all the lies my mother told me." Thomas disregarded what she said and continued in the same tone, pulling a document from the file. "This is a copy of what your father received just before he went to pick you up that day."

"Am I supposed to be impressed?"

"No, but you're going to understand everything a little clearer now," he said as he began to read.

Eleonor sat in silence as Thomas read. She fidgeted in the chair, but Thomas pressed on. The previous fury rose again as she didn't believe his words, but she didn't interrupt him. When he finished, he handed her the paper from the file. She looked at the page and saw the letter head from Banco de San Juan.

"Read it aloud," he commanded.

She looked down and began to enunciate the words.

Dear Thomas,

Thank you for sending Mr. Cuesta my way. I agree with your assessment of his properties, and I am, quite frankly, surprised that no one ever saw the potential of several of his properties. While the buildings may be old, many of the properties are adjacent to one another and the potential for remodeling and creating much bigger shopping complexes is apparent. That fact gives the bank the comfort it needs to refinance the properties in the amounts necessary to pay off the existing mortgage, outstanding debts, and to fund modernizing the buildings. In some cases, we will underwrite the creation of bigger complexes. We have been in touch with the existing lenders and, under these circumstances, and given Mr. Cuesta's experience, they are willing to hold

*some of the debt. Again, thank you for sending Mr.
Luis Cuesta our way.*

Feliciano Torres.

"You want me to think you're a hero now?" she said with a scoff. "The reality is that this nobody gave my mother a penny and we lost it all. When my father died, I had to leave my school, my house, my things, and move into a tiny place in a different neighborhood where I knew no one. I lost everything, even my dad kissing me goodnight was gone too." She sat panting as the color in her face flushed red. Thomas listened and processed, allowing her emotions to settle with each passing moment. When the panting stopped and the color faded, Thomas reached into his coat breast pocket and retrieved a photograph he had not shown in ten years.

"Do you see this family?" asked Thomas, showing the Zubizarreta family.

"Yeah, what about them?"

Thomas pointed at the little girl in the photograph.

"This is the Zubizarreta family. This little girl is Enara Zubizarreta, the lone survivor of this family. They were involved in a six-car pileup on the expressway years ago. Enara lost her brother, her mother, and her father that day. She lived in an orphanage for two months before she was sent back to Spain to live with her uncle, Eneko. Her life went from tragic to worse when Eneko started drinking and ruined his life. She was all alone and despite all of that, she overcame this trauma. This is her now," he said, retrieving a second photograph from the same pocket. "This is her on her wedding day."

Eleonor looked at the two pictures that Thomas held in front of her, one in each hand. She saw the smile Enara had in both photos, one as a child and the one as a married woman.

"This is the life that she chose to live; despite losing everything and more, she chose this life. You can say all you want, but in the end, the place you lived in didn't really matter and what you ate didn't matter. The thing that mattered to you was that your father died. You decided to stop your life the moment your father died. You decided to resent the little house your mother got for you instead of being grateful. You decided to hang out with the wrong crowd, and you decided to substitute life with drugs. Fate played its hand in both of your lives, but she chose to be the hero of her story, and you chose to be the victim of yours." His words pierced her, and she looked down at the floor, the defiance vaporized inside of her. "Enara repaid her mother by working hard and making a life for herself. You've repaid yours by ruining all the sacrifice she's made for you."

Eleonor did not retaliate. She sat motionless, knowing the truth of his words. Thomas continued, his words coming faster as he spoke.

"Maybe your father wasn't paying attention to the road like he should have, but it wasn't because he was losing it all, it was because he was dreaming of the future. With the remodeling and reconfiguration of the properties, he was going to be able to take care of you beyond his wildest dreams." Thomas breathed hard. "Your father was not in a deep depression, in fact, he was optimistic about the future. You don't have to believe your mother, and you don't have to believe me but believe him."

Thomas,

I met with Feliciano Torres today at the Bank and wanted to thank you for your assistance in referring me to him. He explained that you saw the value of my assets, which many bankers had failed to see. Feliciano believes that the properties will appraise at values which will allow me to refinance them and will free up a considerable amount of cash, enabling me to remodel them, and save my holdings. Thank you for giving my family and I a second chance.

—*Luis Cuesta*

"You made up your own story of what happened and decided to believe the story you created despite your mother's warnings that it was not what happened."

She looked up at the lawyer's cerulean eyes through his wire rimmed glasses, and a tear escaped her left eye. Another followed, her body trembled, she sobbed, and then it all came at once.

"There is a very good man out there waiting for you," he breathed the words. "His name is Moses Akouala. He is an assistant state attorney. He has seen the tape of what you did with the child and all your medical records. You will also meet Rodrigo Vivar, your defense attorney. Together they have found a program where you can get clean and sober, so you can live a more normal life."

She moved to speak, but Thomas cut her off.

"We know, you were aware the couple was about to arrive and that they would see to the child, but still, that does not completely excuse your actions. My guess is that if you complete the program they have in mind, and you stay clean, all of this will go away, and you won't have a record. You will have to stay here with the sisters for a while and do community service, but your mother will be there with you in your new life. You can then begin again."

"Why are you doing this?"

"I feel partly responsible for what you have been through even though I know I'm not. Sometimes I think that maybe I should have known on the day of the deposition, when we bumped into each other, that you had been listening to the proceedings. I still regret not having asked Raymond or your father who you were. Sometimes I think I should have come to the funeral sooner and talked to you instead of just your mother and grandmother or even visited you in the hospital. Maybe if I had done any of those things, I would have saved you a lot of grief. Maybe at that age it would have made no difference, but I did none of it and for that, I am truly sorry."

Thomas put the documents inside the file, then walked over to the door as Eleonor did not move nor make a sound. He turned back to her. "Your lawyer, Mr. Vivar, will be here in a moment. You can decide whether to accept his services or find someone else to help you solve this, but in any event, I wish you luck."

She rotated in her chair and stared at him. Not knowing what to say, she waved goodbye and that was all he needed. He waved back and left, closing the door behind him, setting off to find the young lawyers.

Finding Moses and Rodrigo speaking a few doors down, he passed through the doorway and greeted them.

"Thank you, both of you. Rod, she's a little shaken up, but she's ready to talk to you."

Moses nodded to Rodrigo. They both stood up and strolled down the hallway, Rodrigo to Eleonor while Moses walked with Thomas until they found Gabriel in the church speaking with Sister Carmela. After saying goodbye to Sister Carmela, the men walked toward the double doors of the church. For the first time Thomas noticed a sign on the inside of the door on the right. It said, *Judas left early too.* Thomas chuckled as he saw it.

"Don't worry, Dad. You've never left early with anything, even now. Come on, I'll buy lunch this time."

"It had better not be cheap!"

"How about Joe's Stone Crab on Miami Beach?"

"Joe's Stone Crab? –You can afford that?"

Gabriel nodded at him.

"Oh, I'm paying you too much, but I'll take it."

They chuckled as Gabriel entered the car. Joining his son, Thomas sat in the Mustang, and they took off toward Miami Beach.

Chapter 63: The Departure

Miami, Florida: November 1982

Gabriel turned into Coral Gables from South Le Jeune Road, passing the Granada Golf Club as he made his way to Sarah's house on Sorolla Avenue. As he drove along in the Mustang, relief washed over him as he recounted the events of the past day, knowing that he would enjoy Thanksgiving with Abuela and his parents without the stress of any of his cases. When Sarah called him last night, he told her everything that had transpired with Eleonor, how Moses had worked out a deal with Rodrigo, and how his father had finally put this to rest after so many years. As he turned onto Granada Boulevard, he enjoyed the overarching trees that lined the streets alongside the unique houses.

As he turned onto Sorolla Avenue, he drove a little way until he made it to Sarah's, staring at the large tree in the front yard next to the driveway of the Spanish-styled home. He parked the Mustang, turned off the engine, and exited the car. A few moments later, Sarah opened the front door carrying a carry-on and a duffle bag with her purse hanging from an arm. He moved to help her and smiled as the strands of red in her brown hair shone beneath the sunshine. They locked eyes for a moment, and he gave her a kiss.

"Let me get those, Sarah," he said, reaching for the suitcase and the duffle bag. She smiled, handing him the bags which he placed in the trunk of the car, and taking a moment to thank him.

"You seem happy," she said, noticing his refreshed aura.

"You have no idea," he began. "I can't begin to tell you how much relief I feel. I don't have any major cases from here until the end of the year. No court dates, no major contracts; nothing. And, best of all, I was so slammed over the year that I made more than enough for the firm to get me through to the end of January if I needed."

"That doesn't sound too bad, Counselor."

"Do you know how much more free time I'll have now?"

"I can only imagine," said Sarah. "Enough to take me to the airport?"

"More than enough," he confirmed, laughing. "What time is the flight?"

"Not for another three hours," answered Sarah, moving to the passenger door, waiting to get in.

"Wait, close your eyes," began Gabriel.

"Why?" she asked.

"It's a surprise, I can't tell you."

"Okay, I'll play along." She closed her eyes and Gabriel opened the door, reaching in the back seat for the gift he got her on the way home. Holding it in his hand, he adjusted it to perfection and told Sarah to open her eyes.

"They're beautiful, Gabriel," she admitted, staring at the bouquet of flowers he got her.

"I remember you telling me a while back that you really liked Tulips, so I thought that maybe you'd like Daffodils and Tulips instead of Roses."

"I love them, I'll carry these with me on the plane, and I'll put them in a vase at my sister's. I'll get to enjoy them over Thanksgiving. Thanks, Gabriel," she said, tearing up.

"I didn't mean to make you cry, Sarah. Come here," he said, walking over to her and squeezing her in a tight embrace. "I have something else for you too," he said, reaching into his pocket and retrieving a small box. Sarah blushed as he opened it, revealing Sapphire earrings.

She stood speechless, admiring them. She took the earrings in her fingers, holding them in front of her eyes.

"They're beautiful," she murmured.

"I know that blue is your favorite color, so I when I saw them, I knew that they were perfect."

"Thank you," said Sarah, embracing him.

"Come on, let's get you to the airport."

Sarah wiped her eyes as Gabriel reached over and opened the door for her before heading over to his side and firing the Mustang to life. They departed Sorolla Avenue, taking the scenic route. Gabriel reached for Sarah's hand as soon as they left the driveway, playing the radio and lowering the windows of the Mustang to take in the cool November air. They took their time driving, talking about Sarah's holiday plans with her sister in Atlanta and his plans with his family in Miami. When they made it to the parking garage at Miami International Airport, Gabriel got down, helped Sarah out of the car, and grabbed her bags from the trunk.

"Ready?" he asked.

"For?" she inquired.

"To head to the gate."

"Sure, but why are you grabbing my bags?"

"Because I'm going to walk you to the gate," he answered, smiling.

"Really?"

"Yes, Sarah. Is everything alright? You seem a little tense."

"I just didn't expect it. You're always so busy."

"It's the day before Thanksgiving, Sarah. I'm allowed to splurge every now and again. Shall we?" He asked, sticking out his arm to lead her.

Sarah nodded and took it, permitting him to carry her bags and lead her to the entrance of the airport, talking as they strode from the garage over to the terminal.

"So, is this enough to go to your sister's for a week?" asked Gabriel, realizing how little he carried.

"She and I are the same size, so we tend to share clothes. Those will serve, at least, until I have more clothes up there and let's face it, at this time of the year the temperature up there is very different than here."

"You do this often?"

"Often enough to know I can get away with it for at least a while," she said, allowing her teeth to show through her smile. Her dimples appeared and Gabriel took it as a good omen.

"So, when do you return?"

"I don't know. I don't have a return date yet."

"I thought that you were coming back in a week?"

"Originally I was, but my sister arranged it so that I could stay longer."

"Is that okay with your office?"

"Yeah, they're fine with it, Gabriel. I have more than enough vacation days since I was so busy with cases too."

"Oh, that must be nice."

"It is. It'll give me more time with family which is what I really need right now."

"Did something happen?" he asked, pulling her over to the side, in front of the check-in line.

"No, but it's going to," she said, taking her hand to her eyes.

"This must be really bad, whatever it is, because I've never seen you like this. You don't even cry with your clients. Do you have something in your eye?"

"Just sadness."

"Why are you sad?"

Sarah didn't answer. She could only stare at him as the tears welled in her brown eyes. He took a hand and placed it on her cheek, wiping it with his thumb. She laughed nervously and held his hand in hers for a moment before it all clicked in his mind. Before he could say anything, she spoke up.

"I am going up to my sister's house north of Atlanta for Thanksgiving," she began, "but I am staying the extra days because I got my dream job there. The director and board members reviewed my resume and interviewed me because, according to my brother-in-law who set this all up, I am exactly what they are looking for," she said, her voice breaking as she finished.

"What are they looking for?" he asked, curiosity getting the better of him.

"An assistant director for the legal aid society of the county and if all goes well, director-in-waiting."

"Fulton county?"

"No, Gordon, a much smaller county a little over eighty miles northwest of Atlanta. You know I come from a small town on the outskirts of a big city so it will be like home."

Suddenly Gabriel had no more questions and did not want to ask any more. He knew what all this meant. She read his mind and blurted out.

"I made up my mind on the spur of the moment." Her mouth slowed down, "Gabriel, I knew instinctively, it was right for me and right for you, so I gave the go ahead two days ago for John, my brother-in-law, to follow up the initial contact with the administrator who is his golfing buddy. The position opened suddenly, and I had to decide one way or another. So, I did." She rambled nervously. "They needed someone in place for the new year and the new budget."

"What about your job? Aren't you happy here?"

"I resigned yesterday, and they allowed me to use the rest of my vacation days as the last weeks of my job since I have no cases with pending matters and the transfer to another lawyer will be simple."

The reality of it all came crashing down around him. Not knowing what to say, he said the only thing he hadn't yet.

"What about us?"

"Do you remember the last time we had a meaningful conversation about something that wasn't about the law?" she asked gently.

He was quiet for a second, remembering the conversation they had from Monday night.

"I don't," he answered.

"Neither do I. We're both workaholics, Gabriel; stuck in our professions and when we get together, we mostly talk shop. It's fun now, but eventually it'll be toxic and boring and neither of us wants to reach that stage and sour the wonderful times we had. I think we would get there in a few short months if we stayed together and I don't want that for us. Over the last ten months, you've been the most dazzling part of my life, and I don't want anything to spoil that. You raised the bar to a height that'll be hard for anyone else to reach. But in the end, neither of us is ready yet and we have no balance in our lives. We'll reach a time when we will and then each of us will find someone and begin our real lives. You aren't ready to open your heart to me or anyone else. I don't know why, but there's something unresolved in your past and I can't continue dating only one side of you."

Gabriel stared into space, processing everything she had said, knowing in his mind that she was right, but it still burned all the same.

"I'll miss you," she said reaching for his hand. He turned back to her where she met his eyes, "I'll miss you like no one else, but we both need to go on with our lives. We are going to different places, and it took me a long time, but I finally realized the truth of it," she acknowledged, lowering her eyes. She reached into her pocket and retrieved the box of earrings he had given her.

The muscles in Gabriel's cheeks tensed as he processed her tone and struggled to keep himself together. Somehow, he managed to smile.

"Keep them, Sarah. One to remember me by and, the other to make sure you don't settle for less," he said, smiling with all he could muster.

She smiled through water covered eyes, brushed his lips with hers and whispered, "Classy till the end, Counselor."

He broke on the pet name but composed himself.

She took everything with her as she strode down to the check-in line for Air Florida, carrying her suitcase, duffle bag, and purse too. He stood motionless and empty, watching her for a few moments before reality set in and instinct told him it was time to go.

Gabriel walked, broken and in pain, all the way back to the garage where he sat in the Mustang and looked over to the seat where she had sat so many times before. As he came to his senses, he ran his sleeve across his face and turned the ignition. He exited the spot and then the garage, and with that, she was gone.

Chapter 64: The Landing

Miami, Florida: November 1982

Gabriel stood in front of Rodrigo's building, hearing the crash of the waves on the rocks and staring out toward the ocean while watching the flight of nearby seagulls. The door buzzed, and he entered, walking over to the main desk where an old man with gray hair sat. They greeted each other as Gabriel gave him Rodrigo's last name and the old man allowed him through, pointing to the elevator at the end of the hallway. He pressed the button and when it opened, he tapped the 7th floor, and the car transported him from the lobby to Rodrigo's floor. He exhaled a few times on the ride up and when elevator doors parted, Gabriel exited and strode down the hall to Rodrigo's door.

He checked the time and wondered if Arlene had gotten off from her shift at the hospital. *If she's here, she's probably helping Rod with Thanksgiving dinner*, he thought. He only had to knock once before the door creaked open and Arlene stuck half of her face between the door and the frame.

"Gabriel, come in," she said, widening the entryway and allowing him admission. Gabriel ducked slightly as he came in. "Rod's on the balcony if you want to join him."

"He was expecting me?"

"He's been out there at least an hour. He hasn't slept well these last few nights and when he saw you pulling into the parking lot, he asked me to let you in. Go out and join him, I'm almost done with the coffee."

"Thanks, Arlene. I could use another cup."

Gabriel moved toward the balcony and opened the sliding glass door. Rodrigo sat in the corner, wearing an Andy Warhol tee shirt, shorts, flip-flops, and wild hair.

"Damn, I thought I was having a rough day," kidded Gabriel, pulling up a chair beside him.

"You've never come at this hour," he said, not taking his eyes off the horizon before him.

"Arlene said that you haven't slept well."

"It's a case I've got. I can't get the pictures out of my head. Too much blood affects the soul, and the forensics team recorded every drop of it."

"I'm sorry, Rod."

"Perspective, you know. Arlene sees those images daily in the emergency room as patients, but I see them in a court of law as bodies. Guess which one of us sleeps easier."

"She's desensitized, Rod."

"No," he said, shaking his head and dismissing Gabriel's assessment, "she's not desensitized, she just has hope when she approaches her work. I have been thinking about our work for Joaquín last year, and though I was scared that I might not get him off, I had hope in defending a man that I *knew* was innocent."

"Do you want to talk more about changing your practice?"

"No, you're here because you need a friend. We'll save my stuff for another day."

Gabriel grimaced and Rodrigo turned to him, taking his eyes off the horizon for the first time since Gabriel arrived.

"Weren't you supposed to take Sarah to the airport?"

"I did, earlier."

"You're missing her already?"

"Sarah said goodbye."

"Well of course she did, that's what people do when they leave."

"No," said Gabriel, suppressing a chuckle and analyzing the Mexican tile on the floor of the balcony. "She *really* said goodbye and she's not coming back."

"Why?" asked Rodrigo without a hint of surprise in his voice.

"She got an offer for her dream job."

"That's nice. Again, why did she say goodbye?"

"The job is in a county north of Atlanta near her sister and nephews."

"Is that all?" asked Rodrigo, his eyebrows climbing up his forehead.

"No. She said two workaholics is not a good match, especially when they are both lawyers that can't stop talking shop. I guess it was fate."

"The signs were all there," said Rodrigo, "but it wasn't fate."

"You didn't even know her well." argued Gabriel.

"I didn't have to. I know you."

Gabriel shuffled in his seat and leaned forward. He paused, contemplating Rodrigo's words.

"What do you mean?" he asked, looking at Rodrigo's tan face, waiting for an explanation.

"For starters, she was always looking for a position she wasn't going to get in Miami until she had at least fifteen years' experience. Because your world is in Miami and hers is somewhere else. One could say that it was a recipe for goodbye, but the truth is that, under other circumstances, she would have stayed here with you and gone to visit her sister every few months."

Gabriel looked up from the floor and at his best friend.

"Do you have to be so blunt?"

"Listen man, you're my best friend and I love you to death. What we have is a childhood friendship that we developed as older men and that is rare. I know you, and what I can tell you is that your future with Sarah was always going to end before it ever got serious."

Gabriel didn't reply, and listened to Rodrigo, letting him say what he needed to hear.

"She was never going to be important enough to you because even with as amazing as she was, and probably could have been, she could never compete."

"Compete? What do you mean?"

"Give me your wallet."

"What do you need my wallet for?"

"Give me your wallet, Lock."

Gabriel retrieved his wallet and handed it to Rodrigo.

"This is not the problem," he said raising it to Gabriel's eyes. He grabbed the wad of cash inside the wallet and held it up. "You probably bought the flowers with this." He returned the cash to the wallet and grabbed one of Gabriel's credit cards. "You probably bought the painting with this," he said, holding up an American Express credit card.

Gabriel nodded.

"And you probably bought the earrings with this," continued Rodrigo, holding up a Mastercard.

Gabriel nodded again. Rodrigo took the remaining credit cards and the wallet and put them on the table between them.

"You could have bought anything to make a girl happy with all of these things, but all this money and all these cards mean nothing if you still have this," he said.

Gabriel looked up to see Rodrigo holding the picture of the one that got away.

"But I thought about Sarah all the time."

"How could you not? –She was in your daily life. You even shared a client at the same time, so when was she not going to be on your mind? Regardless of how often you thought about her, you never removed the picture."

"I started to, several times."

"But you didn't. Every time you chose not to."

Rodrigo turned as the sliding door opened, and Arlene emerged with two cups of Cuban coffee. "I think you could both use this," she said, and put the tray down on the small rectangular table between them.

"Thanks, babe," he said to her as she walked back inside. "Look," he continued, turning back to Gabriel, "Sarah was incredible, smart, funny, beautiful. She was ten out of ten. A real keeper, but it didn't matter how great she was because you were only going to give her the part of yourself that was comfortable in the shallows."

"It was more than just the shallows, Rod. We could talk about anything," said Gabriel, defiance rising in his voice.

"You could talk to her about anything, but in every conversation, you would always go back to a case you had, or a client's problem. You never learned how to turn off the law because that was the cover, the reason neither of you had to look at the underlying emotional problem. This works when you first meet someone, but after a while, you have nowhere to go. It only happened faster because neither of you could leave work behind." Rodrigo paused to catch his breath.

"She warned me about that," admitted Gabriel. He stood up and walked toward the railing, leaning against it.

"She warned you about it because she only sensed the truth, she didn't know about her. The truth is that you can't have a future because you're still in love with the past. Until you resolve that, all you'll have is your work and we weren't built for just work, we were built for more. Gabriel, you're not a man that can simply love the one you're with. You must be with the one you love."

"But she didn't come back. No explanation, not a word," countered Gabriel, defensively. "I called her for a year, I even sent letters, but never got an answer, Rod, not once."

"Yeah, but you didn't go after her and so you didn't settle the past." said Rodrigo, pointing to the picture. "Someday, not today, not tomorrow, and probably not for some time, but someday you're going to have to go and get the answers." Rodrigo stood up and walked over to his friend, leaning on the railing of the balcony and handing Gabriel the picture. Gabriel stared at the image in his hand, seeing the woman he had loved since he was young.

"She can't be your hope and your past, Gabriel. She has to be one or the other, and until you face that you'll be a passerby in your own life."

Gabriel's thoughts lingered on Rodrigo's words. Knowing he had no other choice, he surrendered. Rodrigo hugged him and squeezed hard. They broke and, turning toward the glass door, Rodrigo pulled it to the side as Gabriel followed behind him. Arlene waited for them in the kitchen and when Gabriel neared the bar counter, she walked up to him and hugged him tightly. A lone tear escaped his eye as she held him and told him that he would be alright.

"Would you like to stay for lunch?" she asked.

"Very much."

"We'll always be here for you, Gabe."

"I know. I'll always know."

The Righteousness of American Law

Gabriel and Thomas are not heroes endowed with superpowers like much of what we have seen in pop culture in the last decade. They are not lawyers characterized by the common Hollywood tropes. They are individuals driven by morals and purpose.

They depend on blind justice. The Locks use the law as a means of advocating for their clients before an impartial authority that guarantees fairness. Without this one element there is no justice, and without justice, a society has no hope. Like fair-mindedness, most of our legal concepts originate in one ancient book, the Bible.

On the 30th of October 2024, my father and I traveled to *Campbell Law School* in Raleigh, North Carolina where he gave a seminar on the *Ins and Outs of Owning Your Own Firm*, sponsored by the Hispanic Law Student Association. After giving the seminar, we walked downstairs and took the opportunity to see the campus. When we did so, we came across this quote:

> *"You shall do no injustice in court.*
> *You shall not be partial to the*
> *poor or defer to the great, but in*
> *righteousness shall you judge*
> *your neighbor."*

Leviticus 19:15

The quote impressed us so much that we knew immediately that we needed to put it in our second novel. There is a chapter where Gabriel represents a client who struggles financially and makes a bad decision. Gabriel and his best friend, Rodrigo, defend the client criminally and later civilly. This exemplifies the principle that our legal system considers only the acts people commit, not who they are or what they believe.

David N. Cancio
10th of October 2025

About the Authors

Humberto was born in Cuba in 1953 but immigrated to the US at 6. At 12 he moved to Spain where he attended the American School of Madrid for six years. Upon his return to the states, he graduated from Duke University with a BA in Political Science and Public Policy Studies. He attended the University of Florida obtaining a JD. He has practiced law for over 40 years in Miami Florida representing multicultural civil and family law clients and is AV rated pre-eminent. Humberto is married with four grown children and two grandchildren.

David, co-author and son, was born in 1991 and has lived in both Florida and North Carolina, graduating from NC State with a major in Spanish. Additionally, he is native in English, fluent in French, and can communicate in Portuguese, German, and Italian. On his way to being a writer, he has made his living through training, sales, and client success. Among other things, David is a practicing Catholic, and a Knight of Columbus.

Acknowledgments

To our wonderful readers, thank you for your incredible commitment to the Gabriel Lock series and for joining us on this journey through its second installment. We truly hope that Bound By Fate gave you even more enjoyment than Bound By Law. As writers, our greatest wish is to keep growing with every story we tell, and we like to think Bound By Fate shows that growth.

This book was a labor of love—filled with late nights, rewrites, and plenty of coffee. Its depth and emotion challenged us to dig deeper into Gabriel's character, to make his adventure not just about solving a case but about facing another person—and his own past. And yes, somehow, we managed to pull it all together in less than a year before the deadline!

We sincerely hope you've felt the heart and care we poured into every page. Of course, we couldn't have done it alone. Behind every word are the amazing people and organizations who helped bring this story to life, and they each deserve their moment of appreciation. You'll find them listed below, with our deepest thanks.

Atlas Elite Publishing Partners

Dar Dowling   Michael Beas   Tom Colleran

Editor

Angela Schutz

Barnes & Noble

Kaye Pellegrino   Sally Amador   Shirley Marmolejo
Danny Carrasco

And

Evelio Vega

St. Jude Catholic Church

Rev. Kevin Nelson   Rev. Gabriel Ghanoum

Father Daniel Barica

And

Deacon Les Loh   Deacon Paul Gianella

Publius Inc.

A.J. Rice   Drew Allen

Young Catholic Professionals

Mitch Heaton   Jackson Messick   Mercedes White

Knights of Columbus

Council 6569

The Gabriel Lock Team

Xavier Primus   Duy Huynh   Kristie DeLouise

John Matland   Ntchwaidumela Thomas

Robert Cancio   Enrique Martin   Giancarlo Benítez

Individual Acknowledgments

1. Adam Nathan
2. Aitor Gastón
3. Alex Fahmy
4. Alex Rabre
5. Alexander Navarro
6. Alicia Soler-Cancio
7. Alicia Macias
8. Amanda Cancio
9. Ana María Cancio
10. Anna Medvedeva
11. Anna Shope
12. Ashley Travers
13. Brad Lynch
14. Brittney Leggett
15. Brooke Salgado
16. Cara Suco
17. Carlos Florián
18. Charles Suaris
19. Christina Cancio
20. Daniel Bello, Esq.
21. Darlene Garcia, Esq.
22. David Flanigan
23. David Torrens
24. Diana Franco
25. Dragica Dodevska
26. Edward P. Cancio
27. Erica Gomez
28. Fernando Santos Vital
29. Fred Suco
30. Gabri Dobre
31. Iván Sánchez Gómez
32. Joel Currá
33. Jorge Gomez
34. José Manuel Alvarado Díaz
35. José Antonio San José
36. Kate Sybilrud
37. Kevin Javor
38. Krithika Ramesh Kuhn
39. Marcus Pauling
40. Mark Mullauer
41. Michelle López (Dr.)
42. Nathan Kuhn

43. Nicolás Sánchez Cuerda

44. Omar Acosta

45. Pepe Llorente

46. Rafael Marrero (Col., Dr.)

47. Rodrigo Villarán

48. Sha Hinds-Glick, Esq. (Prof.)

49. Sofia Cancio

50. Stephanie Cruz

51. Trevor Lee

52. Ty Prentice

53. Tyler Lambert

54. Veronica Cancio De Grandy

Verso l'alto perché non Io, ma Dio